MULBERRIES AND MURDER

"What kind of berry product do you need?" I asked.

"I need berries, not berry products. Mulberries."

"This isn't the season for fresh mulberries. But I can order bags of dried mulberries in various quantities. How many do you want?"

"Enough to cover my house."

My heart sank. Speaking to a crazy woman was not how I intended to start the day. "That's a lot of dried mulberries. I couldn't even estimate how many mulberries you'd need." I hesitated, not certain I wanted to get further involved in this conversation. "Can I ask why you want to cover your house with mulberries?"

"To protect me."

"Protect you from what?"

"From danger." Leticia leaned so close, her long tangled hair brushed my cheek. "Someone wants to kill me . . ."

**Books by
Sharon Farrow**

DYING FOR STRAWBERRIES

BLACKBERRY BURIAL

KILLED ON BLUEBERRY HILL

MULBERRY MISCHIEF

Published by Kensington Publishing Corporation

Mulberry Mischief

Sharon Farrow

KENSINGTON PUBLISHING CORP.

www.kensingtonbooks.com

KENSINGTON BOOKS are published by

Kensington Publishing Corp.
119 West 40th Street
New York, NY 10018

All Kensington titles, imprints, and distributed lines are available at special quantity discounts for bulk purchases for sales promotions, premiums, fund-raising, educational, or institutional use. Special book excerpts or customized printings can also be created to fit specific needs. For details, write or phone the office of the Kensington sales manager: Kensington Publishing Corp., 119 West 40th Street, New York, NY 10018, attn: Sales Department; phone 1-800-221-2647.

KENSINGTON BOOKS and the K logo are Reg. U.S. Pat. & TM Off.

ISBN-13: 978-1-4967-2261-4
ISBN-10: 1-4967-2261-2

First printing: September 2019

10 9 8 7 6 5 4 3 2 1

Printed in the United States of America

Electronic edition:

ISBN-13: 978-1-4967-2263-8 (e-book)
ISBN-10: 1-4967-2263-9 (e-book)

To my cousin Jim Hanson
Who has never given up the search for Bigfoot.

And to my fellow Halloween babies—
There is no better day to be born.
Every birthday is a costume party.

Plus there's always cake and candy.

Chapter One

A ten-foot-tall pumpkin figure glared down at me.

"Can't we have a normal fall festival for once?" I asked, recalling last year's Trick or Treat bike race, which ended in a pileup at the Monroe Farm's corn maze.

"How dull would that be?" Piper Lyall-Pierce stepped back to get a better view of the colorful sign that guarded the entrance to River Park.

It depicted a figure with human arms and legs, but an enormous pumpkin head. Given that Halloween was a week away, a pumpkin person seemed appropriate, except for its attire: a white lab coat accessorized by a stethoscope curled about its neck.

"There's nothing dull about Halloween. You're working too hard to put your own stamp on it. Or do I have to remind you about the trail bike race you dreamed up?"

"I am so tired of hearing about that race. Blame the corn maze, not me. And anyone can throw an ordinary fall festival. Not enough towns think to combine Halloween and healthy living. And a health fair is perfect." As head of the Oriole Point Visitor Center, Piper had first—and final—approval of any festival or fair that took place in our lakeshore resort village.

"Halloween's not a day devoted to sensible eating." I looked up at the Haunted Halloween Harvest Health Fair banner billowing in the gentle breeze. "And while I admire your alliteration, one less word beginning with 'H' might have sufficed. Especially since everyone will end up calling it the Harvest Health Fair."

"You're all philistines. My facialist thinks a health fair is perfect for Halloween."

I laughed. "Well, if Sonya says it's a good idea . . ."

"We need a health fair at this time of year to convince people to eat less candy. I'd certainly love it if Lionel ate healthier. He refuses to listen to his doctor about the dangers of too much sugar. Last Halloween, he polished off an entire bag of Twizzlers." Lionel Pierce was Piper's husband, and the mayor of Oriole Point.

"Maybe Lionel needs a doctor as intimidating as this pumpkin guy. Or is it a she?"

"Isn't it obvious? The lab coat is tapered at the waist. And she has long lashes. I instructed the staff at Greer Sign Painting to hint that she was female. After all, a giant pumpkin man puppet leads off the Halloween parade. We need a pumpkin woman to balance him out."

"You're the only one in town worried about gender disparity among pumpkin people."

"I'll tell you what you should be worried about and that's your booth at the fair." Piper led me into the park, now bustling with activity as vendors set up displays at their tented booths.

Despite the early hour, visitors already showed interest. The beautiful weekend weather helped, as did the locale. On the other side of the park ran the Oriole River. Many owners didn't put their boats into dry dock until November, so I wasn't surprised at the variety of watercraft making their way past the white stone lighthouse and out onto Lake Michigan. The lake view, combined with the park's maple trees at peak autumn color, turned the scene into a dazzling vista. Then again, I'd be hard pressed to find a spot in our village that wasn't picturesque.

Hailed as one of the most scenic beach towns in the country, Oriole Point, Michigan, had been dubbed "the Cape Cod of the Midwest." Also the home of a famous summer art school, Oriole Point drew tourists and art lovers in equal numbers. And Chicago was only a two-hour drive away, making our village the perfect weekend getaway for stressed-out city dwellers. However, those of us who had to work with Piper had more than enough stress in our lives.

"Send Gillian back to the store for more products," Piper instructed as we approached The Berry Basket booth currently overseen by my employee, Gillian Kaminski. "You're selling little more than elderberry tea."

"Not true." I scanned our merchandise table. "We brought a nice selection to the park."

"Marlee's right," Gillian said, stacking berry-flavored protein mixes on a table beneath the tent. "I've already sold a few things. And the fair doesn't officially open for an hour."

To confirm her statement, the newly installed clock bell tower at city hall began to toll. Piper appeared giddy at the sound. Another brainchild of hers, the bell tower was not only unnecessary, but cacophonous.

When the ninth and final chime faded away, Gillian peeked at Piper over her wire-rimmed glasses. "Please make that tower bell quieter. It's deafening."

"And turn it off at night," I added. "It wakes up everyone who lives above the shops."

"Need I remind you that our original city hall had a clock bell tower that tolled the hour? Built by my ancestor Bernard Phinneas Lyle in memory of his mother, Ada Trent, who died in a tragic freak accident."

The last thing we needed was another reminder about the homicidal grandfather clock that fell over and killed Bernard's mom while she napped in her rocking chair. Since Piper was a descendant of the oldest family in Oriole Point, we never stopped hearing about the dubious misadventures of her ancestors. However, this one seemed more absurd than most of her tales.

"Why did he honor his mother with a clock tower if a clock was responsible for her death?" I remarked. "Seems a bit dark."

"On the contrary," Piper said. "Every time it tolled the hour, people remembered her. A pity the bell tower burned down in the fire of 1899."

If it was as loud as this one, I suspected arson.

"This bell tower might not last too long either." Gillian retied her blue chef apron, mandatory garb for Berry Basket employees. "Old Man Bowman is threatening to bring his shotgun into town and use the bell for target practice."

"I'll have that fool locked up for lunacy if he dares. And you two should spend less time concerned about the bell tower and more time worrying about your booth." Her gaze swept over the berry teas, lozenges, hand creams, and bottled juices arrayed on two long tables. "We have vendors here from as far away as Texas. As a local business, you should be better represented."

"As a local business, my shop is a five-minute walk away. If they want to see the rest of my inventory, they can stroll up the street. Or grab one of these." I nodded at the Berry Basket mail-order catalogs stacked on the table. "But I'm not hauling piles of merchandise out here for a weekend event. Bad enough I took Gillian off the Saturday store schedule to work the booth."

"I don't mind." Gillian fished a plastic hair clip out of her apron pocket. She expertly twisted her mass of curly hair atop her head, then secured it into place "When the weather is this warm, I prefer to spend every moment outdoors. Especially now that I'm back at school."

Twenty-one-year old Gillian attended Grand Valley State University, working only weekends at the shop during the school year. She was my most dependable store clerk, and I regretted losing her full-time presence once summer came to an end. My other sales staff, the Cabot brothers, were capable and fun, but reminded me of Fred and George Weasley in the Harry Potter books. Which meant they could sometimes be a little too much fun.

Piper watched as a growing number of people headed toward the park along Lyall Street. "We lucked out with the weather. The forecast is seventy-two degrees and sunny straight through the weekend. But things are due to cool down soon."

"October's good for tourism," I said. "The lake is still warm enough for swimming *and* it's leaf-peeping season. The maples have put on a quite a show this year, too."

"Don't forget all the people coming to town for the parade."

Piper shot Gillian an injured look for that comment. I knew Piper hated any reminder about how big an event the Halloween parade was. Although two Halloween parades actually strutted through downtown: a kiddie parade in the afternoon, with one for adults that night. The adult parade had grown in such renown and inventiveness, it had become like Mardi Gras along the lakeshore. And one of Oriole Point's biggest tourist draws.

"The town needs more than a garish Halloween parade," Piper said.

The parade had not been Piper's idea, and its success served as a constant reproach. Instead, Odette Henderson, owner of Lakeshore Holiday, organized the first adult Halloween parade a decade ago. Envy over the parade probably lay behind Piper's fevered determination to come up with ever changing events and festivals. I only hoped the town wouldn't be subjected to another Roller Blade Bunco Party. Three people sprained ankles on the roller rink that night.

I looked around at my fellow vendors in the park, many sipping a drink from Coffee by Crystal, our local version of Starbucks. A wide array of "good for you" products were on sale, including aromatherapy candles, home blood-pressure monitors, flax heating pads, bamboo kitchen utensils, organic pet food, and magnetic therapy jewelry. Some booths offered services such as bicycle repair or a chiropractic adjustment.

As Piper's ideas went, a health fair seemed perfectly serviceable. Although I wasn't convinced of its tie-in to Halloween or autumn. I was even less convinced The Berry Basket needed to set up a booth. Especially since Elderwood Farm had one of the biggest displays here.

Piper followed my gaze. "Eyeing the competition, Marlee?"

"I don't regard Elderwood Farm as competition. They only sell elderberry products, and they're overpriced. They also claim their berries are organic. Which is questionable. That's why I had Gillian bring so many elderberry products today. Lots of people in the area know what happened at the farm. They'll prefer to buy our elderberry products, not theirs."

"What are you talking about?" Piper asked.

"Two years ago, people got sick from their elderberry tonic," Gillian said in a low voice, mindful of the visitors exploring the park booths. "Lab tests revealed a high arsenic content."

"Arsenic?" Piper threw an alarmed look at the man running the Elderwood Farm booth.

"The groundwater near their farm was contaminated," I explained. "They avoided cleaning it up for years and ended up paying hefty fines. I'd like to think they've fixed the problem. Still, I buy my elderberry products from other sources."

"Now I regret accepting their request to be part of my fair. Too late to throw them out though. This sort of thing always happens, no matter—" A trilling ringtone cut short Piper's rant.

She opened her Birkin bag to hunt for her phone. One of the things Piper spent her considerable wealth on were the classic Hermès bags; she owned an endless supply in every color. Today's Birkin was a fuchsia pink that matched her manicure, leather pumps, and silk blouse. The fashion term "matchy-matchy" could have been coined for her.

After a quick swipe at her phone, Piper listened to the caller with an exasperated expression. "Are you joking? Of course the speakers for Slime Rhyme are expected to wear costumes! I can't believe you even have to ask." She tossed the phone back into her purse. "That's the last time I hire my cousin's son to assist me."

Gillian and I exchanged puzzled glances. "Dare we ask what a Slime Rhyme is?" I said.

"Are you serious? How can you not know?" Piper shook her head. "If it wasn't for me, this entire town would vanish into the mists like Brigadoon. Not that either of you would notice. Any more than you've noticed all the promotion I've done for every activity connected to the fair, *including* the Slime Rhyme."

"Sorry," I began. "But this past month—"

"I've hung posters everywhere," Piper broke in. "Not to mention the promo I've done on Oriole Point's Facebook page and Twitter account." She lifted an eyebrow at Gillian. "Your father's newspaper ran a full-page ad this past week." Steven Kaminski was the editor of the *Oriole Point Herald,* one of two weekly papers in town.

"I've got a heavy class load for my senior year. And since moving closer to campus, I only come to Oriole Point on weekends to work at the store. No time for Slime Rhyme." Gillian grinned. "Hey, that rhymed."

"Fine. I'll give the college girl a pass." Piper turned to me. "But what's your reason for being so uninformed about our latest holiday event? You're usually pretty festive."

"I haven't been in a festive mood. Last month, a pipe burst in my upstairs bathroom. The plumber discovered the copper water lines have corroded. He called in a contractor to tear up the bathrooms, which is when I learned the electrical wiring has never been totally rewired. Putting me in violation of about five housing codes. Every minute I'm not at the shop, I've been overseeing an army of plumbers and contractors." I shuddered. "Along with visits from the Historic Preservation Committee. They haven't made the process easy."

Piper winced. "You have my sympathies. They're a tough crowd."

Both Piper and I lived in historic homes: an 1891 Italianate mansion for Piper and a charming Queen Anne overlooking Lake Michigan for me. But along with the turret, original wainscoting, and spectacular lake view, my 1895 Painted Lady also came with ancient plumbing and wiring. And every repair or upgrade needed to pass muster with the members of Oriole Point's Historic Preservation Committee. My latest requests before the committee made me feel like an accused witch pleading my case before a tribunal of witch hunters.

"I don't blame you for being distracted," Piper continued. "The renovation and repair process can drag on for months."

"This time it only took weeks. The contractors

swear today is their last day. With luck, I can now pay attention to something other than my house."

"Then it's time to bring you up to speed." Piper pulled a stack of shiny flyers out of her bag. After placing the pile on our display table, she took one and handed it to me. "Next week is packed with activities."

She hadn't exaggerated. The flyer listed a dizzying number of events scheduled to take place at the Lyall Conference Center, named after the family of its principal benefactor: Piper. Because our town only held four thousand residents, most of us doubted the necessity of a conference center. But Piper found enough Oriole Point citizens with deep pockets who agreed to help finance the project. And in the year since the Lyall Center opened, it had brought increased visitors and their money to our small town. So chalk up another one for Piper.

"I thought the fair was only a weekend event." I said. "This looks like a mega-convention. I'm surprised *and* impressed."

Gillian whistled as she read the flyer. "I recognize some of these speakers. I can't believe Ellie Vaughn will be here."

My mouth fell open. "Ellie, the Pilates queen? I use her machines at the gym."

Piper seemed pleased with herself. "She's holding workshops all week."

My amazement at the list of speakers grew. "And how did you convince Dr. Cameron Sable to appear at a small-town health fair? His wife Ingrid, too. They're famous!"

Cameron Sable was a best-selling author on nutrition and healthy living, widely known for his Sable

Diet. His wife, a board-certified dermatologist, had cornered the market on skin-care products reputed to be free of harmful chemicals. I knew Piper had connections in Michigan, but I never dreamed her influence extended all the way to Palm Beach and the family who ran a diet, cosmetics, and natural supplements empire.

"Wow," Gillian said. "My Uncle Woody lost eighty pounds on the Sable Diet. He still orders their protein drinks. And I love Ingrid Sable's skin toners and moisturizers."

"Their two sons are giving workshops as well. In fact, the whole family arrives tonight. I've organized everything at the center to revolve around their appearances, which should be standing-room only." Piper's smile turned sly. "Best of all, they waived their fees."

I looked up from the flyer. "Why in the world would they do that?"

"It all came about because I booked Victor Kang to give a five-day workshop."

"*The* Victor Kang?" Kang was a motivational speaker as famous as Tony Robbins.

"Yes, *the* Victor Kang," Piper told me. "His speaking fee was exorbitant, but I thought the expense well worth it. Then Mr. Kang canceled due to some family emergency. Since we had a contract, I was about to call my lawyers. But he spoke to the Sables and they offered to take his place. Apparently, Mr. Kang is close friends with Patrick Sable, the eldest son."

"How generous of the Sable family to do such a thing," I said.

She shrugged. "I doubt it's entirely charitable. Their company launches two new products this season. All of them to be showcased at the fair. And they booked a number of TV appearances in Chicago afterward. In addition, Patrick Sable's wife's new book just hit the bestseller list. She's set up book signings in the area for *Beauty's Bounty*."

"I still think they're being charitable. You may want to express a little gratitude. Gratitude's a cornerstone of Victor Kang's philosophy." I winked at Piper. "I've read his books."

"I *am* grateful," she said. "Grateful he had to cancel and the Sable family stepped in."

"You should be grateful they're not charging you," Gillian said. "Experts are expensive."

"So I've learned." Piper snapped her fingers. "Wait a second. You're a berry expert, Marlee. How would you like to participate in a Holistic Hints session on Wednesday? You could explain the health benefits of berries."

"I don't know." I gave a mock sigh. "My speaking fee is pretty high."

"Very funny." She pulled out her phone and began texting. "I got an email last night from a sleep expert I booked. She agreed to give a talk about the hazards of too little sleep. But last night she fell asleep at the wheel and crashed her car. How's that for irony? Now she's in the hospital so I'm handing over her time slot to you. Two o'clock on Wednesday. Come prepared for a forty-minute talk, and twenty minutes of Q&A."

"Hold on, Piper. I need to check my schedule and—"

She ignored me. "Wednesday, two o'clock. Be there fifteen minutes early." Piper's phone rang in the middle of her text. Her attention now shifted to her caller.

"I want the sports armbands to me by five o'clock!" she shouted. "No excuses!" Piper stalked off to continue her harangue.

I looked at Gillian. "Guess I'm giving a talk about berries on Wednesday."

Gillian smiled. "Look on the bright side. You may find out what a Slime Rhyme is."

"I only hope I don't end up taking part in it." While I rearranged the bottles of berry iced teas, Gillian greeted a trio of customers interested in the dark chocolate raspberry granola bars.

Time to get to my shop. I had a pile of spreadsheets to go over before I opened my doors.

After giving Gillian a quick wave, I turned to go. But I didn't get far.

"Marlee Jacob, I need to talk to you!" The hoarse voice shouting after me seemed unfamiliar. And friends weren't in the habit of calling me by my full name.

Curious, I looked over my shoulder and almost stumbled. A thin woman wearing faded Bermuda shorts, a baggy white blouse, and an oversized white cardigan hurried in my direction.

"Marlee Jacob, I need to talk to you," she repeated.

I waited at the park entrance until she reached me. Even from a distance, I would have recognized the woman by her tangled mane of orange hair, which always looked in need of a comb. Every resident of Oriole Point knew who Leticia the Lake Lady was. Out of the coterie of eccentrics who lived in town, we viewed Leticia as the most mystifying. Certainly, she was the most aloof. She rarely came into the village itself, preferring to wander along the public beach and stare at the lake. So why was she here now? And what did she want to speak with me about?

She came to a halt in front of me. "You're the girl who owns The Berry Basket?"

"I am." Since Leticia was around sixty, I wasn't surprised she called me a "girl," even if I would turn thirty-one this December.

Leticia cocked her head at me. "You cut your hair."

"Yes." I reached up and touched the ends of my hair, which grazed my shoulders. Last month I'd chopped off about eight inches in an impulsive response to my broken engagement to Ryan Zellar. Luckily, I didn't regret cutting my hair. Nor did I regret ending things with Ryan.

"I don't like it," she said. "Women should keep their hair long. It gives them strength."

I smiled. "I thought that only worked for Samson."

She didn't smile back. "If you keep cutting it, you'll look like her." Leticia threw a disgusted glance at Piper, who still marched about the park, shouting into the phone.

Piper always wore her impeccably coiffed ash-blond hair in a stylish short bob. "I like Piper's hair. And I'll be lucky to look that good at fifty."

"She's a Gorgon," Leticia snapped. "Stare into her eyes and you'll turn to stone."

I hoped she never said that to Piper. Although Piper would never have stopped to speak with her. Indeed, I knew no one who had talked to Leticia the Lake Lady. Except for her visits to the lake, she appeared to lead the life of a hermit. I couldn't help but be curious as to why she was in the middle of town criticizing my haircut. And Piper's.

"I'm sorry you don't like my hair. Is that what you wanted to say to me?"

"Don't be ridiculous. I've come to ask for your help. I need berries. I heard you know a great deal about them."

"That's true. My store sells products made from all sorts of berries." The Berry Basket stocked a wide variety of berry food items, which included berry-flavored coffees, teas, wines, muffins, salsas, and baking mixes. I also sold objects decorated with berries, such as aprons, ceramic ware, jewelry, and lots more. If Leticia the Lake Lady needed a specific item related to berries, I felt confident I could supply it.

"What kind of berry product do you need?" I asked.

"I need berries, not berry products. Mulberries."

"This isn't the season for fresh mulberries. But I can order bags of dried mulberries in various quantities. How many do you want?"

"Enough to cover my house."

My heart sank. Speaking to a crazy woman was not how I intended to start the weekend. "That's a lot of dried mulberries. I couldn't even estimate how many mulberries you'd need." I hesitated, not certain I wanted to get further involved in this conversation. "Can I ask why you want to cover your house with mulberries?"

"To protect me."

"Protect you from what?"

"From danger." Leticia leaned so close, her long tangled hair brushed my cheek. "Someone wants to kill me."

Chapter Two

Not the answer I expected. For a moment, I considered simply running away. But Leticia's ivy green Bermuda shorts revealed a pair of muscled, sinewy legs. She might have no problem catching up with me, despite our age difference. Also I had never been this close to her. Now that I was, I realized she wasn't as old as I had believed. Closer to fifty, not sixty.

I decided to play along. "Exactly who wants to kill you?"

"An enemy. One of the shadow people who wish me to remain silent." Her hoarse voice lowered to a whisper. "And my ghost is in danger, too."

As someone who lived in New York City for a decade, I was familiar with unbalanced people who wandered—and sometimes lived—on the streets. In a crowded city, I could hurry past or drop a few dollars into their hand. Not so simple in a small town when the delusional individual knew your name.

"Silent about what?"

"Dark deeds." Leticia gave me a knowing look.

"A visit to the police might be a better idea than buying mulberries." I took a step back.

She grabbed my arm. "The police can't help me. They think I'm crazy."

Worried it might agitate her further, I didn't pull away. "If you have proof, the police won't be able to say you're crazy."

"You think I don't know what the town says about me? All of you believe I'm insane, including the police. But I'm not insane. Nor am I a fool. I am as clearheaded and focused as an assassin."

I wished she'd chosen a different analogy.

"I must protect myself." Leticia tightened her grip. "I need mulberries."

"Please let go. You're hurting me."

"Sorry." She released me. "I'm in danger. You're the only person who can help."

I glanced over her shoulder, hoping to see a friend I might wave over. No such luck. Since River Park lay so close to the beach and river, only tourists ambled down the sidewalk toward us. My fellow shopkeepers were either at their stores or manning the park booths.

"You're not afraid of me?" Leticia seemed disappointed. "I'd heard you were a young woman to be reckoned with. One who helped catch more than one murderer in Oriole Point."

"I'm not afraid of you," I said with more conviction than I felt. "But I've had a few brushes with danger recently. Not sure I'm up for another one so soon. However, if all you require for protection are mulberries, I can provide them." I did a quick estimate in my head. "Covering your entire house with berries won't come cheap, though."

"Cost is unimportant. I'm trying to save my life." She seemed deadly serious.

I felt saddened by her belief that mulberries could

protect her. And why did she think someone was trying to kill her? Was she a paranoid schizophrenic, prone to delusions? I did know she lived alone in a log home near the woods, like a character in a Grimm's fairy tale.

As far as I knew, she had no friends or family in the area. Such isolation would worsen whatever condition she suffered from. I wished I had more information about her. But Leticia was not an Oriole Point native. I hadn't grown up with her, as I had the other local eccentrics like Old Man Bowman. Leticia had moved to my hometown while I was off pursuing a career in New York City. When I returned two years ago, Leticia had already taken up residence in Oriole County. At the time, I'd been busy setting up my Berry Basket business and took little interest in the occasional rumor about her. I should have paid more attention.

"Do you know who wants to kill you?" If she gave me a name, I could pass it on to Gene Hitchcock, Oriole Point's police chief. Although Kit Holt of the sheriff's department might be a better choice now that he and I were dating.

"If I do, you'll tell the police," she said in that distinctive, throaty voice. "And as soon as the police know, my enemy will be alerted."

"Despite that, the police can protect you far better than any berry."

She gave me a contemptuous look. "A real expert on berries should know better."

"I'm sorry. I don't understand."

A group of tourists bumped into us as they hurried past.

"Let's talk somewhere quieter." Leticia once again

took my arm, but much more gently. "At this hour, there won't be many people out by the lighthouse."

The Oriole Point lighthouse stood guard at the end of a long stone pier, where it had guided traffic on Lake Michigan since 1906.

Her suggestion made me uneasy. Did I really want to walk out on the pier with an unstable woman? Although if Leticia did push me off, I was a good swimmer.

It took several minutes to make our way along the river to the concrete ramp leading to the pier. I stayed close behind Leticia, who glanced back to make certain I followed. My spirits lifted when I saw at least a dozen people strolling along the pier. In addition, two cabin cruisers, a pontoon boat, and a motorized dinghy were currently headed up the Oriole River and past the channel markers. I recognized the people on the pontoon and waved.

Another several minutes passed as we stepped carefully beneath the skeletal elevated catwalk that connected to the lighthouse's second story. The catwalk had been built a century ago to protect the lighthouse keeper from high waves when he ventured out on the pier during bad weather. The keeper would have had no need of the catwalk this morning. There was only a gentle breeze and no sign of whitecaps. Instead, the calm waters of Lake Michigan reflected a cloudless sky, glittering like liquid diamonds as it stretched to an unbroken horizon.

It appeared Leticia had no intention of speaking until we reached the lighthouse. Even after we did, she stood with her back to the white structure, gazing out at the endless expanse of blue water. I stood beside her, relieved we were not alone.

A trio of fisherman sat on collapsible chairs at the

end of the pier, their equipment and nets scattered about them. They had set up an array of rods and lines, with two buckets at the ready for the next catch. One of the anglers suddenly reeled in a small-mouth bass.

"Congratulations," I told him and received a wink in response.

Leticia still said nothing. I glanced up at the green-capped lighthouse, which towered thirty-five feet overhead. This may have been a mistake. I was the only one scheduled to work at The Berry Basket today. And I needed to open its doors at ten. That left no time for disturbing conversations with disturbed individuals.

I looked sideways at her. She boasted sharp, pro-nounced features that gave her an air of haughtiness: a long, narrow nose, thick pale lashes, deep-set blue eyes, and hollowed high cheekbones normally seen on famished supermodels. This close I could also see the sun damage to her skin. A pity she neglected her appearance. Sunscreen, along with a comb and brush, might work wonders. She also needed to rethink her pumpkin orange hair color. Peeking at her pale lashes again, I suspected she was a natural blonde.

"Why are you looking at me?" she asked, her gaze still fixed on the lake.

"Not much else to look at." I gestured at the water. "My house is on the lake, so this is a common sight."

"And I'm an uncommon sight?" She shrugged. "I suppose that's true."

"You don't come into the village much. I've only ever seen you on the public beach, staring at the lake as you are now."

I thought back to the times I'd glimpsed Leticia at

the water's edge. Always alone, pacing along the shore before she stopped and looked out over the water. She ignored everyone else on the beach. She also seemed oblivious to the weather. Leticia had been spotted on Oriole Beach during drenching down-pours and zero-degree weather. I'd waved at her once or twice, but never received a response.

"I need to look at the lake." Her hoarse voice grew softer. "It's how I face my fears."

"Are you afraid of drowning?"

"Not anymore," she said brusquely. "I'm afraid of forgetting. And I cannot forget."

"Forget what?"

"The past." This was followed by more silence.

Okay, I'd wasted enough time. "If we came out here to admire the view, I'll have to cut it short. My store opens soon. We can talk at The Berry Basket when you're ready."

"Not possible. I've stayed in town too long as it is." Leticia shot a wary look at the fishermen, but they were occupied with their own conversation. "I went to your house this morning. The workmen told me that you had left to meet the mayor's wife at River Park. I came straightaway." She turned to look at me. "I need someone who has devoted their life to berries."

That made me sound like a medieval nun. "I haven't devoted my life to berries. I simply sell berry products."

"But you know more about berries than anyone else in town."

"Probably. Then again, we live in Michigan's fruit belt. Over a dozen orchards and berry farms lie within a few miles of the village. The farmers will know even more than me. Although for over a century, my family did grow fruit in the area, including berries. But my father and his sister lost the orchards to the bank years ago."

This turn of events came as a relief to my parents, who moved to Chicago. My mother was now a professor at Northwestern and my father ran a boutique hotel. At the same time, I went off to college, followed by several years as a producer for the Gourmet Living Network in New York City. My television career came to an end while I was producing the hit cooking show *Sugar and Spice.* The meteoric rise of the show's stars, John and Evangeline Chaplin, fizzled out after John had an affair with one of the show's interns. His wife Evangeline didn't take his betrayal well. She served him an anniversary cake laced with poison.

The notorious murder trial involved everyone connected with the show and led me to rethink my career choices. I returned home to become an entrepreneur, assuming this spelled the end of any involvement with murder. So far, that had not been the case.

"But you sell berries," Leticia insisted, "even if you don't grow them yourself."

"I've always loved berries. And I have fond memories of playing in the family orchards. A berry-themed shop seemed like a good idea. It's proved to be just that." I gave her an indulgent smile. "But I still wouldn't say I'm *devoted* to berries. My interest is professional."

"Either way, you should know why I need mulberries to protect me."

I felt both confused and intrigued. "Like most berries, mulberries provide significant health benefits. They contain calcium, iron, vitamin K and vitamin C, as well as riboflavin. They're rich in antioxidants, especially the anti-inflammatory agent resveratrol, also found in red wine. The components in mulberries help slow down the aging process."

I made a mental note to include this information in my Wednesday Holistic Hints talk. "Mulberries regulate cholesterol and blood sugar levels," I continued. "Their carotenoids may help prevent vision problems like cataracts and macular degeneration. I have an aunt who uses mulberries to treat her blemishes and age—"

Leticia held up her hand. "Is that all you know about mulberries? A list of nutrients?"

She had a point. Leticia came to me because she believed someone wanted to kill her. The nutritional content of mulberries didn't offer protection from that.

"Give me a minute." The first thing that came to mind was the English nursery rhyme "Pop Goes the Weasel." But I doubted any form of protection could be derived from a monkey chasing a weasel around a mulberry bush.

"Mulberries produce their buds quickly," I said. "Observers in the Greco-Roman world believed this speedy process must be magical. To the Greeks, the mulberry represented wisdom and expediency. They dedicated the mulberry bush to Athena, goddess of wisdom."

"Wisdom." She closed her eyes. "Expediency. Magic."

Uncertain of what she required, I added, "The Japanese fed mulberries to the silkworms that produced the fiber for kimonos. In fact, the only food silkworms will eat are mulberries. In Japan, mulberries symbolize self-sacrifice, as well as the desire to nurture and support."

Leticia opened her eyes and stared out at the lake once more. "Continue."

"Excuse me, but I don't see how any of this stuff about mulberries can help protect you."

"A berry expert would know."

I hated to not do well on a test, and I felt like I was failing now. Rifling my memory once more, I thought back to German folklore, which portrayed mulberry trees as evil. It was believed the devil used the tree's roots to polish his boots. Yet how would that help Leticia? I looked out at the lake. The sun reflecting off the water made me shade my eyes. The sun!

I turned back to Leticia with renewed confidence. "The Chinese associated the mulberry tree with the rising sun. They saw the mulberry as an aid against evil. In fact, arrows shot from a bow made of mulberry wood were believed to drive away evil."

Her face lit up. "Exactly."

Now I understood. "Wands made of mulberry served the same purpose. They were a magical source of power and strength."

"If used correctly, mulberries act as a shield against dark forces." She examined me closely. "I knew you would understand."

"In a way. But covering your house with berries doesn't seem practical." It might be time to lighten the mood. Encouraging this fantasy seemed unwise. "Maybe you need a bow and arrow made of mulberry wood." I smiled. "Or a mulberry wand."

She did not return my smile. Instead, her expression grew more somber. I regretted my joking comment.

Leticia might very well have stockpiled a few arrows and wands.

"Elderberries are even more powerful in the magical world than mulberries," I went on. "J. K. Rowling featured an elder wand in the Harry Potter books for that very reason. And the people who run Elderwood Farm are in the park right now. I'm sure they could supply you with enough elderberries to cover your house." I'd prefer Elderwood Farm cater to her delusions.

She shook her head vigorously. "That farm is an abomination. They corrupted their land. Poisoned it! Their elderberries are tainted and drained of power. No. I need mulberries. And no berry possesses as much power here in Oriole Point. The village was founded because of orioles and mulberries. That's why I moved here. Mulberries protect the town."

Leticia knew her local history. In 1830, Piper's ancestor Benjamin Lyall camped along the Oriole River. When he awoke the next morning, the first thing he saw were flocks of orioles eating the berries of a nearby mulberry tree. This inspired Benjamin to found a town right where he had camped and to name it Oriole Point. Because of this story, Piper regarded orioles as the avian version of angels. So how could I blame Leticia for thinking mulberries might hold special sway in Oriole Point?

There didn't seem to be any way around this but to give her what she wanted. "I have a reliable vendor near the Indiana border. He's open on Saturday. I'll call this morning and get a price on bags of dried mulberries. Assuming he has enough in stock." I frowned. "Do you need to cover every inch of your house? That many mulberries could take time to order and ship."

"More would be better, but the need is urgent." Leticia didn't look happy about this. "Order enough bags to place around the borders of my windows and doors." She gave me the number of doors and windows at her house, and their approximate sizes.

I tried to calculate how many bags to order. "If the berries are in stock, he can ship them directly to you. With luck, they could be here by Tuesday."

"I won't allow a stranger to come to my home. Have the berries sent to your shop. I'll pick them up. My scooter has a storage box."

Ah, yes. Her scooter. The only other times I'd seen Letitia anywhere but the beach was when she motored through town on her purple scooter.

"Your scooter's storage box won't be able to hold that many mulberries. If you like, I can deliver it to your cottage."

"Only if you bring it. No one else." Leticia told me her address, which I entered in my phone.

"Could I have your phone number, too? In case there's a problem with the order."

Leticia looked conflicted about this request. After a moment, she gave me her phone number, but added, "I rarely speak on the phone. I'd feel safer if you sent me an email."

Learning she used email surprised me. Did Leticia the Lake Lady have a presence on Twitter and Instagram, too? I was even more surprised at her email address. The name "Leticia" did not appear anywhere in it. But "Mulberry Mischief" did.

"Looking at your email address, it appears you love berries as much as I do."

"Only mulberries. I have no use for the others."

I slipped my phone back into my cross-body bag. "Too bad you didn't come to me this summer. Mulberry trees grow in front of my house. My lawn is littered with mulberries when they ripen. Especially from the big trees that shade my Adirondack chairs. I could have given you hundreds of my own berries then."

Her face took on a beatific expression. "You live among mulberry trees? It is a sign that I have chosen well."

I didn't know how to respond to that so I simply said, "When I get a price on the berries, I'll email you. A thirty-pound case might cost about two hundred and fifty dollars. That doesn't include shipping, of course."

"This should cover shipping." She reached into the pocket of her cardigan and pulled out a wad of cash. When she unrolled it, I saw they were all hundred-dollar bills. I felt my eyes pop out of my head. She tried to hand me four hundred dollars, but I waved her away.

"That's too much," I protested. "I'll get the exact price and email you."

She pressed the money into my hand. "If you need more, I'll pay you upon delivery. Please. I have no time to argue."

I suspected it would be pointless to refuse. "Okay, I'll email your receipt. Any discrepancies in cost can be handled when I deliver the berries."

"Good. I should not be seen in town for a while."
She looked behind her. "It's not safe."

I tucked the money into my bag. "How did you
become so intrigued by mulberries?"

"I had a roommate once. The most intelligent
person I ever met. She spoke six languages. And she
taught me about the natural world, a world of mystery
and magic. She spoke with plants and trees. They
imparted their secrets to her." Leticia leaned nearer.
"Never harm a beech tree. They are vengeful and will
tell the other trees to injure you."

I didn't ask how. I saw no purpose in encouraging
revenge fantasies, arboreal or human.

"She communicated with berry trees and bushes,
too. Each type of berry possesses mysterious properties, like crystals do."

"Such as?"

"Blueberries draw harmony into your life." She
pointed at my red enamel earrings in the shape of
strawberries. "I don't want to alarm you, but strawberries bring strife."

I wasn't alarmed. In my experience, strawberries
brought pleasure, especially when baked in a pie. "Do
you remember the special properties given to other
berries?"

"Cranberries are for romance. Blackberries evoke
vivid dreams. Raspberries provide solace in troubled
times." She raised her eyebrow at me. "And mulberries produce magic."

"According to your email address, mulberries also
cause mischief."

"Each berry has more than one power. For mulberries, it's magic *and* mischief."

All this alliteration made me think of Piper's health fair and the plethora of words beginning with "H." I hoped the alliteration for mulberry stopped with "magic" and "mischief." Because after my conversation with Leticia, I feared mulberries might also be tied to madness.

Chapter Three

"Trick or Treat!"

I smiled at Minnie. I doubted there was an African gray parrot with a better vocabulary in Michigan. Maybe even the Midwest. Since adopting her in June, I'd counted over three hundred words in her repertoire, with new ones added weekly. She was a quick learner. Especially since I often brought her to The Berry Basket, thereby exposing her to endless conversations from the staff and customers.

"Trick or Treat!" she repeated from her wooden perch. "Andrew is sweet!"

I turned to the front counter where my employee Andrew Cabot sat laughing. "When did you teach her to say that?"

"Don't blame me. Minnie's smart enough to recognize my sweet nature on her own."

"You're such a liar. What other phrases have you taught her? They better be G-rated."

"I'm the boss," Minnie said, then whistled. "I woke up like this."

I chuckled. "I see you're playing Beyoncé for Minnie when I'm not here."

"I sing the songs to her, too. Throw in a few dance moves." Andrew did a quick demonstration behind the counter. "Minnie and I have to do something when things get slow."

"Hi ho, hi ho," Minnie sang out from her perch near the window. "Kiss for Mommy."

"Mommy wants a kiss, too." I kissed the top of Minnie's gray feathered head, then gave her a scratch. She closed her eyes in contentment.

I kept a four-foot-tall perch in the store, along with bird toys and her favorite foods. When she grew sleepy, I let her nap in the travel cage in my back office. My regular customers now expected to be greeted by Minnie and were disappointed on the days when I left her at home.

"Give me a cashew," she murmured, prompting me to take a cashew out of my apron pocket. I always carried around a supply of her favorite snack.

After eating the cashew, Minnie gave a perfect imitation of the high-pitched bark of my friend Natasha's Yorkie. Not one of my favorite imitations since Minnie liked to bark almost as much as little Dasha did.

As the barking continued, I turned my attention outside the shop window. The lovely weather we had enjoyed over the weekend had ended. I woke to cloudy skies and rain. It had rained steadily all day, giving me a case of Monday-morning blues.

"A good thing Piper's health fair is being held indoors for the rest of the week. My weather app says there might be more rain tomorrow. And temperatures are dropping."

"It better stay dry for the parade on Saturday. Oscar and I spent a lot of money on our costumes." Andrew held up his iPad to show me a photo of two cast members from the musical *Hamilton*. "Oscar's dressing as Hamilton, and I'm Thomas Jefferson."

Oscar Lucas owned a florist shop in neighboring Saugatuck, where Andrew also worked part-time. The two had quickly become a romantic couple, even though Oscar was seven years older. I had hoped the age difference might help Andrew move out of his extended adolescence. So far there was no sign of it. For his twenty-fifth birthday last month, Andrew celebrated with a laser tag party. Followed by an hour at the arcade.

"I'm surprised you're letting Oscar appear as the title character while you take second billing."

He made a face. "Please. We had the original Broadway costumes replicated. Thomas Jefferson has a much better wardrobe. My costume is velvet. With cuffs! Oscar's Colonial uniform can't compete with that."

"Dare I ask what costume your brother is wearing?" Dean Cabot also worked at my shop and was even more fashion conscious than Andrew.

Andrew's reply was cut short when someone called the store phone, which spurred Minnie to leave off barking and imitate the ringtone. As Minnie grew louder, I struggled to hear what the caller said. I heard enough to know it was good news.

"You look happy," Andrew remarked after I hung up.

"That was Chris Farnsworth, the vendor I ordered all those dried mulberries from. He and his wife are coming to the health fair. His wife is a big fan of the Sable products. She insisted they drive up to Oriole Point so she could meet them. This means he can deliver the mulberries to me in person." I glanced up at the red wall clock shaped like a strawberry. "He's only an hour away. Says he'll drop the berries off here before they check into a B&B."

"Good news for the Lake Lady. You can deliver her mulberries earlier than planned."

"I'll drive them over as soon as I load the berries in my SUV. You should be fine handling everything here on your own."

He scanned the empty store, "Ya think?"

Indeed, I could count today's customers on one hand. In fact, there was no need for both of us to be at the store. But I felt a responsibility to offer my staff hours even when business turned slow. And I had spent so much time at my house during all the repairs, I welcomed the chance to putter about my shop. However, I had already cleaned every surface, filed invoices, sliced the cranberry coffee cakes left by my baker Theo, then rearranged every last tea tin, jelly jar, oven mitt, and wine bottle in the shop.

I even trimmed Minnie's nails. I might have turned my attention to her wings next, but the vet clipped them last week. Too bad I had already decorated the shop for Halloween. I would have welcomed the distraction of putting out more jack-o'-lanterns, cobwebs, stuffed scarecrows, and bats. But I had overdone the Halloween décor. The store was festooned with so many decorations, customers might think they had entered a haunted house, not a berry emporium.

"I didn't expect a lot of business during the health fair. Not with all those celebrities Piper booked." As I straightened the chairs at the bistro tables near the ice cream counter, my glance fell on the ice cream, especially chocolate caramel raspberry, my current favorite. I'd eaten lunch two hours ago. Enough time had passed to justify a small scoop.

Andrew looked up from his iPad. "If you're getting ice cream for yourself, I wouldn't mind a boysenberry swirl cone."

I began to scoop ice cream while Minnie sang out, "Ba-ba-ba ba-ba ba-ran." No matter how many Beyoncé songs Andrew taught her, Minnie's heart belonged to the Beach Boys.

"If I keep eating this ice cream, I may need the Sable Diet. Gillian's uncle lost eighty pounds. And Tess's sister-in-law lost fifteen pounds in one month. It must work."

"Of course it works. You fast all week, then binge on the weekend. And no dairy. Not even yogurt. Thanks." He took his ice cream cone with an eager smile. "I tried it once when I wanted to lose five pounds. I quit after two days. And you know me. I love a good fad diet."

"Doesn't sound like a healthy diet. I wonder why it's so popular."

"Because most people are desperate and lazy," he said. "That diet's certainly made the Sables rich. The younger son Keith is in charge of all the diet supplements. Saw him on a home-shopping network last month plugging their frozen diet meals and protein bars. I've eaten a few. Too bland. The only product with any real flavor is their espresso chocolate protein bar."

"I don't think I've ever tried anything by the Sable company."

"The skin-care products are first-rate. I use a ton of it to stay this flawless." He patted his smooth cheek.

"Their foaming watercress facial cleanser is the best. Gluten-free, too."

"Why would there be gluten in facial cleanser? And why is your brother taking such a long time at the police station? How much could your mother have to say about the Lake Lady?"

Because I'd worked alone at the store this past weekend, I didn't have the chance to talk to Andrew or Dean until today. Curious about Leticia, I hoped the gossip-loving Cabot boys might know something I didn't. But they were as clueless as me when it came to Leticia's background. However, Andrew and Dean's mom, Suzanne Cabot, worked as the police department's receptionist. That was her official title. Unofficially, she was known as Oriole Point's treasure trove of gossip. Which was why I sent Dean over there an hour ago to pump her for information about Leticia.

"Maybe Mom has so much dirt on Leticia, it requires a good hour to pass on. Or Dean got distracted and is now interviewing someone for his blog."

Andrew's older brother ran a popular blog called The Dean Report. The blog's witty, irreverent take on life along the lakeshore had made the Top 25 Blogs List in *Chicago Magazine.* And Dean had just begun his own podcast. A year from now, I expected he would be too busy to even work his part-time hours at the shop.

"I'm not looking for dirt on Leticia." I finished scooping my ice cream and took a moment to enjoy that first delectable spoonful. "I'd just like to know more about her before I deliver the mulberries. Her full name would be a good place to start."

After my encounter with Leticia on Saturday, I

called my best friend Tess and my aunt Vicki. Neither had much information on her. Aunt Vicki believed she kept bees. Like everyone else in town, they had witnessed Leticia staring out at the lake like the melodramatic heroine of *The French Lieutenant's Woman*. Although I doubted a tale of troubled romance lay behind Leticia's fascination with the lake.

Denise Redfern, owner of the Tonguish Spirit Gallery next door, did have a little info. Three years ago, Leticia fell off her scooter and badly scraped her arms and legs. Because the accident took place right outside her shop, Denise tried to help. But Leticia would not get into the ambulance that was called, nor would she let Denise take her into the gallery to clean her wounds. Instead, she accused the paramedics and Denise of trying to trap her. In the end, they'd had no choice but to let Leticia get back on her scooter and drive off.

Whatever story lay behind Leticia's behavior, it must be a sad one.

The shop door swung open, revealing a rain-drenched Dean. A tall thin man with a receding hairline stood behind him.

"It's about time," Andrew said.

Dean and the stranger stepped inside.

"Welcome to The Berry Basket," I said to the man, who gave me a cursory nod. I wondered if he was a customer or someone Dean knew.

"Why are you even open, Marlee?" Dean pushed back the hood of his rain jacket. "Every local news station along the lakeshore is at the conference center. Along with most of the people who live here. Half the shops on Lyall have closed for the day."

"Are you serious?" I hurried over to the door and

peeked out. He was right. Many of the stores had taken down their OPEN flags. I kicked the door closed. "Well, that is just bad business. I'm sure there are lots of out-of-town visitors here for the fair. They might think our shops don't stay open past the summer season."

Minnie cocked her head at Dean. "Whassup, punk?"

He grinned. "Glad you asked, Minnie. At this very moment, Cameron Sable should be speaking at the Lyall Center on the pursuit of happiness. The Pilates Queen is demonstrating her latest machines. The winners of last season's *Dance with Me* are giving tango lessons—"

"No way! I love that show." Andrew shot me an accusing look. "Marlee, why are we open? We're missing all the fun."

"He has a point. No one will be interested in shopping while the health fair is in full swing." When Dean spied Andrew's ice cream cone, he made a beeline for the ice cream counter, where he proceeded to scoop some for himself. Of course he chose the same flavor as Andrew.

Although eleven months apart, the Cabot boys looked and often acted like twins. Both were tall, attractive, auburn haired, and obsessed with fashion. The only difference is that Andrew was gay, and Dean was a straight man with impossibly high standards in women.

I turned to the fellow who had followed Dean into the shop. He seemed occupied with shaking the raindrops from his umbrella. "Please let me know if I can help you with anything. Unless you're a friend of Dean's."

"Oh, no. I never met the young man before." He finally turned his full attention to me.

"He came into the police station when I was there," Dean said. "He's been asking around about a person he thinks lives in Oriole Point."

"I got into town last night," the stranger said. "I'm looking for a woman, but I only have her PO box address. And her phone number."

"Why don't you simply call her?" I asked.

"She's not answering my calls. I need to get in touch with her about business." He stepped toward me, hand outstretched. "I'm sorry. My name is Felix Bonaventure."

I shook his hand. "Your parents gave you a fortuitous name."

He smiled. "Literally."

"How so?" Andrew asked.

"'Bonaventure' means 'good fortune' in Latin," I said. "And 'Felix' is Latin for 'lucky.'"

"My father believed our last name was responsible for what he regarded as his charmed life," Felix said. "To increase our family's good luck, he chose his children's names with care. My sister is called Felicity."

"My mother's taste in names is more whimsical," I said. "She was rereading *A Christmas Carol* when she went into labor with me on Christmas Eve."

He looked dismayed. "Your name's Ebenezer?"

The Cabot boys laughed. "No, thank the Lord," I said. "Our last name is Jacob, so I was named after Scrooge's miserly partner, Jacob Marley. Only with the name switched around to Marlee Jacob."

"If my father were here," he said, "he could probably explain what your name means."

"We're pretty sure it means trouble," Andrew told him.

"Ignore him," I said. "Why don't you tell us who you're looking for?"

He sighed. "No one has been able to help me so far. And I've been to almost every shop in downtown Oriole Point, although many were closed today. None of the shopkeepers had a clue as to how to help me track this woman down."

"What's her name?" I asked.

"Ellen Mulberry."

Andrew made a strangled sound behind the counter.

"When I mentioned Ms. Mulberry's name, several shopkeepers recommended I stop at The Berry Basket." Felix scanned the items in my store. "But I can see that you simply sell berry products. Unless you do know a person by the name of Mulberry."

I sat down at the bistro table. "I've never heard of anyone called Ellen Mulberry."

"That's what I told him," Dean said.

"She has to be somewhere in the area. I receive mail from her postmarked New Bethel."

"New Bethel lies at the northern tip of the county," I explained. "Why are you looking for her in Oriole Point?"

"I spent the morning in New Bethel, which as you no doubt know, is much smaller than this village. No one knew who Ellen Mulberry was. And the woman working at the post office refused to release any information about the people who have boxes there."

"Again, why come to Oriole Point? The county has a number of small towns."

"Ms. Mulberry has mentioned Oriole Point to me several times. She calls it her home."

I snuck a peek at Andrew and Dean. "Maybe if you told us what she looked like."

"We've never met in person. All our business is done via phone and email."

"What exactly is your business?" Dean asked.

Felix opened his mouth to speak, then stopped. "I'm not at liberty to say. We have a confidentiality agreement. Only some of our business details have gotten complicated recently. Even though Ms. Mulberry prefers we not have a face-to-face meeting, I'm afraid circumstances now demand that we do. If you have any clue as to where she is, I'd be grateful."

Andrew, Dean, and I once more exchanged looks. All three of us shook our heads.

"Sorry," Andrew said. "Never heard of her."

Felix reached into the pocket of his brown jacket and took out a business card. "Let me leave my card with you. I'm staying in South Haven at the Hampton Inn. All the hotels in Oriole County were booked due to that health fair."

I ran my finger over the embossed lettering on the card.

"If you hear anything about Ms. Mulberry, please call me. I must find her."

After he left, we sat in silence. Except for Minnie repeating, "Never heard of her."

"I assume we all think Ellen Mulberry is Leticia the Lake Lady," I said finally.

"She must be." Andrew leaned over the counter. "Although before this weekend, I would never have connected the Lake Lady to anyone called Ellen Mulberry. But now . . ."

I nodded. "It's too much of a coincidence. A strange

man shows up looking for a woman by the name of Mulberry two days after Leticia asks for enough mulberries to cover her house. And 'mulberry' is part of her email address."

"What if she's right about someone wanting to kill her?" Dean asked.

"Do you think this Felix guy is the one she's afraid of?" I tapped the business card.

Andrew shrugged. "Who knows? What does his card say?"

I looked down at it again. "It only contains basic contact information. No mention about any sort of business."

"That's weird," Dean said. "Where's he from?"

"Philadelphia." I slipped the card into my jeans pocket. "I thought Leticia was delusional. But Mr. Bonaventure has made me rethink that assumption. And he didn't really explain *why* he needs to find her. Saying he's here on business is pretty vague."

"Can you fly?" Minnie asked me.

"Even though I promised Leticia I wouldn't go to the police, I should let Kit know." Atticus "Kit" Holt was an investigative officer for the sheriff's department. For the past two months, he had also been my boyfriend. I would have told him already, except three days ago, he flew down to Texas for his brother's wedding.

"When's he coming home?"

"Tonight," I told Dean. "He doesn't go back to work until Wednesday, so I can spend time with him tomorrow. If he's not too tired, he says he might join Theo and me on our early morning hike with the Lakeshore Birders."

"You're such a nerd," Andrew said.

"This from someone who wore face paint and camouflage to his laser tag birthday party."

Dean laughed. "You tell him, Marlee."

"Now that you've finished scooping your ice cream, how about giving us the scoop on Leticia the Lake Lady?" I asked him. "What did your mother say?"

"Nothing. She wasn't at the police station." Dean took a big bite of ice cream.

"What do you mean Mom wasn't there?" Andrew threw his brother a frustrated glance. "Where have you been for the past hour?"

"Oh, I've been at the police station."

"Let me guess," I said. "Your mother is at the conference center."

"Got it in one," Dean said. "Officer Davenport was the only person left at the station."

I made a face at the mention of Janelle Davenport's name.

"Janelle told me that Mom went to see the dance couple and get autographs," he continued. "And Chief Hitchcock signed up for the happiness workshop Cameron Sable is giving. Who knew our police chief was interested in pursuing criminals *and* happiness?"

"Did Janelle have any information about Leticia?" I asked.

"Oh, I got an earful when I mentioned her name. Janelle went off on a rant about the weirdoes and degenerates in Oriole Point, which includes Leticia and Old Man Bowman. She'd like to see them all run out of town."

"By a mob waving pitchforks, no doubt." I had little use for Officer Davenport, who had moved here from Milwaukee several years ago. Her suspicious and often hostile attitude seemed more suited to the mean streets of a big city. "What's her beef with Leticia? She keeps to herself, except for her visits to the beach."

"It seems she's got cats running all over her property. And a bunch of wild turkeys."

"Big deal," Andrew said. "The Carver couple have fifteen pet squirrels. And they're hoarders. The Carvers, I mean. Not the squirrels. Although the squirrels probably hoard nuts."

"What else did Janelle say?" I asked.

"In the middle of her rant, a call came in about a fender bender on Huron Street. It sounded like road rage was involved. Janelle took off, leaving me alone at the police station."

"Where I hoped you did your duty and snooped around," I said.

"Of course I did. First, I logged onto a couple computers—"

"How do you know the police passwords?" I asked.

"Hello? Mom has worked there for twenty years. She knows everyone's password."

"She tells us the passwords, too. In case she forgets." Andrew finished his cone.

I wasn't sure I wanted too many details. "What did all this covert activity produce?"

Dean wiped his mouth with a napkin before answering. "There was nothing on any of the computers about Leticia. Although there's a file on Chief Hitchcock's computer named BURIED TREASURE. Do you know there are supposed to be three buried hoards of gold in the county?"

Andrew whistled. "Maybe we can put together a treasure hunt. I'd love that. So would Oscar. Marlee, are you in?"

"Forget about the buried treasure right now. I want to know about Leticia or Ellen Mulberry or whoever she really is. Dean, did you learn anything helpful?"

"I sure did. After I searched all the computer files, I went through those ancient filing cabinets. And lo and behold, I found a LAKE LADY file folder."

Andrew and I waited. Dean clearly enjoyed dragging this out.

"Her real name is Ellen Clark. Married to an Anthony Clark, who died four years ago. She moved to Oriole Point a few months later and bought those fifteen acres by the woods."

"Fifteen acres doesn't come cheap. I wonder how she afforded it," I said. "She also walks around with a wad of hundred-dollar bills in her pocket."

"Insurance policy?" Andrew looked at his brother. "Was her ex-husband some rich guy?"

"The file says he was a correctional counselor." Dean paused. "At the state prison."

"Uh oh." I bit my lip. "Some ex-convict who knew Anthony Clark might be after her. Does the file say anything about what her maiden name is? Or when she was born?"

"Didn't have time to go through the rest of it. Chief Hitchcock came back. I barely got the file drawer closed in time. Luckily, Felix Bonaventure arrived and distracted the chief long enough for me to get the file folder back and sneak out of his office."

This information had increased my worry. "So Leticia was married to a man who worked in a prison. Now she fears for her life. Think of all the criminals her husband worked with who may had have a grudge against him."

Andrew looked concerned. "What if a homicidal maniac is on his way to Oriole Point?" What if he's just been in the store talking to us?"

"Poor Leticia," I murmured. "I need to tell Kit. He'll know what to do to keep her safe."

"I saw enough of her file to know that Leticia isn't defenseless," Dean said.

"What do you mean?" I asked.

"Leticia, a.k.a. Ellen Clark, was one of the criminals Anthony Clark counseled at the state prison. She was an inmate there. He married her after she was released."

For a moment, neither Andrew nor I spoke. Even Minnie remained silent.

"What was she in prison for?" I asked finally.

Dean frowned. "Murder."

Chapter Four

"You can't go out there alone," Andrew said to me as we loaded boxes of dried mulberries into my SUV.

Chris Farnsworth and his wife had arrived fifteen minutes earlier with Leticia's order. Eager to check into their B&B, the couple dropped off the boxes and were off again with barely twenty words exchanged between us. The Cabot boys made up for it by trying to dissuade me from driving out to the cabin.

"At least let one of us go with you." Dean gave me a worried look.

"Speak for yourself," Andrew said. "I have no intention of visiting some woman who was in prison for murder. Call me kooky, but there it is. And neither of you should either."

I didn't wholly disagree with him. Still, Leticia was frightened for her life, rightly or wrongly. And having these mulberries might bring her some comfort. Besides, I had given her my word that I would deliver them.

"If she was going to be dangerous, don't you think it would have happened by now?"

"Maybe all she needed was some sort of trigger."

Andrew grew more exasperated. "What if she knows this guy is looking for her? What if her terror pushes her over the edge?"

"Why should Marlee be a target?" Dean asked him.

"Oh, I don't know. Because Leticia is crazy!"

I rearranged the boxes in the back of the SUV, then slammed the door. "If she was still a threat to society, why would they release her from prison?"

Andrew looked frustrated. "Right. Because ex-convicts never repeat their crimes."

Dean sighed. "I wish I'd had more time to go through her file. Maybe she killed someone out of self-defense. Or she was under the influence."

"Don't sugarcoat it, big brother. She was in prison for murder."

"What I read didn't specify if it was first- or second-degree murder. That makes a difference, doesn't it?"

"The longer I put off going out there, the more nervous I'll be." I held up my cell phone. "I already texted to let her know I was bringing the mulberries."

"Did she reply?" Dean asked.

"No. But at least I won't take her by surprise."

"Marlee, I'm tempted to go to Chief Hitchcock right this minute to tell him that you're about to visit a murderess," Andrew warned.

"Don't you dare," Dean said. "Hitchcock would figure out you only knew that because I'd snooped in his files. After all, he just saw me at the police station."

"What's he gonna do? Jail you for snooping? Marlee's safety is more important."

"Thanks for your concern, guys." I zipped up my sweater jacket. The temperature had dropped below sixty. "But I'm off to deliver these berries."

While Andrew protested, I got into my SUV. For a

moment, I was afraid he might throw himself in front of my vehicle. Mercifully, he did not.

As I pulled away, Dean shouted, "Text me when you leave!"

While touched by their concern, I felt unnerved by it. Was Leticia a danger? There was no doubt she had been at one time. But how long ago? And under what circumstances? I told myself that I'd already been face-to-face with more than one killer and lived to tell the tale. I could handle one quick visit to Leticia the Lake Lady.

On the way there, I listened to a Native American flute music CD I'd bought at Denise's gallery. By the time I drove the thirty minutes to Leticia's property, I felt like I'd sat through a relaxing meditation session. The drive took me almost to the border of Oriole County. Given the mix of farms and woodland, traffic was light. The rain had stopped and the sun made attempts to break through the clouds. I took that as a good sign.

After a glance at the GPS on my phone, I slowed down and turned onto a small graveled road. After a minute, the trees lining the road stopped and I found myself in a clearing. An attractive log home stood at the end of the drive. My arrival startled an enormous flock of wild turkeys pecking on the ground. As their gobbles pierced the air, they headed for the trees.

I braked to a stop and rolled down the window. I heard nothing but turkeys and meows. I spotted several dozen cats and assorted kittens between here and the front porch. My heart sank.

These cats must be constantly reproducing. My aunt ran a rescue organization called Humane Hearts, and I knew how heartbreaking the lives of feral cats were. With luck, I could convince Leticia to let my aunt and her volunteers trap the animals in order to spay and neuter them.

I got out of the vehicle. Trees stood off in the distance with a wide field in between; some of it held wooden beehives. The property looked well cared for. Flower bushes clipped, front lawn mowed. As for her house, it qualified as a custom-built log home. Several friends owned log homes, and I recognized this one as built in the traditional Hearthstone design.

Now that I saw how she lived, I felt better. I expected her residence to be as neglected as her physical appearance. But Leticia lived in a lovely single-story house with bronze and gold mums planted out front. Although there were far too many cats and turkeys running about.

I walked up the steps to her front porch and knocked on the door. No response.

Although I peeked in her front window, I couldn't see through the plaid curtains. Next, I called her phone. If she were nearby or in the house, I might be able to hear the ringtone. I heard nothing but the turkeys restive in the trees and the angry yowls of the cats who glared at me below the porch.

Maybe I should look for her scooter. If it wasn't here, neither was she.

I checked out a small shed behind the house that held garden tools. Since she had no garage or barn, I suspected it sheltered her scooter when there was bad weather. But her purple motor scooter wasn't in the shed, nor was it anywhere to be seen. A number of plastic dishes did ring the wooden shed, each filled with the remains of cat kibble. Three large water bowls sat on the grassy path. I spotted two cats peering out at me from beneath the leaves of a dying hosta.

I felt relieved she was gone. All I had to do now was unload the boxes and be on my way.

In case it rained again, I placed all the boxes on her covered front porch. After I put the last box below her front window, I took out my phone and called her again. No answer. As I waited to leave a voicemail, I recalled Felix Bonaventure's visit to my shop. Was he a threat to Leticia? Was she right to be afraid? I decided to give her a heads up.

"Leticia, this is Marlee Jacob again," I said after the phone beeped. "I've left the mulberries on your front porch. I also thought you should know a man called Felix Bonaventure is in town looking for Ellen Mulberry. I don't know if you're the woman he's asking about, but the name 'Mulberry' made me think of you." I pulled his business card out of my jeans pocket. "I'll give you his phone number in case you want to contact him."

After I hung up, I wondered if this would make her even more fearful. But if Bonaventure was the person she believed wanted to kill her, she should be warned.

One of the cats went up to the front door and scratched at it with a long, piteous meow. "Do you want to go inside?" I asked.

The gray cat looked at me and meowed again. Maybe all the cats weren't feral. I stepped closer and it didn't move away. Did the cat live in the house? Another cat joined us. A sleek tortoiseshell with huge brown eyes. This one, too, stretched against the door.

"I think it's locked," I told them. Although I didn't know that.

I gripped the doorknob and turned. The door opened and the two cats ran inside. I poked my head in. "Hello?"

Although most Oriole Point residents left their doors unlocked, I would not have thought the misanthropic Leticia would be among them. I looked about. The living room was neatly furnished with a rocker, sofa, wooden coffee table, and brass floor lamps. Shelves crammed with books bordered a flagstone fireplace. My eyes widened at the big-screen TV.

At the risk of being caught as a trespasser, I went over to the TV and saw the satellite TV box. Why had I assumed Leticia lived like a survivalist or the Unabomber? I scanned her bookshelves, intrigued by the eclectic mix of titles—everything from Lee Child to Joseph Campbell's *The Hero's Journey*. The blue-and-white kitchen was visible from the living room.

Another cat darted inside, scooting past me as it ran into a hallway I assumed led to the bedrooms. I had no business being in Leticia's house uninvited, even if I was trying to help her cats. I also hoped she allowed the cats in here, otherwise she might be upset to find three felines inside. I'd leave her another voicemail, explaining that I had opened the door for them.

I suddenly remembered the money in my bag. Leticia paid me too much for the mulberries on Saturday, and I'd brought her the change in an envelope. I scribbled a note on the envelope and left it on the coffee table. I hoped she didn't mind that I had rudely entered her house. At this rate, I'd be hacking into the computers at the police station next.

When I turned to go, my gaze fell on an Apple laptop that sat on a desk by the door.

At that moment, the cats ran back into the living room, chasing each other. One leaped on top of the couch, then jumped onto the adjacent desk. The cat hurled itself off as the other cat raced behind. This flurry of activity caused the stack of papers beside the computer to be dislodged. Several pages fluttered to the hardwood floor.

I picked them up and put them back on the pile. As I straightened the stack, my eyes fell on the top page. It looked like a title page and read, *Mischief and Murder* by Ellen Mulberry.

More confused than ever, I stepped back. According to the police file, she was a murderer. Was Leticia a writer as well? Who was Felix Bonaventure? And who were the shadow people she mentioned? The most pressing question, however, was what was I doing in her house? After all, I'd done what I promised and delivered the mulberries.

Best to leave any murder or mischief to her.

Chapter Five

What I had learned about Leticia troubled me, but the monthly outing of the Lakeshore Birders was scheduled for the following morning. I loved birds and never missed a chance to tramp along the shore or through the woods with my binoculars. So I put aside questions about Leticia's murderous past and looked forward to the search for golden eagles and horned larks.

I rose earlier than usual, threw granola bars in my backpack, and went to meet my two favorite bird-watchers: Kit Holt and Theo Foster. Theo arrived at The Berry Basket before four every morning to bake the daily selection of berry pastries, so it was no surprise to see him waiting impatiently for me at the shop door. And I was impatient to sample the snacks he'd brought for us: warm-from-the-oven raspberry crumb bars.

Because Kit lived in New Bethel, he agreed to meet us in the parking lot of Bell Lake State Park. He'd only been gone since Friday, but when I caught sight of his curly brown hair and crooked smile, I literally felt my heart skip a beat.

His tight embrace and lingering kiss told me the feeling was mutual. I reminded myself to take the relationship slow. It was why I didn't accept Kit's invitation to attend his brother's wedding in Texas. We'd only been dating two months, not long enough for me to feel comfortable accompanying him to an out-of-state family wedding. Especially since I had recently canceled my own wedding.

This past August, my engagement to Ryan Zellar ended in betrayal and shock. Part of me was still reeling. I mistrusted my romantic instincts now, even with someone as sweet and caring as Kit. He'd been burned in love before, too, and understood my caution. Still, the attraction between us continued to deepen.

"Are you two done?" Theo asked. "Everyone's watching."

We broke apart with an embarrassed laugh. The other birders waited near the park's trail map sign. The group's president waved us over.

Kit took my hand as we walked toward them. "I missed you."

"Missed you, too. You looked like James Bond in the wedding photos you sent. Sexy and dangerous. More secret agent than best man."

"Exactly the look I was going for. Too bad my brother wouldn't let me wear my gun holster with the tux."

"If you're not quiet, you'll scare away the birds," Theo warned.

"Shhh," Kit told me, then pulled me close for another kiss.

Once we joined our fellow birders, everything got a lot louder.

We were a friendly group, and birdwatchers are always bursting with tales of the latest addition to their "list." Last week I'd added a sedge wren to my life list of birds and couldn't wait to tell everyone. Kit announced that two days ago in Texas, he'd seen a yellow-billed cuckoo in a willow grove. We were all suitably impressed. I was again gratified to be dating a man who had been a birder years before he met me. If that wasn't kismet, what was?

"It's seven o'clock," Theo reminded us. "We should start."

A flurry of activity followed as we removed lens caps from our binoculars and patted the pockets of our jackets to make certain our field guides were with us. Bending down, I tucked my jeans into my socks. I didn't want ticks crawling up my legs while a white-eye vireo diverted my attention. Four of our members had contracted Lyme disease. I did not plan to follow suit.

Jenna York, president of Lakeshore Birders, held up her hand. "Keep an eye out for American kestrels. They've been seen this week in the park. And a flock of turkey vultures over a thousand strong."

Theo turned to me with a rare smile. "Turkey vultures," he said in a hushed voice.

I was happy that he was so happy. I regarded Theo like a kid brother, even if he was older than me. Kit and Theo were both thirty-seven, but Theo's slim frame and nervous, tentative nature made him seem much younger. I had learned his sometimes childlike responses were a result of a head injury suffered when he was a toddler. And although he had excellent baking skills, his social skills needed honing. I had hired him almost a year ago, and it had taken months before he felt comfortable around me and his fellow Berry Basket employees.

Theo had recently included Kit in the tiny circle of people he trusted—something Theo never did with my ex-fiancé. Proving his instincts about men were better than mine.

Once we entered the woods, conversation faded as we listened for the chirps and calls echoing around us. One never knew if this was the day to encounter a rare shorebird or brown birds we called LBJs, otherwise known as little brown jobs difficult to identify. Bell Lake State Park held a second-growth oak-hickory forest, stretches of prairie, and an inland lake. These varied habitats made it a favorite spot for birders. Within the first thirty minutes, Kit and I spotted a Cooper's hawk, three hooded warblers, and a broadwinged hawk. Theo, however, was on a mission to find the turkey vultures.

As always happened on these outings, members began to wander off on their own. Theo remained with Kit and me, although he disapproved of our quiet conversation and stayed a good distance ahead.

We kept our voices down, but between his brother's wedding, the celebrity-laden health fair, and that yellow-billed cuckoo, we had a lot to talk about. I didn't even mention Leticia the Lake Lady for a good thirty minutes. When I finally told him about her request for mulberries and Dean's discovery about her past, I was met by a long silence.

A thrush landed on an overhead branch. I focused my binoculars on the gray bird. Only after it flew away, did I turn to Kit.

"You look puzzled," I said.

"I am. I thought the Lake Lady never spoke to anyone. Why did she approach you?"

"I told you. She thinks someone is trying to kill her."

"And you went to her house alone? After you learned she had been in prison for murder?" His expression shifted to one of concern. "Not a good idea."

"I promised to deliver the dried mulberries. And she didn't want strangers coming to her house. Only me."

"I don't care what she wants. I only care that you don't put yourself in a dicey situation." He squeezed my shoulder. "You've had a few close calls this past summer. I think you've met your quota for the year. Leave Leticia and her mulberries alone."

"I've done what she asked. Only I can't help but be curious." I lifted my binoculars and aimed them at a pair of blue jays. "What if she really is in danger? Seems fishy that some man shows up looking for a woman called Ellen Mulberry. Then I find a manuscript in her house written by an 'Ellen Mulberry.' With the title *Mischief and Murder*, too. You work for the sheriff's department. Don't you find it suspicious? And worrying?"

"I do. If Leticia comes to you with another request, call me. As for Mr. Bonaventure, I'll see what I can find out about him. Are you sure that's his name?"

"I'd hardly forget it. He told me how both his first and last name meant 'good luck.'"

"What did he look like?"

"Brown hair, receding hairline. Big dark eyes. About five ten, five eleven. Thin. Long, bumpy nose. He reminded me of Fredo in *The Godfather*." As someone named after a literary character, I often associated people with their fictional doppelgänger.

He chuckled. "A police sketch artist would love you." As a distinctive call rent the air, Kit turned his binoculars in the direction it came from. "Pileated woodpecker. Female, I think."

After a moment, I spotted the bird. "You're right. That's a female." I lowered my binoculars. "Kit, you live in New Bethel. As it's even smaller than Oriole Point, you must know most of the residents. Leticia lives on the outskirts of New Bethel."

"Remember I only moved here a few years ago. I rented an apartment in New Bethel because a friend in the department owned the building and gave me a deal on the rent. Most of my time is spent at work, or hanging out with Greg and my sister. Although you take up most of my free time now." He leaned over and kissed me. "I couldn't tell you much about anyone who lives in New Bethel."

"Leticia has long orange hair and drives a purple scooter. She'd be hard to miss."

He looked surprised. "Is that the Lake Lady? I see her scooter parked outside the New Bethel post office sometimes."

"That's her."

"Well, she hasn't done anything to attract the attention of the sheriff's department . . . yet. I advise staying clear of her. Bad enough you broke into her house." He raised an amused eyebrow at me. "Please don't do it again. I'd hate to arrest you."

"I didn't technically break in. The door was unlocked. I was only trying to help her cats get inside." I sighed. "I do feel guilty about walking into her living room. Only I was so surprised to see how nice everything was. She had satellite TV. A laptop, too. The desk and manuscript were by the door. I couldn't help seeing it."

We walked along the trail for a few minutes, scanning the trees with our binoculars.

"Did you hear anything when you were inside her house?" Kit asked finally. "Someone moaning, perhaps? Leticia may have been in one of the bedrooms, sick or injured."

"I didn't hear a sound, except for the cats. And I never went anywhere near the bedrooms." I bit my lip. "I did call her phone. I think I said 'hello' when I went inside. I don't remember. I guess she could have been in the house. But her scooter wasn't on the property. I assumed if her scooter was gone, she must be, too."

"Maybe." He now wore what I had come to learn was his sheriff investigator's expression. "Give me the address. I'll stop by her house on the way back to New Bethel today. Have a look around."

"I should go, too. Leticia came to me for help, so I'm part of this case."

He looked amused. "There's a case?"

"There might be. If so, it involves Leticia, Felix Bonaventure." I paused. "And me."

"Turkey vultures are my new favorite bird." Theo closed his spiral notebook. He'd spent the past few minutes recording the birds he had identified that morning. Despite the impressive number of birds he'd seen, he'd talked about little else but the turkey vultures since we left the park. "How can I get turkey vultures to come to my feeders?"

"Leave dead animals on the grass."

"What!"

I put my turn signal on as I approached the next cross street. "They're vultures, Theo. Vultures eat carrion. Your feeders filled with millet and sunflower seed won't interest them."

I almost added "thank God," but didn't want to diminish Theo's newfound joy in turkey vultures. The huge flock of vultures we saw at the park made an impression on me as well. Especially their unpleasant appearance.

"That's too bad." He pulled out a raspberry crumb bar from the paper bag in his backpack. "I have one more crumb bar left. I'll split it with you."

"No thanks. I ate two at the park. And a granola bar. I'm good." I checked my rearview mirror to make certain the green Camry was behind us. "Kit really enjoyed them. He ate four."

"Sometimes he calls himself 'Atticus.' But you call him 'Kit.' Why?"

"Like me, he was named after a famous character in a novel: Atticus Finch. His mother's favorite novel, in fact. *To Kill A Mockingbird.* 'Kit' is a nickname."

"I've never seen a mockingbird, have you?"

"I saw one in Central Park a few years ago."

He finished his bite of raspberry crumb bar. "I'd never kill a mockingbird. There shouldn't be a book that tells you how to do it."

I smiled and said nothing.

Theo looked out the window of my SUV at the passing mixture of farmland and woods. "Will the Lake Lady mind that we're stopping by her house? I don't like when anyone visits my cottage without telling me first." Theo rented a small riverside house called Crow

Cottage. I was one of the few people who had ever been welcomed as a guest.

"Few of us like a pop-in," I agreed. "But Kit and I want to make sure she's okay. I haven't been able to get ahold of her for the past twenty-four hours. I'm a little worried."

"You worry too much. My dad says people have to learn how to take care of themselves. That's what I do."

"And you do a good job of it. But all of us need help now and then." I slowed down as the road leading to Leticia's house came into view. I hoped the first thing we spotted when we pulled up her gravel drive was that purple scooter.

Instead, I immediately saw multiple cats lazing in the late-morning sun on Leticia's front lawn. I needed to call my aunt as soon as I got to the store. The other thing I saw was a blue car parked near the pebbled walkway that led to the log home. Did Leticia have a visitor?

"Look at the wild turkeys!" Theo pointed out the open window.

I had barely braked to a stop before Theo jumped out and ran toward the turkeys on the lawn. His approach caused them to move away. A wave of gobbles filled the air.

Kit arrived a moment after I did. He got out of his car and looked around. "Don't see any scooter. Maybe she traded it in for this Ford Focus."

"I doubt she suddenly acquired a car. Someone is here." I joined Kit as he looked through the closed windows of the car. The upholstered seats were empty. "And it doesn't explain where Leticia's scooter is. Maybe she parked it behind the house."

"Before we go snooping around her property, let's

knock on the door. This way we'll also be able to find out who her visitor is."

We walked up to the log home, bypassing three cats on the porch steps.

Kit looked in the front window. Those closed plaid curtains revealed nothing. Next, he stepped to the front door and knocked. "Ms. Clark, are you home? It's the sheriff's department."

I bit my lip. If Leticia was home, his announcement was sure to spook her.

While he knocked again, I glanced over the side of the porch in time to see Theo trail after the wild turkeys. All of them seemed headed for the beehives in the back field. Theo must have spotted an interesting bird, because he stopped and raised his binoculars.

"Hello? Is anyone there?" Kit said in a loud voice.

"Maybe we should go inside to make certain she isn't sick or hurt." I grabbed the doorknob and turned. It was locked. "That's funny. It wasn't locked yesterday."

"Maybe you locked it when you left."

"No. I made certain not to. I didn't want to lock her out of her own house. After all, I have no idea if she even carries around a key." I jiggled the doorknob. It wouldn't budge.

Kit gave one last attempt at the door. "If her door is now locked, she must have returned to her home since your visit yesterday afternoon."

He and I walked down the porch steps, accompanied by a chorus of meows.

"Or someone else came here and that person locked the door. Maybe the driver of that blue Ford." I turned to face the log home. "What if he's in there with her right now, waiting for us to leave? We have to do something. None of this feels normal."

"Marlee, you barely know the woman. How can you speculate on what is or isn't normal about this situation?"

I pointed at the log exterior of her home. "There are no dried mulberries on the walls. Instead, the boxes are piled where I left them. She was desperate for me to order the berries because she wanted to put them around her doors and windows. For protection, she said. Yet she hasn't glued one berry up there."

"It rained most of yesterday."

"But the rain stopped by the time I delivered them. The sun was out by five." I glanced up at the blue sky. "And it's been sunny all morning. Besides, she has a covered front porch and a screened back porch. Even if it had rained, she would have been able to get mulberries around most of her doors and windows. Something prevented her from doing so. Or someone."

Kit raised an eyebrow. "Felix Bonaventure?"

"It's possible."

"Marlee! Kit! Come here!" Theo waved at us. He had made his way about forty yards in his pursuit of the wild turkeys. I assumed he'd spotted a rare bird.

Kit and I walked over to him. "What's up?" Kit asked.

"There was an eastern screech owl in those trees." Theo nodded at a stand of birch. "I tried to follow the owl with my binoculars, but it flew away. Then I looked at those wooden boxes in the field. The ones you said were beehives. But I didn't see any bees."

"It's late in the year," I said. "That's to be expected."

"Maybe the bees are gone because someone shot an arrow into the hive," he suggested.

Kit and I looked at the hives. Even without binoculars, we saw an arrow sticking out of one of them.

"There's an arrow in the ground, too. Not really in the ground though. It's stuck in something." Theo looked nervous. "I think it's a body."

"Oh no," I cried.

The three of us ran into the field. As we neared the wooden hives, we saw a body lying faceup in a clump of tall grass. An arrow stuck out of the man's chest. Blood stained the shirt around it. Kit and I knelt beside the body. Even though the person was clearly dead, Kit felt for a pulse.

I immediately scanned the field and surrounding woods. If the person had recently been killed, was the murderer still on the property? Were we being watched? And where was Leticia?

Kit pulled out his cell phone to call the sheriff's department. With a heavy heart, I once more looked down at the dead man.

"Do you know who it is, Marlee?" Theo asked as he stood over us.

"Yes." I gave a deep sigh. "His name is Felix Bonaventure."

I had no idea who killed him with an arrow. Nor did I know where Leticia the Lake Lady was. One thing I knew for certain. Despite his charmed name, Felix's good fortune had run out.

Chapter Six

I soon found myself surrounded by police, cats, and wild turkeys. Neither the agitated animals nor the police made the situation pleasant. However, Theo seemed content to while away the time observing the noisy birds. I wished I was as easily distracted.

Although Kit made his first call to the sheriff's department, he followed up by notifying the state police. No surprise there. The two departments often worked together. And Kit's brother-in-law, Greg Trejo, also happened to be a detective for the state police.

But the arrival of Gene Hitchcock, Oriole Point's police chief, did surprise me. Leticia lived near the county line, which wasn't under the legal jurisdiction of my village. Then again, Oriole County saw few murders, this past year notwithstanding. When one did occur, maybe it became an "all hands on deck" situation for local law enforcement.

And every state police and sheriff's car looked to be on the property. The cats and turkeys didn't know in which direction to run as officers searched the field and surrounding woods. I hoped they didn't find another dead body, especially one with orange hair.

An ambulance came for the body while Greg Trejo questioned me. We had become friends over the summer. But when Greg was in police mode, he conveyed all the warmth of a menacing robot, despite his good looks. I no longer took it personally. I had just finished relating my encounters with Leticia and Felix Bonaventure when Chief Hitchcock joined us.

"Do you mind if Marlee goes over all this with me?" he asked Greg.

Greg nodded. "Go ahead."

Even though it was still morning, I felt drained and exhausted. I'd seen too many dead bodies this year. And my legs needed a rest. If you included all the hiking I did earlier at the state park, I had been standing for hours.

I sat down on the grass and looked up at the police chief. "My legs are tired."

"I hear Leticia approached you in the village on Saturday morning," Hitchcock began.

Kit joined us before I could reply. "I called the judge to request an affidavit for a search warrant. He just emailed me the signed warrant."

"Good." Greg's Vulcan-like expression grew even steelier. "This may be easy to solve. A man murdered on the property of a highly eccentric woman. One with a past."

"Killed with a bow and arrow," Kit added. "An eccentric choice of weapon."

"Don't rush to judgment, boys," Chief Hitchcock said. "Especially with what's going on this week at the health fair. Have you learned anything about this Bonaventure fellow? He must have had ID on him." He gestured at the Ford. "Anything in the car?"

"It's a rental from the airport in Grand Rapids," Kit

answered. "And the car is clean. Nothing in it save for the rental-car registration. Thankfully, he gave Marlee his business card yesterday, which had his Philadelphia address. We called authorities there and asked them to search his home. Marlee also remembered he said he was staying at a Hampton Inn in South Haven. We sent a car to search his room."

"Did they find anything?" Hitchcock asked.

"Heard back from the officers about ten minutes ago. Nothing in his room except for several changes of clothes."

"Any sort of device?" Hitchcock looked frustrated. "Computer, iPad?"

"Nothing. Not even a cell phone."

In this day and age, that seemed as bizarre as living without electricity.

"To make things more suspicious," Kit continued, "there isn't a scrap of paper in the car or in the room to let us know what he did for a living."

I thought back to how he looked like a character from *The Godfather*. "A hit man, maybe," I suggested.

The three men looked down at me with surprised expressions. They'd momentarily forgotten I was sitting right below them on the grass.

"If so, he doesn't appear to have been a good one," Kit answered.

"Maybe you two should go inside while I talk to Marlee," Hitchcock said.

"What does the health fair have to do with any of this?" I asked after Kit and Greg left with several other officers.

"We don't know. Maybe nothing." Hitchcock crouched beside me, not looking happy about getting down to my level. Our police chief not only bore the intimidating name of a famous director of suspense movies, he also boasted a six-foot-five frame and too many pounds. I doubted he'd be comfortable in that position for long.

"And you're not going to tell me anyway."

"Correct." He bit back a smile.

I looked over as the officers entered the house. "How did they get in? Do the police have a special gadget to break locks?"

"Don't worry about the lock. Tell me what happened with Mr. Bonaventure and Leticia."

I repeated my conversation with Leticia on Saturday, Felix Bonaventure's visit to my store yesterday, and my delivery of the dried mulberries later that afternoon. After a moment's hesitation, I admitted how I'd opened her front door to let the cats in—then walked in myself.

He didn't seem any more fazed by this confession than Kit. Maybe both men expected me to bend the rules. "I didn't stay more than a minute or two. I took a quick look around her living room, then left. No one seemed to be home, and her scooter was gone. Like it is now."

"Did either Mr. Bonaventure or Leticia appear threatening to you?"

"But her real name isn't Leticia, is it? It's Ellen."

"You didn't answer my question."

"You didn't answer mine." I'd grown up with Gene Hitchcock as the town's police chief. My aunt was his wife's best friend and we'd celebrated more than a few holidays together over the years. I felt comfortable enough to push back a little. "I have reason to believe she went by at least one other name: Ellen Clark. And that she served time in prison for murder."

He shook his head. "Now I understand what Dean was doing in the police station yesterday. He was snooping around. Probably at your bidding."

"Getting Andrew and Dean to do my bidding is like herding cats." Four cats took this moment to prove my point by streaking past us. "The only time they're amenable is if I ask them to do something they can later gossip about."

"You told Dean to go through our filing cabinets?" Hitchcock asked in a warning voice.

"Of course not." Thank God he didn't know Dean hacked into the police computers. "I sent Dean to see what he could find out from his mother. I had no idea she'd gone off to the health fair. What Dean got up to in her absence is none of my doing."

"Whatever he did, I bet it involves the discovery of Leticia's real name."

"True. He did learn her married name: Ellen Clark. And finding out she was in prison for murder seems worth a little subterfuge."

He hesitated, as if weighing his next words. "The woman paid her debt to society long ago. I don't want her past to become a topic of nasty gossip."

"Neither do I. But she came to me for help because she believed her life was in danger. She worried the ghost was in danger, too. Whoever the ghost is. And she talked about shadow people. It sounded like paranoia to me. A paranoia that now seems warranted." I waved a hand at the field when Felix's body had been found. "She's gone missing and a man is found dead on her property. With a bow and arrow, no less, which is disturbing."

"Bow-hunting season kicks off soon. There could be a homicidal hunter in the area."

"I doubt it. And the police lab needs to ascertain what kind of wood the arrow was made from. If it's mulberry wood . . ." I let my voice trail off.

Hitchcock narrowed his eyes at me. "Explain."

"She thought all things mulberry would protect her from danger. Especially from this person she believed threatened her. Not just the berries either. Objects made from mulberries."

"Like arrows?"

"Yes." I recalled my conversation with Leticia. I had mentioned mulberry arrows and wands in jest. Did I give her the idea of acquiring mulberry arrows? Or did she already have the arrows in her possession? And had she used them to protect herself?

The same idea must have occurred to Chief Hitchcock. "If she was obsessed with mulberries and felt threatened, it's possible the arrows found in the hive and in the victim belong to her. The next assumption is that she shot the arrows."

"And killed Felix Bonaventure," I finished for him.

"The longer she remains missing, the worse it looks for her." With a grunt, he stood up.

I got to my feet as well. "I should never have agreed to order the dried mulberries. She has emotional issues. It was wrong to humor her."

"Don't be hard on yourself, Marlee. She was a customer with an unusual request that involved berries. Who else would she go to in town? And you were able to get what she wanted."

"It's not only that. I suspected the woman Felix was looking for could be Leticia. That's why I didn't tell him anything."

"Makes sense to me."

"When I delivered the berries yesterday and saw

Leticia was gone, I got worried. I wanted to warn her so I left a voicemail telling her a man called Felix Bonaventure was in town looking for Ellen Mulberry. And that the name 'Mulberry' made me think of her."

"I see." His expression turned grim.

"What if Felix was the man she was so afraid of? What if he somehow found out where she lived? He did know she got her mail in New Bethel. Perhaps he finally found someone at the post office to tell him where she lived. What if he came here and Leticia was waiting for him? With a bow and arrow?" I felt ill. "What if I spooked her so much, she ended up killing a man?"

"Sounds like a lot of 'what ifs.' Where's the proof?"

Kit came out on the porch. "If you two are done, we'd like Marlee to show us exactly where she was in the house yesterday."

With a heavy heart, I followed Chief Hitchcock onto the porch. Could my voicemail have led to Felix Bonaventure's death?

Loud yowls erupted from the corner of the porch. As several cats raced past us, one of them leaped onto the boxes of mulberries. When the cat jumped off, I noticed the lid of one of the boxes flapped.

"Someone opened that box." I went over to inspect it.

The boxes had been taped shut when I left them on the porch yesterday. This one had been slit open. I counted the bags inside.

"Maybe this one wasn't taped all that well," Kit said, watching me go through the box.

"No. Someone came here and opened it up. Four bags are missing."

"Do you think Leticia took them?" Hitchcock asked.

"Who else?" I cast an eye over the log wall of her home. "But I'm not sure why. She didn't put a single mulberry around her door or windows."

"Maybe she put them in the house." Hitchcock gestured at the front door. "After you."

Once more I stepped into Leticia's living room. A state trooper stood in the kitchen, his back turned toward me. I spotted another officer in a room down the hallway, while Greg Trejo lifted sofa cushions. The next thing I noticed was the envelope on the coffee table.

I pointed at the envelope. "If Leticia did return, she didn't bother to open the envelope I left for her. It contains the hundred and sixty dollars she overpaid for the dried mulberries. And I left three cats in here yesterday. Are they still inside?"

"No cats," Greg said. "That means she must have come back."

"Or someone else did. I am surprised Leticia lived in such a new custom-built home." I waved in the direction of the kitchen. "One with quartz countertops and high-end cabinets."

"This house was built by a young couple from Detroit," Hitchcock said. "They moved here six years ago with plans to start a goat farm. Didn't take long for them to figure out the bucolic life wasn't for them. They sold it to Ellen, furniture and fancy kitchen included."

"If you touched anything in here yesterday, let us know," Kit instructed. "We're dusting for prints." I noticed only now that he wore plastic gloves.

"I didn't touch anything except the doorknob of

the front door." I froze when I looked over at the desk. "Hold on. Did someone move the laptop?"

"What do you mean?" Kit asked.

"An Apple laptop sat right here." I pointed at the desk. "Something else is missing, too."

Greg appeared by my side. "Those papers you talked about?"

"Not just papers. It looked like a manuscript. Several hundred typed pages. One of them was a title page. *Mischief and Murder* by Ellen Mulberry."

Greg turned to Chief Hitchcock. "You've been looking into her case for some time, Gene. Was there anything in her file to indicate she was a writer? Jailhouse memoirs, maybe."

The police chief shook his head.

"If you don't mind my asking, why were you looking into her case?" I asked him.

"Professional curiosity," Hitchcock said. "I investigate any odd behavior in town to make certain it isn't likely to turn dangerous. I have a file on Old Man Bowman, too. Along with about a dozen others. As soon as I heard people talking about Leticia the Lake Lady, I paid attention. She appeared a little strange. Acted strange, too. Standing on the beach to look out at the water. She never did anything illegal or suspicious, only I couldn't figure out how she afforded this property and house. That's what made me dig into her past."

"And discovered she'd been in prison for murder," Kit said.

"Yes. According to the reports, she lost her husband a few months before she came here. Anthony Clark was much older than Ellen and retired shortly after she was released. They spent all the years of their

marriage in his hometown of Huntsville, Alabama."
He picked up a small framed photo on the coffee
table. "I recognize this man from my file. He's Anthony Clark, her deceased husband. He worked in the
Michigan state prison system for thirty years."

"How did he die?" I hoped it wasn't under suspicious circumstances.

"Complications from Parkinson's disease."

"Not murder then," I said with relief.

"She might have bought this property with his insurance policy," Kit suggested.

"Seems likely," Hitchcock said. "He also had a good
pension."

"Why didn't she stay in Alabama?" I asked him.

"Clark's family wasn't happy he'd married an ex-con.
I spoke to some people down there. They said his relatives made her feel unwelcome from the beginning.
And once Anthony Clark died, they put pressure on
her to leave."

I felt even sorrier for Leticia. Losing a husband,
then being run out of town. No wonder she behaved
strangely. "How did she end up here?"

"Ellen is from Michigan, but doesn't have a lot of
family," he said. "A few relatives still live in Coldwater.
When I looked into her case, I contacted her father.
Ellen wanted to move back home after her husband
died, but her family disowned her after the murder.
Except for one cousin, most of them wanted nothing
to do with her. She was dead to them." He frowned.
"They told her the same thing when she reappeared.
Made sure she knew she wasn't welcome."

I shivered. "Her family seems as cold as the name
of the town. So do the Clarks."

"Soon after, she showed up in Oriole Point. And never left."

"Until now," I pointed out.

"We don't know she left town," Greg said.

"We do know someone came to the house in the past twenty-four hours and didn't bother to take an envelope with a note claiming there's money in it." I felt frustrated and uneasy. "But they did steal her laptop computer and the manuscript."

"Or Leticia took it herself," Kit said. "It's possible she's hiding right now. The manuscript and the files on the computer could be important to her. Did you look at any of the pages aside from the title page?"

"No." A pity the Cabot boys hadn't been with me. They would have skimmed through the entire manuscript. And probably photographed a few pages with their phones.

"It's also possible she hid the manuscript and computer somewhere in the house. Officer Huypers is searching the bedrooms. I'll tell him to look for a laptop and papers. " Greg disappeared down the hallway.

"Look around some more, Marlee," Chief Hitchcock said. "You might discover something else that's gone missing."

I doubted I would. I'd been here such a short time and only noticed the manuscript because of the cats.

Kit walked over to the crammed bookshelves. "Does anything here look out of place?"

I scanned the shelves. "I couldn't say. The only thing that stood out was how eclectic her reading tastes were."

"Take a look anyway. I don't want to miss anything."

To oblige him, I started at the top shelf and read every title until I reached the bottom. Next I turned my attention to the bookshelf on the other side of the fireplace. I soon realized the books on this shelf were not as varied as the others. In fact, they were all accounts of true crime.

Although not a big true-crime fan, I recognized a few famous titles: *Helter Skelter, The Stranger Beside Me, In Cold Blood.* My breathing quickened.

"Is it all right if I touch these books?" I asked Kit, who was talking to Chief Hitchcock.

He handed me a pair of plastic gloves. "Put these on first."

After I donned the gloves, I pulled out two books that caught my eye. Then several more on the shelf below. A quick glance at the covers told me that I'd been right to notice them.

"I know what Felix Bonaventure did for a living," I announced. "He was a writer of true crime. He co-authored these." I held up the books.

"I'll be damned," Kit said. "He can't be a well-known one. I don't recognize his name."

"You wouldn't. I'd bet his name never appears on some of his books. When it does, it shows up in small print. Like it does on these." I handed the books to Kit. "He was a ghostwriter."

Gene Hitchcock and Kit examined the covers of the books. Below the author's name appeared the words "with Felix Bonaventure" in much smaller print. They turned the books around and looked at the spines.

"How did you know he'd written these books?" Hitchcock asked. "His name doesn't appear on the spine."

"True. But someone—most likely Leticia—marked the tops of the pages with a yellow highlighter. It caught my eye. Only a few are highlighted, but all of them were written by Bonaventure."

I pulled out another book marked with yellow highlighter. This true-crime book did not include any reference to Felix, but I suspected he had ghost-written it. Otherwise, why had she marked it like the others?

"Did she ask Bonaventure to help her write the book?" Kit asked.

"I think she did," I said. "I also think this proves she didn't kill him."

"How so?" Hitchcock seemed skeptical.

"She was afraid that she and the 'ghost' were in danger. Don't you see? She was referring to her ghost-writer. Now Leticia has disappeared. And the 'ghost' is dead."

"It's time to take the Lake Lady seriously," Kit said. "And listen to what she has to say."

"We have to find her first." I felt a wave of fore-boding. "I only hope she's still alive."

Chapter Seven

All the way back to Oriole Point, I kept one eye out for a purple scooter on the highway. Maybe Leticia simply hadn't returned home yet. None of us knew the particulars of her daily routine. Perhaps she rose early and did errands. She may even have driven to another beach. Why did I assume she only came to Oriole Beach to do all that mournful gazing? It was possible she had a whole secret life going on we hadn't guessed at.

"I almost got one of the wild turkeys to come up to me," Theo said. "If they lived near my cottage, I bet I could convince them to eat from my hand, like I do the chickadees."

Theo sat beside me, going through the photos of wild turkeys he'd taken on his phone. Although he had been startled by the sight of Bonaventure's body, Theo now acted as if we had done nothing today but go birding. After his encounters with the turkey vultures and the wild turkeys, I suspected Theo had gained a new obsession. And relegated the dead body to some dim memory. Unless he found the experience so upsetting, he chose to pretend it never happened.

Luckily, I was now better informed about his background. In July, Theo and I took a road trip to visit my parents in Chicago and his father in Champaign, Illinois. We both were in desperate need of home cooking and parental love after the harrowing Blackberry Art School centenary. Meeting his relatives reassured me that he came from a loving family who had done all they could to help him enjoy an independent and productive life.

And since moving to Oriole Point last December, Theo had been quite productive, helping my business grow by baking the most delicious berry pastries I had ever eaten.

But he did view the world in an idiosyncratic—sometimes baffling—way. I didn't want anything to frighten him into retreating from the world once more.

"Sorry you had to see that body at the Lake Lady's house. It must have been upsetting."

He looked up from his phone. "I bet that arrow killed some sleeping bees, too."

"Do you want to talk about it, Theo? The dead man, not the bees."

"What do you want to say? I never met him. You did, though. Are *you* upset?"

"Well, it isn't a personal loss. He was little more than a stranger. But finding his dead body in the field was upsetting, of course."

"Whoever killed him missed the first time." Theo held up his phone.

I took my eyes off the road long enough to see that

he had photographed the arrow embedded in the beehive. "You're right. The killer's first shot probably struck the hive. It was the second arrow that killed Felix."

"Do you think the Lake Lady shot him?" he asked.

"No," I said in a firm voice, more to convince myself. "She told me the ghost was in as much danger as she was. And we think Felix Bonaventure may have been her ghostwriter. That's someone who secretly helps a person write a book."

"Maybe she didn't like what he wrote and got angry at him."

"I don't think she'd kill him about something like that. Besides, she feared for the ghost's life, too. Someone else is responsible. A person connected to what she called the shadow people. And the book is part of it. Otherwise, where are the computer and manuscript?"

Theo switched off his phone. "Did you pick your costume for the Halloween parade?"

The non sequitur reaffirmed my suspicion that Theo had moved on. I wish I could do the same. At least his question about the upcoming parade gave me the opportunity to talk about something fun.

"I picked my costume weeks ago. I'm dressing up as Daenerys from *Game of Thrones*. I ordered this fantastic silver gown with nice long sleeves so I won't freeze like I did last Halloween. And I bought a white wig *and* a stuffed dragon I can attach to my shoulder. With two other dragons for my skirt. Only don't tell Dean and Andrew. I want to surprise them."

"I understand. They'll tell everyone. Costumes

should be a surprise. That's why I'm keeping my costume a secret."

I almost veered off the road at hearing this. "You're going to be in the parade?"

"Of course. I like Halloween. And I didn't live here last Halloween, so I missed the parade. Andrew and Dean told me it's the best thing to happen in Oriole Point all year."

Theo spent most of his time at The Berry Basket or alone at Crow Cottage. Too many people tended to make him nervous. And thousands of people came to town for the parade. I worried he might not understand what he was getting himself into.

"It is a lot of fun. But there will be huge crowds downtown that night."

"Gillian described it to me. She'll be in the parade, too." He gave me a reassuring look. "I'll be all right, Marlee. I was around all those crowds for the Blueberry Blow Out. I'll be fine."

I felt tears well up. Only a few months ago, Theo had been uneasy when surrounded by strangers. When I first hired him, we saw him so rarely that Andrew dubbed him "The Phantom." Theo would arrive at the shop kitchen before dawn and leave before we arrived. It took the tumultuous events of the art school centenary to encourage him to trust his fellow workers at The Berry Basket. And now he was getting ready to march in the biggest event held in Oriole Point.

It was like watching a child take their first steps.

"We should all march together," I said. "Kit's going to be in the parade. He chose a *Game of Thrones* costume, too. Jon Snow. He'll be all in black."

"Like Darth Vader." Theo was a big *Star Wars* fan.

I laughed. "Except a lot more handsome."

"Gillian's coming as the Little Mermaid." He lowered his voice as though someone might overhear. "She showed me her red wig. It's as long as the Lake Lady's hair. But prettier."

"I wasn't sure you had ever seen the Lake Lady. She doesn't come into town much. When she does, she stays on the beach."

He nodded. "That's where I've seen her. She rides the purple scooter there. My dad says scooters are like motorcycles. They're dangerous. She shouldn't drive one."

"I didn't know you were a beachgoer. You always talk about how much you like to watch the river instead."

"Sometimes I finish baking early and walk to the lighthouse. There aren't many people around then. I stay on the pier and watch the gulls on the beach. They sleep in flocks."

"And you've seen the Lake Lady on the beach?"

"Yes. She stands there a long time. The gulls walk around like she's not there."

"Why do you think she likes to look out at the lake so much?"

Theo turned his attention out the car window as we passed a goat farm. "She's probably afraid of it."

Leticia had said something similar when I asked her. That she was afraid she would forget. But what did that mean?

"I think she's afraid of Piper, too," he added.

I almost veered off the road again. "Why would she be afraid of Piper?"

"Because Piper yelled at her."

"When?" I debated pulling over to have this conversation, but I had already been away from the shop for hours. And I'd promised to get back in time to let Dean interview the Pilates Queen for his blog.

"Last month. I remember because that was the morning I tried the recipe for those triple berry doughnuts. The ones you asked me to bake for the OPBA people."

As a shop owner, I not only belonged to the Oriole Point Business Association, I also served on the board as membership secretary. Our monthly meetings drew every business owner in town, each with a litany of complaints. These complaints often turned into arguments, sometimes heated ones. In July, we decided to take turns bringing in treats. The sugary desserts hadn't stopped the quarreling, but it kept some of our more vocal members from ranting nonstop. And I remembered how everyone had gorged themselves on Theo's doughnuts.

"So you saw Piper and Leticia last month on the morning of the OPBA meeting."

Theo shrugged. "I don't remember the date. Just the doughnuts."

"If you were on the pier by the lighthouse and Leticia was on the beach, how do you know it was Piper who was with her? Especially if it wasn't fully light yet."

"It was light enough to see. And I was walking back along the pier when Piper got there. I paid attention when her car came into the parking lot. That's because the only other thing in the lot was the purple scooter."

"Did they meet in the parking lot?"

"Piper went down to the beach. She had her big dog with her. The one called Charlie."

Piper and Lionel had adopted a lovable Great Dane this past summer and christened him Charlemagne. I found the dog much too playful for such a weighty moniker and gave him a nickname. This displeased Piper since everyone else now called him Charlie, too. If Theo had seen Charlie, there could be no doubt it was Piper on the beach that day.

"Piper and her dog went to meet the Lake Lady," he continued. "They talked for about ten minutes at the edge of the water."

"If you were on the pier the whole time, didn't they see you?"

"I sat under the catwalk to watch them. I don't think they saw me."

I would have bet my life that Piper had never spoken a word to Leticia. The two women moved in circles stratospherically apart. In fact, I couldn't think of two people in Oriole Point more dissimilar. "I can't believe Piper met with Leticia," I muttered.

Theo began to fiddle with the zipper on his jacket. As with the discovery of Bonaventure's body, Theo had grown bored with this topic as well. "It was Piper for sure. The bossy blond lady who's married to the mayor. He was there, too. The mayor got out of the car and watched them from the parking lot while they talked."

"Are you sure Lionel was there? Piper's husband?"

"It was the mayor. He's the tall black man with the really deep voice. When he talks, it sounds like thunder."

I tried to absorb this information as Theo added,

"I think he was there to make sure his wife was okay. Piper and the Lake Lady looked like they were arguing. Piper shook her finger at the Lake Lady a couple of times."

None of this made sense. Although it might explain why Leticia had called Piper a Gorgon. What it didn't explain was why Piper had left her mansion at dawn to huddle with the local eccentric on the beach.

Something else bothered me. Only an hour ago, Chief Hitchcock had cautioned Kit and Greg not to rush to judgment about Leticia's guilt, adding, "Especially with what's going on this week at the health fair."

If the murder was connected in any way to the fair, the connection also included Piper, who had organized the entire event. It looked like Piper's health fair might not be as healthy as advertised.

Chapter Eight

The discovery of Bonaventure's body had shaken me. So did learning that Piper met with the Lake Lady on the beach. I was also worried about the welfare of those cats on Leticia's property, especially the kittens. Leticia had not answered my text messages for twenty-four hours. If she had left town, what would happen to the cats, only some of whom were feral?

I had an hour before Dean's shift at the store ended. Enough time to make a detour and stop at the headquarters of Humane Hearts, the local animal rescue organization founded by my aunt. The twenty-acre farm held kennels, an aviary, dog runs, annex buildings, a barn, and a stable. The grounds were always filled with volunteers and animals. Since Aunt Vicki also lived in a yellow farmhouse on the property. I had a good chance of finding her there.

Theo looked delighted when I told him we were swinging by Humane Hearts on the way back to Oriole Point. Aunt Vicki's rescue llamas fascinated him. Theo also surprised us by bonding with my aunt's trio of Doberman Pinschers: Buffy, Willow, and Xander. I would have thought the Dobermans too intimidating for his tastes, but he adored them.

On the way over, I gave her a quick call to make sure she wasn't too busy for a discussion about Leticia's cats. I also let her know we'd had another murder in the county. This news was met with a long sigh. I knew just how she felt.

I found her waiting on the front porch when I pulled up the driveway; the Dobermans grouped about her like three bodyguards. Every time I saw Aunt Vicki, I thought of my dad, who closely resembled his blond, blue-eyed sister. They also boasted full-figured, robust frames. I took after my mother and her Italian family: dark haired, brown-eyed, with a lean body type. I lucked out with the Rossi gene since I had the appetite of a hungry wrestler.

The dogs' tails wagged as soon as I got out of my SUV, but it was Theo they ran to.

"Can I take them for a walk?" Theo asked as Willow licked his face.

"I've got volunteers out exercising some recent rescue dogs who might get nervous about the Dobermans." She gestured at the corral by the stable. "Let them run around in there. And you can feed the llamas some hay."

As a euphoric Theo left for the corral with the dogs, I explained the situation at Leticia's house.

"There must be at least fifty cats. A lot were hiding in the shrubs and bushes." I sat on her porch swing. "Most are feral with matted, dirty fur. I couldn't get within twenty feet of them. Others look tame. Especially the ones who wanted to get inside the house."

Aunt Vicki sat beside me. "I'm guessing there were

already feral cats on her property when she bought it. That parcel is almost as big as mine. With woods, too. She probably brought a few kittens into her house. The others stayed wild." She frowned. "And kept breeding. I've seen this situation play out a hundred times on the farms around here."

Oriole County was largely rural, and far too many farmers refused to spay or neuter their cats. Many of them mistakenly believed the procedure made the cats less effective as mouse catchers. Their blind refusal resulted in a countryside overrun with neglected cats and endless litters of kittens. Some cold-blooded farmers even drowned newborn kittens, which enraged me.

Humane Hearts worked tirelessly to prevent that from happening. Sterilizing the animals was essential, even if they were feral and had to be released once again. At least that prevented more unwanted kittens. Those kittens we did round up were fostered and eventually adopted.

I described the food dishes by the shed and how Kit and I had found metal trash cans filled with bags of kibble inside the shed. "Before I left, I filled the food dishes and gave them fresh water. But if she doesn't come back, who will take care of the cats?"

She gave me a sad smile. "Cats are good at surviving in the wild, hon. Although to paraphrase Thomas Hobbes, their lives are likely to be 'nasty, brutish, and short.' I'm more interested in trapping them. I can have a team of volunteers there tomorrow."

"We'll have to wait on that. The property is being treated as a crime scene." I pushed back so the swing would sway. "But I do have permission to feed them."

"Let's leave the cats aside for the moment," my aunt said. "What happened at Leticia's house? Who was the dead man? And how is that poor woman involved with this?"

I told her what had occurred since my conversation with Leticia on Saturday. Including my discovery that Leticia, a.k.a. Ellen Clark, had served time in prison for murder.

Aunt Vicki gasped. "Murder? I can't believe it. Who did she kill?"

"Don't know. Chief Hitchcock's spent the most time looking into her past. But he refused to tell me any details about the murder itself. To be honest, I think he regretted telling me as much as he had." I gave her a wink. "I intend to get the rest of the story when I see Kit."

"I knew Leticia must have had trials in her life." Aunt Vicki shook her head. "Only I never thought a murder trial was one of them. I wonder where she is."

"Maybe there's nothing mysterious about her absence. She might be home tomorrow. If she is, I'll convince her to let you take the cats to the vet." A significant portion of cash donations to Humane Hearts were earmarked for this purpose.

She patted my knee. "For now, all they need is food and water. And don't go out there to feed them unless Kit is with you. A man was murdered on that property. Maybe by Leticia. Maybe not. But as much as I care about saving cats, I care about your safety more."

I thought she was being overly cautious. I couldn't imagine why the murderer would return to the scene of the crime. The computer and manuscript were already gone. So was Leticia. What reason would the killer have to come back?

In the distance I heard barking and Theo's laughter. I wondered if it might not be time for him to adopt a dog. Although I'm sure he would prefer one of the llamas.

"You've made me wonder how many cats are on her property," Aunt Vicki mused. "A lot of the cats may spend part of the time next door at the pumpkin farm."

I stopped swinging. "There's a pumpkin farm near her property?"

"The Rasmussen place. Jill and Norbert belong to my church. They've had a pumpkin farm for decades, but once they hit their seventies, they decided to retire. Now they fly off to Arizona at the beginning of October and don't come back until April." She looked at me with a regretful expression. "Too bad they already left. You could have asked them about Leticia and her cats. Jill is allergic to cats. The situation next door is probably unpleasant."

"Then it no longer is a pumpkin farm."

"Jill and Norbert still plant part of the patch. But they don't sell the pumpkins. Instead, they donate them to the church. We have a pumpkin sale in late September to raise money for charity."

I thought it might be a good idea to check out the cat situation at the pumpkin farm.

"By the way, I'm glad I looked at the Haunted Health Fair Facebook page today," she went on. "Otherwise I wouldn't have known you were giving a talk about berries tomorrow."

I smacked my head so hard, I hurt myself. "I forgot about that."

"Joe and I will definitely be there." Joe Coyle was my aunt's latest boyfriend.

When was I going to find the time to prepare a forty-minute talk? And I didn't want to wing it, not at an event with so many heavy hitters holding workshops. "I don't know why I let that woman bamboozle me into 'volunteering' my services so often. Speaking of Piper . . ."

As my confused aunt watched, I called Piper on my cell. She picked up on the third ring.

"This better be good, Marlee," Piper said. "I'm on my way to the catering staff to complain about the Folgers coffee they're serving attendees. Can you believe it? I gave strict instructions the coffee had to be organic, freshly ground, and fair trade. Who do they think they're dealing with? Some nitwit who doesn't know Sanka from a French roast?"

"Piper, we need to talk. Privately. Something has happened. It involves the Lake Lady."

The resulting silence dragged on so long, I thought my phone died. "I was afraid she would do something," she said finally. "But I can't talk now. I'm swamped for the next few hours. Meet me for dinner. San Sebastian. Seven thirty."

This time when I heard silence, it was because she had hung up. Although I was pleased she'd chosen Oriole Point's most upscale restaurant. The food whipped up by chef/owner Diego Theroux was as irresistible as his good looks.

"She must be distracted," I told my aunt. "She didn't even ask for details."

If she had, I would have told Piper that along with Diego's signature dishes, murder would also be on the menu tonight.

* * *

I never dressed casually for dinner at San Sebastian. The elegant décor and Diego's haute cuisine demanded an extra effort. That required time to get cleaned up and go through my wardrobe.

When I finally got home, I began the arduous task of searching through my closet. I normally wore jeans and a Berry Basket T-shirt at the store, both covered by the chef apron. But I had spent ten years as a TV producer in NYC, which demanded a fashionable wardrobe. At the time, I had the disposable income to purchase the designer pieces necessary.

For tonight, I chose a Rodarte leather midi skirt, black silk blouse with a floral print, and a metallic trimmed faux bomber jacket. To complete the look, I slipped on my favorite pair of knee-high boots. When I looked at myself in the full-length mirror, I worried I might be a tad too trendy for Oriole Point. Then I remembered I was dining with Piper, who once met me for scrambled eggs at the Sourdough Café decked out in vintage Chanel.

I did make certain to leave early. Piper did not tolerate tardiness. And I was starving. If I got there ahead of time, I'd ask the waiter to bring me a bread basket or appetizer.

Piper must have been even hungrier than me. When I walked through the door, I spotted her in one of the curved burgundy leather booths near the back. She waved me over.

As I followed the hostess, I noticed all three dining rooms were packed. I did a double take when I saw Ellie Vaughn, the Pilates Queen, seated with several people at a table near the pebbled fountain. In a booth to her right sat the award-winning dancers from *Dance with Me*. They looked even more glamorous in person. I was glad now that I had worn Rodarte.

"It's about time," Piper said when I reached our table. A glass of red wine sat before her.

"You do realize I'm ten minutes early."

She gave me an injured look. "I've been here since seven."

"And if you'd come an hour earlier, you could have eaten dinner and been on the way home by now." I slipped off my jacket.

This exchange got us off on the wrong foot, and we silently perused the menu until our server appeared. "I'll have the bavette steak, medium, with Spanish onions and ramps," I told him. "And the Perigord salad."

"The same," Piper said in a curt voice.

I looked at Piper's half-empty wineglass. "Also a glass of red wine. Rioja."

Although I preferred German white wines, I liked to immerse myself in the San Sebastian experience when I dined here. Diego's family came from the Basque town of San Sebastian, Spain, near the Bay of Biscay, and his menu reflected his heritage. Since dining here, I had gained an appreciation for that region's wines and flavor profiles, which combined elements of French and Spanish cuisine.

I also had an appreciation for his devastating good looks. Looking out over the restaurant, I saw him speaking to a table of guests by the bar. I smiled. Any sighting of Diego in his chef whites brought pleasure to his female diners. And some male ones as well.

Piper cleared her throat to get my attention. "Rodarte?" She eyed my outfit.

I nodded, then examined her dark teal cocktail dress. "Zac Posen?"

Her disapproving expression softened. "At least you've retained a little of your New York fashion sense."

"Along with my subscription to *Vogue*."

We both finally smiled.

"Now why did you want to talk with me? And about Leticia, of all people."

"She approached me the other day. Right after you and I talked at the Berry Basket booth in the park. She asked me to order dried mulberries for her. Enough berries to cover her house."

She rolled her eyes. "The woman is insane. I hope you ended that conversation quickly."

"Actually no." I described my encounter with Leticia, then told her about the visit of Felix Bonaventure to my shop on Monday. Piper listened intently, but said nothing. "Have you ever heard of this man? Or Leticia calling herself 'Ellen Mulberry'?"

"No. I don't waste my time thinking about any of the odd ducks in this village. Unless they cause trouble."

"Speaking of trouble, Leticia thought someone was trying to kill her."

"So you said." Piper avoided my gaze.

"Do you have any idea who might want to harm her?"

"Maybe it was this Bonaventure fellow. And I'd tell all this to your boyfriend at the sheriff's department. By the way, I approve of Atticus Holt. He's far more likable than that dreadful man you were engaged to."

"I agree. Which is why I broke off our engagement."

The server brought our salads and my wine to the

table. Our conversation didn't resume until he left. "I did tell Kit. The state police and Chief Hitchcock know about Bonaventure, too."

"Why? Is he some sort of international criminal?" She lifted up a forkful of lettuce.

"No." I paused. "He's dead."

Piper froze with the fork an inch from her face. "What?"

"He's dead. Murdered. Shot through the heart with an arrow."

She dropped her fork with a clatter onto her plate. "When did this happen?"

"This morning." I put down my own fork at the memory of Felix Bonaventure's blood-spattered shirt. "He was killed on Leticia's property."

She looked dazed. "Is this some sort of sick joke?"

"You know I never joke about murder. I am literally sick of murdered bodies dropping in my vicinity."

"I can't believe this. Murdered? And with a bow and arrow?"

"We've learned Bonaventure was a ghostwriter of true crime books." I described how I found the manuscript in Leticia's house and the books that Bonaventure had co-authored. "Because of her concern about the 'ghost,' I think he was helping her write a book of her own. Maybe about the crime she committed. Now the book has gone missing."

I'd never seen Piper look so shocked. "Are you okay?" I asked her. "You seem upset."

"Of course I'm upset. When is a murder good for any small town? Especially one that has had far too much lurid publicity lately. And right now I am in the middle of hosting the biggest event the conference center has ever seen. How do you think this will look?

All the attendees came here to learn how to be healthy, happy, and holistic. Now a stranger is found murdered."

"He died out in the country, not the middle of town. Most people here will be too busy to give it much thought."

"Some people will." Piper shot a furtive glance at a table of diners in the far corner.

At least sixteen people sat at the table she seemed worried about. I recognized two of them: Cameron Sable and his wife Ingrid. I'd seen them on TV and book covers. Even if they hadn't been famous, the couple would have drawn attention. Eighty-year-old Cameron Sable was bald, slender, and boasted a Roman profile that accentuated his aristocratic bearing. As for Ingrid, I didn't know if it was her Scandinavian ancestors, surgery, or the Sable natural beauty line, but she looked better at seventy-seven than most women half her age.

"Why should they care about Bonaventure? Unless there's some connection to him."

Piper responded with her own question. "Have they arrested Leticia yet?"

"They haven't arrested anyone. And Leticia has vanished."

Her mouth fell open. "They must find her. Immediately."

"Kit told me they put out an APB on her."

She looked disgusted. "As if that ever works. I recall the police doing the same thing after your Russian friend disappeared in June. Fat lot of good that did."

"I hope they do find her. Leticia was afraid of what she called the shadow people, especially one particular person. She was also afraid for her ghost, which must be Bonaventure. Now the ghostwriter is dead and she's gone. I believe she's in danger."

"You don't know anything about her, Marlee."

"I know she was in prison for murder."

Piper gave a start. "How did you find out?"

I waved away her question. "I also know you spoke with Leticia last month, the morning of the OPBA meeting, to be exact. The two of you met at Oriole Beach shortly after dawn."

Despite the low light given off by the tabletop candles, I saw Piper blanch. "What?"

"Lionel drove you to Oriole Beach, where you met with Leticia. You and she talked by the water for about ten minutes. There was a witness."

"You're mistaken. No one else was there."

"Someone was watching from the pier. That person saw you and Leticia argue. You even shook a finger at her. Apparently, the meeting doesn't seem to have been cordial."

Piper grabbed her half-full glass of wine and downed it in one swallow. "Why did that woman move to Oriole County? She's been a ticking time bomb since she got here."

"That's unfair. She hasn't caused any trouble. Leticia has never displayed any violence towards anyone. Never threatened a single person. She seems harmless."

Piper slammed her hand on the table. "For the love of God, she killed the nanny!"

Chapter Nine

Nearby diners threw us nervous glances.

Realizing her mistake, Piper added in a lower voice, "When Leticia was nineteen, she killed the nanny of a prominent family. I can't believe you don't know about this case. Leticia spent fifteen years in prison. About thirteen years ago they released her, heaven knows why."

"That means the murder occurred when I was two. How would I know about it?"

"I hate the young," she said with disgust. "You're all willfully ignorant."

"You can't blame me for not knowing about a murder that happened decades ago."

"Everyone knew about it at the time. It was a notorious case because the family was famous." Piper bit her lip. "They still are."

I looked over again at the table in the corner that Cameron and Ingrid Sable presided over. "They're in town right now, aren't they? You're talking about the Sables."

"Keep your voice down. Two of them are coming this way."

Startled, I looked up to see two men thread their way around the crowded dining room. As they got closer, the taller of the two gave Piper a friendly wave.

She waved back. This prompted the men to approach our table.

"Don't say a word about Leticia," she muttered, keeping a smile plastered on her face.

"Give me some credit," I said in exasperation. "I'm not an idiot."

One of the men overheard me and laughed. "No one would think any friend of Piper's is an idiot. She is a most discerning woman." He held out his hand. "I'm Keith Sable."

"Marlee Jacob." I shook his hand.

Instead of releasing my hand, he gave me a searching gaze. I didn't mind. Keith Sable had dimples, perfect teeth, and a muscular build. His curly dark hair also reminded me of Kit. "Why is that name familiar?" he asked.

"Marlee is the local expert on berries that I told you about," Piper explained.

"Ah, yes. The Berry Basket girl." He squeezed my hand before finally releasing it. "My brother and I were talking about you earlier today. Our company is looking into a product line based on berry extracts. We'd be quite interested in talking with you."

"If you're as knowledgeable as Piper claims," the other man said, "we may wish to hire you as a consultant. I'm Patrick Sable." Unlike his brother, Patrick's smile seemed perfunctory, and his salt-and-pepper hair pegged him as the older of the two.

My head swam. One moment, I was learning Leticia had murdered a nanny associated with the Sables. The next moment I was being considered for a no-doubt lucrative position as berry consultant by the family's heirs.

"Marlee is giving a Holistic Hints workshop tomorrow," Piper informed them. "All about the beneficial properties of berries. Two o'clock."

"Free berry products, too," I added with a smile.

"I'll make sure the family attends." Despite his words, Patrick didn't sound enthusiastic.

Although I had no fear of public speaking, the idea of giving a workshop before all the members of the Sable dynasty gave me pause. When I got home tonight, I needed to go over my notes. Maybe add a few more things.

"I hope the family is enjoying their dinner here tonight," Piper said. "San Sebastian is one of the finest restaurants in Michigan. Diego Theroux is a supremely talented chef."

"Our meal has been excellent," Patrick said. "My wife can't stop eating the tapas."

"Your townspeople have been so friendly." Keith's smile dimmed. "Except for a few."

Piper sat up even straighter. "What do you mean?"

"Our cars were vandalized. One of them just now." Keith jerked his thumb toward the restaurant door. "That's why Patrick and I were outside. Someone let the air out of all our tires while our driver was down the street having a quick bite."

"I blame our driver as well," Patrick said. "When on duty, he should stay with the car."

"In a town as safe as Oriole Point, he shouldn't have to," Piper declared. "I am so sorry this happened. I shall insist our local police be more vigilant."

"Excuse me, but you said your *cars* have been vandalized," I said. "Plural."

"We rented three BMWs at the airport for the family and our assistants," Keith said. "Someone spray-painted one of the cars between midnight and dawn today."

Piper looked as if she wanted to explode. "I am mortified to hear this."

"The vandal painted LIAR all over the car." Patrick seemed grim. "In red paint, too. We had the car replaced this morning."

"How awful," I said. "And highly uncharacteristic of our town."

"Indeed it is," Piper said huffily. "It must be a visitor here for the fair."

"That's what we assume, too," Keith told us. "We occasionally have trouble with disgruntled people who have not had success on the Sable Diet or haven't followed it correctly."

"It wouldn't be the first time someone has accused us of lying when they haven't lost weight on the diet." Patrick sighed. "One of them is apparently in Oriole Point, drawn here by our presence at the fair. The local police agree that's the most likely explanation."

"The same person probably let the air out of your tires," I observed. "You need to keep an eye on the cars from this point on."

"I will send my own assistants to personally stand guard over your cars," Piper said.

Keith waved his hand. "No need for that. We've instructed our drivers to remain with the vehicles during the day. And we've arranged for secure parking during the rest of our time here."

Patrick glanced over at the table where the other Sables sat. Ingrid Sable was watching us. "We should get back to our dinner. Knowing our mother, she has insisted everyone stop eating until we return."

"Nice to meet you, Ms. Jacob," Keith said. "I look forward to your berry talk."

"And I'm sorry to hear about the vandalism. Oriole Point is usually a friendly place."

"Blame it on Halloween." Patrick shrugged. "It's the time of year for malicious mischief. Don't let it spoil your dinner."

Piper and I looked at each other after they left. The word "mischief" rang in my ears.

"Do you think Leticia is behind this?" I asked.

"I'll run her over with Lionel's Hummer if she is," Piper snapped.

"Why does Leticia view the Sables as enemies?"

"I told you. She killed their nanny. And her real name is Ellen Nagy. At least until she married that Clark fellow who worked at the prison. Her family is from Michigan, you know."

"Was that why you met with her last month on the beach? To warn her the Sables would be in town for the health fair?"

"It was the other way around." Piper picked up her fork once more and stabbed at her salad. "She sent a message to the email address I use at the Tourist Center. With 'Nanny Murder' on the subject line. That certainly caught my attention."

"What did she want?"

"To complain that I had invited the Sables to Oriole Point. She'd seen the latest promo I plastered all over town and social media. She told me the Sables should not be allowed to come to Oriole Point and darken the town with their presence. Those were her exact words."

The phrase "darken the town" struck me. Were the Sable family the shadow people Leticia had mentioned? "Did you email her back?" I asked.

"Yes. I told her Oriole Point was lucky the Sables had agreed to take part in the fair." Piper took a bite of salad. She appeared to do this more as a way to keep calm than out of hunger.

"How did you end up on the beach together?"

"Leticia replied that I had been deceived by the Sables. She claimed she had lost years of her life because of them. Now they were coming to town to destroy what was left of it."

This indeed sounded like they were the shadow people she had mentioned to me. I swirled the wine in my glass. As a childhood spelling-bee champion, I should have associated the Sables with darkness. In a color wheel, sable is placed in the section reserved for shades of black.

"She insisted we speak face-to-face," Piper continued. "But on her terms. That's how I found myself on Oriole Beach the following morning. I brought Charlemagne and Lionel along for safety's sake. After all, Leticia's email implied that she was the young woman who killed the nanny. I had no intention of meeting her without witnesses."

"What happened when the two of you met?"

"She tried to convince me to cancel their appearance. After I refused, she warned me that death would be the outcome. *Her* death."

I took a much needed sip of wine. "She actually said that?"

"Yes. And I became angry. After all the effort and money I'd expended on this event, I couldn't allow her to cause a scene at the fair or bother the Sables. I told her that if I saw her anywhere near town while the health fair was in progress, she would be arrested." Piper looked a little sheepish. "Perhaps I overreacted, but she didn't leave me much choice."

"And that was the last time you saw her?"

"It was. No more emails either. I hoped I'd persuaded her to stay away from Oriole Point for the foreseeable future. With luck, she might even find another beach to loiter on."

I mulled over what she had said as the two of us ate our salads. Leticia had known the Sables—the shadow people—were soon to arrive. And she feared one of them more than the others. A person she thought wanted to kill her. How desperate she must have been to come to me with her fanciful notions about mulberries.

"Why haven't you told me about any of this?" I said accusingly. "All these years, you've known the Lake Lady was a convicted murderer."

"I have not. I didn't even put this whole thing together until she wanted to meet with me on the beach. I simply thought she was a strange woman with dreadful taste in hair color. And she became notorious as Ellen Nagy, not Ellen Clark. So googling 'Ellen Clark' produced nothing. I knew she was an oddball. But there was little information to be had about her. Our police chief wouldn't tell me a thing. I should have realized the Leticia the Lake Lady nickname was a clue, but the murder happened so long ago. I didn't connect the dots until last month."

"How and why was the nanny killed?"

Piper took a deep breath. "The whole thing began on Mackinac Island."

"Mackinac?" I looked at her in surprise. Mackinac

Island was a beautiful island on Lake Huron between Michigan's Upper and Lower Peninsulas. Cars were not allowed on Mackinac, only bikes and horse carriages. This helped to literally transport visitors back to a more charming and quaint era. Mackinac's charm was enhanced by historic B&Bs, a Colonial fort, and bike paths that wound their way along the lake and woods. The island was not only one of the top vacation spots in Michigan, a recent poll named it the best vacation spot in the nation.

For a murder to take place in such a tranquil haven seemed particularly abhorrent.

"Ellen and Keith had gone to the island to work for the summer." Piper signaled our waiter for another glass of wine. "They were both nineteen-year-old college students. Vastly different colleges, mind you. Ellen attended some community college in the southern part of the state. Keith Sable had just been kicked out of Purdue. The year before, he had been asked not to return to the University of Virginia."

"Two colleges expelled him in two years? What in the world did he do?"

"Nothing. That was the problem. He never attended class. Keith spent his time sleeping, chasing after girls, and drinking at the frat house. Newspaper reports claimed Cameron and Ingrid Sable cut off his allowance after the latest expulsion. If he wanted any financial support in the future, he had to find a summer job."

"So Keith took a job on Mackinac Island." Like Oriole Point, Mackinac was a vacation destination. The fudge shops, hotels, restaurants, and marinas needed help during high season.

"Patrick got him the job," Piper said. "Patrick has

always been the more responsible son. Princeton grad, a board member of the Sable company by the time he was twenty-five. The same year he married the daughter of the founder of Fontaine Pharmaceuticals."

"Since Keith Sable works for the family now, I assume he got his act together."

"Finally. Also keep in mind he was a teenager back then. Patrick is nine years older. The Sables assumed he would straighten out his life. Keith took the first step when he agreed to work on Mackinac Island for the summer. He was a recreation attendant at the Grand Hotel."

"Of course he got a job working for the fanciest place on the island," I said.

"The week before, Ellen also got a job as an attendant there. Hotel employees claimed the pair were inseparable. It had all the makings of a typical summer romance." Piper shot me a jaundiced look. "Until the murder."

I looked up in relief as the waiter appeared with our dinners. "What was Ellen, a.k.a. Leticia, like as a girl?"

"You'd never know it to look at her now, but she was attractive. There are photos of her online. Like I told you, the case was famous." Piper dug her phone out of the requisite Hermès bag and typed for a moment. "Here. She's the one in the middle. Keith is next to her."

The photo she pulled up revealed a group of teens, all wearing the white shirts and red jackets found on Grand Hotel employees. If Piper hadn't told me to look at the girl in the middle, I may not have recognized her as Leticia. And I was right. Leticia was a blonde. I compared her straggly orange tresses to the mass of smooth, blonde hair in the photo. It flowed over her shoulders like a golden cape. Keith looked much the same. Or maybe it was that devilish grin.

"If Keith and Ellen were working at the Grand Hotel that summer, how does the nanny figure into this? Did Keith's parents have a vacation house on the island?"

"Hardly. Cameron and Ingrid Sable spend their summers in the Hamptons."

I sat back. "I'm confused. Exactly who was the nanny working for?"

"Patrick and his wife Ainsley. They had a four-month-old son at the time of the murder. That summer they were staying at Victor Kang's vacation home on Mackinac Island."

I thought back to our conversation last Saturday in the park. "You said the Sables stepped in when Victor Kang canceled his appearance at the health fair."

"Yes. Patrick and Victor went to Princeton together and remained friends. Victor was born and raised in Ann Arbor. Like a lot of Michiganders, his family spent summers up north. When he became successful, Victor bought a house on Mackinac Island. He invited them to the island that summer to help Ainsley recover."

"What was wrong with her?"

"Postpartum depression. According to trial records, Patrick and Ainsley had visited Victor on the island several times before. He offered them the use of his home, which they accepted." She smoothed the linen napkin on her lap.

I peeked over at the dinner table filled with Sables. I wondered which of the women was Ainsley Sable.

"So Keith, Patrick, and Ainsley Sable all spent the summer on Mackinac Island?"

Piper cut her steak. "Along with the nanny and our crazy lady of the lake."

"Leticia probably didn't appear crazy then. If she had, why would Keith Sable have gotten romantically involved with her?"

She snorted. "As if teenage boys have an ounce of sense, especially with a pretty young blonde wiggling around them."

"Did she act strange back then, too?"

Piper shrugged. "Depends on how you define strange. According to other employees at the Grand Hotel, she was helpful and sweet. But sensitive in the extreme. Prone to panic attacks and crying jags. Everyone did remark on how bright she was. When she wasn't with Keith or working, they said she had her nose in a book. At her sentencing, two psychiatrists testified to her high IQ." She smirked. "Confirming my low opinion of the psychiatric profession."

"This makes me feel even sorrier for Leticia. Her life has changed so much since then."

"Particularly her hair, which was a gorgeous blond. Not that orange rat's nest she sports now. In the photos she looks like Rapunzel." She threw a pitying glance at my brunette locks. "Sorry, my dear, but blondes do have more fun."

"Looks like it can get them thrown into prison, too."

She laughed. "You have a point. Regardless, at the end of the summer Keith and Ellen announced their engagement."

I hadn't expected that. "So they fell in love."

"His parents weren't happy. I don't blame them. The Sables were already quite wealthy. Then along comes some teenager with a lot of cleavage. Do you really think it was love?"

"Why not? They were both young. To them, it probably felt like love." I took another sip of wine. "What about this nanny? Who was she?"

"Laeticia Murier from Lyons."

I choked on my wine. "Wait a second! The nanny had the same name as our Lake Lady?"

"Not so loud." Piper hissed. "The names are the same, but they're spelled differently. Being French, the nanny used the more common French spelling, which starts with 'Lae.' Our Lake Lady dropped the first 'a.' Knowing Leticia, the reason for that must be irrational."

"Talk about burying the lead. Until this past week, I assumed Leticia was simply her real first name. It was only after Bonaventure came to town looking for Ellen Mulberry that I realized she was using an alias. But if she has chosen to call herself after a dead woman . . ."

"A woman she murdered," Piper reminded me. "Let's not forget the real victim in this story. Laeticia Murier was only twenty-one, here on a student visa. Although I don't know how much college coursework she ever completed. She worked as Ingrid's assistant for a year before becoming nanny to Patrick and Ainsley's infant."

"What did she look like?"

"*Une belle femme,*" Piper said with a sigh.

I took out my phone and googled Laeticia Murier. I found her linked to the Nanny Murder. I lingered on the photos posted of her. Laeticia had lively dark eyes, pale skin, and chin-length black hair worn in a feathered style typical of the 1980s. Heads would have turned at the sight of that alluring gaze, upturned nose, and voluptuous bee-stung lips that Angelina Jolie might envy.

I threw my phone back into my purse. "What happened?"

"Cameron and Ingrid Sable flew in for Labor Day weekend and chartered a yacht to celebrate the end of summer. They also wanted to celebrate the fact that Keith had managed to hold down a responsible job for three whole months. An amazing feat for him."

Engrossed in the story, I reminded myself to finish my steak. Heaven knew, it cost enough. After another bite, I said, "Did they celebrate their son's engagement as well?"

"They must have made an attempt to welcome her into the family. After all, Ellen was invited on the yacht trip."

"Where were they traveling to?"

"Chicago. From there, they planned to fly back to Palm Beach." Piper speared one of her potatoes. "Except for Ellen. Keith had rented a car so she could return to college in Michigan."

I frowned. "Why charter a boat when they had the money for a private plane?"

"The boat was a luxury yacht the Sables were considering purchasing. They own several yachts, kept in various marinas around the world. The trip from Mackinac to Chicago was a test run, a way to decide if they wanted to buy it. They even flew in several people who crewed their yacht in Florida." Piper gave me a knowing look. "They also thought a long cruise on the Great Lakes sounded charming. They were wrong."

As magnificent as the Great Lakes were, they were also hazardous. Weather changed on a dime. If the wind picked up, waves on the lake surpassed those on the oceans. And a yacht trip from Mackinac to Chicago could take the better part of a day. Not the place to be if bad weather hit. Especially thirty years ago when Doppler technology wasn't as advanced.

"They left Mackinac behind schedule. Toward evening, they ran into a thick fogbank," Piper said, "followed by rain and high winds. People began to get seasick, prompting everyone to go belowdecks. Soon after, the nanny went missing."

"Why assume she was murdered? If the nanny decided to go on deck in bad weather, she may have accidentally fallen overboard." The steak was delicious. I took a few minutes to enjoy it before adding, "And why assume Leticia did it?"

"She caught Keith in a compromising position with the nanny earlier that day. Everyone on the boat testified as to how upset she was, crying and carrying on."

"I still don't see how that proves the nanny was murdered."

"The police reports claim Ellen was terrified of water. Her relatives back in Coldwater confirmed that she never learned to swim. Why didn't she stay in her cabin during the rainstorm? This was a yacht of considerable size, after all. She'd feel safer below. There was no reason for Ellen to venture out on deck with the nanny unless she meant to harm her."

I thought about this while I ate. Something about the story bothered me.

"By the way, court testimony revealed the nanny was afraid of water, too," Piper added. "Please explain how two girls afraid of drowning were out on deck during a storm? And at night, too. It's clear one of them wished the other harm."

I raised an eyebrow at her. "Or someone else lured them there."

"Then tell me who else had a motive to want the nanny dead," Piper demanded.

"I have no idea, but they weren't the only people on the yacht."

She sighed in exasperation. "One of the crew members heard shouting around the time the nanny went missing. I don't remember the specifics. He may even have seen what happened. Like you said, this happened a long time ago. But Keith Sable told police that Ellen suddenly took a dislike to his family in the week before the yacht trip."

I couldn't help but play devil's advocate. "She might have had good reason. After all, Cameron and Ingrid had misgivings about the upcoming marriage. They probably wanted Ellen Nagy to go back to Coldwater and leave their son alone. I'll bet they made their antipathy known to her. And Keith's brother and sister-in-law may have felt the same way."

"Talk about spinning a tale." She guffawed.

"You also told me that Ainsley's family founded Fontaine Pharmaceuticals. Which means she grew up with a Tiffany silver spoon in her mouth. I wouldn't be surprised if she was less than thrilled to have some kid from Coldwater join the celebrated Sable clan."

"You always insist on thinking the worst of rich people, Marlee."

"They make it way too easy for me. Did they find the nanny's body?"

"Yes. She had a contusion on her right temple, which the police speculated may have been caused by a blow to the head."

"Or by the nanny hitting her head on the boat when she fell."

Piper glared at me. "Why do you persist in taking Ellen's side? You barely know her."

"Why do you persist in thinking the worst of her?"

"Because she killed Laeticia Murier." She looked like she wanted to shake me.

"What if she didn't kill her? What if the Sable family framed her?"

"You're making up quite a colorful story, Marlee. It will make a great Lifetime movie one day. Except Ellen Nagy, otherwise known as Leticia the Lake Lady, murdered the nanny."

"You don't know that for sure."

"Of course I do. Don't you understand? She *confessed* to the crime!"

Piper collected herself before adding in a quieter voice, "Sorry, my dear, but Leticia murdered Mademoiselle Murier. Just like she murdered Felix Bonaventure. She's not simply crazy. She's a killer."

Chapter Ten

By the time I drove to Leticia's house the following morning, I had downed a gigantic vanilla latte from Coffee by Crystal and chewed three espresso candies. I still felt exhausted.

Blame it on Piper's disturbing dinner revelation about Leticia's confession to the murder of the nanny. But I also stayed up long after midnight putting together my berry talk for the health fair. I had created what I hoped was an amusing but informative PowerPoint presentation on the health benefits of berries. Now I only had to stay awake long enough to give the talk. My nervousness over the prospect of doing this in front of the Sables would help keep me alert.

I also wanted to feed the cats before I opened The Berry Basket. The drive to Leticia's home normally took a half hour, but I made it there in twenty minutes. I blamed my speeding on all the caffeine.

On the way, Kit called to say he was at Leticia's house and had fed the cats for me. Touched by his gesture, I decided to go out there anyway. It gave me a chance to see him before both of us got swept up in what promised to be a busy workday. Especially Kit, who planned to drive quite a distance to speak with the staff at the prison where Leticia had been an inmate.

And it gave me the chance to ask Kit about the Nanny Murder and Leticia's confession. He would now be privy to all the details since the sheriff's department had assigned Kit to investigate Felix Bonaventure's death.

A morning mist hung over the fields, which made the changing leaves along the highway even more beguiling. Given our long Indian summer, this was the first week it felt like autumn. The lake breezes held a nip, reminding us the days were growing shorter and cooler. I welcomed the seasonal shift with all that it signaled: apples, cider, fiery foliage, a quieter energy. Life had been intense since June, and not only because summer was high season for our resort town. Too many tumultuous events had transpired. Lives had ended. So had relationships.

I looked forward to autumn's slower pace and the chance to recover and recharge. No wonder the trees and bears needed a long winter sleep. Hibernation sounded appealing, especially after learning of another tragic story of murder and the wreckage it had left behind.

The past few months had taught me that murder destroyed more than the person whose life was taken. If she had killed the nanny, Leticia not only lost fifteen years of freedom, she'd lost touch with reality. And if she was innocent, Laeticia Murier wasn't the only victim.

I thought back to the man who had visited my shop on Monday. Less than twenty-four hours after our short conversation, Felix Bonaventure lay dead in a field. Somehow the tendrils of that long-ago murder had reached out and killed him. Had it also killed Leticia? Or was she at the deadly heart of this?

This time when I pulled up the driveway to Leticia's house, the wild turkeys barely moved out of my way. The past day had no doubt been filled with a constant stream of law-enforcement vehicles. The birds seemed to have lost their fear of us. Knowing what humans were capable of, I wasn't sure that was a good idea.

Kit quickly came to greet me. Today he wore his dark brown sheriff's uniform. It made him look even sexier, especially when paired with the cap. I have a thing for men in uniforms. My first movie crush was Josh Hartnett in *Pearl Harbor,* who left quite an impression on my prepubescent self. So did every Scottish warrior in *Braveheart,* but I rarely encountered kilted men in Michigan.

Three sheriff's cars were already here, but I only saw Kit. After we hugged and kissed, I took a step back and looked around.

"I don't see the scooter. Guess that means Leticia hasn't shown up."

"We're still checking out the woods," he said. "Maybe she's hiding somewhere in the forested part of her property. However, there's no sign of tire tracks anywhere but on her driveway. If she did head for the woods, she walked there."

"Still doesn't answer the question of where her scooter is."

"The county is filled with farms. Some are abandoned. She's lived out here for four years and might know where they are. If so, she could be hiding in one of them."

"Or she's long gone by now."

We looked at each other before Kit said what we were both thinking, "Or she's dead."

I shivered, even though I wore a sweater.

Kit pulled me close. "Are you cold?"

"No. I'm worried. If only she'd been right about how mulberries were protective. They might have protected Felix Bonaventure. Did the police find the bow that shot the arrow?"

"In the field, about thirty yards from the body. The killer must have tossed it there when they left. And you were right about the composition of the bow and the arrow."

I stepped out of his embrace. "They were made of mulberry wood?"

"Yes. Speaking of that, there's something I want you to see." He took my hand.

I thought he was going to lead me to the house or the place where the body had been found. Instead, he pulled me toward the birch grove bordering the left side of the drive.

"Where are we going?" I asked.

"Next door. It isn't far, and there's a path through the birches."

"What's so interesting at the Rasmussen pumpkin farm?"

Busy batting away low-hanging branches, he glanced back at me. "How do you know about the pumpkin farm?"

"Aunt Vicki." I related what she had told me about the retired couple Jill and Norbert Rasmussen. And how we worried there might be even more feral cats in need of rescue there. Since the Rasmussens spent half the year in Arizona, the cats would have the run of the place.

"The sheriff's department sent officers over here yesterday to look around," he said.

We emerged from the trees to find ourselves on a concrete drive. To our left sat a sage green cottage-style ranch house. I shook my head at the cats curled up on the front porch, and those wandering among the bushes beneath the front windows. Humane Hearts would need to send an army of volunteers to round them up.

I eyed the house with suspicion. "Kit, if Leticia knows the Rasmussens leave every autumn, she knows their house is vacant. What if she's hiding inside?"

"Already checked. We contacted the Rasmussens in Phoenix yesterday to inform them a man had been killed next door. Since their neighbor was missing, we needed to search their property, which includes the house. They told us the address of a friend in the area who keeps a spare key and gave permission for us to go inside."

"I take it you didn't find anything."

"No sign of any intruder inside."

Kit led me past the garage toward the field. At one time, the entire acreage had probably been devoted to pumpkins. I did spy something orange as we walked toward what I assumed was the only section that still grew the popular autumn crop.

"Please don't tell me you found another body in the pumpkin patch."

"No." He squeezed my hand. "After we checked out the house yesterday, we did a search of the fields. There aren't many pumpkins left."

"The Rasmussens donate their crop to the church for their annual sale in September."

"A few are still out here." He raised an eyebrow at me. "Along with something else."

A small black cat ran past us. How appropriate for the season. The cat stopped a few yards ahead and meowed. The meow sounded thin and high. Not the sound of a full-grown cat.

I knelt down. "Come here, baby."

The kitten stared at me with beautiful green eyes. I had to gather these cats up soon. Especially any felines that were all black. With Halloween on the horizon, black cats were at risk from sadistic teens who found it fun to torment them. Adult cats had a better chance at escaping, but not kittens. And certainly not this adorable baby who watched me so attentively.

"Maybe if we had a treat to offer. Or something interesting," Kit suggested.

I glanced down at my silver necklace, a Christmas gift from Denise Redfern.

Knowing how much I loved birds, Denise had made a pendant fashioned of three cardinal feathers she found while hiking in the state park. I noticed how the kitten's eyes followed the feathers as they swayed in the breeze.

Slipping off the necklace, I swung it in front of me. The kitten took a few short steps toward me, its gaze transfixed by the crimson feathers. Another endearing meow followed.

I tossed the necklace onto the grass in front of me, then slowly pulled it back.

The excited kitten took a step closer.

With each toss, the kitten came nearer. The last

time, I let it pounce on the feathers. Now that I was near enough to pet the kitten, I did. A purr was the response. A few strokes later, and I scooped the kitten in my arms.

"This baby's not wild," I told Kit with a grateful smile.

As the cat purred against my chest, I took a peek and added, "This baby is a 'he,' too. I think I'll call him Panther because he's as brave as a jungle cat. The superhero, too."

Kit smiled. "Whoever ends up adopting the cat might want to name him."

"So they have. I'm adopting him." I kissed the kitten now batting my feathered necklace.

Although I'd always claimed to be too busy working to adopt a pet, that belief had been shattered when a talkative parrot entered my life this past June. Minnie had brought only happiness into my life. And Panther chasing after us showed that he had chosen to come to my attention. How could I refuse?

I looked back at the house. "I didn't see any black cats yesterday or today. I wonder if Panther's mother has been killed. He looks about three months old. Maybe a little younger. So he's been weaned. But he's in good shape, although the vet needs to check for fleas. I'll drop him off at Aunt Vicki's on the way to the store and have her take him to Dr. Fitzgibbon."

Giving a kiss to my new kitten, I turned to go back the way we'd come. "If I didn't have to speak at the health fair this afternoon, I'd do it myself."

Kit caught me by the elbow. "Wait. You haven't seen what I brought you here for."

"Sorry. I got distracted. Show me what you found."

When we reached the fenced-in patch, I saw only thirty pumpkins remained. A pumpkin roughly eighteen inches in height sat on a weathered fence post. That was not remarkable. But the arrow stuck in the pumpkin was. The wooden fence was studded with three more.

I looked at Kit. "You found this yesterday?"

"After we searched the Rasmussen house."

I turned my attention to the rest of the patch. Arrows stuck out of two other pumpkins.

I knelt down to examine one of the pumpkins on the ground. Panther wriggled out of my arms. I thought he might run off, but instead he sniffed the pumpkin.

"Looks like the same wood as the arrow that killed Felix Bonaventure," I said.

"All the arrows are made of mulberry. We tested the first arrow for prints, but got nothing. We'll do the same for these, but whoever shot the arrows may have used gloves or wiped them clean."

Panther scampered back to me with a plaintive meow. I picked him up. "The pumpkins were used for target practice."

"We asked the Rasmussens if they had shot the arrows before they left, or if they had seen these arrows. They said no. And they were shocked to learn someone had been on their property shooting arrows into their pumpkins."

I shot to my feet. "Oh no."

"What's wrong?"

"Ask your men if they've seen any dead cats on Leticia's property. Or this one."

"They have. A dead cat was found in the field next door. Shot with an arrow."

I held Panther even closer. "A black cat?"

"A female." He scratched Panther's head. "Might have been his mama."

This whole bizarre scenario made me ill. "Why use an arrow to kill someone?" I asked.

"A gun can be traced, but not this." He gestured at the arrows in the pumpkins. "It's also a quiet method of murder. Unless the victim takes a long time to die."

A wave of disgust swept over me. "Let's get out of here."

Kit put his arm around me. "Sorry if this upset you. But you've been involved from the beginning, I assumed you'd want to know the killer had practiced before taking action."

"No. I'm glad you showed me. It may prove Leticia is the killer. After all, she had access to the pumpkin patch after the Rasmussens left."

Had Leticia been so concerned about the coming arrival of the Sables that she practiced how to defend herself? I told Kit what I had learned from my dinner at San Sebastian. As I did, his expression grew more somber.

"Yesterday we were all briefed on the murder of Laeticia Murier," he said when I finished. "Leticia, formerly known as Ellen Nagy, must have known the Sables were coming to town. After all, Piper never stopped promoting their appearance. Even in New Bethel."

This made me feel even more guilty. Immersed in plumbing and home renovation, I hadn't paid a scrap of attention. Apparently, Gillian and I were the only ones in town—or Oriole County—who had been unaware the celebrated Sables were on the way here.

"It makes sense if she had shot one of the Sables with an arrow. According to Piper, Leticia views them as dangerous. And I think they're the shadow people she mentioned to me. But that doesn't explain why she would kill Felix Bonaventure."

"No idea. When the police searched his condo in Philadelphia, there was no computer."

My eyes widened. "What author doesn't own a computer? Someone got to his hotel room and his condo before the police did and took away his computer. Along with the files on it." I stopped. "This is all about the manuscript Bonaventure wrote with Leticia. It has to be."

"Seems likely. He was a true crime writer. Leticia was at the center of a famous true crime. Maybe she wanted her version of the story to be told. It is telling that he arrived in Oriole Point the same week as the Sables."

"He was desperate to meet with Ellen Mulberry. Then I find a manuscript in Leticia's house written by an Ellen Mulberry. They must have been collaborating, and he needed to see her as soon as possible."

"I wonder if the Sables found out the two of them were working on a book together," he mused as we resumed walking. "Maybe the Sables threatened Bonaventure with a lawsuit."

"Maybe." Panther batted at my chin with his paw. "But what could Leticia say now that would matter?

According to Piper, Leticia had confessed to murdering the nanny."

"Not at first. For a week after the murder, she was almost catatonic. The girl had been so traumatized, she was put on suicide watch and medicated. When she finally did speak, she told the police little, except that she was innocent."

"When did she confess?' I asked.

"About two weeks into the trial."

"But why didn't suspicion fall on any of the other passengers that night?"

"The bosun, James Smith, told police that he heard two women arguing on deck. Given the poor weather conditions, he went to check it out. He got there in time to see Ellen push the nanny over the side."

"What! He actually witnessed the murder?" I thought back to last night's conversation with Piper. She thought the bosun might have seen something incriminating. Since he had viewed the murder itself, I had to look on Piper's memory as worse than spotty.

"Apparently. Ellen collapsed in hysterics while he sounded the alarm and tried to rescue Laeticia Murier. By the time they pulled her out of the water, it was too late."

As much as I wanted to believe Leticia was innocent, this piece of news was damning. "I assume there was no reason to doubt the testimony of the bosun."

Kit took a moment to answer. "On the surface, no. At the time of the murder, Smith had worked for the Sable family for almost three years, crewing their yachts in the Caribbean. They hired him when he was twenty-four, as a favor to Ainsley Sable."

"I don't understand."

"Smith was the brother of Ainsley's favorite stylist. He'd gotten into trouble in college when he discovered cocaine. After he went to rehab, he decided he wanted to go into yachting. Ainsley asked her in-laws to hire him for one of their super-yachts. He seems to have been good at his job. He worked his way up to bosun in two years. The year after the murder, he was made Chief Officer." Kit paused. "And the following year he moved up to captain."

We looked at each other. "Was that rapid rise due to his skills?" I asked. "Or a reward for services rendered? The Sables might have asked him to lie about the murder. And they rewarded him by handing over one of their luxury yachts."

"I agree. Entrusting a ninety-million-dollar yacht to a young man, who three years earlier was a cocaine addict? It does look suspicious. But we can't forget that Ellen confessed."

"I wonder why she waited two weeks into the trial before she confessed."

"Most likely on the advice of her attorney. In addition to the bosun's testimony, the accounts given by the Sables about her being jealous of the nanny were difficult to refute."

"Naturally, the family would stick together. And they're rich, famous, and powerful. Who knows what sort of pressure was brought to bear on a teenager accused of murder? And Piper said she was extremely sensitive, prone to anxiety attacks."

"It's not my job to retry the case of a murdered nanny, Marlee. My immediate concern is tracking down the killer of Felix Bonaventure."

"It seems like they're connected. Solve one murder, and the other one is solved, too."

"We know who killed the nanny," he reminded me.

"Do we?" I looked down at Panther, who had fallen asleep in my arms. "What if the bosun was paid to lie? And Ellen was pressured to confess?"

"I still need a viable suspect."

"I can think of several, all with the last name of Sable."

"Before I can go after the Sables, I require evidence pointing in their direction."

I was pretty sure I had held that evidence in my hands two days ago. A manuscript called *Mischief and Murder*.

Chapter Eleven

The pumpkin lady with the stethoscope once again greeted me. Apparently, she was the Haunted Harvest Halloween Health Fair mascot. Although I wondered if I'd forgotten one of the fair's "H" words. The colorful sign's grimace seemed to deepen, as if contemptuous of my arrival at the Lyall Conference Center.

Cars filled the large parking lot, and it took several minutes before I found an empty space. The fair's popularity made me happy for Piper and Oriole Point. A successful event such as this helped to bring people here year-round. In addition, the view from the conference center and its surrounding gardens—which overlooked Lake Michigan—was certain to impress first-time visitors. Piper's own mansion sat on a similar bluff with a view just as spectacular.

However, I still preferred my lakeside home. The bluff wasn't as looming, but wooden stairs led to my private beach. I wondered how Panther would like the lake. Dogs loved to run along the beach, but I had never seen a cat do the same. Maybe Panther would be the first. He seemed both fearless and lovable.

When I left the pumpkin farm this morning, he

immediately fell asleep on the makeshift bed I put together from the beach towels kept in my vehicle. He'd also been playful and affectionate with Aunt Vicki when I dropped him off at her house on the way to work.

The vet was scheduled to stop by Humane Hearts today, a perfect time for her to check out the kitten. I reminded myself to buy kitten chow along with food and water dishes.

Once I parked, I spent a minute picking cat hairs off my sweater. My feathered necklace was gone. Because Panther seemed enthralled by it, I'd given it to Aunt Vicki. If he did get nervous in his new surroundings, a little playtime with my cardinal feathers might distract him. Right now I had to stop being distracted by kittens and focus on my upcoming talk.

Due to my impulsive adoption of a rescue kitten, Aunt Vicki would not be able to attend my workshop today. That suited me fine. The fewer faces in the crowd, the better.

I spotted several school buses in the lot. The fair planned to host a number of events for students; everything from classes on healthy snacking to workshops about how to identify and treat mental-health issues, such as depression, anxiety, and eating disorders. I also knew costume contests were on the schedule, accompanied by various raffles and fun prizes. Piper had been thorough in putting together the event. Yes, she was a control freak, but no one worked harder to keep Oriole Point on the map.

When I reached the entrance to the conference center, a sandwich board stood beside the door listing those workshop sessions scheduled for the day. One of them was *The Benefits of Berries* by Marlee Jacob. The sessions scheduled opposite me included *Feng Shui for the Office, Meditation and Pain Relief,* and *Seasonal Juicing for Good Health.* A separate sandwich board announced the workshops and book signings of the Sable family. Thank goodness I had stayed up late putting together my presentation.

Once inside, I admired the striking design of the center. The glass-domed roof ensured that natural light always filled the building even when an event required portable partition walls to be moved into place, as they were now. To accommodate larger events, two annex wings branched off on either side of the main building.

As a nod to the season, carved jack-o'-lanterns dotted the floor of the main hall. Black bats and owls with amber eyes dangled from wires, fake cobwebs with plastic spiders draped the walls, and two human skeletons hung on either side of the hallway leading to the banquet room.

To underline the Halloween theme, every person sporting a VOLUNTEER badge wore a costume. A zombie handed out water bottles by the door, two vampires blended fruit smoothies at a temporary juice bar in the center of the atrium, and a pirate—complete with fake parrot on his shoulder—offered visitors fresh apples. My friend Tess had informed me that she was volunteering at the fair today. Only she hadn't mentioned anything about coming in costume. I wondered who—or what—she was dressed as.

I glanced down at my black slacks, red cashmere pullover, and black velour pumps. Were we supposed to come in costume? In order to check out the attire of my fellow workshop speakers, I hurried over to the nearest closed session door. The white sign read "Yoga for Weight Loss with Rowena Bouchet." Rowena ran a yoga studio in town and held classes on the beach during nice weather. I attended as many as possible.

Peeking inside, I saw several dozen people stretched on mats as Rowena led them into the next pose. Rowena wore her usual workout clothes. Relieved, I shut the door. Good. I wasn't required to dress in costume. Now I needed to find out where I was supposed to go for my session.

Due to the crowd, I had to crane my neck to see above all the heads. Someone tapped my shoulder and I turned around. Letting out a small shriek, I jumped back.

Pennywise, the terrifying clown from Stephen King's *It,* stood before me.

"Can I help you?" he said in a whisper. A VOLUNTEER badge was pinned to his creepy white clown costume. Not a good costume choice for a wellness fair.

"I'm giving a workshop soon," I said. "Don't I have to check in somewhere first?"

He responded with a chilling stare.

I looked closer, trying to discern which Oriole Point resident lay hidden beneath the heavy clown makeup. "Who are you?"

"Pennywise," he intoned. Then he added in a normal tone of voice, "It's me, marzipan."

Only one person called me "marzipan." My high school boyfriend, Max Riordan, who ran Riordan Outfitters at the town marina.

"Max, you scared me." I gave him a playful punch.

"Great costume, isn't it? I saw your face. You almost screamed."

"What did you expect? And you may want to think twice about who you sneak up on." I looked around at the crowd, a fair number of whom were seniors. "Otherwise someone may need one of the paramedics teaching emergency aid here."

He grinned. "C'mon. Anyone who faced a few killers this past summer can stand up to a fictional clown. Hey, I heard about the body found in Leticia the Lake Lady's field. And that you, Theo, and Kit were the ones to discover it."

"How did you find out? The local news in Holland and Grand Rapids only mentioned that a dead man was found in Oriole County." I caught sight of Dean making his way through the crowd toward one of the wings. "Don't bother to answer. I see Dean, so mystery solved."

"This may come as a shocker, but it wasn't Dean who told me. It was Theo. I spoke to him about fifteen minutes ago."

Max was right. I was shocked. I shook my head at his sinister appearance. "Theo hates horror movies. I can't believe he came anywhere near someone dressed as Pennywise."

"Unlike my former girlfriend, Theo knew who I was right away." Max pointed to the bushy red clown wig. "It seems my actual red hair looks just like this to him."

I laughed. "That must have been a blow to the ego."

"I kinda like the costume. It covers up my freckles. But he told me how worried you were about the Lake Lady. He thought I'd help you find her."

"That was sweet of Theo." I looked around the crowded atrium. "Do you know where he went?"

"He was heading to the parking lot to eat lunch. He bought a sandwich, but wanted to eat it in his car." Max shrugged. "Seemed like something Theo would do."

"Yes, it does. Why did he think you could help?"

"Because I work at the marina and spend a lot of time by the lake. He asked me to keep an eye out for Leticia and her scooter. Sooner or later, Theo thinks she'll come back to the beach. If so, I have a good chance of seeing her. He's not wrong. Me and the boys get to the harbor before dawn when there are fishing trips scheduled. Gives us time to get all the gear assembled for the charters. And I have seen Leticia drive by in the early morning on that purple scooter."

"When was the last time you saw her?"

"The day the health fair had those booths in the park. Only she drove through town later."

"She came to see me." I bit my lip. "Theo is right. I am worried about her. If you or the guys at the marina do see her, let me know."

"Are you going to let *me* know what this is all about, marzipan?"

"I can't right now. It's almost time for my workshop. Luckily, I had Dean bring products from the shop here earlier today. Only I have to figure out where they're being stored."

Max took me by the shoulders and turned me around. "Go to the table where Wonder Woman stands guard. She'll check you in and tell you where to go."

"Thanks." I held up a warning finger. "And try not to scare too many people."

"I can't promise." Max reverted to his intimidating evil clown voice. "But I may sneak in to your berry talk."

"Don't you dare. They won't pay attention to a word I say if you do."

He gave an evil laugh. Honestly, some people didn't know how to handle a Halloween costume.

Before I got waylaid by another Stephen King character, I made my way to the conference check-in table guarded by Wonder Woman. Once I was face-to-face with her, I saw she was none other than Tess Nakamura, one of the finest glass artists in the region—and my best friend.

Like me, Tess normally wore her usual work garb: the Oriole Glass Studio's orange T-shirt and black jeans. Seeing her in a snug Wonder Woman outfit—complete with knee-high boots and golden armguards—came as something of a surprise. Tess didn't often reveal her killer body to this extent. Nor did she ever cover up her short asymmetrical haircut with a black wig, especially one this long and exaggerated.

"You look like a cross between Wonder Woman and Cher," I told her.

Tess laughed. "It's actually a Morticia wig I borrowed from my sister-in-law. And I wondered when you were going to show up. Your workshop will be held in Annex B, Room Ten." She rifled through one of the boxes on the table and pulled out a black lanyard. "Here's your conference ID."

"Thanks." I slipped the lanyard over my head. "I just ran into Max."

Tess made a face. "His costume's a little intense."

"Tell me about it. Anyone else here that I know?"

"Piper and Lionel, of course."

"Of course."

"This morning Denise Redfern gave a workshop on Native American healing traditions."

"Sounds intriguing. I wish I'd been here."

"A whole bunch of Oriole Point people will be at the center all week. Because there was no way to fit glassblowing into a health fair, I thought the least I could do was help out." She gave me a wry look. "Also Piper came to the studio last week and guilted David and me into volunteering. If you visit the vendor room, David is the chipmunk helping to bag purchases."

The image made me giggle. "Where did David get a chipmunk costume?"

"He bought it during our trip to Disney World last year. I knew David loved Chip 'n Dale cartoons, but not to this extent." She sighed. "He plans to wear it when giving out candy every Halloween. And he's wearing it in the Halloween Parade. This means I have to spend all my birthdays in the company of a giant chipmunk."

Like me, Tess's birthday fell on a holiday, only she had been born on Halloween. "It could have been worse. What if he'd been a fan of Donald Duck?"

She smirked. "Six of one, half dozen of the other."

"Is there anyone else I know in costume here today?"

"Natasha. She's a moderator for two of the Sable beauty products sessions. You can't miss her. She's dressed as Cleopatra. There's even a fake asp attached to her gold belt. I'm impressed by her attention to detail."

Hearing Natasha volunteered for Piper's health fair startled me as much as Pennywise tapping me on the shoulder. Former Russian beauty queen Natasha became a rich widow several months ago. Since then she had spent most of her time enjoying her freedom and her newfound wealth. In other words, shopping.

No one blamed her. Natasha's husband had been an obnoxious brute, albeit a rich one. When he died, no one in town mourned, including his young widow. And being a moderator for the Sable beauty products session did make sense. Not only was Natasha the queen of personal grooming, she planned to open a spa soon. By volunteering at one of the Sable beauty sessions, she probably hoped to pick up valuable information, along with free products.

"Drake's holding workshops on astrology," Tess added. "He's lecturing in Room Fifteen right now."

An Olympic medalist in track and field, Drake Woodhill moved to Oriole Point a decade ago to open Gemini Rising, a New Age bookstore. He was also British—and a witch. "What does astrology have to do with health?" I asked.

"I think he represents the haunted Halloween part of the fair. Like having the volunteers wear costumes." She leaned closer. "I also think he's offended by some of the costumes. Three of the girls dressed as witches. Not sexy ones either." Tess gestured at a young woman in a floor-length black dress. I could see why Drake might be miffed. She had painted her skin green, attached a wart to her nose, and brandished a broom in one hand.

"Drake doesn't have a sense of humor when it comes to Wicca," I said.

"I don't think he has a sense of humor at all."

"He does, but it's well hidden."

She raised an eyebrow at me. "I bet he keeps a lot

of things hidden. David saw Leticia the Lake Lady go into Drake's shop last month."

"No way! Leticia never goes into any of the stores."

"I know. It's weird. I wasn't at the studio that day. I had to meet a gallery owner in Lansing about a winter glass exhibition that David and I will be part of." Tess and David Reese met as students at the Rhode Island School of Design and had been a romantic and professional couple ever since. They had no plans to marry, being content with how harmonious their lives had been for the past twelve years. Some people found this odd. My view was "if it ain't broke, don't fix it." Especially given my own checkered romantic past.

"David only told me about it this morning," she continued. "After I mentioned your encounter with Leticia and the dead body in her field."

Drake's bookshop was directly across the street from their studio, which meant David had a clear view of anyone going in or out. "He's sure it was her?"

"Absolutely. She parked her purple scooter right outside Gemini Rising. He says she was in there for about an hour. Came out with a bag, so she bought something."

"Do you remember when this was exactly?"

She thought a moment. "Pretty sure it was the day of the OPBA meeting."

"Did you ever get around to asking Drake about it?"

"No. Drake and I aren't friends. He'd think it strange if I suddenly visited his shop to ask about the Lake Lady. But not as strange as Leticia's visit to his store. No one has ever seen her anywhere in Oriole Point except the beach. Why would she suddenly visit a store that sells tarot cards, crystals, and books on witchcraft?"

"She probably went there to buy something to help protect her."

"Seems mysterious to me," she said before turning her attention to a workshop moderator wanting to check in.

Unlike Tess, I didn't find the visit mysterious. Earlier that morning, Leticia and Piper met on the beach to argue about the Sables' upcoming appearance at the health fair. When Piper refused to stop the Sable family from coming to Oriole Point, Leticia obviously felt she had to take matters into her own hands. The police and city officials wouldn't help her. That left her few options. One of them involved magic, hence the visit to Drake's bookshop. And once she decided on the method of protection, she came to me.

My phone buzzed from the depths of my purse. Pulling it out, I saw a text from Dean with instructions to get my butt over to Room Ten, Annex B. Piper wanted me now!

I didn't waste time with a reply. Best to hotfoot it over there before Piper went into diva overdrive. Luckily, the crowd thinned once I made my way to the annex. A line of closed doors with workshop signs greeted me. Most people in the annex were already attending sessions, although I saw lots of visitors enter the vendor room.

Despite the time crunch, I wanted a glimpse of David in his chipmunk costume. The sight of David as Chip (or was it Dale?) was well worth angering Piper.

The vendor space was vast, but a man-size chipmunk is hard to miss. Although if Tess hadn't told me about David's costume, I would never have recognized him. His face was covered by a gigantic, smiling chipmunk head. I almost went over to him to take a few photos with my phone, but he was busy bagging purchases. An unwise task to give him since his brown furry costume and gloves didn't lend themselves to feats of dexterity.

After a glance at my watch, I decided to risk a quick tour.

The conference center had taken down partitions of several rooms in order to have the space to sell the items showcased at the fair. And what a compendium of products it was: Ellie Vaughn's Pilates machines, standing desks, trail bikes, nontoxic cookware, gluten-free food, pedometers, first-aid kits, organically grown coffees and teas, workout clothes, non-plastic toys, eco-friendly clothing, healing crystals, and more.

Holding court over it all were the displays devoted to the Sable products. The entire back wall of the vendor room had been reserved for the Sable empire, their photos and names displayed larger than life. All of it framed by haystacks, pumpkins, and scarecrows.

I walked past the tables, each featuring a different Sable skin-care line, cosmetic, hair product, vitamin supplement, and on and on. I never realized how many pies the Sable family had their fingers in. Literally, everything *but* pies. Then there were the books.

The Sable Diet hit bookstands in the 1980s, the first in the family's juggernaut of healthy living and natural-beauty products. Since then, family members had published at least one book a year. An entire section of the vendor room was devoted to a display of *Beauty's Bounty* by Ainsley Sable.

It looked like the book signing for it had just ended. A slender brunette in a gray pencil skirt and plum turtleneck posed by a sign that read "*New York Times* Best Seller." A line of people waited to have their picture taken with her, each clutching a copy of her book. I took a closer look at Patrick Sable's wife, whose nanny was murdered twenty-eight years ago.

I had researched the Sables online and knew Ainsley was following in the footsteps of her mother-in-law. While the Sable men concentrated their efforts on natural supplements and diets, Ingrid and Ainsley were the literal faces of the Sable beauty and cosmetics line. Both women also wrote books about skin care, the most recent being *Beauty's Bounty*.

Ainsley in person wasn't as flawless as her publicity photos suggested. Nor was she a natural beauty like Ingrid, who even in her seventies resembled a Nordic goddess. But Ainsley was attractive, if a bit too animated. Her wide smile seemed forced, as though she were gritting her teeth while grinning. Perhaps this latest book tour had taken its toll. Like most female celebrities, she was reed thin, which meant she looked quite good in her pencil skirt and snug sweater. And although she appeared tall, the gray stilettos were largely responsible for that. I judged her to be about five seven once she kicked off her designer footwear.

However, she looked fit and healthy, despite her nervous energy. I was particularly struck by her mahogany brown hair, which literally gleamed. Our hair lengths were identical—just grazing our shoulders—but her hair flowed about her face like a smooth sheet of dark satin. Maybe I should check out the Sable hair-care line.

As I watched Ainsley interact with her readers, my cell phone vibrated in my bag. It was Dean. "Where are you?" he demanded.

"In the vendor room. And what's the urgency? I

have twenty-five minutes before my talk is scheduled to start."

He gave an exaggerated sigh. "It's Piper. She's sure you're going to be late."

"Well, I'm not. Tell her I'll be there in ten minutes. Fifteen if she makes you call me again." I tossed the phone back into my bag.

"Hey, Marlee, what are you doing here?"

I turned to see Mia Norris. Since she was the owner of a popcorn store called Popping Fun, it came as no surprise that she was outfitted as a giant kernel of popcorn.

"I'm giving a talk at two o'clock on berries."

"That's right. I saw your name on the sandwich board by the front entrance. But why aren't you dressed in a costume?"

"I didn't know volunteers were expected to be in costume. And technically, I'm a speaker, not a volunteer. Although, let's be honest, Piper volunteered me again."

Mia giggled. "Piper always makes me laugh."

"Yeah, she can be a real hoot."

"Isn't this the most fantastic thing to happen in Oriole Point? I've never seen so many celebrities in one place. This is the second day I've volunteered. On Monday I got to dance the tango with Rufus from *Let's Dance*. Of course I took the popcorn costume off." She giggled again. "That left only my white bodysuit, which is actually really sexy. Gary was a little jealous."

Gary was her husband, a taciturn fellow who must often be exhausted by the bubbly Mia.

"What are your volunteer duties today?"

She held up a basket filled with small bags of popcorn, each tied with red ribbon. "Passing out free samples of my shop's low calorie, low-sodium popcorn balls." Her smile widened. "It's great publicity for the store. Why didn't you tell some of your people from Berry Basket to hand out berries? I mean, berries are even healthier than popcorn."

"It didn't occur to me. Anyway, it's been a busy week. Besides, I think everyone already knows berries are a healthy thing to eat. My talk today will tell them why."

"Maybe you can tell me something about the berries I've found in this room. At least I think it's a berry. I've stepped on several of them since I came in here." She pointed at the carpet. "There's another one. Do you know what it is?"

I bent down and picked it up. "It's a dried mulberry."

Mia peered at the berry in my hand. "It's white. I thought mulberries were purple."

"Mulberries can be white, purple, red. Sometimes all on the same tree, too." My breathing quickened. "You've stepped on these berries while you were in here?"

"They're sticky, too. Like there's glue on them." Mia's sparkling brown eyes lit up even more as she glanced over my shoulder. "I have to go. I just spotted my friend Shannon. She's a moderator for the *Weight Loss Wonders* workshop. Shannon knows how much I love that show and promised to introduce me to last year's winner."

"Have fun," I said absently as Mia bounced off to meet her friend.

I looked at the mulberry again. Was Leticia here? I could see no other reason for dried mulberries to appear on the floor of the vendor room. Especially white mulberries, which is what I had ordered for

Leticia from Chris Farnsworth. But would Leticia dare show herself in the very place where all the Sables had assembled?

If so, I feared she had something far worse than a flat tire planned.

Chapter Twelve

Clutching the mulberry in my fist, I looked out over the vendor room now crammed with people. It suddenly felt circus-like. The noise level was high because product demonstrations were going on. And the costumed volunteers made everything surreal. I had a terrible feeling things were about to slip out of control.

The day we found Bonaventure's body, I noticed one of the boxes of mulberries I'd left on her porch had been opened, and several bags of berries removed. Only Leticia would care enough about the berries to take some with her. On one hand, I felt relieved. It proved she was alive. It also meant Leticia was still determined to use the berries as a form of magical protection—or as a weapon. I remembered the mulberry arrow shot into Bonaventure's chest.

But why were the mulberries on the carpet? I examined the berry in my hand once again. Mia had been correct to attribute the stickiness on the berry to some sort of glue. Leticia had glued these berries onto something.

I scanned the room, hoping to catch a glimpse of someone with orange hair.

When I turned up nothing, I pulled out my cell phone. The sooner Piper knew Leticia might be here, the sooner she could put security guards on her trail. I began my text with URGENT in caps, followed by my description of the dried mulberries on the vendor room floor and the likelihood Leticia was about to do something nasty. Something connected to the Sables.

After I finished my text, I felt a tap on my shoulder. My heart sank. Who was behind me now? First, I'd been startled by Pennywise, then by a popcorn kernel on steroids. I wasn't in the mood for another Halloween surprise.

But when I peeked over my shoulder, I saw Ainsley Sable. "You're Marlee Jacob, aren't you?" Her wide smile revealed such perfect white teeth, I felt insecure about my own smile.

"Yes, I am. How did you know?"

"I told the volunteer who oversaw my book signing that I wanted to make certain I finished in time to attend Marlee Jacob's talk on berries. He said I couldn't be late because you were still in the vendor room." She held out a manicured hand. "Ainsley Sable."

"I'm flattered you've heard of me." I said, noticing she had a firm handshake.

"Of course. I loved the cooking shows you produced for the Gourmet Living Network."

I hoped she didn't add that I had become a little too famous when one of my celebrity chefs chose arsenic as a baking ingredient.

"I've left that life behind," I told her. "Now I'm happy to be running The Berry Basket."

"Patrick and Keith said they met you last night at San Sebastian. Did they mention our plans for a new product line using berries?" She had enormous eyes, almost saucer-like, which her perfectly applied make-up exaggerated. And they were of a brown so dark, in a certain light I suspected they seemed black. It was a bit disconcerting to have her avid gaze fixed on me.

"Yes, they did."

"Our labs are working on berry-based products." She gave me another hard, bright smile. "Ingrid has asked the whole family to attend your talk. Speaking of your talk, shouldn't you be heading there now?"

"I'm waiting for Piper. I asked her to meet me here."

"When you're ready, we can all go together. I cleared my schedule in order to attend your work-shop. Once I become focused on a project, I am single-minded. Right now the berry beauty line is all I can think about. What a relief to discover Oriole Point has someone so knowledgeable about berries. A woman who once was a television producer, too." She gave me a conspiratorial wink. "That takes brains and survival skills. I think you'd make a great addition to the Sable team. I hope we can convince you to work with us. We'd be thrilled and honored."

Once again, I was struck by the friendliness of the Sable family. It was difficult to reconcile Leticia's dread of them with my experiences. Then again, I had spent all of five minutes in their presence. Easy to be charming for such a short amount of time.

"If you have questions about specific berries, I'll make sure to include information about them in the talk." I peeked at my cell phone. Still no text from Piper.

"We're working on formulas based on blueberries, acai, strawberries, and goji. Are there other berries you'd recommend?"

"Raspberry oil is a good berry extract for any product targeted for sensitive skin. Many sunscreens include raspberries because they reduce melanin production."

Before Ainsley could ask me another question, a quartet of women interrupted our conversation, thrilled to have stumbled upon the author of *Beauty's Bounty*. Like teenyboppers surrounding their idol, the women offered pens for her to sign their books, along with requests for selfies.

Ainsley's smile grew even more strained, but she signed the first book with a flourish, then let herself be positioned for what seemed destined to be a series of cell-phone photos.

She shot me an apologetic look. "Do you mind?"

"Not at all. I'll see you at my workshop. Take your time." I pushed my way toward the door. If Piper wasn't coming to me, I'd better hunt her down.

Suddenly, I stepped on something. Lifting my shoe, I saw a squashed mulberry.

I bent down and searched the floor. Individual mulberries lay scattered about the carpet. Not many, but enough to catch my eye.

Like Hansel and Gretel, I kept my gaze fixed to the berry version of bread crumbs as I pushed through the crowd. The berries had fallen off whatever she had glued them to. But what?

I didn't discover the source until I made my way to

the demonstration of the latest incarnation of the Magic Bullet Blender. The dried mulberries decorated a pair of white sweatpants worn by a person who stood at the rear of the Magic Bullet crowd. The mulberries had been affixed to the cuffs of the pants, glued next to each other to form an unbroken line. But over a dozen had fallen off. Mulberries were also glued to the border of this individual's white sweatshirt. And the person wore a white ski cap, hiding their hair. It had to be Leticia.

My turn to surprise someone. I stood up and tapped her on the shoulder.

When she spun around, both of us cried out. Leticia didn't expect to see me. And I was taken aback by the mime makeup covering her face. Small wonder no one had figured out who she was under the white face paint, pointy black eyebrows, painted black tears, and scarlet red lipstick. It was a toss-up as to who was more terrifying: Pennywise or Leticia as a mime.

"Marlee Jacob, what are you doing in here?" Leticia hissed at me. "You're supposed to be giving a talk on berries."

"For the love of God, will everyone stop reminding me about my berry talk? The real question is what are you doing here?" I lowered my voice to a stage whisper. "And where have you been? The police are looking for you."

Her painted eyes regarded me with pity. "The police will never trap me again."

"Leticia, no one wants to trap you. Least of all, me."

"You have a kind heart, which is why I need your berries for protection. Most people are not kind. And my enemies are the unkindest of all. I can't go

home until the danger is gone and justice is finally—"
The loud whirring of the Magic Bullet drowned out
the rest of her sentence.

After the blending finished, I said, "I've learned
about your past with the Sables. The shadow people."

Leticia smiled. Those scarlet red lips made it a disturbing sight. "I knew you would realize the Sables are
the shadow people. Even the name reveals their darkness within." She glanced at the Sable display, lit by
spotlights and framed by straw and fake autumn
leaves. "One of them is in the room with us."

"Yes. Ainsley Sable. She spoke to me just now about
berries."

"Stay away from them. All of them." She pressed
her face close to mine. "A Sable killed the ghost. My
ghost."

I heard the fear in her voice. It matched my own
growing fear of the situation. "Which Sable killed
him?"

"The most dangerous one, of course. But they're all
dangerous. Don't forget that."

"Tell me who it is?"

"Shhhh. If you know, you will be in danger, too.
Here, take this. It will help protect you. I made it with
your mulberries." She pulled off her bracelet and
pressed it into my hand.

I looked down. It was an elastic bracelet strung with
dried mulberries.

Leticia closed my fingers over the bracelet. "It will
keep you safe from the Sables. They're very angry
now because they want the book. That's why the ghost
was killed."

"I met your ghost."

"Yes. You left a message trying to warn me. But the ghost was helping me. He was my ally. And the shadow people silenced him."

"He was killed by a mulberry arrow. Was the arrow yours?"

She nodded. "I had them made by the man who has a woodshop on Lyall Street."

"Gareth Holmes? The old guy who makes duck decoys?" After four years of refusing to enter any store in Oriole Point, Leticia had braved a visit to both Gemini Rising and Gareth's woodworking shop. Next, I'd probably learn she stopped in for a chai at Coffee by Crystal.

"I needed a mulberry bow and arrows. You see, I knew about the Chinese legend just as you did. I had to protect myself."

Good grief, had Leticia just confessed to me? After stuffing the mulberry bracelet in the pocket of my slacks, I took Leticia by the arm. I had to keep her here until Piper showed up. I also had to know if I had been tragically wrong about her. "Did you shoot Felix Bonaventure with the arrow?"

She reeled back. "I would never kill my ghost."

The blender started up again. I pulled her around the edge of the audience until we reached the back of the stage where the demonstration took place. A curtain hid us from view.

"Someone killed him with that arrow. An arrow you had made. The police will never believe you didn't do it." I didn't believe it, and I had been trying to protect her.

She shook free of my grip. "I lack the skill. When I learned the Sables were coming to Oriole Point, I practiced shooting targets on my property. And the property next door. But I rarely struck the target. Instead, I hit a beehive. Then I killed one of my cats." Her hoarse voice grew ragged. "My companions. And I killed one of them! I didn't mean to. I didn't. The arrow went astray." Leticia's painted face crumpled as she burst into tears.

"It's all right." I patted her on the back. "It was an accident."

She fell against me and wept. I put my arms around her.

"I couldn't bring myself to pick up a bow and arrow after that," she said between sobs. "I just left them out in the field. How could I ever touch those arrows again?"

"Wait." I lifted Leticia's tear streaked face so I could see her. "Your bow and arrows were left outside where anyone could pick them up?"

"Yes. I couldn't bear to look at them after Callista was killed. I didn't even have the courage to pull the arrow from her body and bury her. I was too upset. And I felt guilty. She had kittens! I'll never forgive myself." Tears streaked her white and black makeup, making her visage more unsettling. "Who will take care of my cats if the shadow people kill me? Who?"

"No one will kill you. As for the cats, I'll look after them until you go back home."

She bit back another sob and hugged me. When she straightened, I readjusted her white ski cap, which had gone askew. My maternal urges had kicked into high gear this week. First, those cats. Now this broken woman.

Glancing down, I saw that her white makeup had smeared my red sweater. It was not yet two o'clock, but

I feared Piper had been right. I was going to be late for that berry talk. And I had second thoughts about alerting Piper. I didn't know if Leticia had killed the nanny decades ago, however I wasn't convinced she was responsible for the murder of Felix Bonaventure.

But someone killed him. Despite their charm, a Sable seemed the likeliest candidate.

"Why were you practicing with the bow and arrows in the first place?"

Leticia dabbed at her eyes with her sleeve. "I told you. I needed to protect myself. Piper invited the Sables here. I knew they would find me. Like they found the ghost."

"Did you meet with Felix Bonaventure before he died?"

"No. And he shouldn't have come here. I think he helped lead the shadow people to my house. I sent him a text and told him to stay away. But he didn't. He came while I was gone."

"Where did you go?"

"To the beach. I woke before dawn, which is the best time to go to the lake." Leticia raised her voice as more blending resumed on the other side of the curtain. "But not to Oriole Beach. I couldn't go there with the shadow people so close. I went to Oval Beach in Saugatuck instead. When I returned home, I saw the car in my drive. I knew it meant the ghost was here."

"How did you know it was Bonaventure?"

"While I was at the beach, he left a voicemail saying he had found out where I lived. And that he was going to come over and not leave until we spoke in person. Foolish man. He, more than anyone, should have understood the danger he was putting himself in."

She gave a shuddering sigh. "I knew something was wrong when I saw the turkeys near my beehives. Turkeys are curious. And bold. They found the body before I did."

"Why didn't you call the police?"

"I can't trust the police. They locked me away. Besides, they would never believe me. Not with the shadow people telling their clever lies." Her expression hardened. "They're going to tell lies again. Lies about me. It will be all over TV."

"I doubt the Sables want to discuss the murder of the nanny. On TV or anywhere else."

"You're wrong. The TV lady told my cousin. She said the story of the nanny will be famous again. People who don't know about the murder will now hear the Sable lies." She leaned closer. "That's why I had to write the book. The world must hear the truth this time."

"Who's the TV lady?"

Leticia looked at me as if I was a dolt. "She's on TV all the time. They call her an entertainment reporter. I can't remember her name. It sounds watery."

I feared this line of questioning led nowhere, so I changed direction. "Are you the person vandalizing the Sable cars?"

"Yes." Her chin lifted in defiance. "I want them to go away. I don't want their visit to be pleasant. And I don't want them to come back."

"Is that why you're here now?" I asked her. "Do you have something else planned?"

A sly smile appeared on her painted face. "Mischief," she said. "Only mischief."

I remembered what I had seen on her desk. "Just mischief? Or mischief and murder?"

Her eyes widened. "How do you know about that?"

"I went into your house on Monday. I saw the manuscript. The one you wrote with Felix Bonaventure."

She squeezed my shoulder, as if to reassure me. "The truth will be revealed in the manuscript and the shadow people vanquished. And this time the sailor man is helping me. He lied about me in the past. Said terrible things that put me in prison. All because a shadow person told him to. But he's changed his mind. Now he wants to help."

"Do you mean the crew member on the yacht? James Smith?"

She nodded. "He's very ill. And he doesn't want to die with such a sin on his conscience. My ghost and I talked to him. He agreed to tell the truth. It's all in the manuscript."

"Where is the manuscript now?"

"Safe with the mulberries," she said solemnly. "*Your* mulberries. Your berries are powerful because you devoted your life to them. That is why you found those other murderers. The berries have given you some of their power."

Shouts erupted from the back of the vendor room. "Fire!" a man yelled. "Fire!"

The shouts came from the Sable products display. As did the smoke that billowed above several stuffed scarecrows and a haystack.

More screams and yells filled the air. Fear rippled through the room. "Oh no!" I cried. "Not a fire with all these people."

Leticia tapped me on the shoulder. "Leave now. The mischief is not meant for you."

I grabbed her hand. "Did you start a fire? Are you crazy?"

She pulled away as more screams and shouts echoed around me. Everyone pushed toward the exit doors. I tried to grab Leticia, but too many people from the back of the room had now reached us. Shoved against the stage where the Magic Bullet demo had been going on, I watched helplessly as Leticia's white ski cap disappeared in the frantic crowd.

Before I got smashed against the stage, I pushed my way around the edge. Only now I was in the middle of a terrified mob. The smoke made my eyes water. It had thickened so fast, I could barely see ten feet in front of me. My heart pounded with fear as the overhead lights began to pulsate in conjunction with a robotic voice from the loudspeaker, "Please make your way to the nearest exit door."

This led to more screams, shouts, and frantic shoving. I struggled to stay on my feet. The lights continued to strobe, adding to the confusion. That chilling robotic voice repeated her instructions as the smoke grew thicker. Why hadn't the water sprinklers turned on?

"No pushing!" a woman yelled. It sounded like Piper. "Please walk quickly towards the exit doors! Don't run!"

But the crowd had become a single frightened organism, intent on escape. Coughing from the smoke, I fought my own rising panic. What had Leticia done? It was one thing to want to hurt the Sables for whatever she believed they had done to her. But to start a fire in a crowd was more than madness. It was murder.

"Run!" someone screamed. "There's a fire!"

Men and women on all sides pressed toward the doors. In the chaos, I caught glimpses of normal adults interspersed with oddities like Frankenstein's monster, Little Red Riding Hood, and Freddy Krueger. The strobing lights gave it a nightmarish aspect. Swept up in the mass exodus, there was a moment when I felt like I had been lifted off my feet and carried by the momentum. I prayed no one tripped and fell. They would be trampled for sure.

The crowd moved so swiftly, I reached the exit sooner than I thought possible. Then it got worse as the space narrowed and a bottleneck formed. I remembered reading how most deaths in a panicked crowd occur because the sheer weight of people crushed against the chest and obstructed breathing. *Put your arms up*, I told myself, *protect your chest.*

Smoke was everywhere. I could barely see the person in front of me. I certainly couldn't see the exit.

People pressed even harder against me. Even with my arms crossed in front of my chest, I found it hard to take a breath. This was a dangerous situation. More dangerous than the fire.

An older woman beside me turned a pale face in my direction. "Help me. I can't breathe," she gasped. Then she slumped forward.

I caught her before she fell to the ground.

"Don't push!" I shouted to anyone who would listen. Holding the unconscious woman in my arms while trying to stay upright was proving to be a losing battle.

"Stop." I struggled to breathe. "Stop pushing!"

Spots danced before my eyes as the sounds grew fainter. I wouldn't be able to hold the woman up much longer. But if I passed out, both of us might be crushed in this stampede.

Heads bobbed on all sides. Some of them looked like witches and devils. Even a giant chipmunk. This felt like a dream. No, a nightmare.

Although I saw everyone shouting around me, the screams now seemed farther away. My legs felt like jelly and my grip loosened on the woman who had collapsed in my arms. I tried to say something, but couldn't form the words. And I needed to warn everyone about the mime and the shadow people before it was too late. Maybe it already was.

Then I couldn't hear the screams at all.

Chapter Thirteen

A gust of cool air blew against my body. I realized I was lying outside on the grass, but felt disoriented. Then I remembered the vendor room, my conversation with Leticia, the smoke and cries of fire, the mad rush for the exits.

I opened my eyes and saw Wonder Woman. "Did I pass out? I hope not."

Wonder Woman smiled. "Let's just say you took a brief nap. Thank God you weren't trampled. How do you feel?"

"Tess?" I struggled to sit up, and several people helped me. One was a concerned-looking Dean. The others wore chipmunk and clown costumes. "David? Max?"

"You do lead an exciting life, Marlee." Dean winked at me.

The glass dome of the conference center loomed to my right beneath cloudy skies. I sat on the grass in a landscaped area near one of the walkways. People thronged all about us, some sobbing. Others lay on the ground. I heard coughing and crying. Everyone appeared upset. I didn't blame them.

"How are you feeling, marzipan?" Max put his arm around me once I sat upright.

"Confused. How did I get outside?"

"This chipmunk carried you out." Tess looked up at David, who stood behind her. "He should be the one wearing a superhero costume, not me."

"I only did what any Disney character would do," he said with a grin. David had removed his giant chipmunk head, but still wore his brown furry costume. "I saved the day."

"You certainly saved my day." I reached up and grabbed his hand. "Thank you, David. You can look forward to a lifetime of free pastries from The Berry Basket. And my unending gratitude. I remember trying to help a woman who fainted against me. Is she okay?"

"I was right behind you in that crush. Everyone went berserk once they saw the smoke, so I kept an eye on you. When that woman fainted in your arms, I knew you were in trouble. I tucked both of you under each arm and barreled toward the exit." David crouched beside Tess, who gave him a kiss on the cheek.

"Who knew chipmunks were this strong and heroic?" Tess looked at him with adoration. At that moment, I adored David, too.

I patted his furry arm. "Thank you again, Chip. Or are you supposed to be Dale?"

"Chip, of course." He gave me a mock angry look.

"Chip is the smart one," Tess told me in a stage whisper. "Dale's something of a dimwit."

"Are you sure that woman who collapsed against me is all right?"

David nodded. "She's fine. A little hysterical though. Luckily, paramedics were already here giving workshops. They're checking everyone out."

"Two men were taken to the hospital with chest pains," Max said. "Over a dozen people passed out."

"I heard someone broke their foot," Dean added. "And the strobe lights set off by the alarm caused a couple seizures. I'm relieved I was at the far end of the annex with the Sables. We heard the alarms and the screaming, but none of the smoke reached us. Or the panic."

"It could have been much worse." Tess smoothed back my hair. "A good thing the smoke was confined to the vendor room and the adjoining corridor."

"No fire?" I asked.

David shrugged. "I didn't see any sign of fire when I was in the vendor room. Then again, that smoke got thick really fast. To be honest, I don't think there was an actual fire. Otherwise the heat from the flames would have automatically turned on the sprinklers. We'll know more once the fire department arrives."

Right on cue, sirens filled the air. The people milling about turned their attention to the trucks pulling into the parking lot.

"I think I can stand up now," I said.

Before I could move, a woman in a slinky gold dress emerged from the crowd. She wore a diadem on her head, a snake around her waist, and a black wig even more impressive than the one on Tess. She also had on more eye makeup than a dozen Kardashians.

The woman flung herself beside me, forcing Max to move. *"Moy bednny* Marlee,*"* she wailed in a Russian accent. "My poor Marlee! I am in bathroom when I hear screams and fire alarms. I come out to see people run like KGB chases them. A person dressed as popcorn ball tell me Marlee Jacob has been trampled in crowd! I am *tak strashno*. So afraid. What if my friend is squashed like she is a beet for borscht!" She proceeded to squeeze me as tight as she could.

"They squash beets to make borscht?" Max muttered.

Natasha heard him. "*Da!* Beet must be squashed for borscht. I am Russian. You are not. You know nothing of borscht. And do not talk of borscht when my Marlee is hurt."

I hugged her back. "I'm fine, Natasha. And I'm glad everyone else got out okay. But I do need to stand up."

My friends pulled me to my feet, each of them looking at me as if I might collapse.

"It's okay, guys." I straightened my sweater. "I'll tell you what isn't okay. Leticia was in the vendor room right before the smoke appeared. I believe she's responsible for all this."

"Are you sure?" Max asked.

"Yes. I spoke to her. She said she came here to cause mischief." I watched as the crowd made way for the firefighters. "And she certainly has."

Tess looked worried. "Maybe she has something else planned."

"Or she intended to start a fire," Dean guessed, "but something went wrong. If so, she could make another attempt."

"The police will be here soon," David said. "They need to know Leticia caused this."

"I'm shocked none of us spotted her," Tess added. "That orange hair is hard to miss."

"She has her hair hidden beneath a white ski cap," I said. "And she's dressed as a mime. Scariest-looking mime I've ever seen, and they're already strange looking."

"The Lake Lady as a mime." Max whistled. "Now that must be a sight."

"You think Lake Lady start all the trouble?" Natasha asked me. "That woman with ugly hair? She look like Kikimora."

David cocked his head at her. "What's a Kikimora?"

"Is bad spirit. Russian children afraid of Kikimoras. They are souls of people who drown."

"Could be why Leticia never goes into the lake," Dean remarked.

I thought of the drowned nanny and wondered if the guilt of that death had unsettled Leticia's mind. "Maybe," I murmured.

"Ms. Jacob, there you are," Ainsley Sable said as she approached us. "I worried you'd been caught up in that mess in the vendor room. I'm relieved you're not hurt." Her husband Patrick accompanied her. They both looked troubled.

"A miracle someone wasn't killed in there," Patrick said.

"I'm glad to see you made it out of the vendor room safely, too." I quickly introduced everyone. When I got to Natasha, she waved her hand.

"I know Sables," my Russian friend said. "I take charge of their skin care workshop this morning."

"Ms. Bowman was our moderator. Such colorful comments." Ainsley's voice dripped with sarcasm. "My mother-in-law and I learned things about our products that we never knew."

It sounded like Natasha had chosen to improvise. Half of it was probably in Russian. "How did you make it out of there?" I asked Ainsley.

"I left before anyone saw the smoke," she explained. "In fact, I had joined my family at the end of the annex. Thank God we were nowhere near that insane mob."

"If you'd been trapped in the rush for the exits, you might not be so quick to label us insane," I said with irritation. "Or a mob."

Ainsley narrowed her eyes at me while Dean said. "We were outside the room where your workshop was scheduled. Piper left as soon as she got your text. She seemed upset."

"I'm not surprised." Yet again, I wondered where Piper was.

"I see Chief Hitchcock. I'll tell him what's going on." David hurried off.

"What *is* going on, Ms. Jacob? And what exactly happened in the vendor room? I demand an explanation." Since Patrick hadn't just been crushed by a panicked crowd, I thought his bad mood a tad unjustified.

"They think crazy lady with orange hair start trouble," Natasha replied. "The Kikimora."

The Sables looked confused. "What are you talking about?" Ainsley asked.

"It's nothing," I said. "We have a town eccentric who likes to pull pranks."

"Starting a fire is hardly a prank." Patrick regarded me with disapproval.

"I agree, however—"

"Marlee, I saw the Lake Lady! She was here!" Theo ran up to us. "I was eating my tuna sandwich in the car when I saw her in the parking lot."

This wasn't how I wanted the Sables to learn about Leticia. I took Theo's hand and pulled him close. "I know. I saw her, too. We'll talk about it later."

"But the police said to tell them if we saw her," he insisted. "And she was here. I saw her walk to her scooter. She had white paint on her face."

"How did you know it was Leticia?" Tess asked.

Patrick and Ainsley looked suddenly alert. "What did you say?" Ainsley asked.

"I asked him how he knew it was Leticia," Tess told them. "Leticia is one of our more unusual residents. We call her Leticia the Lake Lady because she likes to look at the lake."

Ainsley gasped, while her husband barked, "Are you certain her name is Leticia?"

"Yes." Unlike my friends, I understood why the Sables were shocked to hear the name Leticia.

"This is impossible," Patrick said to his wife, who now wore an expression of dread. "Who would dare be this vicious and unkind?"

Tess shot me a confused look.

"Are you sure it was the Lake Lady, Theo?" Max asked.

"Her hat fell off," Theo said. "That's when I saw her orange hair. And only the Lake Lady has hair that color. She drove right past me just as the fire trucks got here." The mention of the fire trucks made Theo look around. "Is there a fire?"

"We don't think so," I reassured him. "Only smoke."

"If he is speaking about the woman who pulled this so-called prank—a prank that could have gotten people killed!—then I insist you inform the police," Patrick ordered.

"Does this Leticia person have a last name?" Ainsley's shock had turned to outrage. "And where does she live? She needs to be arrested."

"She is Kikimora," Natasha said in a hushed tone. "It will be hard to arrest her. They travel through keyholes."

Theo looked disapproving. "No one can do that. You shouldn't tell lies, Natasha."

Natasha reeled off something in Russian to him. Given her tone, I'm sure it wasn't polite.

"Why don't we let the fire department and the police secure the building first," Max suggested. "Then we can talk about whoever may have caused it."

"Did I miss your berry talk, Marlee?" Theo glanced down at his wristwatch. "Am I late?"

"I never got the chance."

"The building has been evacuated," Tess said. "If I had to guess, the rest of today's workshops have been canceled."

"Postponed. I refuse to cancel a single event." Piper appeared in our midst looking as aggravated as an avenging angel. For the first time, Piper's lacquered blond bob was mussed. And her black silk pantsuit wrinkled. I recalled hearing her voice in the vendor room, which meant she'd been trapped in there along with me.

"When am I giving my talk?" I asked her.

"Tomorrow morning at nine o'clock. And if you'd been at the meeting room fifteen minutes early as I requested, you would not have been caught up in the stampede. Instead, I got your text and had to play traffic cop in there. It's a wonder I wasn't flattened to the floor."

"Exactly what was so urgent about Marlee's text message?" Patrick inquired.

Piper's severe expression softened at the sight of the Sable couple. "Marlee informed me that a person of interest had been spotted in the vendor room."

"This Leticia woman, I assume." Patrick looked angry.

"How do you know about Leticia?" Piper turned to me. "Did you tell him?"

"I didn't have much choice. Since she's the person who caused the mayhem in the vendor room, that won't remain a secret for long. Especially now the police have been called."

Ainsley cleared her throat. "Is there some reason we shouldn't know?"

Piper and I exchanged uncertain glances.

"We need to tell the police, Marlee," Theo said with emphasis. "If they find her, maybe they'll find the book her ghost wrote, too."

"What book?" Ainsley looked as if she wanted to shake all of us.

"This is a matter for the police," I said.

"Marlee's helping the police," Theo broke in. "She's helping the Lake Lady, too."

"That's not quite true, " I said. It took all my will-power not to clap my hand over his mouth. Theo had not only lost his fear of people, he seemed well on the way to spreading gossip faster than the Cabot boys.

"But you did help her when you gave her the mul-berries." Theo turned to the rest of the group. "And we've been trying to find her. That's why I had to let Marlee know I saw Leticia leave a few minutes ago on her purple scooter."

"She got away?" Piper swept a hand through her already-mussed hair. "Again?"

"Does this crazy woman have something to do with our vandalized cars?" Ainsley asked.

"Yes," I said. "And I suspect she planned for the smoke to begin at the display of Sable products. She has a grudge against your family."

"Then she admits she knows us?" Patrick asked as Ainsley reached for his hand.

Chief Hitchcock and David arrived in time to hear his question.

Hitchcock nodded at the couple. "David informed me that you're members of the Sable family. That means your family does indeed know this woman, only not under the name Leticia. You knew her as Ellen Nagy."

Patrick shut his eyes. Ainsley took a step back. "Ellen Nagy is here?" she said in a stunned voice.

Piper took a deep breath. "She's lived in Oriole Point for the past four years. As nutty as a Christmas fruitcake, of course, but she's never posed a threat to anyone. Until now."

"She told me she's only doing this so that you and your family will go away," I said.

At this moment, Ainsley's large dark eyes did indeed look black. And filled with anger. "Ingrid and Cameron have to be told," she said to her husband. "Your brother will be upset."

Patrick frowned "Do you think Scarlett is in danger?"

"Who's Scarlett?" I asked.

He turned an irritated face in my direction. "Scarlett

Beckford is my brother's fiancée. The last time Ellen Nagy was with our family, she killed a woman out of jealousy. Who's to say she still doesn't harbor an obsession for Keith? After all, she's dangerous!"

"If so, she may come after Scarlett." Ainsley sighed. "Will this madness never end?"

"I know Scarlett Beckford," Natasha piped up. "She is at workshop this morning. I recognize her as model who wears wings on runway."

"Your brother is engaged to a Victoria's Secret model?" Tess asked.

"Yes, he is," Patrick said impatiently. "And by bringing her to Oriole Point, he has inadvertently put her in harm's way. She must leave as soon as possible."

"I don't think Leticia cares about any of that," I said. "When I've spoken with her, she never brings up your brother. Or any women he's involved with. She seems afraid, not jealous."

"You don't know a thing about Ellen Nagy," Ainsley spat the words at me. "Because you don't, you should stay out of this whole affair. Unless you're helping her. For all we know, you helped her vandalize our cars. Maybe you set off the smoke bombs in there, too!"

That set all my friends protesting on my behalf, even Piper.

"Are you joking?" I said above the babble. "You do realize I was almost trampled."

Piper squeezed my shoulder. "Marlee would not sabotage my health fair. She knows I would never allow her a moment's peace afterward."

"She's right," I agreed.

"All I know is that we were gracious enough to come to Oriole Point after Victor canceled," Patrick said. "As thanks for our generosity, my family finds itself targeted by a murdering madwoman. And none of you have done a thing to prevent it."

"Patrick, that isn't true," Piper began. "I have tirelessly worked to—"

Chief Hitchcock held up his hand. "This is a police matter, one I would rather not have discussed on the front lawn of the conference center." He looked at Patrick and Ainsley. "Once your family is assembled, I need all of you to come with me to the police station. The situation is growing worse by the second, and I intend to stop this nonsense before anyone else dies."

"Who died?" Natasha and Ainsley asked at the same time.

I leaned towards Natasha. "It's a long story."

"Has Ellen killed someone else?" Patrick asked Hitchcock.

"Let's do this at the police station," he said. "Please find your parents and brother."

Pulling out their phones, the aggravated Sable couple walked off, texting furiously.

Hitchcock turned his attention to me next. "While they're tracking down their kinfolk, I have some questions for you. First, what exactly did Leticia say to you in the vendor room? Second, why does Leticia trust you? Third, how do you survive getting into so much trouble?"

I looked at everyone circled around me. "I'll answer the last question first. I have wonderful friends." I gave David a wink. "And one of them is the finest chipmunk in the world."

Chapter Fourteen

"I missed out on all the excitement!" Andrew was inconsolable to learn about the drama at the conference center. "It's not fair. I'm stuck here babysitting Minnie and selling muffins while everyone else is in the middle of an action movie."

"A little too much action," I muttered.

Beside me, David stretched out his legs beneath the bistro table. "Trust me, not even Tom Cruise wants to be part of a stampede."

All of us had reassembled at The Berry Basket. As soon as we got there, I put the CLOSED sign up. For the past twenty minutes, we had downed a variety of berry teas and coffees, while enjoying the four different pastries Theo baked earlier that morning. Inspired by all the talk of mulberries, Theo had whipped up a batch of mulberry thumbprint cookies using the mulberry jam sold in the shop. A clear favorite, since most of the cookies were now gone.

We must have looked a motley crew to Andrew. Although still in costume, Tess, Max and Natasha had tossed their wigs onto an empty chair. David's chipmunk head rested on the front counter. White paint streaked my red sweater, and a glance at the mirror by the door told me I looked as shell-shocked as I felt.

"It wasn't exciting, Andrew." I reached for a boysenberry fritter. "It was terrifying."

"Row, row, row your boat," Minnie sang on my shoulder.

I'd dropped Minnie off at the store this morning and had been gone for several hours. Minnie always grew more loquacious after my absence, as though she were eager to fill me in on her day. In order to keep her quiet while the rest of us talked, I placed her on my shoulder. Being in close proximity to me sometimes reduced her contributions to the conversation.

"Only by the grace of God was no one killed or seriously hurt," I added.

Theo looked up from where he was rearranging fritters in the pastry case. "Did the Lake Lady want to kill everyone?"

"*Da,*" Natasha said between sips of tea. "She is Kikimora. An evil spirit."

Minnie whistled. "*Da.* I want cashew."

"With all due respect to the world of Russian folklore, I don't think she meant for anyone to die." I fed Minnie a cashew. "But it could have easily gone deadly wrong."

"I don't understand." Andrew leaned over the front counter. "Was there a fire, or not?'

"Not," David and Tess said at the same time.

Max turned to Andrew. "She placed smoke bombs beneath the tables holding the Sable products. The fire department found the canisters."

I shuddered. "It was a horror. And I don't use that word lightly."

"Marlec's right." David squeezed my hand. He and I were the only ones in the room to understand what that mass hysteria and fear had been like.

"Oh my Gawd," Minnie said.

"How did no one see her place the smoke bombs?" Tess asked.

"She wore a VOLUNTEER badge on her sweatshirt." I nodded at the white badge on Tess's Wonder Woman outfit. "And she was smart enough to come in costume, like all the other volunteers. If she was puttering around the tables, people would assume she was helping out."

"But she still had to smuggle the smoke bombs into the place," Andrew said.

"The place is swarming with hundreds of people," Max explained, "with products being delivered and moved around constantly. All she had to do was bring in a tote bag with the stuff."

Theo looked over at me. "Do you think the Lake Lady went back home, Marlee?"

"No. She said she couldn't return home until she was out of danger and justice had been served. And since the Sables are still here . . ."

"Sounds like she has more tricks up her sleeve," Andrew observed.

"Trick or treat!" Minnie shrieked.

"Or what she calls 'mischief.'" I said. "That's the only reassuring thing in all this. I believe she has more pranks planned, but nothing she thinks will get anyone killed."

"See you later, alligator," Minnie sang out.

Tess didn't look convinced. "The fact that she uses the word 'mischief' to describe her actions should make you uneasy."

"How so?"

"As former spelling bee champions, we both know words can have radically different meanings. Including mischief."

Tess and I became friends when we tied for a regional spelling bee in fifth grade. We still played word games with each other, and employed the occasional obscure word as a form of secret code around others.

I thought about the dictionary definition. "Mischief: playful misbehavior, an action meant to irritate, cause trouble, or annoy."

"Etymology, please?" She threw me a challenging smile.

"It comes from the Old French word *meschief*." Now I understood. "You're right."

"Give me scritch," Minnie murmured in my ear.

"How about if you two whiz kids let us in on this?" Max said.

I scratched Minnie on the head. "*Meschief* is the Old French term for 'disaster.' It was derived from the word *meschever*, which means 'to meet with calamity or grief.'"

"If that's how Leticia views mischief," Tess said, "the Sables better watch their back."

"Her manuscript was titled *Mischief and Murder*, too. I thought it was a curious title, combining those words. But it makes more sense now."

Dean held up his hands. "Let's get a grip. Most people aren't word fanatics like you two. How would the Lake Lady even know about these old definitions of words?"

"Piper followed this case years ago. She said the press made a big thing about how intelligent the teenaged Ellen Nagy was. Super high IQ." I shrugged.

"Who knows? Maybe all this time our Lake Lady has been some sort of mad genius."

Andrew and Dean snorted in obvious disbelief. Minnie imitated them.

"Don't forget about all those years she spent in prison," Tess reminded them. "Not much to do there but think, stay alive, and use the prison library."

I thought back to my first conversation with Leticia. "She told me that she learned about magic and berries from a roommate. Someone intelligent and multilingual. Obviously, she meant her cellmate. The same one who filled her head with mystical nature lore."

"Sounds possible," Max agreed. "Leticia seems both unstable and clever."

"A clever person might take pleasure in using wordplay to both reveal and conceal," I surmised. "It's like she's telling us she means to bring calamity, only we're too obtuse to see it."

"Hiding in plain sight," David said.

"If I were the Sables, I'd leave town tonight," Andrew said.

"If she is Kikimora, she will find them," Natasha warned us.

Minnie let loose with a few deafening wolf whistles. So much for the parrot staying quiet while on my shoulder.

"The police should have arrested her years ago." Andrew downed the rest of his iced tea.

"But until this week, she hasn't done anything except stand on the beach."

"Tess is right," I said. "She's acting up because she believes the Sables want to kill her."

"Don't forget about Felix Bonaventure," David said. "Someone did kill him."

"Exactly." Restless, I got up from my chair and began to walk about the shop. Minnie made kissing sounds in my ear. "I don't believe she killed her ghost-writer. The manuscript must reveal what she believes really happened to the nanny. She may have witnessed the crime and the Sables somehow forced her to keep quiet."

"They probably scared her," Theo suggested.

"Yes. They probably did." I paced back and forth. "She also told me the yacht crew member who testified against her has now admitted he lied. And that he had talked to both her and the ghostwriter."

"All we need to do is contact him ourselves," Max said.

I frowned. "That might not be so easy. His name is James Smith. With a name that common, it might take some time."

"I'll bet you the Sables know exactly where he is," Tess said.

"I bet they do. What if they found out she was writing a tell-all book about the Nanny Murder? A book that implicates one of them. That would put Leticia *and* the ghostwriter in danger." I thought back to my conversation with Leticia. "This Smith fellow might also be in trouble. However, she said he was dying. So he may not care if the Sables threaten him."

"We definitely need to track down this guy," Andrew said. "And the manuscript."

"You said something about an entertainment reporter." David reached for the last cookie.

"The one with the watery name." Tess looked amused. "Whatever that means."

"I know." I shook my head. "First, she tells me about the ghost and the shadow people. Now a watery reporter. A reporter who told her cousin the Nanny Murder was going to be famous again. Since this is an entertainment reporter, a movie or a miniseries about the murder is probably in the works."

"Makes sense," Andrew said. "True crime is really hot now. But I've been googling the Sables and Nanny Murder and haven't come up with anything about a movie or series."

"Could still be in the early stages. But the prospect of this murder being dragged out for public view again pushed Leticia into telling her side of the story."

"She did confess to the crime," Max said.

"What if it was under duress? If I could figure out who this reporter is, I can try to get in touch with her. After all, I spent a few years in TV myself."

"A watery sounding name," Tess mused. "Rivers, perhaps? Is there a reporter with the last name of Lake or Bay or Ocean?"

We all thought a moment as I continued to pace.

Dean and I suddenly looked at each other. "Delta Marsh!" we shouted at the same time.

"She's a reporter for a network morning show," I said excitedly. "Covers all the red carpets, TV, movies. And she's based in Manhattan. She interviewed me once during the Chaplin murder trial. I'm sure I can track down someone who can help me contact her."

"Delta Marsh." David grinned. "Can't get more watery than that."

"Yes, and she may help me answer some questions about this murder. It's about time we get a few answers. For example, why are the Sables here?"

"Uh, Piper commanded their presence," Max said.

"But she didn't command their presence," I informed him. "Originally, Victor Kang was scheduled to be the health fair's headliner. He dropped out due to a family emergency. The Sables stepped in as a favor to him. Patrick Sable and Kang went to school together."

"Doesn't sound all that sinister, Marlee," David said.

Tess and I glanced at each other. "But it does seem a little too convenient," she said.

"Exactly," Minnie piped up.

Stroking my talkative bird's head, I replied, "I agree with you and Minnie. I don't care how friendly they are with Victor Kang, why is the entire Sable family willing to come to a health fair in a small resort town? A town I bet they never even heard of before last month."

"Kang, Kang, Kang, Kang," Minnie repeated.

"Do you think they came to Oriole Point to find the manuscript?" Dean righted one of the cloth pumpkins on the floor I had knocked aside while pacing.

"Yes. Given that Bonaventure is dead, they plan to permanently silence Leticia, too."

"I think she's smarter than they are."

Max turned to look at Theo. "Why do you say that?"

"Because no one can find her," Theo said. "Not us. Not the police. Not the Sable people. She is smart to find such a good hiding place."

"She is what I tell you." Natasha brushed muffin crumbs from the front of her spangly gold costume. "They will not find her."

"The next best thing is finding the manuscript." I sidestepped a scarecrow propped against the shelf of berry syrups. "I think she hid that, too. She told me the manuscript was safe with the mulberries. *My* mulberries." I halted in my tracks.

"What's the matter, marzipan?"

"Whassup, punk?" Minnie muttered.

"The manuscript is hidden with *my* mulberries. Leticia made a point of saying that. And she ordered the dried mulberries from me because she thought I possessed some kind of special power bestowed on me by the berries."

"You heard it here first," Andrew announced. "Marlee's the latest Marvel superhero: the Berry Basket Bomber."

Dean threw a cloth pumpkin at him.

"The dried mulberries on the vendor floor—the same ones she glued on her clothes—they came from the boxes of berries I ordered. She took several bags from one of the boxes, but the other boxes appeared not to have been opened. Only maybe she did open them, then sealed them up so no one would notice."

"You think the manuscript is hidden in one of the boxes of dried mulberries," Tess said.

I nodded. "Like David said earlier, it could be hiding in plain sight."

"I love you," Minnie said.

Andrew frowned at me. "If you even think of going back to Leticia's place alone, I'll tie you up with a string of Halloween lights."

"Don't worry." I resumed pacing while Minnie repeated, "la la la la la la." "Kit is coming to my house for dinner tonight. I'll ask him to drive me over. This way, the police can't object about me interfering with a crime scene."

Max chuckled. "Even though that's exactly what you'll be doing."

"How can I interfere if a sheriff's deputy is helping me? Besides, once we find the manuscript, we'll know which member of the Sable family we should be most afraid of."

Natasha shook her finger at me. "You must be afraid of Kikimora, too."

Minnie gave a loud whistle, then added, "Be a good girl."

I kissed the top of her gray feathered head. "I'll try, sweetie. I'll try."

"Why does your Kikimora like mulberries so much?" Natasha asked. "In Russia, mulberry is not favorite berry to eat."

"It has nothing to do with their taste," I told her. "The Lake Lady thinks mulberries have protective powers." I suddenly remembered the mulberry bracelet Leticia gave me in the vendor room. I pulled it out of my pocket, running my fingers over the dried berries. "She wanted them because she's worried the same person who killed Laeticia Murier may end up killing her, too."

Natasha sat up so straight, her diadem fell off. "Laeticia Murier?"

"She's the French nanny who worked for the Sables almost thirty years ago. Our Lake Lady went to prison for pushing her off a boat." I stopped in front of Natasha. "Why do you look so funny?"

"Is because of name. Murier." She seemed baffled by our lack of response. "I don't understand. None of you know French?"

"Not unless a French word came up in a spelling bee," I said, a bit embarrassed.

"*Smeshnoy*. Ridiculous. I learn three languages by the time I am ten. You Americans can be so *lenivyy*." She gave an exasperated sigh. "*Murier* is French word. Means 'mulberry tree.'"

The rest of us looked at each other, while Minnie repeated, "Be a good girl" in my ear.

"So our Leticia not only adopted the dead woman's first name," Tess said, "she took her last name as a sign that mulberries could protect her."

I shook my head. "I wish I'd taken French in high school instead of German. If I had, I would have understood her obsession with mulberries sooner."

"I doubt it would have kept Felix Bonaventure alive," Dean said.

Perhaps not. But with luck, mulberries might lead me to Leticia. Before the killer found her first.

Chapter Fifteen

"I've never heard Minnie be this quiet," I joked. "Not even when she's sleeping."

Kit smiled. "She doesn't know what to make of the little fellow."

Minnie sat on her perch, watching the black kitten scamper about the kitchen floor. It was hard to read avian expressions, but it looked like Minnie didn't know whether to be excited by this adorable furry creature, or nervous about him. I stopped by Aunt Vicki's to pick up Panther on the way home. Minnie was happily singing *Barbara Ann* from her travel cage in the backseat when I brought the kitten into the SUV. She'd been silent or muttering to herself ever since.

Instead of Minnie's comments, the sound of tinkling bells filled the air as Panther batted a little plastic ball with bells inside. Aunt Vicki not only reassured me that the vet had given the kitten a clean bill of health, she insisted I take enough cat food, dishes, and toys to fill a small pet shop. Meanwhile, I had eaten enough Kung Pao shrimp to satisfy three people.

I intended to cook dinner for Kit, but he got back from his trip to the prison earlier than expected and was as ravenous as I was. After taking a quick shower, Kit appeared at my front door with a big carryout bag from a local favorite, Peking Palace.

Both of us were famished. For the first few minutes, we kept our conversation confined to the animals and things like "pass me another egg roll."

The kitten dashed after the ball again, prompting Minnie to murmur, "No, no, no, no."

After wolfing down my second serving of rice and shrimp, I finally sat back. "That tasted good. I never got around to lunch."

Kit took a swig of root beer. "How did your berry talk go at the health fair?"

"Postponed until tomorrow." I launched into an account of my conversation with Leticia in the vendor room, the smoke bombs, and the mad rush toward the exit doors.

When I was finished, Kit got up from his tall stool and gave me a tight hug. "I think I should handcuff you to me so I can keep you safe."

I laughed. "David the chipmunk did a good job of that today."

"I may have to deputize him."

"He'd love that, especially if he can wear his costume." I patted his chest. "Finish your General Tso's chicken while I tell you about my plans. Don't look worried. They include you."

"Please don't say you want to help Leticia." Kit sat back down at the kitchen island. "I know you feel sorry for her, but this stunt shows how dangerous she is. To others *and* herself."

"I agree. But I don't believe she killed Felix Bonaventure. And I doubt she killed the nanny. The answers are in that manuscript she took with her. A manuscript she hid with my mulberries. And I did leave four huge boxes of dried mulberries on her porch."

The kitten pounced on the ball, letting out a triumphant little meow. Minnie whistled in response, then said, "Whassup, punk?"

"You think she hid the manuscript in there?" He looked doubtful. "But only one of the boxes had been opened. You told us several bags of berries had been taken."

"The berries she took were the same ones glued onto her clothes. She probably thought pasting them onto her body would protect her."

"We looked inside the opened box. And the other boxes were taped shut."

"Were they? It wouldn't be difficult to slice open one of the boxes, hide the manuscript inside, then seal it up with tape to make it appear it hadn't been tampered with."

"Maybe."

"Have the police been watching the house since we discovered the body yesterday morning?"

Kit smiled. "Marlee, it's a crime scene, not a stakeout. We had law enforcement all over that property yesterday. A half dozen officers searched the woods again today. There's no reason to watch the house constantly. We'll check the property again tomorrow, but our time is better spent trying to track down Leticia."

Panther scampered toward me. When he reached my kitchen stool, he sat down, looking up at me with those beautiful green eyes. "Meow!"

I scooped him up just as Minnie mimicked the kitten's meow.

"Good job, Minnie," I told her, cuddling the kitten against my neck.

In response, Minnie let out a series of high-pitched barks.

Kit chuckled. "Minnie has found her voice again. Only it sounds canine."

"And I think we may find the manuscript in one of those boxes on her porch."

"It won't hurt to look."

"Good. Since we ate so early, we can go before it gets dark." I hopped off the stool. With one hand, I cuddled Panther and cleared the dishes from my side of the island with the other.

Kit held up a dish. "Do you want another egg roll?"

I kissed him on the cheek. "They're all yours. Go ahead and finish dinner. That will give me time to bring Panther's litter box, food, and water into my bedroom. Until he and Minnie get accustomed to each other, it's the safest place for him to be when I'm not around."

It took five minutes to set things up in my bedroom, followed by five minutes of playing with Panther. I had already changed my clothes from the ones I wore to the health fair, so I didn't have to do anything but brush my teeth and give Panther one last kiss.

When I returned to the kitchen, Minnie's vocalizations were in full swing, "Give me a kiss!" she ordered. "Ba-ba-ba Ba-ba ba-Ran."

"She's making up for the half hour of silence." Kit looked up from stacking the dishwasher. I loved men who cleaned up after themselves.

"So I hear." I scratched Minnie's head, eliciting several lip-smacking noises.

Since Kit had finished clearing the kitchen, I busied myself with wrapping up the leftover shrimp, chicken, and rice. "You didn't tell me what you learned at the prison."

"Not as much as I expected. Most of the staff has turned over since Leticia, a.k.a. Ellen Nagy, was released. And she was initially incarcerated in another prison, which has since shut down. I had better luck at the state psychiatric hospital. One of the psychiatrists assigned to the prison now works at the hospital. Given the notoriety of the case, she remembers Leticia. She saw her off and on for two years. Usually when Leticia's complaints about being in danger from the so-called 'shadow people' became too much for prison personnel to handle."

"I don't think there's any doubt the Sables are the shadow people."

"She could blame them for having her locked away."

I put the leftovers in the refrigerator. "Only she confessed to the murder."

"A shame you didn't ask her about the confession when you had the chance."

"If I see her again, I will. Did the psychiatrist allow you to look at her medical records?"

"I'd need a court order for that. But she did paint a general picture of her former patient."

"What exactly is wrong with her?" I asked. "Paranoid schizophrenia?"

Kit closed the dishwasher door. "The psychiatrist says no. However, Leticia does suffer from persecutory delusions. People afflicted with this disorder are convinced someone is trying to harm them. They feel compelled to report these fears to the authorities. Her prison record does note that she often complained people wanted her dead."

"Sounds like schizophrenia."

"Except she doesn't hear voices and seems perfectly capable of taking care of herself. She also doesn't imagine that things are happening to her, at least not to our knowledge."

"Leticia is convinced the Sables are the real threat. What if she's right?"

"That's why we have to track her down."

"We also need to track down James Smith, the bosun." I explained how Smith had apparently decided to come clean and admit he had lied to the police. And that he had spoken with both Leticia and Bonaventure. "The sooner we find him, the sooner we'll learn the truth."

"I'll get the department right on it." He gave me a rueful look. "I only wish he had a name other than James Smith. It is literally the most common name in the U.S."

The doorbell rang through the house.

Minnie called out, "Who's there?"

"Are you expecting someone?" Kit's expression instantly grew wary.

"No. Besides, none of my friends would ring the doorbell."

The bell rang again, inspiring Minnie to imitate the sound. I made my way to the door.

"I'll answer it." Kit strode ahead of me.

"It's my house. I'll do it." I pulled him back. "But you can stand behind me and glower."

I opened the door to see Keith Sable on my front porch. A tall, beautiful young woman stood beside him.

"What do you want?" Kit asked in a gruff voice.

Keith looked startled by Kit's presence and his tone.

"Mr. Sable, I'm surprised to see you," I said. "Is there something wrong?"

"My fiancée and I would like to speak with you. If you don't mind."

His fiancée sent me a disarming smile. She was dressed as I thought a supermodel should be: beige scoop-neck sweater, matching pants, a long fitted jacket, and caramel brown heels. Except for the shoes, I'd bet my entire wardrobe she was outfitted in Stella McCartney. And although Natasha said she was a famous Victoria's Secret model, I had no memory of her on the VS runway or in their lingerie commercials. But her flawless oval face had stared out at me from a number of ads, the most recent ones for Sable beauty products.

The name Scarlett Beckford did ring a bell. I vaguely recalled her bio: Jamaican father, English mother. And too young for forty-seven-year-old Keith Sable. My internet research on Keith this past week had turned up three divorces and three children. None of his marriages had lasted longer than two years; apparently long enough to father another child, allowing the ex-wife to depart with sizable child-support payments. Clearly, he wasn't an ideal lifetime partner. Now he was preparing to take on Wife Number Four. I hoped Ms. Beckford wouldn't regret being next in line.

"Please come in." I ushered them inside.

With Minnie chattering from the kitchen, I thought it best to seat them in my living room. Because I actually enjoyed cleaning, I knew my house was neat and dust-free. I'd also spent an entire year decorating the ground floor and liked to show off the results. Scarlett scanned the living room with an air of approval. The polished wood floors and creamy white walls accentuated the bold tartan green colors of my furniture, the modern light fixtures, the fireplace, and the array of ferns along my bay window. Patrick and Scarlett sat in a loveseat, prompting Kit and me to settle on the leather club chair and glider across from them.

I felt underdressed next to the couple. Keith was outfitted as stylishly as his model girlfriend, while Kit and I wore jeans and sweatshirts. Kit's sweatshirt trumpeted the Detroit Tigers; a bright orange pumpkin decorated mine. Not our finest sartorial look.

"Would you like something to drink?" I asked.

"Let's cut to the chase, Ms. Jacob," Keith began. "My family and I have been at the local police station this afternoon. We've learned Oriole Point has been harboring Ellen Nagy for the past four years, although she apparently goes by the name Leticia the Lake Lady."

"When you use the term 'harbor,'" I said, "you make it sound like she's a fugitive. Which she isn't."

"Marlee's right. Ms. Nagy paid her debt to society many years ago and can live anywhere she likes." Kit didn't mention that he was a sheriff investigating the case.

Keith gave him an irritated look. "And who are you, if I might ask?"

"Atticus Holt," I answered for him. "My boyfriend."

"As Ms. Jacob's boyfriend, I assume you want to keep this young lady safe." Keith nodded at me. "As

I wish to protect Scarlett. Only I can't do that with a homicidal maniac running around the county. A woman who has already killed a young girl out of jealousy."

"If Leticia wanted to kill any of you—"

"Stop calling her that!" He glared at me. "Her real name is Ellen."

"Fine. If Ellen wanted to kill any of you, don't you think she would have done so already?"

"She's not in her right mind. Who knows what delusion she currently labors under? Whatever it is, it involves our shared past. Bad enough she's vandalizing cars and setting off smoke bombs to sabotage our product display. Today I learned she's calling herself by the same name as the young woman she murdered. That alone is cause for concern."

He had a point. "It is troubling," I said.

"Quite bonkers, if you ask me," Scarlett added.

"Far worse than bonkers," Keith said. "She's criminally insane. Twenty-eight years ago, Ellen killed my brother's nanny out of jealousy. She feared my attention was wandering."

"Was it?" Kit asked.

Keith shot him a suspicious look. "Of course not. There was never anything between Laeticia Murier and me. When my mother hired her as an assistant, I was away at college. Which is also where I was when Patrick and Ainsley asked her to be their nanny. They thought she'd be great with kids." His expression saddened. "And from what I could see, she was. She loved babies, especially their baby."

"Something must have happened that summer you were all on Mackinac Island," I pointed out. "Something to make Ellen jealous."

"I didn't do a damn thing," he shot back. "My only mistake was becoming romantically involved with Ellen Nagy. I fell hard and fast when I met her. But I couldn't help myself. Back then, Ellen seemed like an angel: pretty, sensitive, kind, smart. I'd never met anyone like her. The Sables aren't the warmest people in the world, and most girls I had known up to then cared more about my family name and money than me."

Scarlett took his hand. I wondered if she did truly love him. Or was she bowled over by the family fortune, too?

"By the time I went to college, I'd grown cynical," he went on. "That changed when I met Ellen. She was different."

"How so?" I knew what was different about her now, but couldn't picture her as a lovestruck teenager.

He looked frustrated. "I don't know. Different. Like she had been raised by fairies or something, which doesn't make sense. Her family are a bunch of working-class stiffs. I have no idea how she turned out so sweet. Anyway, I fell in love with her."

"And did she love you?" Kit asked.

Keith gave Kit another puzzled look, as if he couldn't understand his interest. "She did. When I proposed that August, she said yes right away. I knew my parents would put up a stink. But I promised we'd wait until we both finished college before getting married. That seemed to placate them." He snorted. "I'm sure they thought I would grow restless within a few months and move on to the next girl. But I don't think that's true. I think I really loved her."

His visit confused me. "I'm not certain why you're telling us this."

"To make you understand how unpredictable Ellen is. How dangerous. You know her as the town eccentric, someone you probably laugh at or gossip about."

"Or feel sorry for," I said.

"Instead, you should be on your guard. I spent all summer with her and thought she was the gentlest creature in the world. Until the last week on Mackinac Island. Things began to change then. She changed. Although she wasn't the only one."

Kit and I glanced at each other before I asked, "What do you mean?"

"Everyone seemed tense. Maybe because it was the end of summer and we were about to leave the island and go back to the real world. Ainsley spent half her time crying. No surprise there. My sister-in-law was being treated for postpartum depression. Patrick was on edge, probably because of Ainsley. My parents stayed with us that last week. They were in bad moods, too. And the nanny seemed the most upset of all."

This was the first I had heard about the emotional state of the nanny. "Laeticia Murier was upset? Why?"

"Maybe dealing with an infant and Ainsley's depressed state was too much for her. After all, she was in her early twenties. A lot to handle for someone that young. And she was far away from home. When we weren't working at the Grand Hotel, Ellen and I spent a lot of time at the lake house. We couldn't help but notice how miserable everyone was. It began to affect Ellen. She grew quieter and wouldn't tell me why."

"If she was as sensitive as you claim, she probably was shaken by everyone's bad mood," I suggested.

"I certainly was. Several times, I tried to comfort Laeticia, who was crying even more than Ainsley. Ellen found me holding Laeticia the day of the yacht trip. There was nothing romantic about it. I only wanted to find out why the family nanny was so miserable. But Ellen wasn't happy to see me with my arms around Laeticia. She told me to stay away from the nanny. We had our first argument that day."

"You're saying she was jealous," Kit said.

"Of course Ellen was jealous. Laeticia was all frothy and feminine. Very French. But I've always been immune to Gallic charm." He smirked. "I don't even like French food."

"Do you really believe Ellen killed her because she found the two of you in an embrace?" I couldn't keep the skepticism out of my voice.

"She confessed, Ms. Jacob. And our bosun actually witnessed the murder! Shock is too mild a word for what I felt then. And still do. That tragedy taught me to be far more certain of people before I let them into my life. I'd fallen for Ellen within a week. You see, I never knew who Ellen Nagy really was. Any more than you do. I never understood how fragile her emotional state was. Laeticia Murier paid the price for my stupidity. As did my family."

"Why do you think Ms. Beckford is in danger?" Kit said. "Marlee spoke recently with Ms. Nagy. She never mentioned being jealous of any woman associated with you."

"Ellen just wants you and your family to go away," I added. "And she doesn't know how to protect herself, except with pranks and mulberries."

"Pranks!" He sat forward, as though about to spring out of his seat. "Have you not heard a word I said?"

"You promised you wouldn't get upset again, luv." Scarlett made him sit back. "Ms. Jacob, I don't understand what mulberries have to do with any of this. The police chief mentioned mulberries had been found on the floor of the vendor room."

"Ellen believes mulberries have the ability to protect her." I sighed.

Keith swore under his breath. "She's unbalanced. And a danger to us all."

"If you're worried about your fiancée's safety, it might be best for her to leave town."

"I'm not going anywhere," Scarlett said. "Honestly, the way everyone is carrying on about this loony woman. Even if she were a danger, I can take care of myself." She shook her head. "Keith spends too much time in Palm Beach. The only thing to worry about there are hurricanes and skin cancer. I spent the first ten years of my life in Kingston, Jamaica. Do you really think I'd run away from someone who sets off smoke bombs? Not bloody likely."

I liked this supermodel with an accent that combined a Jamaican lilt with posh London. A pity she was involved with the Sable family.

"The Harvest Health Fair will be over on Saturday," I said. "Although Piper won't be happy, I'm sure she'd understand if all of you left ahead of schedule. Given the circumstances."

"It wouldn't help. We have several days of promotion and publicity lined up in Chicago. Ellen would find a way to follow us there." Keith nervously twisted his signet ring. "I just need to know how closely you're working with Ellen."

"I'm not working with her at all. She ordered mulberries from me. That's my job. I sell berry products. Beyond that, I haven't done a thing for her."

"You met with her at the conference center this afternoon, where she probably told you what she had planned. You found the dead body of the man who was her ghostwriter. A man Ellen no doubt killed. My family and my fiancée are at risk. Yet you are still protecting her."

"I'm not. If I knew where she was or what she has planned, I'd tell the police."

"Liar!"

Kit shot to his feet. "That's enough. Raise your voice one more time or attempt to intimidate Marlee, and I will arrest you."

Keith looked dumbfounded.

I cleared my throat. "Captain Holt is head of Investigative Services at the sheriff's department."

"What! You both trapped me." Keith straightened his jacket. "Let's get out of here, Scarlett. The whole town is lined up against my family. Including the police."

"If you continue to overreact," Kit warned, "we will get nowhere in this case."

"Oh, I doubt very much local law enforcement will get anywhere. Not with such a careless attitude about the safety of anyone who isn't a resident."

Scarlett got to her feet with a sigh. "He's upset. The last thing he expected to find here was a crazy woman from his past."

"Of course I'm upset! We should all be upset. She's a killer!"

I stood up, too. "I'd keep an eye out for more pranks. I don't think she's done causing trouble. But I also don't believe she means to kill anyone."

Keith gave me a long, searching look. "Are you a hundred percent certain of that?"

"A hundred percent certain?" I paused. "No. I'm not."

"Exactly." His smile was chilly. "The police chief

told us that both a manuscript and Ellen's laptop are missing. Since a ghostwriter has been found murdered on her property, I assume he helped Ellen write a book. And she killed him when the book was done."

"No one knows who killed Felix Bonaventure."

He threw me a disbelieving look. "Can we stop the pretense, Ms. Jacob?"

"Back off, Mr. Sable," Kit said in a commanding tone I had never heard before.

"I don't know where the manuscript or the laptop are." I had no intention of telling him that both might be hidden in a box of mulberries on Leticia's front porch. "I wish I did know because I think the manuscript will answer a lot of questions."

"Such as?" Scarlett looked bewildered.

"Why does Leticia fear the Sable family? What does she have planned?" I hesitated before I added, "And what really happened the night Laeticia Murier died?"

"How dare you imply Ellen didn't kill Laeticia?" Keith shouted, his face red with anger.

Kit stepped in front of him. "Time to go, Mr. Sable."

Scarlett took Keith by the arm. "If I'd known he was going to cause a scene, I would never have let him come."

"Whose side are you on?" He now turned his anger on her, but this supermodel had both hauteur and moxie to spare.

"Yours." She smoothed down his jacket. "Until you start acting like a bloody idiot. Now say good-bye. We've bothered these poor people quite enough."

Kit and I followed the couple to the front door. Scarlett had pulled him over the threshold when Keith turned back and said, "You don't know what you're dealing with, Ms. Jacob. You think you do, but you don't."

"I agree. I'm not sure what is going on, to be honest."

"I know one thing, and this is no threat." He glanced over my shoulder at where Kit stood guard. "All of us are in danger, Ms. Jacob. But you might be in the most danger of all."

Fifteen minutes after Keith and Scarlett left, we were on the way to Leticia's house. Because Kit was still fuming about Keith Sable's aggressive behavior, I thought it wiser if I drove. To distract Kit, I tossed him a bag of candy corn when I got behind the wheel. Piper told me that Twizzlers were irresistible to her husband. Kit's sugary Achilles' heel was candy corn. Snickers bars ran a close second.

"Where do you think Leticia is hiding?" I turned on my headlights. I was mistaken about the sunset time. Halfway to Leticia's house, dusk turned into darkness. A reminder of the shortening days and longer nights ahead. Cooler temps, too. I had chosen a quilted jacket to keep me warm on the drive.

"You told me she pulled out a roll of hundreds that day on the pier. With that much cash, she could find lots of cheap motels in any of the surrounding counties."

"Why a cheap motel?"

"More upscale places would require ID. We're sending officers to hotels and motels in the area. Because this is a tourist destination, there are lots of them. If she suspects the police are doing that, she may only spend one night at a particular motel, then move on." He threw back a few more candy corn. "If she owned a car, it's likely she'd be sleeping in there."

"What's to stop her from doing that anyway?"

"Sleeping in random cars is an easy way to get caught."

"Not necessarily. For example, my next-door neighbor has gone to Chicago for the week and left one of his cars in his driveway. He always does that when he's away because he likes people to think someone's at home."

He munched on candy for a moment. "She'd still have to figure out how to get into a locked car."

I laughed. "None of the residents lock their cars. Few of them even lock their houses, at least during the day. I'm an oddball. I may leave my vehicle unlocked, but never my house."

"Marlee, please lock your car. Do you know how easy it is for some man intent on harming you to hide in the backseat?"

"I always check my backseat before I get in, and let's not get off the subject. Leticia could be staying in cheap motels or someone's car. But I don't think she's far away."

"Why?"

"Because the police put out an APB on her. They're looking for her purple motor scooter, which Theo saw her driving only a few hours ago. She wouldn't want to be on the road too long for fear of being spotted. That means she's hiding somewhere close. Close enough to get to the conference center without being seen."

"Right under our noses maybe," he said, more to himself than to me.

We discussed all the possible hiding places in

Oriole Point, but after twenty minutes we ran out of ideas. "For all we know, she has a tent and spends the night in the woods. Maybe even the state park." Kit resealed the candy corn bag. "I need to stop eating this. Thank God I only eat candy corn at Halloween. Is this what we're giving out to the kids?"

I smiled at his use of the word "we." Because Kit lived in an apartment, he had suggested the two of us dress in costume on Halloween and hand out candy to the parade of children who would be trick-or-treating in my neighborhood. Not only was that a cozy idea, but both of us planned to march in the Halloween parade later that night, so it also was convenient.

"I'm mainly giving out M&Ms and peanut butter cups." I peeked over at him. "Snickers bars, too."

He chuckled. "They'll never get their hands on a single Snickers bar if I'm there."

We compared notes on favorite candies. By the time I made the turn onto Leticia's property, I felt more relaxed. Until I saw the log home in my head-lights. The lights also reflected numerous pairs of glowing eyes.

"As soon as the sheriff and police give the word, I'm sending Aunt Vicki and her volunteers to round up these cats." I switched off the car.

The darkness was startling. Since her property was far from town, there were no streetlamps or nearby homes to provide any light. And her house was completely dark.

I got out of the SUV. The grass rustled with the movements of cats. "You should have left a light on inside. Or turned on the front porch light."

"Since I've got the key, I'll do it now." Kit pulled out his keys.

When we climbed the steps to her porch, I spotted several shadowy shapes. Shapes that couldn't be cats since they didn't move. I bent down. With my eyes now more accustomed to the darkness, I could see they were bags. I picked one up.

"It looks like one of the bags of dried mulberries."

Kit hurried to the front door and unlocked it. A moment later, the porch light went on.

I gasped. The remaining boxes of mulberries had been ripped open, their contents strewn everywhere. None of the bags had been unsealed. Instead, whoever did this had flung the bags all over the porch. And there was no evidence of claw marks on the bags or boxes, eliminating the cats as the culprits.

Not that I had suspected the cats. Only the person who feared whatever was in Leticia's manuscript would have reason to rip open boxes whose labels claimed they were dried mulberries.

Kit crouched down beside me, his gaze sweeping the length of the porch. "I spoke to the department when I returned today. The officers left the property at two this afternoon. The boxes were taped up at that time. Between now and then, a trespasser has come looking for something. Most likely, the missing manuscript and laptop."

"The question is, did they find what they were looking for?"

"The ghostwriter of the manuscript has already been killed. If this person found the manuscript and computer hidden among the berries, there's only one thing left to do. Assuming this whole thing is about keeping a murderous secret."

"I know." I felt helpless and worried. "The only other person who needs to be silenced now is Leticia. Maybe it's a good thing she can't be found."

"You're wrong." Kit didn't look happy. "Keith Sable basically accused you of knowing where the manuscript and laptop are. If he believes that, so do the other Sables."

Which meant Leticia might not be the next person silenced. That dubious honor could fall on me.

Chapter Sixteen

The next morning, Abraham Lincoln introduced my Holistic Hints workshop at the conference center. It took me a moment to recognize our local chiropractor beneath the black frock coat, stovepipe hat, and beard. Who knew Dr. Jason Orsini had such a flair for public speaking? Indeed, his introduction to my talk exceeded my expectations.

Dr. Orsini began his intro by declaiming, "Nine score and nine years ago, Benjamin Lyall founded Oriole Point beneath a grove of mulberry trees."

As soon as he said that, I knew my intro was going to be far longer than the Gettysburg Address. My mind wandered as he described my college degree in marketing, my years at the Gourmet Living Network, and the opening of The Berry Basket two years ago. I only hoped he didn't mention my broken engagement and the murders I had helped solve this past summer.

I looked out over the room. Despite the early hour, every seat was taken. Aunt Vicki and her boyfriend Joe waved at me from the third row. Denise Redfern sat behind them. Andrew and Oscar were in attendance as well. Although I'd bet Andrew was only here to take a selfie with the host of *Hard Bodies*, Chad Nixon, who was giving a strength-training workshop in this very room after me.

Piper stood against the back wall, arms crossed. Her steely expression told me that if anything went wrong today, her response would be nuclear. I noticed added security measures when I arrived an hour ago. Costumed volunteers checked everyone's bag. A sensible precaution, even if I found it hard to take the situation seriously when a werewolf asked to paw through my tote bag. And I hoped no one dared to dress as a mime. Piper had probably given instructions for all mimes to be shot on sight. If Leticia was as smart as court records suggested, she wouldn't risk another visit to the health fair.

Yesterday's incident had been publicly passed off as a Halloween prank, accompanied by assurances that the guilty party would soon be arrested. I saw throngs of people when I arrived this morning, so few had been dissuaded from coming. Piper must be relieved.

And I felt relieved that, despite their earlier interest in berries, none of the Sable family were in attendance. Given Keith's hostile attitude toward me last night, I assumed the entire clan now viewed me as Leticia's co-conspirator.

Or their absence could be connected to the pillaged boxes of mulberries we found last night. Maybe one of the Sables had gotten there first. Probably not Keith. He'd left my house only fifteen minutes before Kit and I began our drive out to Leticia's property. But what if another member of his family had the same thought I did about those boxes? Whoever wanted the manuscript feared its contents. Feared it enough to kill the man who helped write it.

"And here's our own Berry Girl, Marlee Jacob!" Dr. Orsini bowed in my direction.

I acknowledged the scattered applause with a smile, glad to finally be able to get on with this talk. Dean stood off to the side, ready to help with my slide presentation. He looked like he couldn't wait for it to be over, too.

"Thank you so much for that delightful introduction, Dr. Orsini." I took the microphone from him. "And thank you all for coming. To reward everyone for attending such an early workshop, I've brought a few berry goodies to pass around. Cranberry mini-muffins, sample bags of elderberry lozenges, and chocolate strawberry teabags."

The crowd perked up as volunteers passed out the freebies. I hadn't intended to bring baked goods, but after yesterday's panicked debacle, I wanted to make an extra effort for attendees—and Piper. Last night I asked Theo to add a big batch of mini-muffins to his predawn baking schedule, leaving him to decide which berry to flavor it with. I should have known he'd choose cranberry, his favorite berry.

"Because we are about to enter cold and flu season, let's start things off with a berry that should be in everyone's winter medicine cabinet: elderberries." I held up a bottle of elderberry cough syrup as Dean clicked onto a photo of elderberries and a list of its health benefits.

"Most people use elderberries to help alleviate coughs and respiratory ailments, but as you can see from the chart, the berries also affect blood pressure, the gastrointestinal system, bone strength, cholesterol, weight loss, and even the quality of your skin."

One of the workshop doors opened. A line of Sables marched in.

"Since I've already heard a few sneezes in here, I should explain why elderberries may be of use." I kept my gaze fixed on the family who took their seats in the back row. "It has long been an herbal remedy, but medical research suggests the anti-inflammatory flavonoids in elderberries help reduce swelling in the mucous membranes."

They were all here, even Scarlett. Since the group comprised more than six, I assumed the others were personal assistants, publicists, etc. Piper obviously hadn't expected the Sables to attend this morning. She hurried over to them, exchanging whispers with Ainsley and Patrick.

"This is why many doctors recommend taking a product that contains elderberry extract as a preventive measure at the first sign of trouble." Behind me, a slide appeared showing items containing the extract.

Keith looked as hostile today as he had last night in my living room. Scarlett stifled a yawn. But it was the presence of Cameron and Ingrid Sable I found most unnerving. Even from the length of the room, it felt like they were so focused on me that they had forgotten to blink.

"I must add that none of the berry products I will talk about should be given to children without a doctor's consent. That includes elderberries." I held up a warning finger. "Despite the health benefits of elderberries, the raw berry contains a toxic compound related to cyanide. If you eat raw elderberries or those not properly cooked, you may end up being poisoned."

Ingrid and Cameron finally blinked. And their expressions now turned as poisonous as the cyanide I had mentioned.

The Sables had stopped viewing me as simply a berry expert who might consult with them on future products. After my conversation with Leticia in the vendor room, it was clear they now saw me as her partner in crime. I fought to focus on my talk and the list of berries I had yet to go through. But I couldn't forget that the last person who helped Leticia was killed with an arrow through the heart.

Maybe I should start wearing that mulberry bracelet Leticia gave me.

This whole week had not only turned murky and murderous, it was bad for business.

Sitting before my laptop on the store counter, I opened up my computer file and compared sales figures for the same week last October. We were way down.

Usually our festivals—and the crowds they attracted—benefited everyone. In warm weather the beach was an even bigger draw. But no one could resist all those celebrities at the conference center. Piper had done her job too well, rustling up reality TV stars, fitness gurus, motivational speakers, even professional athletes. I was stunned to learn two players from the

Detroit Tigers were giving sports-injury workshops this afternoon. Small wonder I had had a grand total of three sales since I opened my shop today. Granted, I opened an hour later than usual due to my berry talk, but the first customer didn't enter my store for another hour after that.

I looked out over my empty shop. It was too quiet.

I'd left Minnie at home since Aunt Vicki planned to stop by the house and check up on Panther. She promised to keep the animals company for a while, and let Minnie get more accustomed to the presence of a frisky kitten. Afterward, she and Joe would visit Leticia's property to check out the feral cat situation. Kit said he would let the department know a visit from Humane Hearts was forthcoming.

Another downside of the Harvest Health Fair: Rowena's yoga classes had been canceled for the week. I attended her beach yoga classes five days a week before I came to work. My fellow practitioners and I braved the weather up until the lake breezes turned too brisk in November, when we decamped to her downtown studio. But Rowena had numerous yoga sessions set up at the conference center, far too many for her to also hold any in her own studio. I felt the loss of those daily asanas and stretches.

At least my berry talk had gone well. People had so many questions, the next workshop was delayed by ten minutes. Dean passed out Berry Basket brochures to everyone and I hoped some of them might decide to visit the shop or order items from my website.

Bored, I considered updating my website. I had little else to do. Yesterday I sent out emails and texts to my friends still working in television. I explained that

I needed to get in touch with Delta Marsh regarding an upcoming production of the Nanny Murder. I didn't see any point in being coy. Better to let everyone know what I was interested in. And if Delta had contacted Leticia's cousin about this, there was a chance I might get a response from her.

My glance fell on the spot where Felix Bonaventure shook raindrops from his umbrella only three days ago. Poor man. Kit told me some basic facts about the writer: forty-five, born and raised in Philadelphia, divorced, no children, two brothers, mother deceased, his father retired and living in Sarasota. How shocked and grief-stricken his family must be. And if no one was arrested for the crime, they would have to deal with the horror of such an injustice.

I walked over to the door and peeked out. I saw only two people about a block down; both locals. A shame. Lyall Street looked especially charming and colorful this week with all the hay bales, pumpkins, and scarecrows decorating the storefronts.

Too bad everyone was indoors at the Lyall Center getting autographs from baseball players and having their backs adjusted by a chiropractor dressed as Lincoln.

A man came out of the post office. Both his trimmed goatee and impeccably tailored suit set him apart from every other Oriole Point resident. As did his British accent and esoteric interests. At the moment, there was no one I would rather speak to than Drake Woodhill.

I ran inside my shop, grabbed my bag, then locked up, making sure to hang the BE RIGHT BACK sign on the door. Even though Drake had won a bronze medal in track and field twenty years ago, I was confident I could catch up to him.

As I sprinted across Lyall Street, I yelled, "Drake, wait up!"

He turned. "Adding 'please' to that sentence would make the command more palatable."

"Please wait up. I want to ask you something."

"I'm not in any hurry. Not until the health fair has folded up its tents and stolen away." Drake busied himself going through the mail he'd picked up at the post office. "Except for my regular clients, I haven't had a customer at Gemini Rising for the past two days. Thankfully, I'm holding workshops and readings at the conference center. But I'm not fond of crowds."

"Neither am I." I flashed back to yesterday's scary stampede. "I assume you've heard about the man found on Leticia the Lake Lady's property."

"Every shopkeeper is talking about it. What else do we have to do until business picks up?" Drake finished going through his mail and finally looked up at me. "I've been informed you were among the people who discovered the body. You may want to have your chakras readjusted. Along with your priorities." He gave a droll chuckle. "If you spent more time at The Berry Basket, you might avoid the next grisly discovery."

"So says the man not currently in his own store," I observed. "And since you're holding bags from Spice Tent and Michigan Mudworks, it looks like you've spent a lot of your workday shopping."

He smiled. "Touché."

"If you've heard about the dead man, I assume you also know Leticia is missing."

"I hadn't heard. Given her unusual habits, how do

we know she is missing? Perhaps she is simply taking her version of a lakeshore walkabout?"

"I'm guessing the dead body on her property points to something sinister afoot."

"How Holmesian you sound."

"No, I sound desperate. I need to figure out where she is. I want to keep her from harm."

His expression turned quizzical. "I had no idea you and our curious Lake Lady even knew each other."

"And I had no idea she visited your shop last month."

Drake narrowed his eyes at me. "How do you know that?"

"Tess told me. Her studio is right across from your store. Leticia has never visited any shop here, so why did she finally decide to walk into yours?"

"The same reason most of my customers do. She had need of my services."

"Can you be more specific?" I hoped astrologers didn't have a confidentiality pact, like doctors or priests. "Did she want her chart done?"

He shook his head. "She was interested in books about Halloween. Don't look so puzzled. There's always interest in All Hallows' Eve at this time of year. People become curious about the holiday's origin and significance. Leticia required information about the souls of the dead. She wanted to know if it's true they return on Halloween."

"Do they?" I wasn't superstitious, but Leticia no doubt was.

"Yes. The energy veil between our two worlds is at its most porous on Halloween. Those souls with unfinished business find it easier to come back at that time." He cocked an eyebrow at me. "You don't believe any of this. But I have had experience with the Other Side. I know this to be true. And although restless spirits can come back at any time, it is difficult for them. Not on Halloween, however. That night the door is ajar."

"Did Leticia buy books on Halloween from you?"

"Only one that I recall. An out-of-print volume published a century ago. The book focused on the return of the spirits on All Hallows' Eve and how they can be appeased. She paid cash, which surprised me. It was rather expensive."

"I think I know which spirit she wants to appease."

"I hope this has nothing to do with the dead man found on her property." He said, starting to get upset. "I would be loath to think I had sold her a book instructing her on how to appease the spirit of a man she killed. Please tell me I am mistaken."

"I don't believe she had anything to do with Felix Bonaventure's death," I reassured him. "But there is someone she might have reason to worry about. A person long since dead."

"Are you saying Leticia is a murderer?"

"I honestly don't know. My gut says she isn't."

"Oh well, if your gut says so, I guess she's innocent."

"For someone who believes in ghosts, witchcraft, and astrology, you seem far too contemptuous of intuition."

He permitted himself a small smile. "Touché again."

I looked up in time to see the bell tower across the street strike four. "Cover your ears," I warned.

Drake and I did just that as the bell tolled four thunderous times. It took another moment for the echoes to die away. Thank goodness the bell-ringing system was electronic. A human bell ringer would have gone deaf within a week.

"Bloody hell," Drake spluttered. "That bell is louder than Big Ben. It can't be legal."

"Over a hundred complaints have been lodged. But since Piper and Lionel run Oriole Point . . ."

"Those two are despots." He shot an angry look at the bell tower. "And why did she add a balcony to the cupola?"

I knew he wouldn't like my answer. "Piper plans to install a track along there. She wants mechanical figures in historical dress to appear every hour and pretend to strike the bell."

"Insufferable woman. She won't be happy until she turns this charming village into Disneyland. Only she'll change the name to Lyall Land."

"Don't worry about it. Old Man Bowman says the bell is upsetting the wildlife in the area, including the fish and Bigfoot. He swears he plans to get rid of it. I'm sure we'll wake up one morning and find the bell missing."

"If only Piper would go missing, too. I'd view it as a lovely treat for Halloween."

Dead leaves swirled around our feet as the wind picked up. I suddenly felt cold. "I wish Halloween was already behind us. If Leticia was interested in what spirits did on that night, I'm afraid she might have a weird plan in place."

A look of concern crossed his face. "Do you think someone could be hurt?"

I nodded. "Her, for one. And any of the Sables."

"Do you mean that family now presiding over Piper's fair like a gang of corrupt Habsburgs?"

"I take it you don't care for the Sables or their products," I said.

"Of course I don't. A commercial dynasty built on a ludicrous diet that reduces fat *and* nutrition. Not to mention all those so-called natural supplements. Any decent herbalist could whip up better concoctions in their sleep. And don't get me started on the Sable cosmetic line. My clients number among the most reputable beauty experts in the world. All of them will attest that the Sable makeup is little better than paint and chalk. In fact, the results might look more appealing if the products were comprised of paint and chalk."

"How can they be so successful if what they are selling is so low quality?"

Drake gave me a patronizing look. "The advertising world is nothing but smoke and mirrors, my dear. If you tell people something is marvelous enough times, they believe it. And the Sables possess the money to flog their products constantly. The only thing I can find to like about the Sables is that one of them competed in the Olympics as I did. I have a soft spot for fellow Olympians."

He had startled me once more. "One of the Sables competed in the Olympics? Which one?" I assumed it had to be either Patrick or Keith; both looked fit and athletic.

"Ingrid, the matriarch. This was in the 1970s. I believe she was in her early thirties then."

"What was her event?"

"One of my favorites. Archery."

Chapter Seventeen

If I thought I was cold before, Drake's announcement about Ingrid Sable chilled me to the bone. I had no idea she was once expert enough in archery to compete in the Olympics. Despite her age, had she retained her skill? I didn't see why she wouldn't.

I cut my conversation short with Drake and headed for Coffee by Crystal, Oriole Point's favorite coffee hangout. I'd chased after Drake without bringing my jacket. Instead of returning to the warmth of my shop, I decided hot caffeine was even better. I literally ran into Coffee by Crystal, thrilled to see there was no line. The health fair was cutting into everyone's business.

"A large pumpkin spice latte," I told the barista, who was a fellow member of Lakeshore Birders. We chatted about the latest field trip while he prepared my drink.

Just being there relaxed me. Maybe it was the welcoming warmth, combined with the delectable aroma of coffee and pastry. I wondered if I should have something to eat and glanced up at the menu board. Although Coffee by Crystal concentrated on coffee drinks, it also offered sandwich wraps, hard-boiled eggs, a daily soup, egg bakes, and hummus. I decided coffee was what I craved, even if I did have a soft spot for their Greek egg bake.

Outside, the wind picked up and the leaves left on the trees trembled. I was glad I'd come to the coffeehouse, where it was warm, and there were people, and of course coffee.

The wood-frame building had previously been a millinery shop in the nineteenth century, and it retained a quaint historic charm. Antique photos of Oriole Point hung on the sections of the walls not reserved for bags of coffee beans and Coffee by Crystal mugs. Divided into four rooms, each was filled with mismatched tables and chairs collected over the years from antique stores and estate sales. In nice weather, many customers sat on the café's front porch or in the back garden, but the lake breezes held a bite today.

After my barista handed me the latte, I made for the back room, where it was coziest. It was also the only one that didn't have at least one customer currently hunched over their laptop or a book. I settled onto the cushioned bench before one of the three tables in what I called the nook. The window behind me looked out over the bricked garden now ablaze with orange, yellow, white, and maroon chrysanthemums.

I sipped my latte. The flavorful hot coffee sent a wave of warmth through me. I hoped the caffeine would help me sort out the tangled mess I'd been drawn into. And a mess it certainly was if an accomplished woman in her seventies now figured as a prime suspect in a murder. But the idea that famed dermatologist Dr. Ingrid Sable had tracked Bonaventure and shot him with an arrow seemed ludicrous.

Yet an arrow had killed him, shot by someone with expert aim.

I didn't know a lot of people skilled in archery. Maybe only Old Man Bowman, who had spent half his life hunting Bigfoot. However, Felix Bonaventure had looked nothing like a hairy missing link, so I crossed Old Man Bowman off the list.

Nearby footsteps made the wooden floor creak. I looked up to see Patrick Sable and a young man. They were talking to each other and didn't see me until both reached the back room. Patrick saw me first, his expression hardening.

"I didn't know you were here." His tone implied that he wished I wasn't.

His companion had the opposite reaction. "Ms. Jacob! We were at your talk this morning. I thought it was great, especially all the stuff about how many varieties there are of each fruit. I never knew there were over two hundred varieties of raspberries." He pointed at the two chairs at my table. "Do you mind?"

"Please do." I gave him a welcoming smile.

He plopped in the chair across from me, carefully setting down his own coffee drink and a plate holding a banana nut muffin. Patrick hesitated before taking the seat next to him. He held a white mug with a teabag floating in it.

"I'm glad you enjoyed my talk," I added. "And if you were impressed about raspberries, you should know strawberries are available in over a hundred thousand varieties."

His smile widened. "I was the one who proposed to the family that we create a product line with berry extracts. Your talk confirmed my idea was right. Think of the possibilities."

I looked at Patrick. "Is this your son?"

But it was the younger Sable who answered me. "Yeah, sorry. I should have introduced myself. I'm Joshua Sable. It's my first day in Oriole Point. I had a business meeting in New York yesterday, but flew into Grand Rapids last night." He unwrapped the paper holder on the muffin. "I needed to check out the health fair before my own talk tomorrow. I'm giving a workshop with my mom on anti-aging supplements."

Patrick cleared his throat. "My son has a Ph.D. in chemistry. He's been working in our labs on anti-aging formulas."

"I planned to be a geochemist. I've been a rock and mineral hound since I was a kid. But both sides of my family have a real need for chemists. It took me awhile to decide whether to join my mom's relatives at Fontaine Pharmaceuticals, or throw my hand in with the Sables. In the end, the Sable products seemed more diverse and interesting." He took a big bite of muffin.

"You must be pleased," I said to Patrick.

"Of course I am. Josh is a gifted chemist with innovative ideas. He has already proved an asset to the company." Patrick regarded his son with the first warmth I had seen him display.

"Some of my ideas are a little too innovative for Mom and Dad. Luckily, Grandpa loves them. And if Grandpa approves . . ." He returned his attention to the muffin. I didn't blame him. The baker at Coffee by Crystal was almost as talented as Theo.

"My father is quite fond of Josh." Patrick removed

the teabag from his mug. "He's never been able to deny him anything."

Joshua chuckled. "He means I'm spoiled rotten. And I am. But I'm also hardworking, trustworthy, and adorable."

"If you say so yourself," I said with a laugh.

There was an engaging quality about Joshua. He didn't have the practiced charm of his uncle Keith, or the forced bonhomie of his mother. As for his dad, I found Patrick Sable an enigmatic figure. A man with a calm reserve, but one who seemed to struggle to maintain it. Not having met Drs. Cameron and Ingrid Sable, I couldn't vouch for their friendliness. But I had a feeling Joshua might be the only appealing member of the family.

And he had to be close to my age. Since he was an infant when his nanny was killed, that made him twenty-eight now. He vaguely resembled his father and had inherited the aquiline profile of the Sable males. Darker hair than his father, of course, since gray peppered Patrick's hair. Definitely a Sable, though. I saw little trace of his mother in his dark good looks.

He was also more attractive than the other male members of his family, even his uncle Keith. Joshua had beautiful eyes, with thick long lashes I envied. He was almost pretty, like one of those erotic young men painted by Caravaggio. The Sables were lucky he had decided to join the company, especially the skin care and anti-aging division. His handsome looks and natural charm made him the ideal spokesman for the Sable promise of eternal youth and beauty.

"I was impressed with the lineup at the health fair

today." Joshua swiped at his mouth with a napkin. "A couple of Detroit Tigers, Ellie Vaughn, about a dozen reality-show stars, the host of *Hard Bodies,* and three Olympic gold medalists from the American gymnastics team. That Piper woman knows how to pull off a conference."

I sat up at the mention of the gymnasts. "Speaking of Olympians, I had no idea your grandmother once competed in the Olympics."

Patrick set his mug down on the table with so much force, tea splashed onto the table. "I'm surprised you didn't know. Her bio always includes it."

"I guess I concentrated on her work with the Sable company." I didn't add that I had never given much thought to any of the Sables until they arrived this week.

"Mormor's the best," Joshua said. "She's done so many fantastic things in her life, it's easy to forget some of them."

"Mormor?" I asked.

"Sorry," he said with a sheepish smile. "Mormor is what I've always called her. It's Swedish for Grandma. Mormor's family live in Mariefred, which is about thirty miles from Stockholm. She grew up with a lot of siblings, and everyone was super athletic. You should see her on the slopes at Telluride. She even snowboards! I mean, c'mon. How many grandmothers in their late seventies do that?"

"My mother is an extraordinary woman," Patrick said. "But she prefers to be known for the advances in skin care she has launched."

"Being an Olympian is nothing to sniff at," I said. "Especially in an event as unusual as archery."

"And she did it at the age of thirty-two. Mormor is

like Iron Woman." Joshua finished off his muffin. "My mom is an archer. Mormor is her role model. Anything Mormor does, Mom wants to do, too." His expression turned impish. "I think Mom believes she can qualify for the Olympics one day. She spends a lot of time at the Gold Coast Archers Club in Palm Beach."

"He exaggerates," Patrick said. "My wife also loves to golf and ski."

"Don't listen to him." Joshua leaned forward. "Mom always talks about Thomas Scott. He competed as an archer in the Olympics when he was seventy-one, the oldest person to ever compete in an Olympic archery event. He's Mom's other role model."

"I wish I was good enough to qualify for the Olympics," I said. "In anything."

Patrick looked bored. "I don't see the Sables competing in the Olympics in the foreseeable future. Least of all, my wife. And don't be impressed by her interest in archery. Everyone in the family knows how to hit an archery target. When you grow up with a mother who competed in the Olympics, there's no escaping being handed a bow and arrow."

"Are all the Sables good archers?" I asked.

"Good enough," Patrick said curtly.

"Not me." Joshua set down his coffee. "But Dad, Grandpa, and Uncle Keith go bow-hunting for deer every fall in Georgia." A ringtone sounded. Josh pulled his iPhone from the front pocket of his shirt. He peeked at the screen. "Sorry, I have to take this."

He got up and walked into the other room.

Patrick and I stared at each other. "I know what you're doing," he finally said.

"Really? Because I don't."

"You're trying to implicate us in a crime. My family has been informed a man was killed with a bow and arrow on Ellen Nagy's property. The woman you call Leticia the Lake Lady."

"I am well aware of the crime. As I am aware the victim was killed with a bow and arrow. Shot through the heart. The murderer was therefore skilled in archery."

"Olympic-level archery, perhaps?" he asked. "Isn't that what you're hinting at?"

"I'm not hinting at anything. And I only just learned your mother was an Olympic archer." I took a moment to sip my latte, giving Patrick more time to seethe. It might make him careless enough to say something incriminating. "Now I discover the entire Sable clan is conversant with bows and arrows. I don't have to be a police detective to be curious about the timing of your visit to Oriole Point. And the murder of a man by such a method."

He pushed his mug of tea away, causing much of it to splash onto the table. His controlled exterior had begun to fray. "If I needed further proof you are working with that madwoman, you've just given it to me."

"I've spent less than thirty minutes in her company, so stop saying that."

"I will as soon as you stop defending her. How many times do you need to be reminded that Ellen Nagy murdered an innocent young woman? She spent fifteen years in prison. And according to many residents in your town, she has behaved like an unbalanced mental patient for the past four years."

"I'd describe her behavior as eccentric."

He balled up his napkin and swiped at the tea he

had spilled. "I don't give a damn what you think about Ellen. You know nothing about her or my family. Or how much my poor brother has suffered all these years."

"He's rich, attractive, successful, and about to marry a Victoria's Secret model. He doesn't seem to be suffering all that much."

"You're an insolent woman," he said with far too much hatred.

"You make me sound like a character from a Victorian novel. Jane Eyre, maybe."

"Oh, I think of you as a character all right. One desperate to involve herself in things that are none of her business. Maybe that's how people behave in small towns, but elsewhere it's regarded as rude. Even hazardous."

"Is that a threat?"

He pounded his fist on the table, making me jump. "If I was threatening you, you'd know it. Which is why I advise you to stop looking for ways to link Mr. Bonaventure's murder with my family. He was killed on Ellen's property. According to police, he may have collaborated on a book with her. Those are the links that matter. Links that prove Ellen killed him."

"She's also linked to your family," I said. "And the murder of your nanny."

"I'm sick of hearing about that damned nanny!" He looked down, as though trying to regain his composure. "Look, my family had nothing to do with her death or the ghostwriter's."

"Then you have nothing to worry about. But once the police know that all the Sables can hit a target with a bow and arrow, you and your family members will be under suspicion."

He gave a hollow laugh. "I'm sure you'll be happy to inform them."

"I'd advise your family to do that before I can. For the optics, if nothing else."

He pushed back from the table, the chair legs making a scratching sound. "And I'd advise you to think carefully. The Sables are not residents of some sorry hick town in Michigan. If a Sable is attacked or threatened, we know how to protect ourselves."

"Insulting Oriole Point won't help your cause," I said, "especially with local law enforcement. By the way, we're known as the Cape Cod of the Midwest."

"If you smear my family, we'll make certain Oriole Point is known for something far worse." His tone left me in no doubt that he was serious.

I recalled the fear on Leticia's face when she spoke of the Sables. What must it have felt like to be a frightened teenager faced with the power and influence of this family? A teenager whose own family quickly disowned her. Was pressure brought to bear on her to confess? I could certainly see how.

"Threaten me if you like," I said. "But I will get testy if you threaten Oriole Point."

"I know something about you as well, Ms. Jacob." His voice grew soft, which seemed more unsettling. "I think you like publicity. Any kind of publicity. That's why you've inserted yourself in several recent crimes in this ridiculous town. I also know you were involved with a murder back in New York when you produced cooking shows."

I took another sip of my latte. "Sorry to disappoint

you, but I was not the one who put arsenic in John Chaplin's cake. That was his wife. Or maybe you missed the trial."

"I don't miss anything. That's how I know why you're coming after my family. It's a way to get further attention, like some twisted serial killer who loves to read about his sordid crimes."

"Oh, please. Now *you* sound like a character in a Victorian novel."

"You're playing with fire, Ms. Jacob, only you're too stupid to realize it. Ellen Nagy is a cold-blooded killer. She killed my nanny and she killed that man found in her field. I believe she also plans to kill a member of my family out of revenge."

"Because she went to prison? Since she confessed, that doesn't make sense."

"Ellen's behavior won't make sense. She's insane. Perhaps you need further proof."

He pulled a folded piece of white paper from the inner pocket of his suit jacket. With a weary sigh, he held it out. "This was left at our hotel this morning."

I unfolded the piece of paper. A message had been pasted onto the page, using letters cut from newspapers and magazines. It looked like the notes kidnappers leave in movies.

The message read: "The dead want justice. Confess before you are exposed. Tell the truth. Now!"

I looked up at Patrick. "How did it get to your hotel?"

"It was sealed in an envelope and taped to the revolving door of The Beekman. Scrawled on the envelope were the words 'Deliver to the Sables.' An employee who arrived for his morning shift found it and handed it to the front desk. They gave it to us."

I handed the note back to him. "I assume no one saw who left it."

He tucked the note back into his pocket. "No. It must have been delivered before dawn, since the employee found it at six a.m. And I don't think there's any mystery about the identity of the person who left it."

Since I agreed with his assessment, I said nothing.

"Ellen wants to destroy my family," he went on. "With lies, rumors. And given her unstable state of mind, probably another murder. She's killed twice before."

Although I didn't think she meant to kill the Sables, I did worry about her next move. So far she had pulled a "prank" on the Sables for each of the past four days. "Have you shown this note to the police yet?"

"That's why I'm in town. To hand it over to your police chief." He looked disgusted. "Although there was some debate in the family about that. Your local law enforcement hasn't impressed us so far. My father and I believe this is best dealt with internally, but we were overruled. However, we all agree on one thing. Our patience is at an end."

"What does that mean?"

He stood, no doubt for the chance to loom over me. "It means you and the police better start taking this more seriously."

Joshua looked up from his phone in the next room. "Dad, we need to go somewhere private and call the lab in California. One of the serum batches has gone missing."

"Be right there," he told his son. Patrick turned his attention back to me. "Looks like yet another thing has gone missing. I'll handle the serum batch. But I recommend you find Ellen and the manuscript she wrote. And do it before we leave on Saturday." He stomped out.

If I had any doubt a Sable was behind Bonaventure's death, this conversation dispelled that. Someone in the Sable family murdered Bonaventure. And probably the nanny. I had no idea which one, but Patrick Sable was a front-runner.

Chapter Eighteen

When I returned to The Berry Basket, I called Chief Hitchcock and told him about my conversation with Patrick and Joshua Sable. He already knew about Ingrid Sable's Olympic career but wasn't aware that all of the Sables were skilled in the use of a bow and arrow. I had a feeling the Sable family were going to be visited by the police later today. If nothing else, it would keep them out of trouble—and Leticia and me out of danger. At least while the police were with them.

I didn't have time to worry about the Sables for the next hour. A group of women came into the store. And they were in town for a long girls' weekend, not the health fair.

In the mood for a good time, they loved everything in the shop and bought bags of berry-flavored coffees, teas, wines, Theo's pastries, berry hand lotions and soaps, berry syrups, and much more. By the time they left, I had sold more in one hour than I had all week.

Their visit seemed a happy harbinger as customers trickled in for the remainder of the day. Maybe everyone had begun to have their fill of all those celebrities. I hoped so. The fair continued tomorrow and

Saturday, the two biggest shopping days of the week. In addition, the people coming here for the Halloween evening parade would start to arrive. Halloween visitors were in a party mood. That meant lots of food and drink . . . and retail therapy.

At five, I closed up, pleased at the day's sales. I had just stapled the receipts and credit-card slips when my cell phone rang. It said Unknown Caller.

"Hello," I said with a degree of caution.

"Is this Marlee Jacob?" a female voice asked.

"Yes."

"Delta Marsh here. The booker on *Wake Up America* told me to contact you. Apparently, you have questions regarding an upcoming production about the murder of Laeticia Murier, otherwise known as the Nanny Murder." She laughed. "Had it been anyone else, I wouldn't have bothered. But how can I refuse a request from the former producer of the *Sugar and Spice* show? The show and the murder trial that ended it were epic! You may not remember, but I interviewed you for *Wake Up America.*"

"Of course, I remember."

Hundreds of reporters had interviewed everyone connected to the Chaplins, particularly those of us who worked on the popular cooking show. At some point, they all became a blur, but Delta had left an impression. She managed to make our interview seem like a cozy chat between friends, rather than a savvy reporter determined to get answers from a beleaguered TV producer caught up in a scandal. Although I'd revealed more than I meant to, it was an honest interview, maybe the best one ever conducted about the Chaplin case. For that I had to credit the talented Ms. Marsh.

"What have you been doing since you left New York?" she asked. "I hear you're a businesswoman now. And in a lovely beach town along Lake Michigan. I'm so jealous."

We spent a few minutes catching up. I summarized the past two years for her, then asked polite questions about her own career, which had continued to rise. An entertainment correspondent for the morning show, Delta covered everything from George and Amal Clooney's twins to royal marriages. I expected her career to reach even greater heights. She was twenty-nine, vivacious, smart, and ambitious.

"Now what's all this about the Nanny Murder?" she asked finally.

I explained how the Sables were in town for a local health fair, and that I had heard a possible series or movie about the murder of their former nanny might be in the works. To encourage her to confide in me, I added that the woman convicted of the murder lived in Oriole County, and I thought she might be upset to learn the case was about to go public once again.

Delta gave a throaty laugh. "Leave it to you to live in a town with a famous murderess. I'm also not surprised Ellen Nagy is upset the Nanny Murder is about to go viral again."

"Then it's true?"

"Yes. A deal was signed with a premium cable channel for a limited dramatic series about the murder of Laeticia Murier. I'm not at liberty to say which one until the executive producers make the announcement. The Sable family tried to stop it, but couldn't.

After all, the case is a matter of public record. They should be flattered. I've heard Saoirse Ronan has been asked to play the young Ainsley Sable. Producers want Nicole Kidman for the role of Ingrid."

My heart sank. If they put together a cast that stellar, the series was sure to be a hit. Making the details of the nanny's murder once again public fodder. "When did you contact Ellen Nagy's cousin?"

"Earlier this year, as soon as I learned a series was being put together. I had no idea where Ellen Nagy was, especially since she married after she got out of prison. But I did remember she had family in Coldwater, Michigan. I could only get a cousin to talk with me: Sarah Nagy. They're the same age and grew up together. She and Ellen have stayed in contact. I told her about the upcoming series and asked her to get a reaction from Ellen." Another throaty laugh. "She told me to go to hell and hung up."

"Well, she did tell Ellen about the series, and Ellen's not happy about it. I spoke with her about it yesterday."

"Do you remember Ellen's exact words?" Delta's voice grew serious. "A quote from the killer would be fantastic."

I sighed. "I don't think of her as a killer. Just a sad woman."

"I was a baby when this whole thing happened, but I've read enough about it. Don't get too sentimental, Marlee. Ellen Nagy murdered that French girl. Speaking of murder, weren't you all over the news this past July? I seem to recall a killer chased you during a road rally. Girl, you must be a magnet for danger."

"Yeah, lucky me. Getting back to the Nanny Murder, do you know any journalists who covered it way back then?"

"Not really. Although I did some asking around when I heard you wanted to talk with me. The only person who remembers much about the case is our producer on *Wake Up America*. At the time of the trial, she was an intern at *Harper's Bazaar* and helped research a feature about Laeticia Murier. One thing that stuck with her was that the French nanny loved the color orange. Apparently, she often wore something orange, even if it was just a piece of jewelry in that color. Weird, huh?"

"I guess she just had a thing for orange," I said. Although neither Delta nor I understood why Laeticia Murier had such a fondness for the color, it did explain why Ellen dyed her hair pumpkin orange. It was yet another way for her to keep Laeticia's memory alive.

"What can you tell me about the Sables?" I asked. "Have you ever met any of them?"

"Sure. One of the Sables is always walking some red carpet function in New York. And Keith Sable shows up on Page Six whenever he gets married and divorced. I've lost count as to how many Mrs. Keith Sables there have been."

"I met the soon-to-be Number Four last night."

"Ah, yes. Scarlett the model. All his wives have been models. You'd think these girls would stick to rock stars and Leo rather than get hooked up with Keith Sable."

The distaste in her voice made me sit up. "You don't like him?"

"God, no. Hard to like someone so enraptured with himself. I've interviewed him a few times. He spent the whole time flashing those dimples and pouring on the charm. But beneath all that charm is a talent for manipulating people. Takes after his mother."

I thought back to the icy beauty of the Sable matriarch. "She does seem formidable."

"More like indestructible. I guess you'd have to be if you're married to Cameron Sable. Her husband's the best salesman I've ever seen, and I've seen them all. He never stops selling. And I don't mean his products. He's always selling himself. Trying to convince us that he's the final authority on everything from magnesium supplements to the meaning of life."

"In other words, a narcissist."

"Big-time. And so demanding. We did an interview last year on the anniversary of that damned diet. He refused to be filmed unless we obtained an Eames chair for him to sit on! Along with his favorite make-up artist, who had to be flown in from Florida. He also insisted on a specific camera filter." She gave a rueful chuckle. "It was like working with a bald Henry VIII."

"Do you like any of the Sables?"

"Not really. Joshua, the younger one, seems the most decent. But his parents are a joke. Ainsley is a brittle socialite pretending to know something about skin care and beauty. A trust-fund baby who married into another rich family. She's as shallow as a wading pool."

"What about Patrick Sable?"

"The man possesses all the *joie de vivre* of Eeyore. He reminds me of an unhappy soldier awaiting his next order."

"And who would order him?"

"One of the Sables, of course." She sighed. "If only the public could see past their polished facade and the skills of their public-relations team. Those products are nothing more than twenty-first-century snake oil."

I was glad I had never jumped on the Sable bandwagon. "I remember liking one or two Cameron Sable cookbooks back when I was at the network. And now he's become just as famous for his motivational books. In fact, all of them seem to be continually writing books."

"You don't believe they actually write them? The Sables are like most celebrities. They pay people to write their books."

"You think they're all ghostwritten?"

"I'd bet my new apartment in Tribeca they are."

"Do you know a ghostwriter called Felix Bonaventure?"

"I've certainly heard of him. He writes true crime now, but he started out doing celebrity memoirs. Don't know if he ever worked for a Sable. It's possible. Try checking the acknowledgments page in their earlier books. Some famous people feel guilty about not including their collaborator on the cover. They throw an occasional bone by mentioning their name in the acknowledgments. Without specifying why they're being acknowledged."

"I'd love to know if Bonaventure worked with them in the past."

"Why?" Another pause. "Don't hold out on me, Marlee. I did you the professional courtesy of contacting you *and* answering your questions. It's only fair you reciprocate."

She was right. The business was built on quid pro quo. And Delta had a reputation as a woman who could be trusted. "Fair enough. But until things here have been resolved, all this is off the record."

"Agreed." I heard paper rustle. She was getting ready to write everything down. I was also sure I would be recorded.

The Sables, Leticia, and the Nanny Murder were about to take center stage once again. And not simply because of the TV series. A man had been murdered and a woman was in hiding because of the Sables. It wasn't yet All Hallows' Eve, but I suspected the ghost of that dead nanny had come back, demanding the truth be known.

And if Ellen Nagy and I failed to reveal her hidden secrets, maybe a woman with a watery name—and a big public platform—could.

Chapter Nineteen

On the way home, I thought over what Delta said. Not only about the personalities of the Sables, but her claim that their books were ghostwritten. Half the Sable display in the conference center's vendor room consisted of their bestsellers. If they had been co-authored, maybe the name of their collaborator appeared somewhere in the book. Delta said Felix's first ghostwriting job was twenty years ago, and that he had concentrated on working for famous people then. One of them might have been a Sable.

Even though I wanted to go home, eat dinner, and play with my animals, I decided to take a peek at the Sables' early books. Before I could talk myself out of it, I took the next turn and headed for the Lyall Center.

Once I entered the vendor room, I second-guessed my decision. The last time I was here, I'd been caught up in a terrifying rush for the exits. Not enough time had passed for me to forget the fear that swept through the room. Luckily, it was after five thirty and most attendees were at the various celebrity Q&As set up in the early evenings. I hoped some of those celebrities were Sable family members.

I also saw no evidence of mulberries scattered on the carpet. Fingers crossed, a mime wouldn't pop up either.

I recognized the volunteer who sat at one of the tables in the Sable book section. It was Kim, a young cashier at Lufts' Grocers. She gave me a brief smile before returning her attention to a Sable instructional book on makeup.

Going over to the first table, I picked up the famous *Sable Diet* and leafed through the opening pages. The acknowledgments page mentioned various doctors, the publishing house's editor, and Cameron Sable's agent. I did the same with the next six titles; none of them included a name on the dedication or acknowledgment pages that didn't also explain who that person was.

"Looking for something in particular?" a familiar voice asked.

I turned to face Ainsley Sable. "Checking out publication dates. I had no idea the Sables had written so many books."

"It looked like you were more interested in the dedication and acknowledgment pages."

"I find it interesting to see who authors choose to thank." That was certainly true.

"No doubt you were hoping to find Felix Bonaventure mentioned."

"If I had, it would have been rather telling."

"What would it have told you? That we were too lazy to write our own books?" Those jet dark eyes narrowed at me. "But not too lazy to murder him. Because that's why you're rifling through the pages. Trying to find a link between us and that dead man. Well, page through all of them. You won't find a single mention of his name. Or any ghostwriter. The Sables are quite capable of penning our own books." She shot me a disdainful smile. "All bestsellers."

"I am impressed. But it appears you did seek assistance from other professionals." I held up the book I'd been looking at. "This one mentions a dozen doctors and therapists."

"What did you expect, given the subject?"

I wished I'd paid attention to the titles of the books. I opened the book once more and flipped through the pages. It allowed me see the title: *The Natural Path of Pregnancy . . . and the First Year.* The author was Ainsley Sable.

"I've heard that after you had your son, you went through postpartum depression."

"An experience that inspired me to write this." She tapped the book I held. "That's what all of us in the family do: help others make better choices to improve their lives. Choices that don't include harmful chemicals, toxins, and negative thinking."

"So the Sables are all about positive thinking?" I tried not to sound disbelieving.

"Yes, but it can be a struggle. We write about that, too." She took a deep breath. "The family has certainly found it difficult to maintain an uplifting attitude this week."

"I'm not surprised." I kept my attention on the pages, most of which mentioned coconut oil and babies. I was skimming too fast to figure it all out.

She snatched the book from me. "You seem fascinated by the book. Are you expecting?"

"No. Simply curious. For a book about pregnancy, it mentions coconuts an awful lot."

"This book launched our coconut oil supplements for expectant and new mothers."

"Did coconut oil supplements help with your post-partum depression?"

"They did. But it took time to find the right combination." She paused. "I was the guinea pig, you might say."

"I met your son today. You must be very proud of him."

She clutched the book to her chest. "I am. Josh has been the perfect son. I'm very lucky."

"And yet you never had another child."

"I didn't want to risk going through postpartum depression again, especially once I had a child to care for."

I thought it an opportune time to bring up the nanny. "At least you had the nanny to help you in those early months."

Ainsley flinched. "It's debatable how much help Mademoiselle Murier was to any of us. The girl was hardly Mary Poppins."

"I'd heard she was fond of the baby. And took good care of him while you were ill."

"Joshua has always been lovable. How difficult would it be for her to look after him? But she was also selfish, immature, and calculating. Quite full of herself. She expected to get her way, as long as she pouted prettily enough. Especially at men." Ainsley frowned. "I know we're not supposed to speak ill of the dead. And ever since the girl was murdered, everyone refers to her as if she was a martyred saint. But Laeticia Murier was no saint. Not by a long shot."

I was sure my face reflected my surprise.

Ainsley leaned closer to me. "I'll let you in on a little secret. I wanted to fire her long before we ever got on that yacht. I had had quite enough of her tantrums. It was starting to upset the baby. She had already upset Ellen. And Ellen was not an emotionally stable teenager. If Ellen hadn't confessed to pushing her off the boat, I would have thought Laeticia threw herself off. That's how out of control Laeticia's behavior had grown that summer."

"And yet you didn't fire her."

"Ingrid and Cameron talked me out of it. They said I wasn't thinking clearly due to my depressed state. But I was thinking quite clearly. That girl was maddening. She deserved to be fired." Ainsley gave me a challenging look. "Her death was a blessing in disguise."

"Convenient, too," I remarked. "It also seems convenient that you didn't tell the police you wanted to fire the dead girl."

Ainsley shrugged. "It didn't seem relevant. After all, *I* didn't kill her."

"That's usually something the police like to determine for themselves."

"And so they did. They decided that a jealous teenager pushed the nanny overboard. I only wish Ellen had fallen into the lake as well. She and that French train wreck landed this family in the middle of an awful scandal. Now all these years later, Ellen is intent on doing it again. Will we never be free of that damned nanny's death? And the lunatic who killed her!"

"What is going on here?" Dr. Ingrid Sable joined us, her presence heralded by the sandalwood fragrance of what I recognized as the expensive Shalini perfume.

My mouth fell open to see her this close. Taller than both Ainsley and me, Ingrid's statuesque height was magnified by a massive white bouffant wafting about her face like a cloud. Her impeccable bone structure gave her an air of haughtiness, and I marveled at how a seventy-seven-year-old woman's skin could remain this unlined. I didn't see a hint of a wrinkle.

No matter how many supplements she used, only the world's best plastic surgeon could work such wonders. That, or she bathed in the blood of young virgins.

While all heads turned in the vendor room, no fans dared come close for an autograph or selfie. I didn't blame them. Outfitted in a black dress that skimmed her knees, a gold silk jacket, and ropes of gold necklaces, with a gigantic turquoise cross as the centerpiece, she seemed like a modern-day Catherine the Great. Or whatever the Swedish equivalent was.

"You are speaking too loudly, Ainsley," she said. "And about matters better left unspoken."

Ainsley ducked her head, as if embarrassed to be caught misbehaving. "I'm so sorry, Ingrid. But Ms. Jacob brought up Laeticia Murier's death and I became upset."

She placed her hand on Ainsley's shoulder. "This has been a difficult week for all of us." Ingrid turned to me. "And Ms. Jacob should not be upsetting you further."

"I didn't mean to," I said. "I asked about the Sable coconut oil supplements, and whether they eased her postpartum depression. Since I knew Laeticia Murier had been her nanny, I simply mentioned her. I assumed the girl had been of help during that period."

"I tried to explain how terrible that time was for all of us," Ainsley said in a tearful voice. "But she refused to listen."

She looked up at the older woman like an adolescent girl seeking her mother's protection and approval. Odd behavior for a fifty-something socialite. Then again, Joshua Sable told me that his mother tried to imitate Ingrid. So much so that she hoped to compete as an Olympic archer as well. An unlikely achievement for someone in her sixth decade.

Ainsley was quite the actress, I decided. No doubt she'd been playing the obedient daughter-in-law since the wedding day. I wondered what her endgame was. To become the Sable matriarch when Ingrid died? Assuming Ingrid ever died. Those Swedish genes looked pretty powerful.

"I didn't know Ainsley was so sensitive." I didn't conceal my sarcasm.

"Now you do know," Ingrid told me. She turned to Ainsley. "We'll be leaving the center in fifteen minutes. Join the others at the side exit. I'll be along shortly."

"Yes, Ingrid." Ainsley's nod looked less like a gesture of agreement and more like an act of deference.

"Does everyone follow your orders so quickly?" I asked after Ainsley left. "I'd love to know your secret."

"My secret?" She lifted an already arched eyebrow. "My secret is that I possess years of experience and the wisdom to learn from it. Everyone in my family has endeavored to do the same." With a sweeping gesture, Ingrid directed my attention to the Sable products and books.

"Quite an output. The Sables have created an empire."

"And we will defend it when it comes under attack."

"I hope you don't think I'm a threat to the Sable empire."

"You? Even if you wanted to, you couldn't. Ms. Jacob, you have a quaint little business in a quaint little town. Go back to what you do best: selling berry products. But if you continue to aid and abet that madwoman, the consequences could threaten us both."

"How?"

"Scandal. If scandals can topple governments, think how easy it would be to topple a mere company. Or a berry shop. Maybe you've forgotten how the scandal of the Chaplin murder forced you to give up your successful TV career and run back to your hometown to hide."

"My years in television were not as pleasant as you imagine. The Chaplin trial was simply the last straw. I came back to Oriole Point to start a new life. A happier one." I gestured to all those books. "Just the sort of thing I hear you Sables are always preaching."

She stiffened. "Neither of us needs another scandal. My family suffered through the tragic death of Mademoiselle Murier twenty-eight years ago. We have no wish to deal with it again. Any more than you want to have the Chaplin murder trial unearthed."

Now that I had gotten accustomed to her striking looks and natural hauteur, I felt comfortable enough to challenge her. "You seem to regard your daughter-in-law as someone who is easily upset. That hasn't been my impression of her."

"Your impression is irrelevant."

"I've done some background reading on your family. All of you are strong, self-confident individuals. Ainsley's only struggle appears to have been post-partum depression."

"While pregnant, Ainsley was plagued with morning sickness for almost the entire nine months. Once the baby was born, we hoped everything would return to normal. Only the depression set in. It was a painful time." Ingrid looked off into the distance.

"It seems to have been a difficult time for the nanny as well."

Ingrid instantly returned her attention to me. "What are you talking about?"

"Your son Keith came to my house to discuss Ellen Nagy and the murder."

"What an extraordinary thing for him to do." Her tone indicated displeasure. "He didn't say a word to me about it. Keith never talks about Laeticia or Ellen. He must be more upset than I realized if he spoke to you about the murder."

"Maybe he needs to talk about it. Learning Ellen lives in Oriole Point may have brought up all the bad memories. He was only a teenager when the nanny died. And the girl he asked to marry him was sent off to prison. Think how it must have traumatized him. Trauma needs to be dealt with openly if everyone is to recover."

"I didn't realize you offered berries *and* counseling, Ms. Jacob. Don't irritate me further by giving advice on matters you know nothing about."

"But I want to know. Especially since Ellen came to me for help."

Ingrid's exquisitely made-up eyes scanned the

room. Probably to make certain no one could listen in. The nearest person was Kim several tables away, and she now chatted on her cell.

"How do you think the murder affected my family?" Ingrid asked in a low voice. "A young woman in our employ lost her life due to my son's jealous fiancée. You're too young to remember the sordid publicity, the speculation, the horror of being associated with murder."

"I do know something about that," I reminded her.

"*Även efter att anklagelsen har väckts, sitter ändå misstanken kvar,*" she said softly.

"Excuse me."

"A Swedish proverb. 'Even after the accusation is refuted, the suspicion still remains.' The scandal from the murder followed us long after Ellen confessed to her horrible crime. Tabloid reporters loved to speculate about what happened on the yacht that day. They didn't like the way the story ended. Instead, they preferred to hint that one of my boys had done it. Or poor Ainsley, who was so depressed she could barely speak."

I was struck by what she didn't say. At the time of the murder, Ingrid would have been forty-nine, and Cameron fifty-two. Both hale and hearty enough to have pushed someone off a boat. "Did the speculations ever include you or your husband?"

She seemed to consider whether to answer that question. "Of course they did," she said finally. For the first time, I heard a slight accent in what had been perfect English.

When she didn't elaborate, I dared to go on. "Reports at the time suggested that you and your husband were not happy about Keith proposing to Ellen."

"Keith was too young to become engaged. And to a girl he barely knew. We never made any secret of that. Not to the police or the reporters. What no one understood is that we didn't bother to protest his engagement too much. My youngest son has a short attention span and a wandering eye. As his subsequent entanglements with women have shown." She revealed the hint of a sneer. "Keith would have grown tired of Ellen soon. There was no necessity for Cameron or me to obstruct the pair. Time would have handled that."

"It looks like it did. Ellen was sentenced to prison for fifteen years. Why such a short sentence? The murder was famous. Judges like to make an example in such cases." Indeed, Evangeline Chaplin was currently serving a life sentence.

"Her young age. And we asked the judge for clemency during sentencing."

That startled me. "You did?"

"Although shocked by the murder, Keith still labored under the illusion that he was in love with Ellen. Because she confessed to the crime, we knew prison was inevitable. Keith begged us to help her. He couldn't bear the thought of Ellen dying behind bars. My youngest son is sentimental to a fault. But we've always indulged him. So we did as he asked."

Despite what Ingrid believed, it appeared Keith had truly loved his teenaged fiancée.

"That is why Ellen is now free to create havoc for our family once again," she went on. "Something she seems to be doing daily."

"Yes. I spoke with your son Patrick earlier. He showed me the note."

"You seem to be spending more time with my family that I am. But if you saw the note, you realize Ellen is determined to harass us. Even though she knows we were responsible for getting her sentence reduced." She sighed. "No good deed goes unpunished."

"Perhaps. But Ellen certainly was."

"We were all punished. Especially Laeticia Murier, who did nothing to deserve her fate. Lovely girl. Bright, personable, and with an accommodating nature. Perhaps too accommodating."

"How so?"

Ingrid frowned. "A few months after I hired her as my assistant, I broke both legs while skiing in Zermatt. Because I take pride in my athleticism, the injuries were difficult to accept. I became irritable during my convalescence. Laeticia took the brunt of my bad behavior."

I suspected Ingrid was controlling at the best of times. Injured and frustrated, she had probably been as irascible as the Red Queen in *Alice in Wonderland*.

"I was too out of sorts to focus on the business at that time," she continued. "This was the same period in which Ainsley became sick in her pregnancy. Ainsley and I spent the last few months of her pregnancy at our villa in St. Lucia. I have a fondness for the Caribbean, as does my daughter-in-law. But Laeticia was quite miserable."

"Why?"

"She was afraid of the water. When she was a child, some ridiculous fortune-teller in France told her she would die by drowning. And our villa has a private beach. Wherever she looked there was water. I should have sent her to work in our offices in New York or LA."

"When did you finally leave St. Lucia?"

"A month after Joshua was born. The arrival of

the baby put Laeticia in a better mood. Ainsley and Patrick planned to hire a nanny once we returned home. However, it quickly became apparent that Ainsley suffered from postpartum depression. So it was Laeticia who cared for the infant. I regretted losing her as my assistant, but we agreed she would be of more use as Joshua's nanny. And she was wonderful with the child. Certainly Laeticia preferred catering to a baby rather than me." She shrugged. "As I said, she was a bright girl."

I heard an announcement over the loudspeaker regarding the Q&A session with Chad Nixon of *Hard Bodies*. At least a dozen people in the vendor room headed for the exits.

Ingrid smoothed her jacket. "I've answered enough rude inquiries for one day."

"I have one more question."

She frowned so severely, a hint of a wrinkle appeared. "Don't abuse my kind nature."

There were a lot of ways to describe Ingrid Sable, but the words "kind nature" didn't factor onto my list. "You say Laeticia enjoyed being a nanny. But Keith mentioned she had grown unhappy that last summer on Mackinac Island."

Ingrid took a deep breath. "Keith appears to have been quite talkative during his conversation with you. I must speak to him about that."

"Ainsley claims she wanted to fire the nanny, and you and your husband talked her out of it. If Ainsley wanted her gone, and the nanny was unhappy, why not let her go?"

"I don't owe you anything, Ms. Jacob. Least of all answers."

"True. But I'm good friends with Oriole Point's

chief of police. I was there when the body of Felix Bonaventure was found. I'm dating the investigative officer handling his murder for the sheriff's department. And Ellen Nagy has so far chosen to communicate through me. I'm involved whether I like it or not. That means I have questions I am determined to find answers to. If you don't wish to answer any of them, fine. But someone will."

Although Ingrid's blue eyes flashed with anger, her voice was calm when she replied, "Yes, Laeticia was unhappy that summer. Who could blame her? She spent months taking care of me while I recovered. She helped Ainsley during her bouts of morning sickness. All while being anxious about the sea lapping outside our door. She was then entrusted with the care of an infant. It was a great deal of stress to put on someone so young."

"And then she spent the entire summer on Mackinac Island," I said. "More months surrounded by water. I'm surprised she stayed as long as she did."

"As I said, the girl was too accommodating. But she wasn't afraid to speak her mind. She announced several times that summer that she wanted to go back to France. None of us believed her. She often threatened to return home when things became stressful. But she never did."

"Why did Ainsley want to fire her?"

"My daughter-in-law began to resent the girl. Because of her postpartum depression, the baby spent most of his time with Laeticia. Ainsley felt excluded, and she blamed the nanny. But Ainsley would have changed her mind as soon as we returned home and she had to look for someone to replace her. Nor did I think Laeticia meant to leave whenever she threatened to quit."

"Why not?"

"The Sables live a most luxurious life. As do the employees who cater to our daily needs. Laeticia would have missed the perks."

"Maybe she was more unhappy than everyone realized."

"You think she threw herself off the boat?" Ingrid shook her head. "Impossible. Laeticia was terrified of water. The last thing she would have done is willingly gone into the lake."

"Ellen was afraid of the water, too."

"Ellen's fears were never my concern. Although if she was so afraid of water, why did the foolish girl take a summer job on an island?" she said with contempt.

I thought back to Leticia staring at the lake and how she told me that she did so in order to face her fears. Maybe she'd done that as a teenager, too. Forced herself to live surrounded by water, hoping she would grow less afraid.

"You may not have cared about Ellen's feelings, but why include the nanny on that yacht trip?" I didn't bother to hide the disapproval in my voice. "I would never force anyone terrified of drowning to go out on Lake Michigan. And on a boat trip that took hours."

"It was a thoughtless thing for us to do. And I regret it. As I regret this conversation."

Long after she left, I stood there thinking about how frightened Laeticia Murier must have been on that yacht. Especially after it ran into bad weather.

And how did anyone even convince her to go up on deck?

The decision to take the nanny on that boat ride was more than thoughtless and cruel. It was deliberate. Someone wanted to get rid of Laeticia Murier and a long yacht trip on Lake Michigan served as the perfect opportunity. Ellen Nagy was just an unwitting passenger.

One of the Sables did come up with that idea, however. And carried it off so well, the nanny ended up dead and another person blamed for the crime.

I needed to find Leticia, or Ellen Nagy as I now thought of her. If I couldn't, I feared the killer would. But where was she?

Ellen didn't think or behave like the rest of us. She was eccentric in the extreme. Some people thought she was crazy. It might take another crazy person to find her.

I knew exactly who to ask.

Chapter Twenty

The head of a black bear looked down at me from the opposite wall.

"I hope you didn't kill that bear," I said to the older man by the stove.

Old Man Bowman chuckled. "Do you think he died in his sleep outside my tent? Took two days of tracking in Menominee County to finally bring him down."

"I'm not a fan of hunting for sport." I sipped coffee in the blue enamel mug he'd given me. He'd brewed it so strong, this one cup might keep me up for days.

"Don't get on your high horse with me, young lady. You ain't no vegetarian." He gestured at the bacon frying on the stove. "Unless you don't want this bacon to be part of the breakfast I'm making for us. Or the eggs neither. If so, all you're gonna get are the bread and dried berries I put on the table."

My mouth salivated at the smell of the bacon. "I'm not about to turn down bacon."

"Exactly." He flipped the bacon strips in the cast-iron pan. "And don't mistake me for some damned trophy hunter. I use every part of an animal I kill: hide, meat, bones, fat, fur. The meat from that black bear kept me fed over the winter of ninety-nine. Along with my venison."

I eyed the various pelts that accompanied the mounted bear head. "Do you plan to do the same thing with Bigfoot if you ever find him?"

Old Man Bowman snorted. "I'm no murderer. And Bigfoot's as close to a human as anyone in Oriole Point. Hell, he's more human than a few of them, especially the politicians. Nah. I'm gonna trap the big fellow. Keep him alive to show the world the legends are true. And prove that those of us who believe he exists have been right all along."

Now that I'd mentioned Bigfoot, he launched into his latest sightings in the forests up north. I'd heard these tales before, and directed my attention instead to the thick slices of brown bread on the table, the butter in a ceramic butter keeper, and a wooden dish of dried cranberries. All of which tasted delicious. And he hadn't even brought the bacon and eggs to the table yet.

"Did I tell you the Kiefer boy saw a young Bigfoot up in Tawas last spring?"

"I don't recall."

While he proceeded to describe the Tawas Bigfoot, I slathered butter on another slice of bread while examining the room. I'd never been inside Old Man Bowman's home. He lived in a real log cabin, not a modern-day facsimile like Leticia's. The three-room structure looked much older than Bowman, who was seventy. Since the Bowman family came to the area in the nineteenth century, it likely belonged to his ancestors. They would have felt right at home.

He cooked on a woodstove. Kerosene lamps hung on the walls and sat on rough-hewn shelves.

An ancient refrigerator hummed in the corner, so he did have electricity, but the kitchen sink had a pump, not a spigot. The wooden furniture looked hand-made, and when I arrived, I spotted an outhouse in the woods out back. The weird thing was that he had built a state-of-the-art treehouse in his yard. It not only had running water and electricity but Wi-Fi, too. I'd asked him about it once, and he said he'd built the treehouse for guests.

However, the only treehouse guest I knew about was Natasha, the widow of his deceased nephew, Cole Bowman. She lived here for a month after her husband was murdered, Old Man Bowman viewing himself as the young widow's protector. Looking at the number of wild animal carcasses hanging on the walls, I thought Natasha should feel quite secure. And if my high-maintenance Russian friend felt comfortable living in that treehouse, it had to be plush.

Wendall Bowman, known as Old Man Bowman since he was in his fifties, could afford to *zhuzh* up a dozen treehouses. He made a fortune decades ago with one of his inventions. Something to do with the adhesive used in automotive engines. Whatever it was, it made him rich. However, he continued to live like Davy Crockett.

"I came by yesterday," I said. "But you weren't home."

"What time?" He cracked eggs in the pan. The sound of sizzling grease filled the air.

"Close to six."

"That's fishing time. They like to bite at dusk in my lake out back."

Bowman lived a couple miles inland on a patch of forested land that included Sumac Lake. I steered

clear of the lake, assuming the name meant poison
sumac flourished in the vicinity.

I'd been disappointed to not find him home last
night after I'd left the conference center. Old Man
Bowman didn't believe in phones, so there was no way
to call him. Because he kept pioneer hours, I woke at
dawn this morning, skipping breakfast in order to
arrive before seven.

When I pulled up his dirt drive, he had been outside chopping wood. I lucked out when he offered to
make breakfast, which he now set before me. I took
my first bite of bacon, crunchy and blackened. Exactly
how I liked it.

He sat across from me with a grunt, pouring a cup
of coffee from the enameled coffeepot on the table.
"What did you want to see me about? I know Natasha's
fine. I saw her yesterday afternoon when I dropped
off the maple syrup I tapped earlier this year."

"You have homemade maple syrup?" I said with my
mouth full.

"I'll give you a bottle before you leave. Now why are
you up so early?"

"I need your help. I'm trying to find someone who
doesn't want to be found."

He shrugged. "I'd respect that and leave 'em alone."

"She's hiding because she's afraid of some people
who are in town this week. I want to find her before
they do."

"Do I know these people?" He raised an eyebrow
at me, always a distracting sight. He had jet black
bushy eyebrows—so thick they resembled dark fuzzy
caterpillars. They stood in sharp contrast to his snow
white hair, which he wore in a long twisted braid
down his back.

Before I could answer, something moved in the corner. "Uh, there's a raccoon in here."

He sipped his coffee before answering, "That's Mamie. Pay her no mind. Tell me about these people this lady is hiding from."

"Funny you used the word 'lady,' because Leticia the Lake Lady is the one who's hiding. And the Sable family are the people she's worried about. With good reason, I might add."

My attention was diverted once more when a small brown rabbit hopped from behind a feed bag by the sink. Since a raccoon sighting seemed common in the Bowman kitchen, I saw no reason to point out the rabbit.

"If Leticia has good reason to be worried, you should be, too." He pointed his fork at me. "Don't go looking for trouble."

"I'm not looking for trouble. I'm looking for Leticia. Of course, that might be the same thing. But she's pulling pranks on the Sables. She's got them all riled up. If one of them is a murderer, that person might find her first. I want her to come out of hiding and tell the police what she knows about the Sables. I think it's her only chance to be safe."

"They haven't found her so far." He scooped up a large piece of fried egg with his bread.

"I've had enough experience with the criminal mind this past year. Murderers who think they might be caught are more dangerous than that black bear on the wall."

"Why do you think I can help you?" He chuckled. "Wait. Don't tell me. You think since I'm as much of an oddball as Leticia, I'll be able to figure out how her mind works."

I shrugged. "Basically."

He laughed again, then turned his attention to his breakfast. I did likewise. When we'd eaten every morsel of food on our plates and mopped up the grease with bread, we both sat back.

"That was the best bacon I've ever had," I said.

"Get it home cured from the Kiefer hog farm." He refilled both our enameled coffee mugs. "All right. Tell me what you know about these Sables and the Lake Lady."

I related everything I'd learned about the Nanny Murder, Leticia, and the Sable family since last Saturday. His expression didn't change, except when I mentioned how Felix Bonaventure had been shot.

"Not many with the aim to shoot a man clean through the heart with an arrow," he said.

"Ingrid Sable could. At least well enough to qualify for the Olympics back in the seventies. And her daughter-in-law has spent years emulating her. In addition, both Sable sons and the father go bow-hunting for deer every fall. Any of the Sables could have made that shot."

A tapping noise drew our attention to the kitchen window. An enormous crow sat on the outside ledge. He peered in and used his beak to tap on the glass again.

"Hold on." Old Man Bowman stood up. "Edgar wants his morning hard-boiled egg." He grabbed an egg from a bowl near the sink, then opened the window. As there were no screens on the window, I expected the crow to fly inside. Instead, Bowman cracked the shell of the egg, broke it in two, then laid it on the outside sill. Edgar the crow dove in with that large pointy beak, and Bowman closed the window once more.

I felt like I was having breakfast with Hagrid at Hogwarts.

"Edgar?" I asked when Old Man Bowman sat down again.

He grinned. "Always had a fondness for Edgar Allan Poe. And crows and ravens belong to the same family. Corvids."

"Let's get back to the death by bow and arrow. Leticia told me that Gareth Holmes crafted a bow-and-arrow set from mulberry wood for her. But she needed to practice shooting targets first. After she accidentally shot one of her cats, she got upset and left the bow and arrows out in the field." I took a sip of coffee. "Where the killer must have found them."

"And killed this ghostwriter fellow?"

I nodded. "Bonaventure was in Oriole Point last Monday asking for a woman called Ellen Mulberry. The Sables knew her real name was Ellen Nagy. I think they'd found out she was using a ghostwriter to put together a book on the Nanny Murder. And I bet at least one of the Sables was following Bonaventure. He led them straight to her house, only she wasn't home."

"How did Bonaventure end up out in the field by the beehives?"

"I suspect he was running for his life. If someone suddenly appeared with a bow and arrow, I'd start running, too."

Bowman looked thoughtful. "If this person wanted both Bonaventure and the Lake Lady dead, why not wait until she showed up, too?"

"She wasn't home when Bonaventure arrived. And

the police estimate he was killed shortly before we got there. Around eight a.m. All the Sable family members have had talks and events scheduled at the health fair from nine o'clock on. If one of them didn't show up, it might seem suspicious. Especially if Leticia went public with her accusations against the Sables." I frowned. "But if she handles it wrong, she may wind up dead."

"I've met Leticia. Don't see how you think you'll convince her."

"I haven't had a lot of opportunity to do so. And she's pulled some sort of stunt on the Sables every day this week. Vandalizing their cars twice, setting off smoke bombs. Leaving a threatening note. Each time she does this, she risks getting caught."

He tried to top off my coffee but I waved him away. I already felt as alert as that brown rabbit nervously watching me from the corner.

"Whoever is the killer in the Sable family wants her dead," I continued. "And they want that manuscript she and Bonaventure wrote. Someone tore open all the boxes of mulberries on her porch the other day. That may have been where Leticia hid the manuscript or her laptop. I doubt she'd be foolish enough to conceal both of them on her porch."

Although I had to admit that Leticia's logic often eluded me.

"You think she's still got a copy of that manuscript with her?"

"Yes. Either printed off or on that computer. At least I hope so. It may be the only thing keeping her alive. Once the Sables have that, she's expendable."

"You may be right." Bowman cleared the plates, cups, and coffeepot from the table.

"No one in Oriole County knows the back roads and woods better than you do. Where could Leticia safely hide? She can't have gone far, not without taking the risk of being seen on her purple scooter. Do you think she's holed up in an abandoned barn by the orchards? Maybe a vacation home closed for the season. She could even be camping out. Unless she has a friend I don't know about. Someone willing to hide her. Do you know of anyone?"

"Sure do." He shot me a mischievous look as he placed the plates in the sink. "Me."

"You?"

"Always did have a soft spot for damsels in distress." I stood up. "Where is she?"

"Where all my guests stay. In the treehouse."

My giddiness at discovering Leticia's hiding place dimmed as soon as Old Man Bowman and I went outside.

"I told you. She ain't here. Took her scooter about an hour before you got here." He walked me over to the ladder that led to the treehouse. "Go on up and see for yourself."

I did just that. The trapdoor had been left open, and I emerged into a room illuminated by dappled sunlight on the plank floor and braid throw rugs scattered about. It was airy and bright, probably less so in spring and summer when leaves covered the branches outside the windows.

The main room contained a loveseat, chair, desk,

TV, and bookshelves. A chandelier made of deer antlers hung near the stairs, which led to an open loft with a bed, reading lamp, and a rattan chest of drawers. An electrical baseboard had been installed to provide heat in cold weather. I spotted a bathroom sink along one wall, a rustic mirror hung above it. I could figure out how he wired the house for electricity, but had no idea how he got water up here. He'd even built an outside patio deck furnished with a small table and four chairs.

I was impressed, but disappointed. Leticia wasn't here. Although I took heart at the sight of what must be several changes of clothes piled neatly on the coverlet of the bed. However a quick look through all the drawers revealed they did not contain a manuscript or a laptop.

When I climbed down the treehouse ladder, Old Man Bowman was leaning against the tree that held the house. He gave me a knowing look. "I told you she wasn't there."

I looked around the wooded lot, spying the waters of Sumac Lake off to the left. "Did she tell you where she was going?"

"Never says anything to me about how she spends her days. It ain't my business to ask. But I do know how she gets in and out of here 'cause I showed it to her." He pointed to a small trail that led into the woods.

I walked closer to the trail and saw single tire marks on the dirt. "Where does it lead?"

"It's an old Potawatomi trail. Takes you to the big lake. Once you're there, it's easy to get on an access road to anywhere in Oriole Point."

"How long is the trail?"

"A little over two miles. Big enough for a scooter,

but not a car. That's what makes it safe. No car's gonna sneak up on you in there. That's why I told Leticia about it."

"How did Leticia wind up in your treehouse?" I asked.

"Saw her at Oval Beach early Tuesday morning. I was there with my metal detector. You'd be surprised what you can find in the sand with one of those. Last year Gil Palka found a Lincoln-head copper penny from 1943 there. They issued them by mistake during World War II, which makes them real valuable. He ended up selling it for over fifty thousand dollars!"

I needed to get him back on track. "We don't have time to talk about numismatics. You must have spoken with her right before she came home and found Bonaventure's body."

"She and I aren't total strangers. Two years ago I asked for permission to go hunting on her woods. Heard word that Bigfoot spoor had been spotted nearby. She was nice enough to let me track on her property. I owed her a favor. So that morning, I re-minded her that if she ever needed anything to just come to me. A few hours later, she came up my drive in that scooter, wanting to know where she could hide for a few days." He gestured at the treehouse above us. "Told her she could be my guest as long as she needed."

Despite his odd beliefs and pioneer lifestyle, Wen-dall Bowman was quite the knight in shining armor. "Did she have a laptop or a manuscript with her?" I asked.

"Not that I could see. But she brought a big back-pack."

"I saw her backpack on the bed. Nothing in there

but socks, underwear, a scarf." I kicked at the dirt in frustration. "You said she left about an hour ago."

"That she did."

Edgar the crow chose to strut up to us, bold as brass. Old Man Bowman bent down and stroked his head. I needed to bring Theo here. He'd be thrilled with Edgar.

"If I took the trail, I'd come out on the lake." I turned toward the opening in the woods.

"Sure will. The lake will be right below the bluff. The trail dead-ends there. Been that way since the Beekmans cleared the land to build their fancy resort."

I bit my lip. "Oh no. The Beekman is where the Sable family is staying."

"She better be careful when she leaves the trail there. One of 'em could spot her."

I thought they might want to be careful as well. Yesterday she had delivered a note to the front door. Who knew what she intended for today?

"I need to walk the trail. If that's how she's coming and going, I may meet up with her."

He gave a great sigh. "Then I'll have to come with you."

"Why? I can easily walk two miles there and back. And I'm dressed for a hike." I looked down at my jeans, blue pullover, denim jacket, and sneakers. My cross-body bag held my cell phone, small water bottle, and several pieces of dark chocolate. It was also a sunny day in the upper fifties. Even if I weren't trying to find Leticia, I'd enjoy a morning hike in the woods.

"The trail branches off along the way. If you take your eyes off the main trail, you could end up hiking for a lot longer than you want. Besides, I'll be able to point out the poison sumac bushes." He grimaced. "You don't want to trip and fall into one of those."

"Okay. You convinced me." I'd twice suffered a bout of poison ivy. I had no wish to repeat the experience with the even more toxic poison sumac.

I wanted to mention that he wasn't properly dressed for a hike in the woods, but it would be pointless. Old Man Bowman refused to wear anything but cargo shorts and a baggy shirt. And Birkenstocks on his bare feet. However, he made a concession to winter by adding woolen socks. I had no idea how he hunted while outfitted like that.

He set off for the opening in the trees. "If we keep up a good pace, we'll get to the end of the trail in less than thirty minutes. More than enough time to tell you about the UFOs I saw over Grand Traverse Bay last Christmas. The same week there were four Bigfoot sightings in the U.P. One of 'em by me."

It promised to be a long two miles.

Old Man Bowman was wrong. Our hike took more than thirty minutes, mainly because he kept stopping to point out suspicious animal tracks he thought might be bipedal. I almost prayed for a sighting of a hairy hominid if only to forestall another hunting tale. The last one involved the time he heard the hoots of a Bigfoot while he was gutting a deer. All of it involved too much descriptive detail, especially the gutting part.

I kept myself distracted following the tire tracks of Leticia's scooter. I also hoped to catch the distinctive sound of her scooter coming toward us, but all I heard was my companion's voice.

The hike did teach me how to identify poison sumac. Old Man Bowman had twice prevented me from using my hand to bat away a branch from the poisoned shrub. The least I could do was listen to his Bigfoot hunting monologue with good grace.

"Are we almost there?" I sounded like a cranky child on a road trip.

"Almost. If you listen, you can hear the waves on the lake."

If he ever stopped talking, I was certain I could.

He crouched down. "These prints are interesting."

"Animal or Bigfoot?" I yawned.

"Human. And they weren't walking in a straight line."

I knelt beside him. There were partial footprints on the dirt, most of them not discernible among the weeds, rocks, and dead leaves gusting in the breeze.

He stood up and turned in a circle.

Nervous now, I scanned the area for scooter tire tracks. I'd taken my eyes from the ground a few moments ago. Now I regretted it.

"Look!" I pointed at the tracks that now swerved back and forth on the trail. "She was trying to avoid something. Or the scooter went out of control."

We followed the erratic tracks, with Old Man Bowman pointing at an occasional footprint as well. In the tense silence, I finally heard the surf from the lake. We were almost at the end of the trail.

He took my arm. "This doesn't feel right."

We hurried up the remainder of the trail. Suddenly the trees ended. So did the tire tracks.

To our right was Lake Michigan. Up ahead sat the baronial white hotel known as The Beekman. Pines and autumnal flower beds dotted the front lawn. A sweeping driveway led to the wide portico entrance. Behind the hotel were more trees and a parking lot filled with cars.

A taxi pulled up to the entrance. Two men exited the hotel and got in.

Not a sign of anyone else. No surprise. It was only a little after 8 A.M.

"I don't see her or the scooter," I said.

I'd never seen Old Man Bowman so grim. "She never made it to the hotel."

Dread washed over me. "The lake?"

We hurried to the edge of the bluff and looked down. I bit back a scream.

Forty feet below, a woman lay on the sandy slope of the bluff. From this height, we weren't able to see her face. But the long orange hair splayed over the sand told us that we had found Leticia the Lake Lady.

Chapter Twenty-one

Despite his sympathetic manner, the manager of The Beekman looked as if he wished all of us had remained outside with the dead body. Instead, his pristine lobby swarmed with state troopers, local police, and officers from the sheriff's department. Curious hotel guests made the scene even more confusing.

I wanted to leave, a sentiment clearly shared by the Sables, who had been summoned down to the lobby and ordered to wait. Old Man Bowman had gotten the attention of a law-enforcement officer and was expounding on his theory that not only was Leticia's scooter forced off the bluff, there was a likelihood a Bigfoot in the area witnessed it. I hoped this day didn't end with Wendall Bowman being hauled off to the state mental hospital.

After spotting Leticia's body, I called the police on my cell. We couldn't get to where she lay from our initial vantage point on the bluff. The only access was via the Beekman's private beach, which Old Man Bowman and I reached from the stairway that led down to the sand.

Rescue was futile. Leticia had been thrown from her scooter, her fall broken by a shrub jutting from the sandy bluff. Neither of us could get near her on the steep slope. We did get close enough to see that her eyes were open and her body completely still.

The impact had killed her. All we could do was sit and wait for the police. Pieces of her scooter littered the slope and beach. What was left of the machine lay on the wet sand, the front tire gone. I told Old Man Bowman to stay away from the damaged scooter. Let the police ascertain what happened without us compromising the scene.

Until their arrival, I spent most of the time crying. Not because I had been close to her. I'd met her only twice. I mourned not her premature death, but her troubled life.

Fifteen years spent in prison for a crime she likely didn't commit. Although she was only thirty-three when she walked free, the experience had unsettled her mind. I wish I had known the prison counselor she married. I hoped the older man was kind. I told myself he must have been if Leticia not only agreed to marry him, but lived with him until his death. After he was gone, she led a solitary life, disowned by most of her family, seeking companionship with feral cats, watching the lake as if it held answers—or salvation.

I also found myself watching the lake while we waited. The blue expanse of water was the last thing she saw before falling to her death. Had she been suddenly distracted, causing her own death? I doubted it. Some people might surmise that her plunge off the bluff was deliberate. But she didn't seem suicidal. And there was a gang of Sables who wanted her out of the picture, all of them conveniently nearby when she died.

Although Old Man Bowman shed no tears, I knew he was upset, too. We hadn't been able to protect her.

Kit and a fellow deputy from the sheriff's department were the first to arrive on the scene. I fell into Kit's arms for another quick bout of crying. Behind me, I heard Old Man Bowman declare that someone had forced the scooter off the bluff. I stopped crying long enough to chime in, "He's right. It had to be one of the Sables."

More police appeared, including Detective Greg Trejo. Four of the men made their way up the bluff to the body. It took a lot of effort. With each step, they sank up to their ankles in the sand. Walking through deep sand feels like plowing through a snowdrift. I breathed a sigh of relief when they reached her, but I couldn't bear to watch them bring the body down. It was too upsetting. Even Old Man Bowman looked away. We eagerly accepted a state trooper's offer to escort us to the hotel, where we would be expected to give a statement.

Two hours later, we were still in the lobby, along with the Sables. They refused to come near me, even though I sat on a sectional sofa a few yards away. Scarlett Beckford texted nonstop on her phone. Beside her, Keith and Patrick Sable took calls while Ainsley sat on the adjacent sofa, swinging her foot nervously.

Every ten minutes, she asked, "How much longer is this going to take?"

Her son Joshua kept dozing off, making him the most relaxed person in the room.

The Sables remained partially hidden from view

by their team of personal assistants, who provided endless cups of coffee, water bottles, and the occasional serving of continental breakfast. When the crowd around them parted, I caught Ingrid Sable observing me like a raptor. The rest of the family kept deferring to her, except for Cameron Sable.

Oblivious to the hubbub in the lobby, Cameron sat absorbed in a book whose title read *A Guide to the Good Life: The Ancient Art of Stoic Joy*. He did look up once to give me a gracious smile, as if he knew I had been surreptitiously watching him.

If they were afraid of being accused of murder, I didn't discern it. Instead, they appeared irritated, bored, impatient. Everything you would expect of people who didn't give a damn about the woman who had just been found dead. The real hostility from the Sables was directed toward me. When I first walked into the lobby and saw the Sables gathered there, Keith asked, "What in the hell is she doing here?"

"Will we never be free of unstable women while we are in Oriole Point?" Ingrid demanded. Dressed in a long-sleeved black dress, her white hair towering above her, she reminded me of the evil fairy Maleficent in *Sleeping Beauty*.

None of them looked pleased after learning Old Man Bowman and I found Leticia's body. The family began talking at once, the general consensus being that my presence was suspicious and probably criminal.

Weary of the Sables and upset by Leticia's death, I ignored them. I had been questioned by the police and knew it wouldn't be the last time. I also knew each Sable would be taken in turn by Kit and Detective

Greg Trejo and interrogated in the hotel manager's office.

I breathed a sigh of relief when I saw Kit enter the hotel. After speaking with his fellow deputies, he walked over to where I sat. "Come with me," he murmured.

He led me to the lobby bar. At this hour of the morning the bar was deserted. We were the only ones sitting at any of the high top tables.

"Have you learned anything helpful?" I asked.

"Yes. We checked out the trail. As you said, her tire tracks show she swerved and went over the edge. No evidence of anything on the ground that would have caused a problem. We'll check out the scooter for mechanical failure. We found footprints near the place she went over. Yours and Wendall Bowman's, of course. But there are others."

"Can you identify them? Get a shoe size. A marking from the sole of the shoe."

"The prints are indistinct. But someone was lying in wait for her there."

"How do you know?"

"Because of the evidence on the body."

"Didn't she die from the fall?" I nervously drummed my fingers on the table.

"She might have, depending on the impact. But I think she was dead before she ever landed on the ground."

"From what?"

"A blow to the back of her head. Our initial guess was a blunt object of some kind. A rock perhaps. Then we found a two-foot-long tree branch that had been tossed into the woods about fifty yards away. We think someone struck her as she drove past."

I felt dizzy from the horror of it. "Why do you think the branch was used to kill her?"

"The fresh blood on it. If it matches the blood of Ellen Nagy, we have the murder weapon." He grabbed my hand on the table. "I'm sorry. I know you wanted to help her."

I looked over at the Sables, surrounded by lackeys. "Old Man Bowman told me she'd used that trail every day since moving into his treehouse. And the trail ends in clear view of The Beekman, where the Sables are staying. One of them could have caught a glimpse of her and figured out that was how she got in and out of Oriole Point. If murder was their intention, all they had to do was wait for her to drive by again."

"They'll be questioned today. In fact, we need a statement from everyone in the hotel, guests and employees. Someone might have seen something suspicious early this morning."

I went back over the day's timeline. "I got to Old Man Bowman's house right before seven o'clock. And he said Leticia left about thirty minutes earlier."

"Driving that scooter, she would have quickly reached the end of the trail," Kit said. "Not many guests are likely to be outside that early. I'm not confident we'll turn up witnesses. And they wouldn't have been able to see her scooter go over the bluff from the hotel itself. I checked. An eyewitness would need to be by the firepit on the front lawn in order to have seen it."

The Sables had been at The Beekman since last Saturday, time enough for all of them to have a good idea of the early-morning activity on the grounds.

"Unless you can get one of them to confess today, I doubt you'll be able to do more than scare them."

"I don't think they scare easy." He looked frustrated. "According to my deputies, the Sables have called their attorneys. Two of them are flying in today. We haven't even gotten their statement yet, and they're lawyering up. Which is a smart thing to do."

I leaned over the table and said in a low voice, "Did you find the manuscript or laptop in the scooter? It had a storage box."

He shook his head. "Nothing in the scooter's storage box but apples and six identical photos of the dead nanny, Laeticia Murier."

"Photos?"

"Poster size, all folded up. Probably taken from a photo used during the trial. I suspect she meant to post them in town, or at the hotel and conference center."

"Today's prank." It saddened me that a grown woman thought such measures had any weight or power. Then again, it had resulted in serious consequences for her. Deadly ones.

"You've given your official statement, Marlee, so you can go." He squeezed my hand. "And please take Mr. Bowman with you. We've heard enough about Bigfoot for one day."

"Then you didn't find the book she and Bonaventure had been working on?"

His brown eyes regarded me with affection and regret. "I suspect the murderer already has them. Like you said, she probably hid the laptop and manuscript in those boxes of mulberries, which we found pillaged on her porch. If so, her version of the story died with her."

"Any luck tracking down that crew member who testified against Ellen?"

"We traced James Smith's whereabouts during the time he worked for the Sables. He captained a number of their super yachts in the Mediterranean and the South Seas. The year of Ellen's release from prison, he left their employ to run charter fishing boats in New Zealand. After that, he falls off the map. Don't know where he went next, although a fellow yachtie says he got married to a woman called Shelly Zahradnik. That name's a lot less common than James Smith, so there's a good chance we'll be able to track her down. We may have a lead in Hawaii."

I took comfort from that. "I also think it's suspicious he quit working for the Sables at the same time Ellen got out of prison."

"Agreed. It's too coincidental. For his testimony, Smith might have been rewarded with years of sailing around the world on super yachts. He seems to have had quite a bit of money when he did quit. The charter fishing boat companies were run more as a hobby than a business."

"According to Ellen, he contacted her after he became terminally ill. That means he wanted to set things right with her before he died. You need to find him before it's too late, Kit."

"We're doing our best. But if he's dying of cancer, who knows how long he has?"

"It's not just his illness I'm worried about. If the Sables get to him first, you and I both know his death will not be a natural one."

Chapter Twenty-two

"Tie me kangaroo down!"

I opened one eye. Minnie sat on the back of the couch, singing her favorite Australian ditty. Actually it was the only Aussie song she knew, taught to her by former owners. Due to a problem with taking a parrot out of the country, the Australian family gave up their African grey before they returned to Brisbane. Their loss was my gain. But Minnie still remembered her vocabulary of Australian terms. My favorite was "G'day, cobber."

She whistled, then gave a perfect imitation of Panther's meow. This prompted the kitten to respond with the real thing. Panther and I had been napping on the couch. Since Minnie hadn't woken us up until now, I suspected my parrot also took the time for a little shut-eye.

After leaving The Beekman, I went straight home. I'd scheduled Dean to work at the shop. There was no need for me to join him. If I did, I'd have to tell him about our Lake Lady's death. I didn't want to talk about it. Not yet. Soon enough it would be public knowledge and I would be inundated with questions.

For now, I chose to hide away at home with a talkative parrot and an affectionate kitten. When the world turned harsh, I could think of no better retreat. I always had an affinity for Dorothy and her wish to return to Kansas and Auntie Em.

The fireplace mantel clock chimed three times. I'd slept for an hour. Despite the nuclear-strength coffee I'd consumed at Old Man Bowman's, the stress of the day overrode the caffeine and I did something I only resort to when sick: take a nap. I felt much better. Burrowing into my sofa cushions, I resumed cuddling with Panther, who stretched his tiny body beside me.

My cell phone buzzed from where I'd dropped it next to the sofa. It was a text from Aunt Vicki. She and several shelter volunteers were about to leave for Leticia's cottage. Yesterday the sheriff's department gave permission for Humane Hearts to set traps on the property in order to collect the feral cats. She asked if I wanted to meet them there and lend a hand.

I texted back that I would leave now, which meant I'd be there in about a half hour. The sorry news of Leticia's death could wait until I saw my aunt face-to-face.

The day had grown colder, with clouds scudding across the sky. As I drove out into the country, gusty winds blew dead leaves over the road. The weather felt funereal. How fitting, given the circumstances.

After I parked in front of Leticia's log cabin, a sense of unease came over me. I didn't know if it was grief or the fact that Aunt Vicki and her volunteers hadn't arrived yet. My guilt over not being able to protect Leticia returned. Although I didn't believe in magic, I wished my mulberries had somehow been able to protect her.

Because the winds were brisk, I zipped up my suede jacket before getting out of the car. I stared at the porch where I'd left the boxes of berries on Monday. Kit removed them the night we found the boxes torn open and took them to the sheriff's department.

I considered the possibility that Leticia might have taken those missing bags of berries for something other than trimming her costume and making that bracelet. Perhaps she buried the manuscript and laptop on her property, covering the ground with mulberries in case something happened to her. A clue only I would understand, to point out where she'd hidden them.

Before I could begin to search for suspicious mulberries, I heard tires on the graveled driveway. Expecting to see Aunt Vicki and her Humane Hearts van, I watched in surprise as a shiny silver vehicle came into view. It rolled to a halt behind my SUV, allowing me to see it was a BMW. During my dinner with Piper, the Sable sons mentioned that they had rented BMWs for their stay in Oriole Point.

My breathing quickened. I had been so distracted on the drive over, I hadn't noticed anyone following me. I considered getting back into my SUV and racing out of here. But Aunt Vicki and her volunteers would be here any moment. No need to panic.

A tall, husky man got out of the front passenger side of the car. He looked more like a bodyguard than a personal assistant. "My employer would like a word with you," he said.

"Who's your employer?"

The back window rolled down. "He works for me," a cultured voice replied from within.

I walked over to where I could see into the open

window, making certain to keep a healthy distance from the car. "Hello, Dr. Sable. I'm surprised to see you here."

He sat alone in the backseat by the opposite window. "You have spoken with all the members of my family, except for me, Ms. Jacob. Given all that has occurred, I thought it time to speak with you. Privately." He nodded toward the leather seat beside him.

I gestured to the leaf-strewn lawn. "Why don't you join me out here?"

Cameron Sable gave me a thin smile. "Too chilly for my old bones."

The husky man opened the back door. "If you would, miss."

"I'd rather not." No way was I getting into that vehicle.

"Dennis," Cameron said in a tone I recognized as an order.

The man grabbed my arm and shoved me into the car. It happened so quickly, I only had time to land one good kick at his shin. His yelp of pain gave me a tiny bit of satisfaction.

After he pushed me inside, the door slammed shut, followed by the click of the locks. I tensed up, fearful I was about to be spirited away.

"Look, Dr. Sable, I don't appreciate being manhandled by your minions. And if you plan to abduct me, I'm going to put up one hell of a fight."

"No one is being abducted, my dear." His sonorous voice seemed designed to soothe.

"Then why is the car still running? If you want to talk, tell the driver to hand me the keys."

Looking amused by my request, Cameron turned to his driver, who stared out the front window. "Give the young woman your key, Peter. And step outside the car."

"Yes, sir." The driver switched off the motor, then held the key behind his head. Once I snatched the key fob with the BMW logo, he exited the car.

The car felt even more confining after he shut the door behind him. Maybe because Cameron Sable appeared so in control of the situation. He sat, legs crossed, relaxed. His hands, which I noticed were long and tapered, idly stroked the brown scarf that hung about his neck. I hoped he didn't have plans to strangle me with it.

"Do you make a habit of forcing strangers to have conversations with you?" I asked.

"We haven't been formally introduced, but I'd hardly call us strangers. As I said, you've met my family. And I assume you've heard of me." That last was said with a hint of arrogance.

"I also assume you've been following me."

"Me, personally? No. But after the police questioned my family at The Beekman today, I thought it best to speak with you. My driver was taking me to your lakeshore home when you rode right past us. Your Berry Basket vehicle is difficult to miss. Naturally, we followed."

"Naturally." I had to stop daydreaming when I was on the road. "Have I been watched the entire time you've been in Oriole Point?"

"We weren't aware you needed watching until you found Mr. Bonaventure's body." His gaze lazily swept over me. "Although I would enjoy watching you. I have a fondness for spirited, young women with silky black hair and long legs." He leaned closer. "You're quite enticing."

I reached for the locked door, but the husky man was leaning against it. "Let me out of here. Now!"

Being trapped in the car with the Sable patriarch—with his men just outside—sent my heart racing. Would I be the second dead body found on this property?

He gave a low laugh. "Frightened an old man like me will seduce you?"

"Seduction wasn't the word that came to mind. Let me out."

"You will be free to go soon, my dear. As soon as we've had our conversation." He settled back against the leather seat. His calm expression revealed that he was enjoying my nervous reaction. I felt like I was in the car with Mephistopheles, albeit one outfitted in a beige turtleneck, camel brown tailored suit, and cashmere scarf.

Escape seemed problematic. "You haven't put me in the mood for a casual conversation."

"I never said anything about a casual conversation. I intend for this to be a serious one."

"I assume you wish to speak about Leticia."

He bridled. "That is not her name. Please refer to the deceased as Ellen Nagy."

"No matter what we call her, she's dead. The question is why."

"I have a question, too." His smug smile vanished. "Why are you here? What possible reason could you have for coming alone to the property of a woman who died earlier today? You're not a relative, nor are you a policewoman. I can't imagine what would draw you here. Unless you're looking for something."

"I'm here for the cats. My aunt runs an animal rescue organization, and she and some volunteers are on the way here now. We plan to trap the feral cats so we can have them spayed and neutered."

"Cats?" Cameron shook his head. "You can do better than that."

"Just wait." I glanced down at my watch. "They'll be here any minute." With luck.

He cocked his head at me, uncertain if I had told him the truth.

"While we wait, we can discuss Ellen," I said. "And why she died."

"You seem a woman of boundless imagination. Why do you think?"

"I think it had something to do with the death of your former nanny, Laeticia Murier."

He didn't look surprised. "You believe a Sable is responsible for Ellen's death?"

"Yes." If I'd said anything else, he wouldn't believe me. "I think a Sable family member wanted to silence Ellen about what she knew of the nanny's death."

"You are aware Ellen confessed to the crime?"

"I am." I shrugged. "But she didn't confess for weeks. I've researched the case. Reports claim Ellen was in shock when the police boarded the yacht. And she became hysterical once she was arrested for the crime, all on testimony given by your family."

"And one of the crew members," he added. "The bosun."

"Your employee." I gestured at the men who stood guard on either side of the car. "People paid to do as you ask."

"Are you accusing me of bribing my staff to give false testimony?" He laughed.

"I have my suspicions. By the way, I've passed on those suspicions to the police."

"I'd be disappointed if you hadn't. Do you have evidence to back them up?"

"If I did, I'd make certain the right person was arrested for the murder of Laeticia Murier. And Ellen Nagy."

"Ellen died in an unfortunate accident," he said. "No one can prove otherwise."

"Perhaps. But there may be proof Ellen didn't kill the nanny."

Cameron looked bored. "We're back to that, are we?"

"We never left. The nanny's murder is behind Ellen's death. And Felix Bonaventure."

"This is why I needed to talk with you, Ms. Jacob. Such slanderous nonsense must stop before it gets out of hand."

"Two murders in one week?" I said angrily. "It's already out of hand."

"Unfounded rumors can cause this to spiral completely out of control. The Sable brand is dedicated to natural living, holistic practices, positive energy. We cannot be tarnished by a murder. Not again. The financial repercussions could be irreparable. That's why you need to give me Ellen's computer. It contains the file of that book she wrote with her collaborator."

I gave him a suspicious look. "Don't you also want the copy of the manuscript Ellen had in her house?"

His expression turned impish. An alarming sight. "Not any longer."

"So you found it." I felt like the Sables had landed another blow.

"My family and I have been discussing various

hiding places Ellen might have chosen. One of them ended up being correct." He looked over at the porch where the boxes of mulberries recently were.

If only I had thought to look through all the boxes when I had the chance.

He stroked my arm. "Make it easy on yourself and give us the computer."

I slapped his hand away. "I don't have the laptop. And if your family is innocent, why are you so concerned about the manuscript?"

"Truth is a victim in any scandal. And I don't intend for my family to be victimized. The last thing we need is Ellen's bizarre version of events to become public."

"A TV series about the murder is soon to go into production. It will be dredged up regardless."

"Ah, yes. The series." He seemed irritated at the thought. "We weren't pleased to learn that poor girl's murder was about to exploited again. However, we have been assured their script will adhere to what actually happened. One can only hope. If not, we shall take legal action. As I am tempted to do against you."

I looked at him as if he was crazy. "Me? What have I done?"

"If you think we will let you sell that book to the highest bidder, you are mistaken."

"And I think you're deluded. For the last time, I don't have her laptop."

"You're not a convincing liar. Now where is it? We've learned it wasn't in her house." He poked his finger hard at my shoulder. "From what I've gathered, you were one of her few friends. You and that old man who keeps talking about Bigfoot."

"We didn't know her well enough to be friends. She simply came to us for help."

"A remarkable coincidence that she did so the same week we arrived here."

I returned his threatening stare with one of my own. "I don't think there was anything coincidental about it. I suspect your family knew where Ellen Nagy lived. However, I don't know how long you've been aware of her collaboration with Felix Bonaventure."

Where were Aunt Vicki and her volunteers? There was only so long I could keep up this bold front.

He sighed. "We knew Bonaventure had collaborated on a book with Ellen. He and the Sable family shared the same literary agency, although his agent is farther down the company food chain. We were informed as soon as he contacted his agent with the proposal."

"Didn't he know your agents worked for the same company?" I asked.

"If he didn't, he soon realized his mistake. When Bonaventure told his agent he'd written a book with Ellen Nagy about the Nanny Murder, it caused concern at the agency. The Sable books have made a fortune for them. It is in their best interests to keep us happy. A libelous version of the murder would not do that."

"So the agency refused to handle the manuscript."

"Not immediately. His agent informed our own agent there. She told us. We didn't even have to mention lawsuits. They had no intention of angering us. Or losing us as clients."

"But there was nothing to stop him from submitting it elsewhere."

"True. That's why we instructed the agency to hold off on giving him an answer. They told him the proposal would be sent to committee to look into legal issues. It bought us a little time to decide how to handle the manuscript."

No doubt it did. Time enough to arrange an extended stay in Oriole Point, the better to coerce Ellen. And time enough to ransack Bonaventure's condo.

"Eventually he pressed the agency for an answer, which is when he learned he had been dropped as a client." He leaned closer. "That same day, someone broke into his condo and stole his computer and all his copies of the manuscript. Such a shame."

"I'm sure Bonaventure knew your family was behind the break-in *and* his rejection by the agency. Then he learned the Sables would be here for the health fair. He was probably worried you planned to pressure Ellen about the manuscript. Also she had the only remaining copies."

"That she did," he said in that mellifluous voice I had already grown to hate.

"You planned to scare her into giving you the book. But your arrival backfired. It did scare her, but only to go into hiding. Taking the only other copies of *Mischief and Murder.*"

Cameron seemed nonplussed. "Ellen has always been unpredictable."

"And after you sent someone to Bonaventure's home in Philadelphia to remove any trace of the book, you followed him here and got rid of him." A chill went through me.

"Don't be tiresome. It's one thing to retrieve information. It's quite another to kill someone over it." He frowned. "Ellen obviously killed the man out of some paranoiac fear."

I was tired of his suave bullying and his lies. "And I bet you asked Victor Kang to bow out so the Sables could take his place."

He shrugged. "Simply a fortuitous turn of events. And Victor will say the same thing."

My frustration grew. "How long have you known Ellen lived here?"

"Long enough."

"Doesn't the agency have a copy of the manuscript?"

"No. Bonaventure told his agent the general outline of the book and that it was ready to be sent to publishers. He only called so they could discuss which houses to submit it to. All he emailed the agency was a one-page summary of the book."

I glanced over my shoulder, searching for any sign of Aunt Vicki. "If you have both Bonaventure's and Ellen's copy of the manuscript, then you already know what's in it."

"Of course we know," he said in a weary voice. "That's why we need her computer. We sent someone to search Mr. Bowman's cabin and treehouse today while the police had us detained. He found nothing. You're the only other person she would have given it to."

"I'll take you to my house right this minute and you can search all the rooms."

"That was done yesterday while you were at the conference center." He smiled at my shocked cry. "Didn't even know someone was in your house, did you? That's how expert my people are. Able to paw through closets and drawers and not leave a thing out of place. Nor did they leave any prints. They found your parrot and kitten amusing. And they were tempted to eat the leftover Kung Pao shrimp in your refrigerator, but wisely refrained."

To think strangers had invaded my house, gone through my things, and played with my animals sent me into a rage. "Why are you telling me this? To prove how despicable you are?"

"I'm telling you because our patience is at an end. We know you have the computer. Or that you know where it is. We'll pay you well for it. Along with your silence."

The driver rapped on the window and pointed. We looked behind us. Two Humane Hearts vans pulled up the drive. A tsunami of relief washed over me.

"Are we done with our conversation? Or should the animal shelter volunteers join us?"

"We're done," he said. "I've made my position clear. And you can pass on our conversation to the police. It won't matter. There's no way to prove anyone broke into your house. Or Mr. Bowman's. My people are quite adept at their jobs."

"I plan to tell the police the same literary agency handled you and Bonaventure."

"I assume they already know. If not, they soon will. I'm not concerned. Our agency did the rational thing by rejecting the manuscript. The irrational element in all this is Ellen Nagy."

He paused to give me a searching look. "And you."

"Three people are dead," I said in disgust. "Don't you feel any responsibility?"

"My only responsibility is to protect my family from ruin."

"And that justifies the break-ins you ordered? The lies?"

"Ms. Jacob, the truth does not always set you free. In fact, it's much more likely to get one thrown in prison." He narrowed his eyes at me. "Or killed."

"Is that a threat?"

"A warning. My family leaves tomorrow. If you're as clever as I believe, you will hand over the computer. If not . . ."

I didn't ask him to elaborate.

Chapter Twenty-three

Although my day began with a shocking death, it ended with a pajama party. Such is life in Oriole Point.

To be honest, I was as relieved to have overnight company as I was when I saw the Humane Hearts vans pull up behind Cameron Sable's BMW. As soon as he and his thugs drove off, I told Aunt Vicki what had just occurred. It was all I could do to stop her and her boyfriend Joe from hopping into one of their vans and speeding after them.

Instead, I mollified my furious aunt by calling Kit to tell him about my conversation with Cameron. He was even more outraged than Aunt Vicki. And I thought only my maternal Italian relatives could get angry that quickly.

"I'll break his scrawny neck!" Kit shouted over the speakerphone. Aunt Vicki and Joe were listening and nodded in approval. "How dare that bastard threaten you! Then has the nerve to admit he had men break into your house!"

"Not just mine," I reminded him. "Old Man Bowman's, too."

"We'll dust every inch of your place for prints. Bowman's, too."

"Don't waste your time," I said. "The Sables are rich enough to hire people who know how to get the job done. You won't find any prints."

I regretted telling him this on my phone. Face-to-face, I might have been able to calm him down. And now that he knew I was surrounded by seven Humane Hearts volunteers, Kit decided to interrogate all of the Sables again today. This time the Sables would encounter a sheriff's deputy in a much worse mood than just a few hours ago.

Aunt Vicki grabbed my phone. "Don't worry, Kit. We'll swing by Marlee's house, pick up the animals, and bring her to my place for tonight."

I took the phone back. "I'm not letting the Sables make me afraid to stay in my own house. Besides, they've already been inside and found nothing. Why would they come back?"

"To scare you," Kit replied. "Or worse."

The discussion ended when Aunt Vicki and Joe assured Kit they would spend the night at my house. Since I was a little shaky from my encounter with Cameron, I welcomed the suggestion. Kit insisted he would spend the night as well, which was even better. I thought that was that, and I could concentrate on setting out cage traps for the cats, while also searching for suspicious mulberries on the property.

But news travels fast in Oriole Point, thanks to the other volunteers working with us. By the time I returned home, I found Tess and Natasha waiting for me in the driveway.

After our conversation, Kit had informed Old Man Bowman that someone had illegally searched his cabin. An angry Bowman passed the news on to Natasha. Tess found out about the break-ins from Marie the librarian, who heard it from Paige, the sales clerk at Gemini Rising, who heard it from Dean, who heard it from his mother at the police station. In an hour, I suspected the news would reach someone's cousin in Chicago.

By eight o'clock that night, the pajama party had officially begun. After adding a leaf to the antique table in my dining room, I sat down to a pizza dinner with Kit, Tess, Natasha, Dean, Andrew, Aunt Vicki, Joe, Theo, and Old Man Bowman. I didn't even bother to ask how Theo had found out. All of us wore pajamas and robes, even the intrepid Bigfoot hunter. And David promised to join us as soon as he finished working on his last set of glass pumpkins. Natasha brought Dasha, her Yorkshire terrier, whose barking convinced Panther to observe the proceedings from atop the dining-room buffet.

The room was filled with the smells of pepperoni, cheese, and lively conversation. And friends. None of them had to be here tonight, but they were. Simply to make me feel safe, and to help me forget the terrible thing that happened today.

Looking up from his pizza, Kit saw that I was moved. He reached over and squeezed my hand. "I like your friends," he said softly. "And your aunt."

I smiled back. "I like them, too."

Andrew heard us. "She likes me best," he piped up.

"I don't think so." Old Man Bowman took another slice of pizza from the five different pies laid out on the table. He winked at Kit.

"I think you're the favorite," Theo said as he cut his pizza slice with a knife and fork.

Kit and I looked at each other. "I hope so," he said softly.

For a moment, it felt like we were the only ones in the room. Maybe it was a good thing we weren't. Or I might have fallen into his arms again and cried. Lord knows, I had cried enough for one day. It wasn't like me to be so weepy, but my equilibrium had been shaken this past summer. The betrayal by a man I thought I would marry, combined with violent death, secrets, and far too much danger, had left me feeling vulnerable. I knew I could be wounded, physically and emotionally. But I also didn't know how to protect myself. Or if I even wanted to.

And as much as I feared being hurt again, I couldn't let it prevent me from helping someone who came to me for help. Or from letting myself love again.

Kit put down his pizza and gathered me close. "Don't cry, Marlee," he whispered. "I'm here." He hugged me even closer. "And I love you."

That did bring me to tears. "I love you, too," I whispered back.

It was the first time we had admitted our love for each other. Not how I'd pictured it happening, with Dean and Andrew fighting over the last can of Diet Coke, Minnie singing Ba-ba-ba Ba-ba ba-Ran, and Natasha ordering the yapping Dasha to be quiet in Russian. Although it somehow felt perfectly right.

"Get a room, you two," Tess said with a laugh. "Oh

wait a minute. You've got four bedrooms in this house. I'll amend that to, go to your room."

Kit and I broke apart, exchanging smiles.

"Not until we've had dessert," Dean said. "I brought five bags of candy. I say we get a head start on Halloween."

"We shouldn't eat the Halloween candy," Theo told him. "It's for the children."

I looked at Dean. "Speaking of Halloween, I still don't know what your costume for the parade will be."

His brother answered for him. "He stole my Broadway theme. Only he's much cheaper than Oscar and me. Do you know how much we paid for our *Hamilton* costumes? A lot. All Dean is wearing is a white shirt, black tie, and black pants. And he bought a book. Big deal."

"I don't get it," Tess said. "What are you supposed to be?"

I laughed. "You're going as a missionary from *The Book of Mormon,* aren't you?"

Dean nodded in acknowledgment. "Subtle, simple, different."

"And cheap," Andrew repeated.

"I cannot find my golden snake," Natasha wailed. "It is lost at conference center. How can I be Cleopatra without the snake that bites with poison?"

Old Man Bowman picked up his bottle of beer, "Don't worry. I got lots of snakes at home. I'll find you a snake to wear with that costume."

Natasha looked thrilled at the offer. I didn't think she understood that he meant an actual snake.

"After everything that's happened, I'm looking forward to Halloween," I said. "I love when the children come trick-or-treating at the shops. Then I get to watch them in the afternoon parade. They're so cute. And I can't wait to put on my own costume."

Tess sighed. "David plans to wear his chipmunk costume all day and night. I warned him he has to take the head off every thirty minutes, otherwise he'll overheat and pass out."

"If so, people will think he's a zombie chipmunk," Dean said. "He might even win 'Best Costume.'"

"Nah, I'm gonna win," Old Man Bowman announced.

"What's your costume?" Joe asked.

All of us answered at the same time, "Bigfoot!"

The doorbell interrupted our laughter.

Kit grew serious instantly. "If that's another Sable, I swear I'll arrest them. I spent hours today questioning the whole clan and their flunkies. I'm out of patience."

Tess jumped up. "Let me see who it is."

We looked at each other. All evening we had managed to avoid talking about Ellen, the Sables, Felix Bonaventure, and that missing laptop computer. Time enough to worry about it tomorrow. Or the day after. There was a limit to how much danger and sorrow I wanted to deal with. Especially since I had nothing to do with any of the murders, starting with the poor nanny.

Tess came back with a wide smile. She was followed by Piper, Lionel, and five men carrying boxes of equipment.

None of us knew what to say. Even Minnie grew quiet.

"How nice to see both of you." I smiled at Piper and Lionel. "And your friends. Only I'm not certain why you came."

"We came because I heard your house had been ransacked by employees of Dr. Sable." She sounded insulted. "That is unacceptable."

"And illegal," Tess added.

"To think a man of his renown would sanction such a thing!" Piper jerked on her blazer in anger. "And after I invited his family to be our guests. They have abused my hospitality."

Lionel laid a hand on her shoulder. "My wife has been most upset. She blames herself for these break ins. I told her there was no way she could have guessed the Sables would stoop to such levels."

She sighed. "We can't let them get away with this. Who knows what Dr. Sable will instruct his people to do next. Oriole Point and its citizens must be protected."

"If he used professionals," Kit said, "there's no way to prove it. And I'm certain he did."

"They come back to my house again, I got a surprise waitin' for them." Old Man Bowman sent Kit a warning look. "Don't ask unless you really want to know."

"Please don't ask," I whispered to Kit.

"We can at least protect one of our citizens." Lionel gave me a benevolent smile.

"I don't understand," I said.

Piper waved at the men standing behind her and Lionel. "These are the gentlemen who installed my home-security system. They are here to do the same for you, Marlee. No one will ever be able to break into your house again."

"They're going to install it tonight?" I asked.

She snapped her fingers at them. "Immediately."

The five men took off for parts unknown in my house.

"Now I'm afraid we'll never be able to get out," Dean muttered.

I looked down at Kit, who shrugged, "It's not a bad idea," he said.

I didn't know what to think about it, but Minnie spoke for all of us when she said, "Oh my Gawd."

Chapter Twenty-four

I wished I'd scheduled someone besides the Little Mermaid to work the Saturday shift at The Berry Basket. But since Gillian now lived near campus, she only came to town on weekends. Which meant she worked Saturdays.

Today, however, she wasn't much help. She hadn't told me that she planned to come to work wearing a costume. A pity. I could have warned her a slinky fishtail skirt, waist-length red wig, and a necklace of large seashells weren't conducive to making berry smoothies and scooping ice cream.

In fact, I suspected her voluminous wig put us in violation of the health department's rules—at least around the ice cream and pastry counters.

"Gillian, why don't you let me handle the food today?" I suggested as I boxed cupcakes for a customer. "You can take care of the register."

"Thanks, Marlee." She minced over to the register. Her ankle-length green skirt didn't leave a lot of wriggle room . . . literally. "And I'm sorry about the costume. I thought because I'm wearing this for the parade tonight, I might as well keep it on all day. Not my wisest decision."

"Look at it this way. You're the most glamorous person we've ever had in the shop." We exchanged smiles before Gillian turned her attention to cashing out a young couple, while I tied string around the box of cupcakes.

Theo had exceeded expectations with his pastry selections this morning. Because it was Halloween, he made Strawberry Ghosts dipped in white chocolate, Berry Spooky Cupcakes (which I especially loved because of their blood red raspberry puree batter), and the vegan and gluten-free Halloween Bloody Cups, Theo's version of peanut butter cups using raspberry sauce filling. He rounded out the Halloween selection with a surprising choice: mulberry cookie bars covered with orange icing. Theo told me he made them to honor the Lake Lady. All I could think was how much Ellen would have loved them.

I'd sampled all the pastries this morning, along with the Halloween candy on the counter. I fully expected to go into sugar shock by dinnertime.

Only the customers saved me from nonstop snacking. There were a lot of them today, all in a festive mood. It took Halloween to finally draw them away from that Harvest Health Fair. It helped that the day was sunny and sixty degrees, ideal conditions not only for trick-or-treating, but the pumpkin carving contest in River Park and the Children's Parade at two.

Gillian and I were kept busy, but there was an occasional lull. This let me fill her in on all that had occurred since last weekend.

Every few sentences she interrupted me to say, "Are you kidding?"

When I was done, she shook her head and said, "Wow."

"Exactly."

"I feel so bad for Leticia. Or should I call her 'Ellen'?" She frowned. "Now I wish I had tried to be-friend her."

"I don't think it would have mattered."

"What are the police going to do about her death? And this Felix guy? I mean, if one of the Sables killed them . . ."

"They're far too influential and powerful. We need proof, not just our suspicions." I watched out the window as people began to line up along the sidewalk for the parade. "That's why I have to find that laptop. I think she hid it somewhere on her property. Then covered it with mulberries so I'd find it. But I didn't see anything when I was there yesterday. I'll go out to-morrow. Not alone, of course. I'm not making that mistake again."

"Let the police search for it, Marlee. You're already got the entire Sable family believing you have her computer. The last thing you want is to actually find it. If they killed two people for it, they won't stop at you." Gillian gave me a stern look, difficult to do in that wig.

Denise Redfern stuck her head in our open door. "Parade's about to start!"

None of us wanted to miss the sight of all those kids marching down Lyall Street, many accompanied by their leashed dogs, also in costume.

I helped Gillian wiggle her way out of the store, then locked the door behind us. It was already crowded, and we had to search to find an empty space along the curb.

Two thunderous gongs reverberated overhead. Several children screamed, while Gillian covered her ears. I glared at the bell tower down the street.

"I swear, that thing gets louder every day," I complained. "I might end up paying Old Man Bowman to come here and shoot it down."

Gillian straightened her wig. "Let me know if you do. I'll chip in a hundred bucks."

I twirled on my front porch as two young girls clapped. My ankle-length gown flowed about me.

"Are you a fairy queen?" one of them asked with wide eyes.

"Don't be silly," the other said. "She's a dragon queen. Look at the dragons." She pointed to the small dragons attached to my costume. Two on my skirt, one on my shoulder.

"She's right." I exchanged smiles with the girls' parents. "And my name is Daenerys."

Of course I didn't expect the children to recognize my favorite character from *Game of Thrones*. But they got the general idea. And in my silver gown and flowing white wig, I did resemble a queen. I couldn't wait for everyone at the adult parade to see it. Especially Kit. Unfortunately, he couldn't join me for the trick-or-treating at my house. Ellen Nagy's relatives arrived earlier today to claim the body, and the entire department had been occupied with the Nagy family. But he swore he would meet me in time for the adult parade later. Dressed as Jon Snow, as promised.

"Where's Queen Cersei?" the little girls' father asked with a chuckle.

"I made her stay away." I gave them my most imperial look. "I'm the only queen here."

"How about Jon Snow?" their mother said. "I thought he'd be here, too."

"Jon had business at Winterfell." I smiled at the next wave of trick-or-treaters climbing my porch steps. "But I shall see him soon. My dragons will fly me there."

I continued my Daenerys performance while handing out candy from a big wicker basket. The weather continued to cooperate with a gentle breeze, and temperatures dropping oh so slowly as the sun set. Orange lights twinkled from where I had entwined them about my porch and shrubs. Four jack-o'-lanterns also flickered along the path that led from the sidewalk to the porch.

A glance in either direction along Lakeshore Drive revealed costumed children, rushing from house to house. The night air rang with squeals of laughter and cries of "trick or treat!" So far, Halloween had been wonderful. And after the week I had had, I wished the fun could go on forever.

But an hour later, this part of the festivities had drawn to a close. Since the children began trick-or-treating before the sun set, they were worn out by seven. I looked down at the basket. Empty, except for three peanut butter cups, which I quickly ate.

I'd spend extra hours at the gym this week to make up for the candy consumption. Basket in hand, I gave a last look at the street, pumpkins flickering in either direction.

With a contented sigh, I went inside. I'd left Minnie

on her perch in the kitchen, and she greeted me with five consecutive "Trick or Treats." I had a feeling I would be hearing that phrase constantly for the next month. Even though it was a bit early, I decided to put Minnie in her sleep cage. I needed to decompress before the big parade, and conversation with Minnie was not the best way to relax.

She must have been tired, too. When I opened the door to her sleep cage, she quickly hopped on a perch. I placed the thin cover over the cage, giggling when I heard her murmur, "Trick or treat. Andrew is sweet."

I checked on Panther next. I had left the kitten in my sunroom with a mountain of cat toys. It must have tired him out because when I brought him up to my bedroom, he fell asleep after only a few minutes of petting. I left the bedroom before I was tempted to join him.

What I needed next was to eat something that wasn't covered in chocolate or drenched in sugar. I returned to the kitchen where I had earlier put together a kale salad with grilled chicken. I sat at my kitchen island and dug in.

I welcomed the sudden silence as much as the healthy food. Last night's pajama party had been fun and wonderfully distracting. And we had all stayed up much too late. However, I was used to living alone. I needed solitary time. Time to hear my own thoughts.

I glanced over at the small white box that Piper's security team installed on my wall yesterday. It had never occurred to me to worry about security, especially in Oriole Point. But after Cameron Sable revealed that my house had been searched, I saw the wisdom of such measures. At least while he and his cronies were in town.

And they were still a threat. Kit called earlier and told me Ellen's relatives were demanding answers about her death. Too little, too late, I thought. But their demands had compelled the police to instruct the Sables to remain in Oriole Point a few days longer. That sounded great for the investigation. Not so great for me.

While I ate my salad, I went over what I'd learned about the Nanny Murder. Why did Ellen become so unhappy during her last week on Mackinac Island? Ainsley had been unhappy enough to fire the nanny. And given how she described the French girl to me yesterday, it was clear Ainsley had been jealous, and not just over the baby. She implied Laeticia Murier was accustomed to getting her own way with men. Did that include Patrick Sable?

The nanny was unhappy, too, and apparently had been since their extended stay on St. Lucia. She found herself catering to a recuperating Ingrid, a depressed Ainsley, and a newborn. At least she'd found contentment in caring for the infant. In fact, the arrival of the baby helped her forget how miserable she was, at least according to Ingrid. Ingrid also said Laeticia threatened to leave several times that last summer. But she didn't. Why not? Was it really because she had grown fond of the lavish lifestyle of the Sables? Or was there another reason for her to stay?

I stopped eating. What if she had an added reason to care about the child? I thought back to the timeline of the final year of the nanny's life. She, Ingrid, and Ainsley spent the last five months of Ainsley's pregnancy on the island of St. Lucia. And remained there two months longer. Supposedly because they were concerned about Ainsley's extended morning sickness, followed by postpartum depression.

But what if Ainsley had never been pregnant? A child emerged out of the situation, so someone was pregnant. What if it was the nanny? If that were true, who was the father?

"A Sable," I said aloud. It had to be, otherwise why would Ainsley pretend the child was her own? And the rest of the family must have known. Had to have known.

But which Sable fathered the child? The teenaged Keith, perhaps. Or was it Patrick, Ainsley's husband? Joshua did look like the Sable men, even if he was better looking. In fact, there was a distinct resemblance between him and the photos of the young Laeticia Murier. Had Ainsley agreed to adopt the child fathered by her own husband with the nanny? It seemed outlandish, unless one had seen how much Ainsley wanted to please and emulate her mother-in-law. If Ingrid Sable told her to adopt the child, I felt certain Ainsley would.

But there was another Sable male who might have sired the baby. My stomach turned at the idea, but it was possible Joshua was the son—and not the grandson—of Cameron Sable.

This line of reasoning made me lose my appetite. I marched over to the sink to rinse my plate. As soon as I saw Kit tonight, I'd talk this over with him. See if I was completely crazy or if the scenario made sense.

Barking from the front of the house broke my train of thought.

I hurried down the hallway and peeked out the window beside the door. Two chocolate Labradors gamboled on my front lawn. They belonged to Doug Washington, my next-door neighbor. With a relieved smile, I stepped out on the porch.

Clapping my hands, I called out, "Pan! Cleo! What are you two doing?"

They galloped onto my porch, threw themselves against me, licked my face, then jumped off the porch once more.

"Don't mind them." Doug came into view. "I had them inside during the trick-or-treating. Now they've got energy to burn. I thought I'd play a few rounds of Frisbee with them." He held up a Frisbee. "But they prefer chasing each other at the moment."

"Looks like you gave them shots of espresso, too." I laughed as the dogs raced back and forth over my lawn, weaving around the jack-o'-lanterns.

"Big babies. We got back from Chicago this afternoon, where they were cooped up in my brother's apartment. I wanted to be here for Halloween though. I love to give out candy. And of course I can't miss the parade." He lifted up his arms to better display his black cowboy outfit. "I'm the bad guy this year. But you look like the forces of good. Daenerys, right?"

"Right. And Kit is coming as Jon Snow."

The dogs ran up to him, both trying to reach the Frisbee he held. "Oh, now you want to play." Doug sent the Frisbee flying.

The dogs dashed after it. The nearest street lamp was half a block down so I had no idea how the dogs would find the Frisbee in the dark. Doug threw it in the wrong direction too, at least for a game of night Frisbee.

Although my house faced Lake Michigan, Lakeshore Drive ran between it and the stairs that led to my beach. The narrow road didn't see much traffic, and I wasn't worried the dogs would get run over. However, the Labs might have a hard time finding the Frisbee on the wide grassy patch that overlooked the lake.

"Get back here," he called to them. "We'll find the Frisbee in the morning." He turned to me and shrugged. "I think they've lost interest in the Frisbee. They're jumping over your Adirondack chairs. Probably peeing on your mulberry trees, too."

"What did you say?" I said sharply.

"I was only kidding, Marlee. But they shouldn't be running wild on your property anyway. I'll get them."

While he ran to collect his Labs, I hurried into the house. When I ran out again, I held a flashlight. Doug had managed to get the dogs to follow him. They now decided to play Frisbee once more, but on his front lawn instead.

I headed for my mulberry trees. A week ago, I had my first conversation with Leticia. All of it focused on mulberries. When she requested a great quantity of the berries, I told her it was too bad she hadn't come to me in summer when the mulberry trees on my property dropped hundreds of berries. She claimed that was further evidence of the special power my mulberries had. *My* mulberries.

And at the conference center before the smoke bombs went off, I asked her where the manuscript was.

"Safe with the mulberries," she told me. "*Your* mulberries."

I wanted to knock myself on the head with the flashlight for only remembering that now. She knew there were other special mulberries besides those I had left on her porch. And those mulberry trees were literally right in front of me all this time.

When I reached my four Adirondack chairs, the area surrounding both them and the trees was visible in the moonlight. As was the lake glimmering below me. Still, I switched on the flashlight and swept it over the ground. Dead leaves were piled everywhere and I kicked them away. I walked around each mulberry tree, but saw nothing out of the ordinary. The nearby barking of Pan and Cleo continued unabated, which felt comforting.

I debated going to my garage for a shovel. But I didn't see anything suspicious on the ground, so where would I start digging? I almost sat down on one of the Adirondack chairs before remembering I had already slipped canvas covers on them, in preparation for winter.

I looked at the covered chairs. They sat directly beneath the biggest mulberry tree. Kneeling on the ground, I lifted each of the canvas covers. The beam from the flashlight revealed nothing under the first two. Beneath the third chair sat a metal box.

Holding my breath, I slowly pulled it out. The metal box wasn't locked. When I opened it, I saw a laptop computer. Covered in white mulberries.

Chapter Twenty-five

I wanted to make a mad dash to the house with the metal box. But in my long skirt, I worried I might trip and fall, damaging the computer. I also worried someone could be watching from the moon-dappled shadows around me. Clutching the box to my chest, I carefully walked back to the house. Doug and the dogs still played Frisbee on his lawn. Thank God for the boisterous Pan and Cleo. If they hadn't been out there, I might have grown panicky.

Still, my paranoia ran high. I gave a prayer of thanks to Piper when I punched in my new home security code. I'd turned the system on when I ran out to the mulberry trees, and felt confident no one lay in wait for me inside.

Once I locked the door behind me and set the laptop on my home-office desk, my anxiety worsened. If the Sables sent someone to watch me, they would have seen me take a suspicious box from beneath my trees. Under cover of night, too. It wouldn't take a Mensa scholar to know it held the laptop. I listened for any furtive sounds while hooking up the computer.

Fortunately, Ellen and I owned the same model

MacBook Pro. But she had taken no chances and included the charger in the box. Before turning it on, I suddenly hurried to the living room, where I had left the mulberry bracelet Ellen gave me. After I slipped the elastic band onto my wrist, I grew calmer. The bracelet's dried mulberries might not possess any special magical power, but they reminded me that, despite all her troubles, Ellen had wanted to keep me safe. I felt that she was nearby and watching out for me. And on All Hallows' Eve, too.

Sitting down at my desk, I turned on the computer. As the iconic apple appeared on the screen, I phoned Kit. When I got his voicemail, I groaned. I had no idea if he was still at the sheriff's department or had already gone off duty and went home to get into costume.

"Kit, I found the laptop," I said when the voicemail beep sounded. "She left it in a metal box under my mulberry tree. Please call me as soon as you can."

With the computer now on, I sighed when I saw the photo she had chosen for her screen saver: a haunting image of Lake Michigan. It wasn't enough for her to go to the beach to stare at the lake. She looked at the lake every time she used her laptop.

The tragic sadness of her life and premature death struck me again. I told myself this was not the time to grieve. Not when I had the story someone was willing to kill for right in front of me. Leticia had left it in my custody, knowing I would let the public know the truth about the Nanny Murder. First, I had to learn what that truth was.

Although the desktop displayed folders labeled "Felix Bonaventure," "Sable Family," "Mulberries," and "Nanny Murder," the one I clicked on was "Mischief and Murder." In the folder I found the manuscript itself, which began with a dedication: *To Laeticia Murier, who has waited too long for the truth to be known. I have never forgotten you. I never will. I hope this book makes you rest easier. I am no longer afraid. And justice will be done.*

I began to read the first chapter, and soon lost track of time. When my mantel clock chimed at nine o'clock, it startled me. It also served as a reminder that I still hadn't heard from Kit. Maybe he was too busy to check his phone and intended to meet me as planned at my shop before the parade. Since the parade began at ten o'clock, I needed to read faster.

Soon after, I sat back, shaken. I now knew who killed the nanny. When I called Kit again, he picked up. I quickly told him what had happened, and he instructed me to stay put until he got to my house. He had just changed into his costume and could be at my house in less than half an hour.

I listened to the silence in my house. Was it too silent perhaps? No doubt I was spooking myself, but I felt like a sitting duck. Yes, I had a security system, but it wouldn't stop anyone from breaking in. The killer could finish me off and grab the laptop long before Kit even left his apartment in New Bethel.

"I think I'm safer waiting at my store. There are thousands of people right now on Lyall Street, in town for the parade. I'll lock myself inside the store and wait for you there."

He promised to be there as soon as he could.

Picking up the metal box, I got ready to unplug the computer so I could take it with me. I stopped. What if I was waylaid between here and Oriole Point, even if it was only a three-minute drive? I needed to make

certain the manuscript wouldn't be lost even if the
computer was.

Opening Leticia's email app, I attached the manuscript file to a message and sent it to myself. Once I
retrieved the message on my computer, I dashed off
an email of my own. I'd send this message to Kit, the
state police, and Chief Hitchcock. Next, I attached
the manuscript to the message. Just as I was about to
send it off, I remembered someone else I'd be wise to
mail it to. After checking the email address on my
phone, I added Delta Marsh to the message. I hit Send.

The laptop might end up stolen or destroyed. But
I'd made certain the manuscript survived. Now I had
to make sure I survived as well.

I heard the crowds in downtown Oriole Point
before I reached Lyall Street. People came from all
over Michigan and Illinois for this night. With many
more traveling here from Indiana, Ohio, and Wiscon-
sin. It was our version of Mardi Gras. Judging by the
rowdy noise of the thousands thronging downtown, it
was clear they had been celebrating for quite a while.

The cross streets to Lyall were closed to traffic, forcing me to take a circuitous route by the marina, then
illegally drive over a patch of harborside lawn in order
to reach the small parking lot behind my store. Everyone would be fighting for parking tonight, so I'd left
two traffic cones in my shop-owner parking space.
Accompanied by a sign warning people they would be
ticketed if they parked there. It wasn't true, but it
often worked. Tonight it did.

After I went in the back entrance to The Berry

Basket, I made sure to not only lock the door behind me, but placed several rolling bakery shelves in front of it. If someone tried to break in from the back, the falling shelves would alert me.

I looked down at the metal box I held. Kit would be here soon, but I wanted to hide it nonetheless. Who knew what was in the rest of the files? My small cramped office would be the first place someone would look. The storage room ran a close second. There were few places to tuck anything away in Theo's immaculate kitchen.

In pursuit of a hiding spot, I walked into the shop. The only illumination inside came from a string of orange lights I'd draped around the front counter. However, the town put up large lights along the sidewalk for the parade, almost as bright as the lights seen on outdoor film sets. These cast more than enough light inside the store.

I wandered about the shop, taking care to sidestep the decorative pumpkins, scarecrows, and hay bales scattered about the floor. The shelves were too small to conceal a laptop, and they were crammed with merchandise besides. Behind the counter would be as obvious as my office. So where to put it?

I went to the front window to look at the hordes of costumed people on the sidewalk. No one looked back. Indeed, everyone was too busy fighting for a place closer to the curb. The crowd was already three deep and growing. Most of the revelers wore costumes, even if they didn't plan to be in the parade. The restaurants and bars held costume parties and contests afterward, with drinks flowing freely. It was time to party. The noise level was high and not just from the crowd. A sidewalk sound system blared

Halloween music and spooky sound effects. Right now, Michael Jackson's "Thriller" thundered outside.

I wished I could be out there enjoying it as I usually did. This was my favorite night all year. Much more fun than New Year's Eve. Instead I found myself hiding in my store. And hoping the killer avoided downtown tonight.

Someone dressed as a scarecrow walked past. That prompted me to straighten the hat of the scarecrow that sat in my front window display. A scarecrow wearing a Berry Basket T-shirt, of course. I cast a rueful eye at all the straw scattered in the window. I really had gone overboard. There was enough straw in there to bury the scarecrow.

Or a laptop.

After I made certain no one outside was looking at the window, I quickly buried the laptop and metal box beneath a virtual mountain of straw. Placing a big cloth pumpkin over it, I gave it a pat. Then I touched my mulberry bracelet for good luck.

I stood watching the crowd. No one cast a suspicious glance at my store. Good. The laptop and I should be safe until Kit arrived. I didn't bother to call the police. Virtually every officer was on crowd control duty tonight. The parade would be over by eleven o'clock, at which point, I'd find Chief Hitchcock. At the moment he had his hands full trying to control drunken revelers. I just needed to sit tight until then. Besides, I had already told Kit who the killer was, at least according to *Mischief and Murder*. I didn't ask what he intended to do with the info, but I hoped it included sending a sheriff's car to the hotel where the Sables were staying.

The *Phantom of the Opera* walked past my window and peeked in. He suddenly stopped, his mask turned toward me. I hoped it was merely someone who admired my *Game of Thrones* costume. It had been a mistake to stand here in clear view outfitted as Daenerys. Dragons, included. I was hardly unobtrusive.

The Phantom waved. I cautiously waved back. This encouraged him to walk to the shop entrance and pull on the locked door.

I froze, hoping he would go away. He knocked. Maybe it was a friend. Someone I could convince to leave.

He seemed persistent. I went over to the glass shop door. "Sorry, we're closed."

The Phantom removed his mask. It was Theo. "Let me in, Marlee."

After ushering him inside, I locked the door again.

"Why are you in the store?" he asked. "It's more fun out there."

"I'm waiting for Kit." This wasn't the time to explain about the hidden laptop and the killer looking for it.

"If you want to march in the parade, you have to go to the end of the street and get in line." He wore a worried expression. "You don't want to be late."

"We won't. But I told Kit to meet me here."

He pointed at my silver gown. "I like your costume. You should wear the white wig all the time. It makes you look like a princess or queen."

"That's the idea. I like your costume, too." Beneath his long black cloak, he wore a black jacket, white shirt, dark pants, and the replica of the white mask worn by every Broadway Phantom.

He turned around so I could fully appreciate his costume.

"I thought you'd come as a *Star Wars* character," I said. "I know how much you like Han, Luke, and Finn."

"I almost dressed as Kylo Ren. But I remembered how Andrew called me the Phantom when I first moved here. I thought he'd like it if I dressed as the Phantom for my first Halloween parade."

"Wonderful idea. Andrew will be thrilled." I gave him a hug. Theo didn't understand that he had been dubbed the Phantom because he kept to himself so much during his first months here. Indeed, we saw him so little, we used to say we might not believe he existed if not for the berry pastries he left every morning in the shop kitchen.

"Don't tell anyone that the shirt and jacket are attached to each other," he said in a whisper. "It looks like they're two different pieces."

"Very nice. They should make all suits like that. Men could get dressed faster."

"And I added the cloak, even though it belonged to a vampire costume. It makes me look scarier."

"Elegant, too. I love a good cloak."

"Well, I have to go now." Theo slipped on the white mask that covered half of his face. It turned the boyish-looking baker into a sinister character. Amazing what a simple mask can do. "You should leave soon, Marlee. You don't want to miss the parade."

"Don't worry."

I unlocked the door and let him out. But first I gave him another hug. Theo was like the little brother I never had, even if he was older. A most endearing little brother, too.

After he left, I sat at one of the bistro tables and

texted Kit. It would be useless to text or call any of my friends. They were all part of that raucous crowd and would never hear their phones. Someone knocked on the door again.

I craned my neck from where I sat and peeked out the door. The Phantom was back. Theo had left no more than five minutes ago. I hoped nothing was wrong.

I got up and let him in again. He walked past me without saying a word.

After locking up, I went over to him. "You just left, Theo. Why are you back so soon?"

That half-hidden face stared at me in silence.

I glimpsed street clothes beneath the long black cloak. "You're not Theo."

"No. I'm not." He pushed back his mask.

The bright streetlights spilling into my dark shop revealed exactly who it was.

The man who killed Ellen, Felix Bonaventure, and the nanny.

Chapter Twenty-six

Fear swept over me at the sight of Keith Sable. "What did you do to Theo?" I cried.

Frantic with worry, I made a dash for the door. Before I could unlock it, Keith yanked me into the center of the store. He flung me onto one of the bistro chairs so violently, one of the dragons velcroed to my skirt went flying.

"Tell me where the laptop is," he demanded.

"I swear, if you've harmed Theo, I'll shoot an arrow into you myself!"

"He's alive and well. Which is more than will be said for you if you don't be quiet."

"Where is Theo?" I crouched forward, preparing to push past him. "How did you get his cloak and mask?"

Keith stood in front of me, barring my way. "I took it from him. But I asked nicely. Or rather, my assistant did."

"Your assistant? More like a henchman."

"Let's call him an employee. I asked him to stop your friend and pay him for the mask and cloak. He was paid more than he probably makes in a week." Keith looked down at his cloak. "So now I'm dressed for the occasion. And with a mask to conceal my identity."

The store clock hung in the shadows, but it had to be almost ten. Kit swore he would be here before the parade. Any minute, he might turn up. And Keith didn't appear to have a weapon on him, but that cloak could conceal a knife or a gun. Maybe both.

"How did you know where I was?"

"Someone was assigned to watch your house earlier."

I tensed up. Had they seen me take a box from beneath the mulberry tree? "Did they enjoy watching me give out candy?" I tried to sound casual.

"No. Once the children were gone and you went inside, I told them to come to town and watch your store instead."

Thank God they left before I went out to the mulberry trees. "Why?"

"Piper told us that everyone who lives here marches in the parade. I knew you'd show up later on. And your SUV has Berry Basket painted all over it. Hard to miss. One of my men saw you head for the back parking lot." His voice hardened. "He said you carried a box inside."

"Pastries," I replied.

"Don't take me for a fool. You have the laptop. And you brought it into the store. No one but your *Phantom of the Opera* buddy has been here. I saw you let him in. And when he left, he didn't carry a box. That means it's here now. I'll ask you again. Where is it?"

My mind raced through everything in the store that resembled a box. Store pastries not sold earlier were wrapped in plastic in the display case. And a pan of mulberry cookie bars were in the kitchen. I didn't have any boxed desserts in the store at the moment. Except for one.

"If you look in the kitchen, you'll see a sheet cake in a white box. It's a birthday cake for my friend Tess. That's what your goon saw me bring in."

We all planned to meet back here after the parade for cake and champagne. Theo had baked her birthday cake this morning: chocolate with raspberry filling, its frosting decorated with pumpkins, bats, and ghosts. And a single oriole to honor her studio shop, Oriole Glass. Theo had left the cake boxed on the kitchen counter.

"I can go back there and get it for you."

He grabbed my arm again. "We'll both go."

As soon as we reached the kitchen, Keith flipped open the cake box and swore under his breath. Only a birthday cake was inside.

He turned a furious face in my direction. "Where is the laptop Ellen gave you?"

"All she gave me were cryptic clues, like the manuscript was safe with my mulberries."

"I know that. The night Scarlett and I came to your house, you mentioned the mulberries. As soon as I got in the car, I texted my brother. He sent someone over there to rip open the boxes of mulberries on her porch. The manuscript was there, but not the laptop."

"You sent someone that night? Kit and I must have missed him by minutes."

"Lucky you did miss him." The tone in his voice implied that a body or two might have been the result if we had caught the intruder in the act.

"How did you know there were boxes of mulberries on her porch anyway?" I asked, then stopped. "You'd been there before, hadn't you?"

He nodded. "Tuesday morning. Early, so my absence at the conference center wouldn't be noted. My parents sent me there, hoping I could convince Ellen to hand over the laptop and manuscript. But she was gone and her house locked. I would have broken in, but Bonaventure drove up. We had a long talk out on the front lawn. He was most unreasonable."

"In other words, he refused to let you intimidate him."

"He was even immune to an exorbitant offer of money. He insisted he would find a publisher for *Mischief and Murder*, and it didn't matter how many lawsuits the Sables threatened him with. The book would prove Ellen had been wrongly accused of murder, and he was proud to help her." Keith's voice rang with scorn. "There was no point negotiating further with him. I thought fear might be more motivating. So I showed him the gun."

"The gun?" If he hadn't had such a grip on my arm, I would have taken a step back.

"I'm licensed to carry a handgun, a necessity when one is as wealthy as I am. When I pulled the gun out, he ran off into the field, believing I meant to shoot him then and there. Which would have been stupid with a gun easily traced to me."

"You chased after him, didn't you? That's when you saw the bow and arrow that Ellen had left out in the field."

"It was as if the Universe had smiled down on me. Virtually handing me a weapon. A weapon I knew how to use, given my frequent bow-hunting trips. I called for Mr. Bonaventure to stop, and he made the mistake of turning around rather than keep on running. Otherwise I would have shot him in the back, instead of straight through the heart. Poor fellow looked so surprised."

I winced at the image.

"Dead before he hit the ground," he continued with an air of pride. "Only my mother could have hit the target more cleanly."

"I wouldn't brag about such a thing," I muttered.

"Well, I would," he shot back. "My only mistake was leaving right afterward. I should have waited for Ellen. But I couldn't guarantee she'd be alone, and I missed my chance to break into her house. When she returned home and saw the body, Ellen obviously fled. But first she hid her manuscript in one of the boxes on the porch. And took the laptop with her."

Dragging me back to the shop, Keith pushed me against the ice-cream counter. "All right. Where did you hide the computer? I know it's in this shop."

"It's not." Maybe I could pretend I'd hidden it elsewhere.

"You are forcing me to hurt you. And for what? Out of some strange loyalty to a crazy woman who wasn't even your friend? That was the ghostwriter's mistake. And look what happened to him." He stepped away from me, as though trying to control his temper. "My family has already destroyed everything Bonaventure possessed regarding the manuscript."

Including him, I thought.

"And the last printed copy of *Mischief and Murder* was found in that box of mulberries. Now that it's been shredded, the only thing we need is the laptop containing the file."

"You all seem pretty upset over a book written by a so-called crazy woman," I observed.

"Oh, my family thinks the entire book is a pack of lies. But those lies could damage us. Therefore it's imperative we find her laptop. Which I know you have."

"You don't know that at all. You're guessing."

"I'm a good guesser."

If Kit was on the way, he was taking his sweet time. Although time stood still when I was confronted with danger. "You're also a murderer."

"Unavoidable. Mr. Bonaventure would be alive today if he had been smart."

"And Ellen?"

He gave a mock sigh. "Ellen's been a thorn in my family's side for a long time. That's why I was the one asked to deal with her that morning. Ellen and I have a history, after all."

I pretended to think this over so I could move away from my trapped position by the counter. I slowly walked along the edge of the shop, kicking aside the occasional scarecrow on the floor. Keith followed.

"Your family sent you there to murder her?" I asked.

"Don't be absurd. We're not the Borgias. None of them has ever killed anything, aside from white-tail deer on our Georgia hunting trips." His chuckle had a nasty sound. "Except for Laeticia Murier. And that was my doing. Not theirs."

"Are you telling me your family had nothing to do with Ellen's death?"

"I disposed of Ellen. My family had no idea she was living in a treehouse just a short drive away from the hotel. But I knew. I saw her late one evening on that scooter, disappearing into the woods. After that, I waited for my chance to surprise her. My chance arrived yesterday."

Bile rose in my throat. I felt sick at hearing him talk about her murder so casually. "And are the other Sables unaware you killed Bonaventure?"

"They believe Ellen murdered Bonaventure. And why wouldn't they? She's been unstable for years. And she did confess to the murder of the family nanny."

"Not at first." I had now reached the shelves that held my berry wine bottles. A heavy bottle made a good weapon, as long as I chose the right moment to use it.

"No. I persuaded her to confess. She didn't have much choice after I convinced the bosun who witnessed the murder to tell a more plausible story. All about a jealous teenager who pushed her rival off the boat. I warned Ellen that she had no chance of being found innocent. But if she agreed to confess, I'd make certain she got a lighter sentence. And I did. My family had no reason to doubt this scenario." He shrugged. "Perhaps they had a few doubts. But none of them cared for Laeticia or Ellen, therefore it didn't matter."

"How did you persuade the bosun to lie?"

"I have a certain persuasive charm," he went on. "Along with a lot of money. I convinced one of the family attorneys to let me tap into my trust fund earlier than planned. As I said, I can be persuasive. And the attorney was female and easily convinced. I have a way with women."

"Not all women," I said with disgust.

"Well, Ellen was susceptible to my charms. That's why the family asked me to speak with her." He took a step closer. "I told them I found Bonaventure dead in the field. That Ellen must have shot him while in a paranoid frame of mind. She was rarely anything but paranoid."

"No thanks to you and your family. And they believed that?"

"Who wouldn't they? She'd been sent to prison for murder in a shaky mental condition. And she had a long history of emotional problems dating back to her childhood."

"How convenient. Gave you an excuse to pin the murder of the nanny on her."

"And Mr. Bonaventure." He smiled. "My parents instructed me to let the police discover the body. We didn't want to be connected in any way to his death. And I doubt we would have, except for those stunts Ellen pulled. They called attention to us." His smile vanished. "As you did. Always determined to defend her."

"I was right. She was innocent." Anger warred with caution. Then again, how safe was I, locked in the store with a murderer? "And you finally killed her. Like you almost did the night Laeticia Murier died."

He snapped his fingers in my face and I flinched. "I knew you read the manuscript! And you have the laptop. Therefore you already know why I killed Laeticia Murier."

No time for games. "Fine. I read the manuscript. Laeticia became pregnant with your child. A child fathered during one of your visits home from college. You wanted her to have an abortion, but she refused."

"A cunning, selfish girl determined to trap me." His voice shook, as if twenty-eight years was still not long enough to quiet his rage. "But I had no intention of supporting a child I didn't want. I almost killed her when she told me about the pregnancy. Luckily, my family stepped in. Ainsley had miscarried three times. Both she and my brother were desperate to have a child. They offered to adopt Laeticia's baby as their own. After all, the child was a blood relative."

"It was your child, too," I reminded him.

"I look on Joshua as my nephew, not my son. And Patrick and Ainsley have been happy with the choice. My parents love their first grandson. In fact, he's their favorite. It all worked out."

"Except for Laeticia." I inched my hand behind me to where the wine bottles were stacked on the store shelf. "And Ellen."

"They did it to themselves. Laeticia claimed to be in love with me. That was why she wanted to keep the baby. To tie us together. That's why she tricked me into getting her pregnant."

My fingers curled around the neck of the closest bottle. "Sure. You had nothing to do with the pregnancy. Just an innocent bystander."

"Pretty much. I was a horny teenager seduced by a woman in her twenties." He laughed. "A Frenchwoman, too. I never stood a chance. But my parents paid her handsomely to pretend it was Ainsley's baby. Laeticia even got a nice long vacation in St. Lucia out of it. All she had to do afterward was pack her bags and go back to France. If she had, Laeticia would be living in a fancy apartment in Paris right now, with her second or third husband. Instead, she refused to go. Refused to honor the deal she struck with my family."

"The manuscript claims Laeticia didn't want to leave her baby. And she agreed to stay on as Patrick and Ainsley's nanny in order to be near her son."

"Then threatened to sue for custody. Said she wanted us to raise our child together." His anger seemed to grow as he talked about it. Without warning, Keith overturned a nearby display table of Berry Basket sweatshirts, making me jump.

As he kicked at the shirts on the floor, I hid the wine bottle in the folds of my skirt.

"*People* magazine had just done a story on the first Sable grandchild," he continued. "Patrick, Ainsley, and Joshua were on the cover. We'd been pretending for four months that the baby was theirs. Now the nanny wanted to go public and tell the world Patrick Sable's brother knocked her up! And that the family paid her to be silent and go away. How do you think that would have affected our business?"

"You killed the mother of your child to protect the family brand?"

"Damn right I did." If I could have clearly seen his face, I'm sure it would have been beet red. "Did you think I'd let myself be blackmailed by her? But I gave her a chance. Tried to make Laeticia understand we had no future together. That's why I started a relationship with Ellen on Mackinac Island. I even proposed to Ellen, hoping it might make Laeticia realize it was over between us."

I glanced out the window, praying to see Kit. "According to *Mischief and Murder,* she became even more distraught when you announced your engagement to Ellen."

In fact, Laeticia went to Ellen during that final week and told her everything. How the young man Ellen agreed to marry had gotten another woman pregnant the year before and then discarded her.

Even worse, he handed the baby over to his brother like he was a pair of shoes Keith regretted buying. She warned Ellen that Keith would toss her aside, too. All Laeticia wanted now was her baby. And she asked Ellen to help her.

"Now I understand why Ellen became unhappy at the end of your stay on Mackinac Island," I said. "She'd learned you had only proposed because you wanted to push Laeticia further away. And that you were part of the family's web of lies about the baby."

"When we boarded the yacht, I had two demanding women to deal with. My parents told me to handle Laeticia gently. That I should leave it to them to employ their money and their attorneys to keep Laeticia silent. I was not to upset her further. But she was always upset."

"According to the book, Ellen was upset, too," I said.

"More than upset. Enraged." Keith must have decided to search for the laptop. He began to pull open the bottom drawers of a wooden hutch filled with berry jams. "After she learned about the baby, Ellen turned on me. She feared my family would keep Laeticia's child from her. Ellen promised she would do anything she could to help Laeticia."

I had only known Ellen a few short days, but it was long enough to appreciate her steadfast determination. It had gotten her sent to prison. And then killed.

"I warned Ellen." He opened the drawers so roughly, jam jars toppled to the floor in a tinkle of broken glass. "I tried to make her see reason. She was more stubborn than I realized, and vowed to protect Laeticia and the baby. We argued that night while everyone was below in their cabins being sick. She was so caught up being self-righteous, she forgot her fear of water and followed me out on deck."

"Led there by you." I edged my way to the front door. "The manuscript says Laeticia went to look for Ellen because she knew Ellen was afraid of water. She was worried about her. With reason. She found the two of you outside." I paused, recalling what I had read earlier that night. "And you had your hands around Ellen's throat."

He turned his attention from the drawers and stared at me for a long uncomfortable moment. "I hadn't even applied any pressure yet. Before I could, Laeticia rushed over to save her. I had a split second to decide which of the two posed the most risk. I knew Laeticia would always be a threat. A mother's love and all that. The choice was easy."

A murderous choice is always easy for a psychopath, I thought.

Realizing that I had moved, Keith walked over to me. I froze. He now stood so close, his breath moved the white strands of my wig.

"I also knew Ellen had a history of emotional instability. No one would believe her when she told the truth. And no one did." He put his face even closer. "I repeat, the choice was easy."

"So is this choice." I swung the bottle at his head. It landed with a satisfying thunk.

As he fell to his knees, I ran for the door. On the other side looking in stood a man I recognized. Dennis, the man who waited outside the car the day I spoke with Cameron. He looked startled to see me suddenly staring back.

I raced for the back of the shop.

By the time I reached the door that led to the

parking lot, I heard voices behind me. Keith must have recovered from the blow I struck and let his goon inside. I pushed aside the wheeled baking shelves I'd placed in front of the back door to alert me of any intruders. Now they blocked my escape.

"Tear this store apart!" I heard Keith say. "The computer is here. I know it!"

I hoped the shop window was the last place he looked. And I hoped to get the hell out of here before Keith reached me. I pushed the metal shelves out of the way, sending them crashing into the stove. Fingers crossed, Keith had not posted another man out back.

When I unlocked the door, I saw only parked cars. I took off at a run. When I burst out of the side alley and onto the crammed sidewalk, I felt giddy at finally being among so many people. Thousands of eyewitnesses—if Keith Sable chose to pursue me. Unlike the panicked crowd in the vendor room, I welcomed the sight of all these people.

I scanned the mobbed sidewalk in search of Kit's Jon Snow costume. Everyone not in the parade had staked out their viewing spot along the length of Lyall Street. Sawhorses lined the curb to keep spectators from getting in the way of the parade participants.

Because they planned to march, my friends must be at the end of the street. I needed to find them. But I could barely move.

I caught sight of Pennywise the clown to my left, about three stores down. Max stood on a park bench in front of the White Gallery, laughing and making threatening gestures at people. I tried to reach him, but five women dressed as Dallas Cowboys cheerleaders blocked my way. I barely avoided being smacked in the head when one of them did a high kick.

I pulled off the remaining dragon velcroed to my skirt and waved at Max.

"Max! Max, come here!" I shouted. The loudspeakers, now blaring the song from *Ghostbusters,* drowned me out.

He waved back, accompanied by his version of spooky fingers. This inspired the cheerleaders to wave blue and white pom-poms in my face. I'd never get past them. Or the gang of Walking Dead behind them.

Someone snatched the dragon from my hand.

"Hey!" I looked over in time to see Spiderman squeeze through the crowd, holding aloft my dragon. So much for superheroes.

I was also in time to see the white mask of the Phantom appear over someone's shoulder. With his flunky left behind to tear up my store, Keith must feel confident the computer would be found. That made me expendable. He had spotted me and roughly shoved Little Orphan Annie and Princess Leia out of the way.

The beginning of the parade lay to my right, and I needed to head there fast.

"Excuse me, excuse me." I tried to muscle my way to the edge of the sidewalk and onto the street, which had been cleared for the parade. If I could reach the empty street, I could run. Keith wouldn't dare follow me.

But a chorus of protests greeted my attempt.

"We were here first!"

"Who do you think you are?"

"She's the Mother of Dragons," someone replied, spying the one dragon I had left, still clinging to my shoulder.

"Well, she can get the dragons to fly her out of here, cause she's not taking my spot!"

"Let me through!" Unable to reach the curb, I pushed

toward the end of the street where a giant pumpkin man puppet stood overhead. He traditionally led the parade, held aloft by several local puppeteers. Behind him assembled a virtual army of costumed people, many of them locals. And my friends.

Desperate, I stepped on people's toes and shoved. Up ahead I spied the back of Wonder Woman's head. I got as close as I could and touched her shoulder. "Tess!" I yelled.

She turned around, revealing a bearded man dressed as everyone's favorite Amazon. Before I could let out a frustrated sigh, I felt a hand on my own shoulder.

I looked behind me. The Phantom was near enough to stretch his hand out and clamp onto my shoulder. Then he got even closer.

I screamed as his fingers curled around my neck. "This man is trying to kill me!"

"Of course he is," a drunken man yelled, brandishing a beer bottle. "He's the Phantom of the Opera!"

A chorus of laughs and hoots rose up. The crowd viewed us as two costumed people playing our parts to the hilt.

His hand tightened around my neck. There was no way he could strangle me from this angle, but he could keep me from getting away. I sunk my nails into his hand and he cried out.

When his grip loosened, I threw myself forward.

"Out of my way!" I pushed through the crowd like a woman possessed. I also landed a few random kicks to convince people to move aside.

If only I could reach somewhere less crowded, I could get people to pay attention to the danger I was in. But only the bars and restaurants were open, and they lay too far up the block or on the other side of the street.

I had almost reached city hall when I had a light-bulb moment. The city hall building was open because that was where the sound and lighting equipment had been stored before the parade. Along with the giant pumpkin-man puppet. Someone might still be inside. If not, it had a place where I would definitely be seen.

I didn't bother to look back, not when I was so close. As everyone pressed toward the street, I moved in the opposite direction. I tripped forward out of the crowd and fell in front of the front door of city hall. Scrambling to my feet, I pulled the door open.

The lights had been left on inside, but I didn't see anyone. Sidestepping boxes of electrical equipment stacked on the floor, I ran past the closed city offices. Behind me I heard the door open, letting in the noise from the street. Then it grew quiet again. Had Keith followed me? I didn't wait to find out.

I ran up the stairs to the bell tower, which ended in a circular landing. Open arches met me on all sides. Directly overhead was the cupola and Piper's shiny brass bell. It looked even larger up close.

I stepped through one of the arches onto the outside ledge. It was narrower than I imagined. Fortunately, Piper had ordered the renovators to install a two-foot-tall black iron railing. Otherwise I might have toppled over the side. It was only two stories up, but high enough to break your neck if you landed wrong.

Pressed against the back of the bell tower, I looked down. Lyall Street teemed with spectators. All of them focused to my right, where the parade participants were poised to begin. But I needed all eyes on me to stay safe.

I yanked the velcroed dragon off my shoulder and waved. Waved harder than I ever had.

Up here, everyone could appreciate the full effect of my silver glittering gown and long white wig. In addition, my stuffed dragon was fiery orange. Almost immediately, people in the crowd began to wave back. *Please have Kit see me. He has to be out there. Chief Hitchcock, too. Look at me. Look at me.*

"It's Daenerys!" someone shouted. "Daenerys!"

A cry went up and suddenly everyone seemed to be waving at me. They probably thought this was part of the festivities. The Mother of Dragons signaling the parade to start.

I heard Keith step onto the ledge. He was breathing heavy.

"If you plan to kill me, you've got an audience," I said, waving my dragon.

Out of the corner of my eye, I saw his long black cloak swirl in the night breeze as he took a step closer. "When the parade begins," he said, "their attention will be elsewhere, and you and I will go back inside. As soon as Dennis lets me know he's found the laptop, you'll meet with an accident on the way down the stairs. Poor girl, they'll say. So excited to see the parade, she tripped over her costume and broke her neck."

"You'll have to pick me up and carry me off this ledge," I warned.

"Maybe I should just push you off." He moved closer.

I heard the clock hand below us click to ten o'clock as Keith went on, "If I trip you, it will look like an—"

The brass bell rang out.

I was prepared for the deafening noise. Keith wasn't.

He gave a startled cry and jumped back. But there was nowhere to jump to.

Arms flailing, he toppled over the short iron railing and fell from sight.

As the bell continued to toll ten o'clock, I looked down to see him crumpled on the sidewalk below. His white mask had shattered, and his black cape spread about him like the wings of a dead bat. It looked like he had barely missed falling on a woman dressed as a nurse. Which seemed ironic.

Because much of the crowd had been watching me wave my dragon when Keith fell, I was sure screams had gone up. Not that I could have heard them with the loudest bell in the world tolling right above me.

People rushed over to where he fell. Two were police officers. One was a man with a black fur cloak, who knelt beside the body. After a moment, the man looked up at me and shouted something. The bell drowned him out, but I thought he said, "He's still alive."

Leaning back against the bell tower, I smiled. Jon Snow had finally found me.

I rubbed my mulberry bracelet and waited for my heart to slow down. And the bell to finish tolling. When it finally did, I went back through the arch to the landing inside, only to be met with Bigfoot. And he held a shotgun.

"What the hell?" I asked.

Old Man Bowman pulled off his rubber mask, lavishly trimmed in brown animal hair. "I've been meaning to put an end to this bell, Marlee. It's a hazard. And now it's done killed a man. Almost killed you, too. Luckily, I had my shotgun in my truck around the corner. Now I'm going to blow the bell's innards in that box over there." He pointed at the electronic controls affixed to one of the arches.

"The man that fell is Keith Sable. And I think he's still alive. He was trying to kill me. The bell scared him before he could. It saved my life. Literally."

He grunted. "Don't that beat all? It's like that John Donne poem about not asking for whom the bell tolls."

"Yep. Tonight it tolled for me. But in a good way."

Old Man Bowman stared at the blinking electronic box. "It's still too damn loud. And we'll never convince Piper to lower the volume. So . . ."

He raised his shotgun and fired. The control box exploded into dozens of pieces.

My ears already rang from the bell. The shotgun blast sent them vibrating.

"Now maybe we'll have a little peace and quiet in this town." He put his hairy rubber mask back on.

"I doubt it," I said as I followed Bigfoot down the steps. "And when Piper finds out what you've done to her bell . . ."

"Hah! If I ain't afraid of Bigfoot, I'm sure not gonna worry about Piper." Then he let out a mock growl to prove it.

At times like this, it felt like every night in Oriole Point was Halloween. Which wasn't all bad if you factored in the candy.

Chapter Twenty-seven

By the time Halloween officially ended at midnight, I'd had my fill of costumes, candy—and murder. Although we all agreed this year's Halloween parade would be hard to top. What with Daenerys signaling the start of the event and a brutal killer toppling from the bell tower. Followed by Bigfoot exiting city hall with a shotgun.

"How do other towns celebrate Halloween?" Gillian asked us.

"Not like this," Dean said, loosening his *Book of Mormon* missionary tie.

"You have to admit Oriole Point makes it a real thrill fest." Andrew laughed.

"With the accent on thrills," I said, looking out the shop window as costumed stragglers left the bars about to close.

"I feel bad that I sold my cloak and mask to the dangerous man," Theo said for the fourth time. "He used my costume to fool you, Marlee. It's my fault."

"You didn't know what he planned to do with it," Max told him, also for the fourth time. "Don't feel bad."

"Hey, if someone offered me five hundred dollars,

I would have sold him my costume, too." I spun about, enjoying the silver sparkles on my gown. On second thought, maybe I wouldn't have been able to part with it.

"I can't believe you got five hundred dollars for a cloak and mask." Oscar looked down at his Colonial uniform. "Here I am, the spitting image of Alexander Hamilton, and no one offers me a dollar for this costume." He pointed at Andrew's elaborate Thomas Jefferson getup. "Or his."

"Well, I wouldn't part with my Chip costume for double that," David declared, giving a pat to the chipmunk head that sat on the bistro table beside him.

Tess rolled her eyes, busy eating her third slice of cake. Since it was Wonder Woman's birthday, she was focused on overindulging.

Still in costume, Old Man Bowman emerged from the shop kitchen, holding two cups. I didn't know which was more disturbing: the prospect of his industrial-strength coffee or seeing Bigfoot expertly handle my Grindmaster Coffee Brewer.

He handed one cup to Natasha. The extra pot of coffee had been made especially for her. Our Russian Cleopatra had drunk a bit too much birthday champagne. "Is not right the Sable man only breaks his neck," she exclaimed. "For what he does, he should be shot."

"Pennywise would have done worse," Max said with an evil chuckle.

Natasha glared at Bigfoot, her diadem lying crooked atop her head. "Why do you not shoot him in bell tower?"

"Hell, he'd already fallen off the damn thing by the

time I got there." Like a hairy headwaiter, he handed the other cup to David.

"*Net opravdaniya.* Is no excuse." Natasha flung a stuffed snake onto the table. It appeared Old Man Bowman had found a snake to replace her rubber asp. Only this one looked like a mummified garter snake. Which it probably was.

Despite the frightening events of tonight, I felt calmer than I had all week. And at peace. After I gave my statement at the police station, my friends and I decamped to The Berry Basket, where we broke open Tess's birthday champagne and ate that delicious cake Theo baked for her. For the past two hours, we had discussed what I learned from *Mischief and Murder,* interspersing it with requests for me to retell my chilling encounter with the murderous Keith Sable.

It was now two a.m. and the adrenaline of the night still hadn't worn off. No surprise. The past four hours had been filled with enough action for several *Game of Thrones* episodes.

After his plunge off the bell tower, Keith Sable was rushed to the hospital, where doctors discovered he had broken his neck, along with both shoulders, and three vertebrae. He'd live, but a long, painful recovery lay in front of him. As did a murder trial. And, hopefully, prison.

The Sables were in an uproar. Although I wasn't certain if it was because Keith had been charged with the murders of Ellen and Bonaventure or because the contents of *Mischief and Murder* were about to go public. Even worse for them, Kit had tracked down their former bosun, James Smith, now residing in Kauai with Shelly Zahradnik. Because it was six hours earlier in Hawaii, the sheriff's department had spoken with him tonight. And the tale he told resulted in an additional murder charge against Keith Sable. This time for the murder of Laeticia Murier.

All this before midnight. I couldn't help but think that the spirits of both Laeticia and Ellen had been present this All Hallows' Eve. And that their souls were finally at rest. I sent a prayer for Felix Bonaventure, too.

The door opened and Jon Snow walked in. Although we had been together at the police station earlier, Kit and I flung ourselves at each other now. Then kissed for what seemed like five minutes.

When we finally broke apart, applause greeted us. "This is so sweet," Andrew said. "I always wanted Daenerys and Jon Snow to get it on."

"It's really Marlee and Kit," Theo said in a stage whisper.

Kit hugged me close. "Did I miss all the cake?"

"Almost," David said. "But we hid two slices from the birthday girl. Otherwise you would have been out of luck. And cake."

"He's lying." Tess put down her empty cake plate on the bistro table. "There are three pieces left."

"Two," Old Man Bowman said, smoothing down the hair on his costume. "I ate another piece when I was in the kitchen making coffee. And a couple of those mulberry cookie bars, too."

"I'll get you the cake," Gillian announced. She slowly minced her way to the kitchen in her tight mermaid skirt. At this rate, she'd be back with his cake in about an hour.

Kit looked around the shop. "Everything looks fine. Last time I was in here, there was broken glass on the floor, along with sweatshirts and tins of tea knocked from the shelves."

"It wasn't that bad," Dean said. "Took me and Andrew about twenty minutes to clean it all up."

"You got here before Keith Sable's goon had a chance to really tear my store apart looking for the laptop." I glanced at the pile of straw in the window where I'd hidden the computer. "In fact, you must have arrived about three minutes after Keith chased me out of here."

"Wish I'd gotten here sooner. I would have liked to put cuffs on Keith Sable." He gave me a wink. "Or been on the bell tower so I could have pushed him over."

"Hey, I didn't push him." I laughed. "Blame that bell."

"The bell is no more." Old Man Bowman reached for his shotgun.

"Marlee told us that James Smith is dying," Tess said. "Will he live long enough to testify against Keith Sable?"

Kit grew serious. "I don't know. He was diagnosed with stomach cancer earlier this year, and given no more than a year to live. It's why the Sables went after Ellen and Bonaventure first. I think they all assumed Smith would be dead before he could cause any real problems for them."

Dean looked disgusted. "Such a lovely family, those Sables."

"They underestimated Smith," Kit said. "His prognosis made him regret his false testimony in the Nanny Murder case. He told us that he's never gotten over his guilt about letting an innocent girl go to prison. And allowing the murderer to go free."

"I wouldn't want to die with something like that on my conscience," I said.

"He didn't," Kit went on. "That's why he tried to find Ellen. Around the same time the ghostwriter tracked him down for the book he and Ellen were writing."

"Serendipitous," Tess murmured.

"Sure was," Max said. "Smith gets to expiate his guilt, and Ellen had an eyewitness to the murder she unjustly went to prison for. Proof that she was innocent of the crime. A shame she didn't live long enough to see this."

"Without the determination of both Ellen and Bonaventure to keep the manuscript from the Sables, the truth would still be hidden." While sorrowful over their deaths, I admired their courage.

David turned to me. "Despite what Keith told you, it makes me wonder if the whole family isn't complicit. I mean, they had to have realized Ellen didn't do it."

I shrugged. "Who knows? And I don't think they cared." Ellen had been right. Except for Joshua, the Sable family were shadow people, comfortable with the dark sides of their nature.

"Whatever the other Sables knew, the man who actually murdered three people will pay for his crimes," Kit said. "And James Smith's testimony against him will be on record, even if he dies before the trial."

"You look a little tired," Old Man Bowman said. "Let me get you a cup of my coffee. I also think our Little Mermaid needs help walking in that fish tail." Shotgun over his shoulder, he headed for the kitchen.

"Until they return with your cake and coffee, I have something to tide you over." I reached into the front window display and held up a big bag of candy corn.

Kit gave a whoop. "Now it feels like Halloween!"

Before he could tear into the candy bag, the front door to the shop banged open. Piper strode inside. She wore a black Catwoman costume and a furious expression. "Where is he?" she shouted.

"Who?" I asked, although I could take a pretty good guess.

"That hairy devil who destroyed my bell-ringing system! Odette Henderson told me that she saw him in here. Where is he hiding?"

I heard a cup crash to the floor in the kitchen. A second later, Old Man Bowman dashed thorough the shop, shotgun in hand. He was out the door before she could get near him.

"Come back here!" Piper ran after him, leaving her black Birkin behind.

All of us crowded at the front window to watch Bigfoot flee down Lyall Street, pursued by Catwoman, who ran remarkably well in her designer heels.

"Do you think she'll catch him?" Andrew asked.

"Not a chance," I replied. "No one has ever caught Bigfoot."

"Even if she does, he'll be protected," Theo said solemnly.

"What do you mean?" Kit asked.

"He had a mulberry cookie bar in his hand when he ran past. And mulberries protect people, don't they, Marlee?"

"Indeed, they do, Theo." I smiled and looked down at my bracelet. "Indeed, they do."

Recipes

MULBERRY MUFFINS

Since mulberry trees grow on Marlee's property, she has hundreds of mulberries available to her every summer when they ripen. This low-fat recipe is a great way to utilize some of them. Marlee and Theo found the recipe on allrecipes.com and decided to do just that.

- 1½ cups all-purpose flour
- ½ cup white granulated sugar
- 1 teaspoon baking powder
- ½ teaspoon baking soda
- 1 pinch of salt
- ½ cup fat-free sour cream
- ¼ cup skim milk
- 2 tablespoons applesauce
- 1 egg
- ½ teaspoon almond extract
- ½ cup mulberries

1. Preheat oven to 400 degrees F.
2. Combine flour, sugar, baking powder, baking soda, and salt in bowl.
3. Mix sour cream, milk, applesauce, egg, and almond extract in a separate bowl.

4. Slowly add flour mixture to the batter. Stir until smooth.
5. Mix after each addition until well blended.
6. Gently fold in mulberries.
7. Spoon batter into 6 greased jumbo muffin cups, or paper-lined cups.
8. Bake 25–30 minutes or until inserted toothpick comes out clean
9. Cool 5 minutes before removing from muffin pan.

Makes 6 jumbo muffins.

MARTHA'S MULBERRY PANCAKES

If you've never tasted pancakes made with mulberries, this recipe recommended by Martha Stewart is a great place to start. And don't forget the maple syrup.

4 teaspoons sugar
4 teaspoons baking powder
1¼ cups all-purpose flour
1 teaspoon coarse salt
2 large eggs, lightly beaten
5 tablespoons unsalted butter, melted. Additional butter, softened, for serving
1 cup whole milk
Vegetable oil
2 cups mulberries, with more for garnish
Pure maple syrup

1. In a medium bowl, whisk together sugar, baking powder, flour, and salt. Set aside.
2. Whisk eggs and melted butter in another bowl. Gradually add milk, whisking to combine.
3. Pour egg mixture into flour mixture. Whisk until combined.
4. Heat heavy skillet or griddle over medium-high heat; hot, but not smoking. Brush lightly with oil and reduce heat to medium.
5. Ladle 2 tablespoons batter onto skillet, placing 4–5 mulberries per pancake.
6. Cook until pancake edges bubble, 1–1½ minutes.
7. Flip. Cook until set and bottom is lightly browned, about 1½ minutes more.
8. Repeat with remaining batter, cooking 3–4 pancakes at a time.
9. Place cooked pancakes in a 200 degree F oven to keep warm.
10. Serve with butter and maple syrup. Garnish with mulberries.

HALLOWEEN BLOODY CUPS

One of the pastry selections at The Berry Basket for Halloween is this berry version of peanut-butter cups. Not only is this a simple, three-ingredient recipe, but it's gluten free and vegan. So it's guilt-free, too.

> 1 cup frozen raspberries
> 1 tablespoon maple syrup or rice syrup or agave syrup
> 1¾ cups vegan baking chocolate or chocolate chips

1. In a small pot, heat frozen raspberries on medium-high heat until soft. Mash the softened raspberries to remove chunks. Add syrup. Mix and set aside to cool.
2. Melt 1 cup of the chocolate in a double boiler.
3. Place 8 muffin liners in a muffin pan. Spoon approximately 1½ teaspoons of melted chocolate in each muffin liner and tilt so the bottoms are coated.
4. To allow the chocolate to harden, place muffin pan in refrigerator for several minutes.
5. Melt ¾ cup of the chocolate in double boiler.
6. Add a teaspoon of raspberry filling into center of each chocolate coated muffin liner.
7. Once the chocolate has melted, pour it over the raspberry filling so that chocolate completely covers the top. Let it harden in refrigerator for five minutes.
8. After the chocolate is hard, remove cupcake liners. Keep in fridge till ready to serve.

Makes eight chocolate cups.

STRAWBERRY GHOSTS

Once you've melted the chocolate, this is a remarkably fast and easy recipe. And don't worry about being neat. Any chocolate dripping from the strawberries makes a lovely ghost tail.

30 fresh strawberries
8 ounces white baking chocolate

1 teaspoon shortening
⅛ teaspoon almond extract
¼ cup miniature semisweet chocolate chips

1. Wash strawberries and gently pat completely dry with paper towels.
2. In a microwave, melt white chocolate and shortening at 50 percent power in a microwave-safe bowl. Stir until smooth. Stir in almond extract.
3. Dip strawberries in melted chocolate mixture. Place berries on baking sheet lined with waxed paper. Allow extra chocolate to form ghost tails. Immediately, before chocolate hardens, press chocolate chips into berries to form eyes. Freeze 5 minutes.
4. Melt remaining chocolate chips in microwave. Stir until smooth.
5. Dip a toothpick into the melted chocolate and draw a mouth on each berry ghost. Refrigerate leftovers.

Makes 30 ghosts (approximately 54 calories each).

Connect with U s

Visit us online at
KensingtonBooks.com
to read more from your favorite authors, see books
by series, view reading group guides, and more.

Join us on social media

for sneak peeks, chances to win books and prize packs,
and to share your thoughts with other readers.

facebook.com/kensingtonpublishing
twitter.com/kensingtonbooks

Tell us what you think!

To share your thoughts, submit a review,
or sign up for our eNewsletters, please visit:
KensingtonBooks.com/TellUs.